Praise for J. Courtney Sullivan's

Friends and Strangers

A *Real Simple* Best Book of the Year

"What's crucial about . . . *Friends and Strangers*, though, is that [it is] more than 'nanny novels' predicated on a Manichaean dynamic between employer and employee. [It] expertly lay[s] bare the shortcomings of the employers they represent, but . . . allow[s] them humanity too: These mothers are lost, isolated and often have no one else to whom they feel they can turn other than their nannies. More importantly, while [*Friends and Strangers*] center[s] the young women who have been transported into unfamiliar and luxe surroundings under the auspices of care-giving, [it] take[s] care to define [the] protagonists by more than their work."
—*Vogue*

"Literate and smart, but also a heck of a lot of fun. . . . A gimlet-eyed examination of classism and privilege in America and a close look at the complicated terrain between parents and hired caregivers, with the ensuing guilt and resentments that so often accompany such relationships."
—*Portland Monthly*

"Exposes fraught truths about power dynamics, class, and privilege."
—*Marie Claire*

"Sullivan's writing is captivating and witty as the characters observe the disconnects in their respective lives and those around them."
—*New Canaan Advertiser*

J. Courtney Sullivan

Friends and Strangers

J. Courtney Sullivan is the *New York Times* bestselling author of the novels *Commencement*, *Maine*, *The Engagements*, and *Saints for All Occasions*. Her work has been translated into seventeen languages. Sullivan's writing has appeared in *The New York Times Book Review*, *The Washington Post*, *Chicago Tribune*, *New York*, *Elle*, *Glamour*, *Allure*, *Real Simple*, and *O, The Oprah Magazine*, among many others. She lives in Brooklyn, New York, with her husband and two children.

Also by J. Courtney Sullivan

Saints for All Occasions
The Engagements
Maine
Commencement

Friends and Strangers

Friends and Strangers

J. Courtney Sullivan

VINTAGE CONTEMPORARIES
Vintage Books
A Division of Penguin Random House LLC
New York

FIRST VINTAGE CONTEMPORARIES
EDITION, APRIL 2021

The Library of Congress has cataloged
the Alfred A. Knopf edition as follows:
Name: Sullivan, J. Courtney, author.
Title: Friends and strangers : a novel / J. Courtney Sullivan.
Description: First edition. | New York : Alfred A. Knopf, 2020.
Identifiers: LCCN 2019041613
Subjects: LCSH: Female friendship—Fiction.
Classification: LCC PS3619.U43 F75 2020 | DDC 813/.6—dc23
LC record available at https://lccn.loc.gov/2019041613

Vintage Contemporaries Trade Paperback
ISBN: 978-0-525-43647-8
eBook ISBN: 978-0-525-52060-3

Book design by M. Kristen Bearse

www.vintagebooks.com

Printed in the United States of America
10 9 8 7 6 5 4 3 2 1

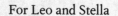
For Leo and Stella

2014–2015

Elisabeth

S HE AWAKENED TO SILENCE. Nobody up at this hour besides mothers and insomniacs. She did not need to look at the clock to know that within seconds the baby would cry, and she would lift him from his bassinet before her eyes were quite open, exhaustion giving way to acceptance, devotion, as she held the warm heft of him in her arms.

A flash of hot rage sparked in her at the sight of her sleeping husband, but just as quickly it was gone, and she was changing the diaper, walking downstairs, wondering what would happen if she dropped the baby, if he died. The answer as familiar as the question: she would go out a window. That settled, Elisabeth kissed the top of his head.

A video affirmation she had found online began, in soothing tones, *Every time I nurse my child, I drink a glass of water. In this way, I remember that I too deserve care.* Filling a glass of water required more than she had at the moment, but she thought it was good enough that she knew she ought to.

In the living room, her eyes adjusted. She saw the black and blue shadows of the glass and gold coffee table with which she would soon have to part, the pair of armchairs, the potted fiddle-leaf fig tree, seven feet tall. She had arranged these items in the exact configuration they had occupied in the Brooklyn apartment, but somehow it all looked different here.

Elisabeth reached under the sofa and pulled out the ugly pillow with the stupid name. My Brest Friend. Someone, she couldn't remember who, had given it to her as a shower gift, swearing that it was a godsend. This turned out to be true, even though she felt like she was wearing a life preserver around her waist whenever she put it on.

She sat down, laying the baby across her padded lap. She lifted her T-shirt, unhooked her bra. He latched on and began to suck, an easy rhythm that had seemed impossible four months ago. In order to be discharged from the hospital after giving birth, she was required to attend an hour-long class about breastfeeding. The entire time, Elisabeth kept falling asleep, waking when her head slammed against the wall behind her.

She held her phone aloft in one hand now, above the baby's head, and used her thumb to navigate to Facebook. Straight to the BK Mamas page, as usual. Elisabeth scrolled until she came to the place where she'd left off before bed. The page buzzed with questions from mothers at all hours. They kept one another company there. She imagined the rows of brownstones in the old neighborhood, bathed in blackness but for the tiny screens, lit up, connecting them all.

There was a post from a woman looking for tips on flying cross-country with a toddler. Elisabeth read all thirteen responses with interest, even though she didn't have a toddler or plans to fly anytime soon. Someone was asking about the flu shot. Someone else needed a unicorn birthday cake on short notice. Mimi Winchester, who had recently purchased a townhouse for three million, was selling a used boy's coat, size 2T, for nine dollars.

Elisabeth had once mocked women like this—women who graduated from prestigious universities and excelled in their chosen fields, only to be felled by the prospect of clipping a newborn's fingernails. Now they were her survival. The only people alive who cared about the exact things she did at this moment, with as much intensity, the people with all the answers. They were learning an evolving language, one you spoke for a week or two before everything changed again. What else to do with that accrued knowledge but share it. Someone with a child six weeks older than hers was a prophet.

She switched sides after ten minutes.

A new post popped up.

Slightly off topic, but . . . last month, as usual, my husband was a no-show on a visit to my parents in Minneapolis. While I was there, I ran into my college boyfriend, recently divorced. Now we're texting at all hours. Is this an emotional affair? Am I supposed to stop? Because dammit, it's FUN, and I think I deserve some fun.

In her profile picture, the woman was blonde and smiling and toned, a tall guy's arms wrapped around her. They stood on a white sand beach, palm trees in the distance. Their honeymoon, maybe. Half the women still used their wedding photos, including, Elisabeth had noticed, the ones who complained most about their useless husbands.

The secrets they divulged to one another amazed her. The group was marked Private, but that only meant that you had to ask to join. There were 4,237 members, and in theory at least, most of them lived within twenty blocks of one another. Yet it felt like a safe space. At once intimate and anonymous.

The same fifteen women commented on everything, each with her own predictable slant on the issue of the day.

When someone asked about whether to have a third kid, the self-righteous environmentalist said that she had not done so because of fears about global warming and her family's carbon footprint; someone posted an easy chicken recipe, and the Environmentalist wrote a manifesto in the comments section about why she was raising her kids vegan.

Mimi Winchester managed to complain about her brownstone (she'd kill for open concept), her cleaning lady (she wouldn't do windows), and even, somehow, her Hamptons house (*traffic!*).

The nanny tattlers loved to report on sitters they saw feeding a child junk food or talking on the phone to a degree they deemed excessive. There were also those who stood up for any nanny's behavior, no matter how terrible.

Elisabeth's best friend, Nomi, said her greatest source of irritation was the friends who didn't come to them with problems but instead posted them to the BK Mamas page. Last spring, their college friend Tanya, who also lived in the neighborhood, spent an entire dinner making small talk, only to post to BK Mamas two days later that she was on the hunt for a divorce attorney.

"I'm not acknowledging it unless she tells me directly," Nomi said.

"I think she assumes you'll see it on Facebook and then ask her about it," Elisabeth said.

"Well, I won't."

Elisabeth, like most people, was a lurker, rarely commenting, never posting, despite the time she spent reading the page each day.

Within five minutes, twelve women said that what the smiling blonde was up to with her college boyfriend was nothing but a harmless flirtation. Ten others said to cut it off immediately.

This sort of question appeared once a month or so, standing out among so many queries about potty training and playgroups. Someone would confess a husband's alcoholism or infidelity, or a disturbing desire to run away, and everyone else would reply in a rush, energized by being in possession of a secret.

They were the posts Elisabeth told Andrew about the next morning, even though she knew he didn't care. Half the pleasure of the group was talking about it with someone in real life. She missed Wednesdays in Brooklyn, when Nomi worked from home and would meet her at the crepe place on Court Street for lunch.

She kept revisiting their last lunch in her mind. How they sat and talked, both unwilling to end the conversation, until the kid behind the counter said it was closing time. Then they lingered on the sidewalk in the sticky August heat, as they had done in the parking lot on the day they left college.

Nomi once swore she'd never live in Brooklyn. The first time she came out from Manhattan for brunch, just before she climbed into a taxi, she swept her hand across Elisabeth's forehead like Barbra Streisand in *The Way We Were* and said, "Your borough is lovely, Hubbell." But it was another two years before she and Brian moved. They bought a three-bedroom in a new high-rise with an elevator and a swimming pool. Elisabeth had only ever lived in dusty walk-ups, with crown moldings and creaky wooden floors. Places that were listed as having *character* and *charm*, if not central air or laundry in the building.

She attributed the longevity of their friendship at least in part to the fact that she and Nomi had opposite tastes in men and real estate. It was impossible for either of them to be jealous of the other.

"Am I making a huge mistake?" Elisabeth said as they parted, locked in a hug, the baby asleep in the stroller at her side.

"Yes," Nomi said. "You are."

"That is not a supportive answer."

"I'm still mad at you for leaving."

"I always said I was going to."

"But you'd been saying it for so long, I stopped believing you at some point."

Elisabeth had been so lucky to have the friend who knew her best right nearby, all that time.

She supposed this was another reason why she clung to a neighborhood Facebook group—it made her forget that she lived 250 miles away now, in a town where she had no friends.

I'm your friend, Andrew said.

Husbands don't count.

He hadn't made friends either, but he at least had coworkers and the odd amusing story to tell.

Most days, Elisabeth took Gil for a walk after lunch and passed a playground where mothers stood in a cluster, gossiping, laughing.

Jesus, you're not the new kid at middle school, she chided herself. *Go over and say hello.*

They were grown women. They had to be nice, at least to her face. But she couldn't do it. Some mix of self-consciousness and fatigue stopped her. That, and the fear that she wouldn't like them anyway.

Even as she talked herself out of wanting to know them, she hoped they might notice her and wave her over, but they never did.

The baby drank himself drunk and closed his eyes, his head an anchor seeking the bottom. Elisabeth carried him upstairs and lowered him gently, deliberately, into the bassinet, as if he was a bomb that might detonate if handled improperly.

In the hours before he woke again, she lay in bed unable to sleep. She knew she should find a way, that the day would be hectic. An interview with a potential babysitter, emails to answer, those stretches of time with an infant that got eaten up by she couldn't say what. But she kept looking at the phone, eager to see how the BK Mamas were weighing in on the blonde woman's emotional affair.

Violet, her therapist, would say that Elisabeth was trying to distract herself—from the secret she was keeping from her husband, from her father-in-law's recent struggles, and from her relationship with her own parents, which had always been a mess, but had become more painful of late.

Elisabeth had gone to see Violet in the first place with no intention of returning week after week. She wanted someone to tell her she was clinically depressed, or anxious, or else that her worries, her spinning thoughts, could be explained by a protein deficiency. She wanted a clear diagnosis and a simple treatment she could buy at a pharmacy or a health-food store and feel working immediately.

That is so not how therapy works, Nomi said.

"Postpartum depression is real," Violet said.

"I know it is, but no," Elisabeth said. "I've always been like this."

She was only addressing it now because of Gil. She had an urge to fix herself before he became aware of all the ways in which she was broken.

Violet said to remember that thoughts are vapor. She said to read Eckhart Tolle.

When Elisabeth googled Violet, she came across an essay she'd written years earlier for an anthology about mothers and daughters, so she knew that Violet had no children, that her mother had died, that her dear old father was lost to Alzheimer's.

Sometimes, when she complained about her family during a session, Elisabeth wondered if Violet was suppressing an urge to scream, *My perfect mother dies, my dad doesn't know who I am, while your shitty parents go on and on. How is this fair?*

Violet yawned a lot, which hurt Elisabeth's feelings.

Her eyes opened. She woke up. This was how Elisabeth could be certain she had slept. For ten minutes? An hour? Impossible to say.

It was five o'clock in the morning. In a moment, the baby would wake. She wondered how long their bodies would remain in sync like this, hers anticipating what his was about to do.

She checked BK Mamas on her phone while she waited.

A woman named Heather had posted around four, asking if, after two glasses of wine, it was necessary to pump and dump. The replies came swift, a resounding chorus of *nos*. Heather thanked them, then admitted that she was feeling guilty. About not getting enough vitamins, about having an Oreo when she had sworn to eat organic for the baby's sake.

Guilt was their common bond.

Stop overthinking it, someone wrote. *Multivariate regression analysis on the impact of that Oreo is a dangerous path.*

Elisabeth considered this, amused.

The baby cried. The day began.

2

THE SUMMER HEAT HAD LINGERED into the second week of September, but early mornings were pleasant. A crisp breeze hinted at the cool days to come.

Before Andrew left for work, they walked around the pond at the nearby college, an approximation of their old routine. In Brooklyn, they had strolled together to get coffee each morning, peering into the windows of new restaurants, greeting neighbors out walking their dogs. Here, there were no coffee shops or restaurants within a mile. Elisabeth reminded herself that she had wanted this—nature, stillness, the sound of birds in trees.

Andrew bought a French press and made her coffee now. On the days they walked at the college, he filled a travel mug for her.

"Where are the actual college kids?" Andrew said the first time they drove down Main Street, which ran through the center of campus.

"I'm assuming these are them," she said.

She gestured toward the young women all around. They were laughing in a group by the stoplight; sitting on the front porch of a dorm; rushing along, hunched forward from the weight of their backpacks. Photos in an admissions brochure come to life.

"No way," Andrew said. "These girls look like they're in the sixth grade."

They crossed paths with a dozen of them now, jogging in formation. Their white windbreakers gave off a satisfying swishing sound as they passed, two by two.

Most of them smiled at the baby, asleep in the sling on Elisabeth's chest.

Elisabeth smiled back, tried to appear cheerful. She had been in a snit since Andrew woke up and said he'd forgotten to tell her they were having dinner at his parents'. The early evening hours after he got home from work were her only chance to be alone, or to have a real conversation with him. She didn't want to give them to her in-laws.

They came to the halfway point of the pond, marked by a rope hanging over the water from a thick branch. Elisabeth pictured drunk teenage girls in cutoffs swinging back and forth, shrieking as they let go. Still making the kinds of bad choices that ultimately didn't matter. Their lives all ahead of them.

"These crickets are disgusting," Elisabeth said. "Is that what they are? Crickets? They're huge. I hate when they land on me, don't you?"

Andrew shrugged. "None have landed on me, I don't know."

"It feels like this," she said, and punched him in the arm.

He raised an eyebrow.

Notice the moments when you feel yourself growing resentful, Violet had said. *Don't assign value to them, just take note.*

Nomi put it more plainly: *You'll probably loathe Andrew for a while after the baby comes. If he touches you, you might want to die. Don't worry. It will pass.*

Elisabeth didn't loathe him. She had been lucky to find a man as kind as Andrew, a partner who understood her like he did. But so much had changed these past few months. Sometimes it felt like they were standing on opposite sides of a crowded room and could see, but not reach, each other. She wasn't sure yet how or when the two of them would fit together again.

And there was the issue of the secret she'd been keeping, which Violet called *toxic*.

"It's never the thing you're holding back that kills the relationship," Violet said. "It's the holding back itself that does it."

"I hear what you're saying," Elisabeth said. "But in this case, I think it could go either way."

After Andrew left for work, she showered.

Children's folk songs streamed from her phone, which she had left on a chair just outside the bathroom door. The baby was strapped into the bouncy seat on the tile floor. He started to cry halfway through "This Land Is Your Land."

Elisabeth rinsed the conditioner from her hair and shut off the water. She had been trying to shave her legs for a week.

She wrapped herself in a towel and picked him up.

She stepped out into the hall and brightened to see a text from Nomi.

Brian's acting weird. He's either having an affair or planning something for my birthday.

Birthday, Elisabeth typed back. She didn't need to think about it. Brian was capable of many things, but he wasn't a cheater.

How can you be so sure?

Because he's the last person on earth who would have an affair.

But isn't it always the ones you least suspect?

No, it's the ones you least suspect when it comes to murder. It's the ones you suspect when it comes to infidelity.

They never had actual voice-to-voice contact anymore. There were no hellos or goodbyes, just an ongoing conversation that they picked up and ended several times throughout the course of a day. If her best friend called her on the phone, it would mean someone had died, or, back when they both lived in Brooklyn, that she was locked out of her apartment.

Any progress on a sitter? Nomi asked.

Interviewing someone in an hour.

Elisabeth's friends in the city hired nannies from the Caribbean or Tibet, whom they paid to be the grandmothers their own mothers were not. You wanted someone who loved your baby and shared her intuition without judgment. Who did not drink wine on your sofa while the child cried, or tell you that you ought to cover your boob in mixed company.

She'd heard every variety of complaint from her friends about their parents' odd post-baby behavior. Elisabeth would have gladly taken any of it over her own situation. Four months in, her parents still hadn't met Gil.

Her father seemed to think she should bring the baby to him.

"Arizona is gorgeous this time of year," he said. "It's the perfect place for kids. They can run all over."

"But he doesn't run," she said. "He can't even sit yet."

Her mother was on a Viking cruise up the Rhine when Gil was born. She sent him a cup and bowl handmade by nuns in Bucharest and had since made no overtures to come see him.

So many people—even people Elisabeth didn't know—made comments about her mother. Nomi brought her own mother over for a visit when she was in Brooklyn. She had knitted Gil a blanket.

"Nothing better than being a grandma," she said. "Your mom must be over the moon."

Elisabeth smiled and nodded, knowing that Nomi's mother was thinking of a different sort of family, one like her own.

Since her early twenties, she had been mostly free of her parents. They did not spend holidays together. Elisabeth never went back to California to visit. But the process of forming her own family had made her reflect more than ever before on the one from which she came.

She didn't think she would care when her withholding, inattentive mother inevitably turned out to be a withholding, inattentive grandmother. But she did care, sometimes. Her parents loomed larger now than they had at any other moment in her adult life.

"We're moving because I'm switching careers, but also to be closer to my mom and dad," Andrew had said again and again in the weeks before they left, simplifying the truth, polishing it. "It will be such a relief to have their help."

Elisabeth pressed her lips closed whenever he said it. In the abstract, Faye and George were thrilled to be grandparents. But they weren't helpful. Whenever the baby pooped in her mother-in-law's presence, Faye would hold him out to her, nose wrinkled, and say, "Somebody needs to be changed." The one time Elisabeth asked her to take care of him while she ran to the store for ten minutes, she came home to find them watching *Dr. Phil*. The baby's eyes were two full moons attached to the faces on Faye's big-screen TV.

Faye was an elementary school teacher, which Elisabeth had assumed would mean she'd make an incredible grandmother. But it felt like Faye had gotten her fill of childcare at work. She would adore Gil, but she would not be responsible for him.

George doted on the baby, but he was distracted by his own problems lately.

From what Elisabeth could tell, most children in their new neighborhood went to day care part-time or else stayed home with their mothers.

Debbie across the way was a housewife married to an insurance salesman. The other women on Laurel Street had the sorts of job titles that might be all-consuming, but could also be clever terms for doing nothing: Melody was a realtor. Pam taught yoga. They seemed to be home at all times.

Elisabeth supposed they could say the same about her. There

were few things more humiliating than meeting a stranger at a party, having him ask what she did for a living. *I'm a writer,* she would say, and invariably the stranger would get an uncomfortable look on his face. *Have you—published?* was always the second question, warily asked, and when she said yes, two books, his expression would grow terrified, like she might be about to try to sell him those books from out of the trunk of her car.

It was better when Andrew was beside her. He bragged in a way she could not about herself. *Her first was a bestseller,* he might say. Or *Simon and Schuster gave her a three-book deal.*

That third book, due in a year and not yet begun, was the reason she needed to hire someone to watch Gil. Elisabeth didn't even have an idea yet. It was unlike her. Usually, as she wrapped up one project, she was already well into thinking about the next and eager to start. She had expected that by now she would want to get back to work. Instead, her ambition was something she remembered vaguely, yet couldn't seem to conjure.

She knew from friends' experiences that the search for a sitter could be worse than dating but similar—some were duds, and you knew right away there was no chemistry, yet you still had to go through the motions of an interview. Sometimes you liked someone who chose somebody else. Nomi had hired a woman on the spot who turned out to be faking her references. That had petrified them both.

When Elisabeth told her neighbor Stephanie that she was looking for someone, Stephanie said this was the best part of living in a town that was home to a small women's college.

"I've used a couple of the students, and they were good," she said. "Good enough. No one burned the house down."

Elisabeth thanked her for the suggestion and suspected that Stephanie didn't love her children half as much as she loved Gil.

But in the end, she decided to try a college student. She could get someone three days a week to start, ease into things. If the arrangement didn't work out, the end of the semester would make for a natural parting of ways.

A week ago, Elisabeth had pushed the stroller over to campus, a flyer in hand.

"Can you point me toward College Hall?" she asked a girl with close-cropped hair.

The girl stared back, then pulled out an earbud.

"Sorry," Elisabeth said. "College Hall?"

The girl pointed to a red-brick building with turrets at the top.

Inside, the space was hushed, dim. Stephanie had told her there was a bulletin board where people from off campus could post requests for help. But the walls in front of her were lined with portraits of the school's presidents—twelve somber-looking white men with varying degrees of hair loss and, at the end of the line, a black woman with a triumphant smile. Elisabeth stared at her until the baby squawked, a reminder of her purpose.

She turned a corner. There, between the open doors of the registrar's office and Alumnae Relations, was a large corkboard, with papers pinned all over. One advertised a potluck supper at the local Presbyterian church. Another, the need for volunteers at the animal shelter. Most were from mothers like her, looking for sitters, though unlike her, the others only wanted someone a few hours a week, or to call on date night.

As Elisabeth took it all in, a man's voice broke the silence. The sound startled her.

He came into view a moment later. Silver haired, handsome, in a gray blazer and dark jeans, walking beside a student who wanted to know if it was possible to get an extension on a paper because, she said, her grandmother had died.

The man showed no sign of sympathy.

"I'll need a copy of the obituary," he said.

Harsh, Elisabeth thought. Peculiar.

You couldn't marry a guy who taught at a women's college. It would be like marrying a gynecologist. There was something pervy about it.

Or maybe there wasn't.

For some time now, she'd been attempting to be less judgmental. While trying for a baby, she read a blog post about how a woman's negative thoughts could harm her fertility. From then on, every time she wanted to say something judgy, Elisabeth said the word *banana* instead. There were entire days when her speech came out like a letter censored during World War II: "And I love my sister, but she can be so *banana*. I know this guy she's dating is *banana*, but does she deserve anything but *banana* after that whole *banana* thing with the *banana* guy?"

One night she dreamed she gave birth to a banana.

Four potential sitters called in response to the ad. She had already ruled out three of them.

The first, Silvia, was, to Elisabeth's surprise, not a student but a woman from El Salvador with grown kids of her own.

Silvia critiqued Elisabeth's way of burping Gil; she suggested he was cold and should be wearing one more layer. This didn't bother Elisabeth. Because she often believed she was the only person who knew what the baby needed, it was an interesting change of pace to have someone come along who thought she had no idea what she was doing.

She planned to offer Silvia the job, but at the last minute, Elisabeth thought to ask how she'd come across the flyer.

"I work nights, cleaning, at the college," Silvia said. "I've been looking for a good second job."

"But if you already work nights and you were to take this job, when would you sleep?"

"I don't need much sleep. I'll nap when the baby does."

Was that normal? For a sitter to nap on the job?

Silvia looked Elisabeth up and down. "You sure that baby came out of you? You're tiny."

Other people had asked the same question, which Elisabeth presumed they meant as a compliment, but it felt accusatory. Though she was naturally thin and petite, her body was foreign to her now. The pouch of skin where her flat stomach had been. Her breasts, still small, yet newly droopy. Her hips were wider, her feet too big for certain shoes. All this, she knew, was supposed to be distasteful to her. It was, sometimes. But it was also the proof of what had happened in that body, the thing she had done that was somehow both ordinary and extraordinary.

The second candidate, a sophomore with a blue streak in her hair, answered her phone in the middle of the interview. She didn't say, *I'm sorry, I have to take this, it's an emergency,* she just held up a finger while Elisabeth was midsentence and said, "Hey."

The third had only ever worked with older kids, as a camp counselor. She didn't support the baby's head when she held him. Elisabeth snatched Gil back, a tad overdramatic, and said she'd be in touch.

The fourth candidate was due at nine. She had sent an email in response to the ad, saying she had spent the previous summer working as a nanny in London. Elisabeth knew better than to get her hopes up, but she could not stop entertaining visions of Gil being adored by a loving, yet firm, British woman.

Julie Andrews as Mary Poppins.

Julie Andrews as Maria von Trapp.

At five to the hour, Gil asleep on her shoulder, she watched a plump young brunette in a baggy T-shirt dress and flip-flops come up the block.

The girl walked past the house without slowing down.

Elisabeth decided it must not be her.

She had made coffee and put out muffins and croissants, as if she were hosting brunch. She did the same for the others. The girl with the blue streak in her hair had asked if she could take the leftover pastries to go.

Elisabeth had never interviewed anyone for a job before. When she was younger, she would have imagined that by the time she was doing so, she'd know how. That just being on this side of things conferred authority, control.

She pulled up her to-do list on her phone. *Dinner at Faye and George's. Shower. Babysitter. WRITE?* She sometimes added things to the list that she had already done, so that she could check them off later. A question mark after an item meant there was no way she was going to do it.

The doorbell rang right at nine, and there stood the girl in the T-shirt dress, a huge smile on her face. Had she kept walking so she wouldn't arrive early? Or had she gotten lost?

"You must be Sam," Elisabeth whispered, pushing the screen door open with one arm as she cradled the sleeping baby in the other. "I'm Elisabeth. And this is Gil."

"Hi," the girl said softly. *Chipper,* that was the word for her tone.

She stepped inside, looked around.

A soft blue rug ran the length of the front hall, exposing on either side the hardwood floors beneath. To the left was the large, sunny living room. To the right, a wooden staircase with a white banister. Midway up the stairs, there was a stained-glass window, which Elisabeth had loved as soon as she walked in for the first time, knowing then, before she had seen a single room, that they would buy the place.

"I love your house," Sam said. "It has such a peaceful vibe."

Elisabeth almost snorted, but then took stock of herself: her plain white button-down and black leggings. Her bare feet, her hair up in a loose bun. The silver tray of pastries; Simon and Garfunkel playing on the Bose. The baby in his soft white pajamas. She could see how it seemed peaceful from the outside.

The girl couldn't tell what was in her head. Elisabeth liked that.

"Oh my goodness, look at his curls," Sam said.

It was what most people said when they saw Gil for the first time. The words filled Elisabeth with a foolish degree of pride, as if she had designed him that way.

He was born with a full head of golden hair, which made him special from the start. Nurses came to her hospital room just to see the curls.

They all called Elisabeth Mom, and Andrew was Dad.

The first time it happened, the nurse was not much older than Sam.

"You should take three Motrin, Mom," she said. And, "Mom, press the button if you need to get up. Don't try to stand on your own yet."

In her stupor, Elisabeth wondered whether the girl really thought she was her mother. *Was she?*

Later, Nomi told her nurses did this so they didn't have to learn the names of parents they would know only for forty-eight hours. Elisabeth thought maybe it was also meant to help the parents catch up to what had happened, saying the words over and over, until they felt like the truth.

"What can I get you, Sam?" she said now. "Coffee? Pellegrino?"

"Nothing, thanks. I'm good."

Sam kicked off her shoes.

"You don't have to," Elisabeth said, but the gesture pleased her. None of the others had thought to do it.

"I should wash my hands," she said.

Elisabeth pointed at a narrow door. "Powder room."

The handwashing seemed to take a long time. It felt odd, oppressive, to wait in the hall. Elisabeth went and sat down on the sofa.

The baby woke up from his nap.

"Hello, my love," she whispered. "There's a friend here to meet you."

It occurred to her then that Sam wasn't English.

When she came in, Gil was sitting, assisted, in Elisabeth's lap, big blue eyes open wide.

Sam gasped.

"He's beautiful," she said, and Elisabeth loved her at once.

"Please," she said. "Sit. Tell us about yourself. You said in your email that you were a nanny in London? So I thought—" She laughed.

"What?" Sam said.

"I guess I thought you'd have an accent."

"Oh. No. Sorry. I was just there for the summer. I worked for a family with eighteen-month-old twins and a newborn. All boys."

"Dear God."

"It wasn't as hard as it sounds," Sam said. "I've been taking care of children my whole life. I'm the oldest of four, and I have nineteen younger cousins."

"My goodness."

"My mother never wanted me to babysit. She wanted me to get a waitressing job. She said it was more respectable. But I love working with kids."

"I was a waitress for years. There's nothing respectable about it, believe me," Elisabeth said with a smile. She pushed the tray of pastries toward Sam. "What did you think of London? I've liked it there, the few times I've been."

"I love it," Sam said. "My boyfriend, Clive, is there. He's English. I'm hoping to get back to see him as much as I can this year. It's expensive, but his sister-in-law works for British Airways, so we can use her discount if we go standby."

"Is Clive a student too?" Elisabeth asked.

"He—graduated."

Elisabeth wanted to ask more, but she could hear Andrew's voice in her head: *Boundaries*.

"What are you studying?" she said instead.

"I'm a Studio Art/English Lit double major. My dad likes to joke that he's not sure which is the more useless degree. He wanted me to major in economics."

"I've worked with a lot of former English majors," Elisabeth said. "They turned out okay. Don't worry."

"What do you do?" Sam said. "If you don't mind my asking."

"Of course not. I'm a journalist. I was at the *Times* for twelve years."

"How exciting."

"It was."

Elisabeth did not say that a year ago, she and half her friends had taken buyouts, rather than risk getting laid off six months later.

"Now I'm writing a book," she said.

"That's incredible. Is it your first?"

"My third."

"Wow."

"Do you know what you want to do after graduation?"

Sam looked embarrassed. "Since I was a kid, I've loved to paint. But that's not a *job*, obviously."

"It is for some people," Elisabeth said.

"I'd love to work in a gallery, maybe teach someday," Sam said. She straightened her posture. "Sorry. I should have mentioned, I have lots of infant experience. I'm CPR certified. I have great references here in town. I did a bunch of night and weekend sitting my first three years of school."

"And three full days a week won't interfere with your studies?"

"Senior year," Sam said. "Not too strenuous. Besides, every other year, I had a campus job in the dining hall and built my classes around that, so I'm used to it."

"Great," Elisabeth said. She had a list of questions, but no idea where she'd put it. She felt like she should be asking more. She had gotten caught up in the pleasant conversation.

Sam looked around the room. "How long have you lived here?"

"A month."

Elisabeth and Andrew had started talking about leaving the city ten years ago, on their third date. They had gone to so many open houses, casting themselves into lives they weren't ready to live—small farms on the Hudson, New Jersey Colonials with big backyards, even beach cottages in Maine, which, in mid-July, they could almost convince themselves they might stay in year-round.

"You shouldn't waste a realtor's time if you're not serious," said her mother-in-law, apparently a champion of realtors' rights.

But Elisabeth could never be sure whether they were serious or not. New Yorkers reveled in complaining about the city: the crowds, the subway delays, the hassle. Every sane person wanted to go somewhere else. New Yorkers could best be understood not by where they lived but by where they talked about escaping to—L.A. or Portland or Austin or wherever they came from to begin with. And yet, when someone left, it shocked her.

Her friend Rachel had moved to a suburb of Cleveland, her hometown. She spoke of its charms whenever they talked, repeating herself.

"On Fridays in summer, they have beerfests at the botanical garden, and you can sit in the grass, drinking craft beers from a bunch of different breweries," Rachel had said on at least five occasions.

It sounded nice, but how often could a person drink beer at the botanical garden? Then what?

To Elisabeth and Andrew, life in the city had never felt permanent, even though they both lived there for twenty years, longer than they'd lived anywhere else, including the places they called home. She had long wondered what would be the thing to make them go. A child, she assumed. But Gil wasn't the reason. It was the situation with Andrew's father; the situation with Andrew himself.

Most days, Elisabeth didn't know what she was doing at 32 Laurel Street. How, after all that searching for the perfect place, she had ended up here, in the middle of nowhere.

Before they left, when anyone asked where they were moving to, Andrew would say, "Upstate."

She felt the need to add, "But not, like, cool upstate. Take wherever you're picturing and add two hundred miles."

She liked that their house didn't look like every other house on the block, at least. Their neighbors had torn down old capes to build monstrosities that extended to the furthest possible edges of their property.

Their house was an original. Small but lovely. A glossy red door, ivy crawling up a white wooden façade that the realtor advised would need to be repainted every four or five years. Elisabeth and Andrew nodded, casual, when she said it, as if they hadn't spent their entire adult lives in apartments, never taking on a home-improvement project more involved than changing a light bulb.

Gil reached for Sam now and cooed, unwilling to be left out of the conversation.

"Is it okay?" Sam asked.

"Of course."

She took hold of him, held him up in the air. In that way one does with an infant, she spoke to Elisabeth through him. "I can tell you are an exceptionally smart young man, Gilbert," she said. "I think we'd have lots of fun together."

He grabbed hold of her hair, and they both laughed.

Elisabeth beamed. "Look how good you are with him."

"He seems like such a sweet one."

"He is. We got lucky."

Her eyes still on Gil, Sam said, almost absentmindedly, "Do you think you'll have more kids?"

A strange thing to ask during a job interview. But then, she was young enough to believe this was a simple, unloaded question. And hadn't Elisabeth recently complained to Andrew that it gave her the creeps how everything here seemed hidden? In the city, she found it unsettling that lives were on display. People fought or ate lunch or tweezed their eyebrows right in front of you on the subway. But her neighbors here, darting out their front doors and straight into their SUVs with plastic smiles and apologetic waves, were worse.

"I only ever wanted one," Elisabeth said. "Andrew, my husband, he'd have five. So, who knows what will happen."

Didn't she sound carefree? Unbothered. Willing to leave it all up to chance. She thought of the two embryos, frozen in liquid nitrogen at a storage facility in Queens.

Andrew had nightmares about them.

Four times a year, they received a bill from Weill Cornell in the amount of two hundred and sixty-two dollars. The storage fee was the same no matter how many embryos a person had, so every time Elisabeth saw that bracketed number 2 on her statement, she felt a tug of annoyance at the cost.

In the early days, when doing IVF was still a theoretical, they read an article that said there were more than a million frozen embryos around the country that would likely go unused. Couples who had produced children in this way and didn't want to have more found themselves in limbo—unable to discard what could potentially become their child, but unwilling to bring that child to fruition.

Andrew said it wasn't fair to create those potential lives and then just leave them there. He made her swear they would never do such a thing.

She thought to tell Sam all this now, but resisted.

"It's time for Gil to eat. I'll get him a bottle," Elisabeth said, rising to her feet. "I do breastfeed, but I supplement with formula."

She went into the usual monologue. "I've always had a low supply. I was taking forty herbs a day for the first three months, and tying myself in knots. Three different lactation consultants. This disgusting tea that made my sweat smell like maple syrup. Pumping after every feed, every two hours, even in the middle of the night. Then I decided to throw some formula into the mix and be done with it."

The intensity of her shame had surprised her at the time. Even now, she'd be loath to say it to another mother.

"I once read that Charles Manson was breastfed," Sam said brightly. "Ever since, I've figured that it can't possibly matter one way or the other."

Elisabeth smiled.

"Are you sure I can't get you anything to drink?" she said. "I made coffee."

"Coffee would be great if it's no trouble."

"It's no trouble at all."

3

As soon as Andrew got home, Elisabeth thrust the baby toward him and said, "Can you hold him for a sec? I have to pee."

When she called him at work earlier to say she had hired a sitter, Andrew said, "I can't wait to hear more about her tonight."

Translation: *I'm busy. Stop talking.*

From the start, theirs had been an egalitarian marriage. He cooked; she washed the dishes. He vacuumed and did laundry and mopped the kitchen floor. She cleaned the bathroom, which most people thought was the worst chore of all, when really it was the easiest. If either of them did more than their share, it was Andrew, no question.

But it sometimes seemed like the baby was only hers. At first, it was a biological thing. But Gil was four months old, could take a bottle, and still she did all the night feedings, all the mental calculations of knowing when he needed more diapers and lotion and clothes.

"His pants are getting tight. I think he's ready for the next size up," she said a week ago, and Andrew made the mistake of asking, "What size does he wear now?"

In part, she knew, this was a function of Andrew's new job and the fact that she was more often physically present at home. She was technically still on maternity leave, though that was a murky concept when you worked for yourself. But Elisabeth couldn't help fearing it was more than that; that parenthood had redefined the terms in a way she hadn't expected.

By the end of the day, she felt exhausted and resentful and spent. Hiding in the bathroom was a greater solace than any spa she had ever been to, as relaxing as a vacation in Saint Barts.

Twenty minutes passed, and she was still on the toilet, scrolling through pictures of the baby on her phone. This was what happened—the urge to escape Gil fulfilled, Elisabeth pined for him. The first day home from the hospital, she got teary at the thought of his moving away to college.

"You're going to live at home and commute," she told him.

She had never before missed something as it was happening.

Elisabeth texted Nomi.

I hired a sitter.

Great! What's she like?

College senior. Wants to be a painter. Adorable. We talked for two hours.

Why?

She was interesting. (And it's possible I haven't had a real conversation with anyone besides Andrew in weeks.)

A moment later, her phone lit up with what she assumed was Nomi's response, but instead her sister's name appeared.

E . . . I HATE to ask, but is there any way you can spot me $200? I'll pay you back ASAP—the deal's going through next week!

A familiar knot in her stomach.

Sure, Elisabeth wrote back. *No prob.*

She hated the feeling this thing with her sister always aroused in her.

She toggled over to the BK Mamas as a palate cleanser. It was an instinct beyond her control, like a stutter or a twitch. Someone had posted the saddest story, about a child abused in foster care.

There was a related online petition. She signed without reading the particulars. Her eyes filled with tears. Why had she logged on to this page? Elisabeth was certain she had come looking for something, but she couldn't remember what.

She sensed Andrew's presence outside the door.

"Hon. You okay in there?"

His polite yet passive-aggressive way of asking why the hell she had been in the bathroom so long.

She stood and flushed the toilet.

"People are monsters," she said when she emerged.

"Hmm?"

"Something I read online. You don't want to know."

"Okay. We should get going, huh?"

"One time years ago, your belt was on the bed, so I hit myself with it to see how it felt, and Jesus Christ, it's barbaric. How could anyone do that to a child? I didn't even hit myself very hard and it hurt so much."

"Well, you have a low pain threshold," he said.

"I do? How do you know?"

"You think a cricket landing on you feels like getting punched in the arm."

On the way to his parents' house, he told her they didn't have to stay for long. His mother had said it would do his father good to see the baby. She was worried about him again.

"He's been holed up with those files for the past three nights," Andrew said. "She says he needs a distraction."

"Or she does," Elisabeth said.

For some time now, her father-in-law, George, had been consumed by an idea. Months ago, he told Elisabeth how it came to him when he overheard a stranger yelling into a cell phone about how America was no longer a global superpower.

"He said, 'This hasn't been the greatest nation in the world for sixty years. That's just something we tell ourselves,'" George recalled. "It pissed me off. For the rest of the day, I wondered why. Was it a feeling left over from grammar school, where each morning we pledged allegiance to the flag and meant it?"

After that, George started to notice a pattern. More and more, the conversations he had came back around to the sorry state of things, how life was getting worse instead of better.

"There's no protection for the little guy anymore. No accountability from higher up," he explained to Elisabeth. "We're on our own. It's like a hollow tree. That's how I think of it. On the surface, this country looks more or less like it always did. But there's nothing inside holding it up. No integrity, no support. Doesn't matter if the leaves are green and the trunk is tall. A hollow tree can't stand for long."

In the downstairs guest room that also served as George's home office were toppling stacks of newspaper clippings and printouts meant to back up his theory, as if someone might arrive at any moment and ask him to prove it. Dozens of handwritten notes, scrawled on Post-its, were stuck to the wall.

Her mother-in-law grimaced whenever she walked in there, like she had stumbled upon a serial killer's lair.

"What is the point of this, George?" Elisabeth heard her say once.

"The point is people blame themselves when it's systemic. The citizens of this country should be taking to the streets, not popping antidepressants."

"And what exactly are you going to do about it?" Faye said.

Since Andrew was in kindergarten, George had made a good living with a small fleet of Town Cars he owned. He and a handful of employees shuttled people to and from the airport and around the valley. Three years ago, George decided to reinvest in the business. He used some of his and Faye's retirement savings to buy three brand-new Lincolns. The timing could not have been worse. Six months later, Uber came to the area, offering cheaper fares and immediate bookings, and wiped out his company.

Eventually, George started driving for Uber himself. Faye told Elisabeth it was awful, diminishing. The pay was an insult. Half the passengers were drunk college kids. George could lug three heavy suitcases through the airport and up someone's front stairs, and still get just a thank-you in return, if he was lucky.

"The app says customers don't have to tip," Faye said, disgusted. Elisabeth was astonished to hear her say the word *app*.

For a while, Faye reported that George was in bed by seven most nights, that he had no appetite, that he wouldn't talk much, which wasn't like him.

Then, instead of being depressed, George became obsessed—with the Hollow Tree, with the plight of the common man. Andrew was annoyed that instead of getting a new job, and facing what had happened, George now spent all his free time on this pointless endeavor. Elisabeth thought the whole exercise was a kind of therapy, a means of exploring what had happened to him, without having to make it personal, which wasn't George's way.

"If you still hate it here in a year, we'll go back," Andrew said now, in the car.

"I don't hate it, exactly," she said. "Besides, I've seen *Bridges of Madison County*. Once the wife moves to her husband's hometown, she never leaves. All she gets is one weekend of passionate infidelity with Clint Eastwood."

"At least you have that to look forward to."

They didn't actually live in his hometown, which was run-down and somehow perpetually gray no matter the weather. Their house was twenty minutes away in the nearest college town, a place where Elisabeth had imagined attending lectures and eating Ethiopian food, and availing herself of all the best parts of an intellectual-adjacent life.

In reality, it felt strange to live in a place that revolved around a college campus when you yourself had nothing to do with it. Everyone in town referred to it as *the* college, just as in their world, New York was *the* city and Gilbert was *the* baby—you knew there were others, but they didn't matter.

So far, Elisabeth had gone to exactly one reading, given by a poet she liked. She expected the room to be full of older women in long cashmere cardigans, but everyone in attendance was a student. They swiveled their heads as one when she entered, taking her in as you might a space alien.

There were three colleges within fifteen miles of their house. The women's college around the block; a state university that was so large she had mistaken it for a city the first time she saw it; and the hippie college where Andrew spent his days, a place where they didn't believe in grades or even desks. During class, students sat on mats on the floor.

After spending so many years in Brooklyn, they had believed themselves to be as progressive as was humanly possible. But they were learning now that they'd been mistaken.

"This kid in my lab told me today that he's pansexual," Andrew said over dinner one night.

"What's that mean?" she asked.

"It means he's attracted to all genders."

"So he's bi."

"No."

"How is he not bi?"

"He doesn't see gender. Or maybe he sees it, but it's not part of what attracts him to a person."

"Okay. But he's attracted to both genders, so basically—bi. Right?"

"No, because gender is a spectrum, not a binary. He said the only reason babies are assigned one gender or the other at birth is because the American medical establishment is stuck in a hetero-patriarchal view of said binary. So really, we shouldn't force Gil to subscribe to these norms. We should let him make up his own mind."

"Huh," she said, considering this.

It felt to her like humanity was on the cusp of something. Maybe the world was becoming a more tolerant place, and their child would grow up with entirely different boundaries than the ones they'd known. Gender-neutral toys were all the rage. Her friends would sooner give their daughters hard drugs than Barbies. She wanted to know how this would shape them as they grew, how Gil's generation would come to think about their own bodies, and one another's.

For a moment, Elisabeth glimpsed her former self—the curiosity, the thrill, that came from asking questions of people whose lives were nothing like her own. It had always amazed her how willing strangers were to open up to a journalist, even on the worst days of their lives. Maybe especially then.

"I'm so jealous of you," she told Andrew. "My most interesting conversation of the last week was with the FedEx guy. I told him our address was 32 Laurel Street. He insisted it was 23."

Locals like her in-laws complained about the colleges. They caused too much traffic; they were full of self-important academics who looked down on regular people. But whatever money those students and their parents pumped into restaurants and hotels and gas stations and grocery stores was the only thing keeping this corner of the world afloat. Each campus was abutted by a few blocks of pretty houses and a downtown full of quirky shops and music venues and vegan cafés. Then, abruptly, things dropped off.

Years ago, George had told her, the area boomed with mills that produced lumber and paper. There was a soda-bottling plant, a toothbrush factory. But when these places closed, nothing came along to replace them. Now half the towns around here were all but abandoned. Stores and bars and restaurants were few and far between, only their signs left behind to remind you of what had once been and was no more.

Immigrants from El Salvador and Mexico and a large Puerto Rican population had settled in certain towns, out where there were still working dairy farms and fruit orchards. In Weaverville, you might go to the old five-and-dime and hear nothing but Spanish spoken. The place sold Mexican spices and sodas and candies.

Elisabeth liked this—the classic architecture, populated with people and things one wouldn't expect. But the town was otherwise depressing. Empty storefronts, houses no one wanted to buy. Not even a school anymore. The kids got bused elsewhere.

Faye, who was raised there, shook her head whenever Weaverville came up in conversation and said, "That town used to be something."

The baby was asleep in the back seat when they arrived.

"Maybe I should stay out here with him," Elisabeth said. "You can bring me a plate."

"Ha," Andrew said. "Nice try."

Gil was alert and craning his neck to take in the new surroundings by the time they reached the back door.

The door opened straight into the kitchen, which hadn't been renovated since the seventies. A yellow linoleum floor, wood-paneled cabinets, and, above them, a border of purple tulips, hand-stenciled by Faye.

She raced over from the stove and took Gil from Andrew's arms.

"Hello, baby," Faye said, raising him to the light.

The dog came in, howling.

"Duke, don't be jealous," Faye said. "You know I love you too."

She looked at Andrew and Elisabeth as if just noticing them.

"Dinner's almost ready," she said. "Beef stroganoff."

"Yum," Andrew said, even though he hated beef stroganoff.

He had wanted to be a chef when he was young, but he was afraid he'd never make any money. Instead, Andrew made cooking a hobby. Elisabeth had often wondered how he got so good at it, growing up with a mother whose recipes all seemed to include Hamburger Helper.

Faye handed the baby back to Andrew, sated by her thirty seconds of quality time. She lowered her voice to a whisper. "We got another notice from our friends at Citibank. We have ninety days to make the payment, or we're out. Your father refuses to care. Like he's going to call the bank's bluff. I try to make him talk to me about a plan, and he says he's busy."

Elisabeth pretended to be looking for something in the diaper bag. Whenever Faye mentioned their finances, she wanted to bury the uncomfortable conversation, to squelch it, to make it disappear.

In the last year, she had realized that George and Faye were homeowners only in the loosest sense. They had refinanced and borrowed against this house so many times that they now owed more on it than they'd paid in the first place.

A thump came from George's office, the sound of something heavy hitting the floor.

Faye straightened, and said, "Anyhow. What's new with you?"

"Elisabeth found us a great babysitter today," Andrew said. "Now she can finally get back to work."

A strange pause as she pondered whether to be offended. He made it sound like she'd been floating on a pool raft drinking piña coladas for four months.

"She's a student at the college," Elisabeth said.

"That's young to be in charge of an infant, isn't it?" Faye asked.

"I thought so too at first. But her references were great. Gil seemed to adore her. And she has tons of experience with babies. Much more than I do."

Faye frowned. "Be careful. I saw on the news this terrible thing. A babysitter killed three children. Drowned them in the bathtub."

She only mouthed the words *killed* and *drowned*, didn't say them out loud, to shield Gil from the horror.

"She did it with her bare hands," Faye continued.

"This happened around here?" Andrew said.

"No, it was in Ohio or someplace."

Faye glowed as she said it. She thrived on the mere suggestion of tragedy. She had once diagnosed Gil as autistic because he stared at a light bulb. "That's one of the signs," she said. "I *think* that's one of the signs."

For each life stage, there existed cautionary tales meant to keep women in their place. Every female in New York was haunted by a story. Not some urban myth, but whatever was on the cover of the *Post* the day she arrived. A girl who stayed late at a bar and ended up raped, her body rolled in a carpet, tossed in a dumpster. A girl who was pushed in front of an oncoming train by some lunatic for no reason. A girl whose roommate came home drunk one night, stabbed her to death, and didn't remember any of it in the morning.

So it was with new mothers. The air was full of threats. On the news: the exhausted, overwhelmed woman who left her baby to suffocate in a hot car. Online: the day-care worker who dosed the kids with Benadryl to make them sleep, accidentally killing them all. Overheard in the produce aisle at the grocery store: the one about the parents who kept putting off that first-aid class, and then watched helplessly as their child choked to death on a grape.

Elisabeth heard George's heavy footsteps coming toward them now. A happy-making sound that drove away all thoughts of small lifeless bodies floating in a tub.

"Lizzy!" he said when he saw her.

He was the only person who had ever called her that, the only one who could get away with it.

George still wore the same uniform he had worn to work for the past thirty-five years: a black suit, the jacket hanging on a hook in the mudroom now, to be slipped into again tomorrow. He had taken off his patent leather shoes. On his feet were black socks with a bright burst of gold at the toe.

Before he shut down the car service, it was George's habit to be out the door by seven at the latest each morning, sometimes four or five if he had to make an early trip to the airport. He started every day by polishing his Town Car's black exterior, vacuuming the floor mats, placing new bottles of water in the cup holders built into the back-seat console, filling a bowl with peppermints. He still went through the motions, even though, as an Uber driver, he could work in sweatpants and drive a beat-up Mazda and no one would care. Something about this pulled at Elisabeth's heart.

George hugged her. He was a wall of a man. When he hugged you, it felt like being a child again. Safe and small. Elisabeth wanted to stay awhile. But George moved away from her, clapped Andrew on the back, then went to the stove and made a big show of inhaling.

He whistled. "That smells delicious."

Elisabeth wondered if he too was lying. To her, the room smelled like an elementary school cafeteria at lunchtime.

George and Faye had a solid marriage. She appreciated this. Her own parents had been miserable together, and perverse in their misery. All she ever wanted was for them to be normal, to wake up one day and realize they loved each other after all.

Elisabeth spent her childhood playing referee. She could walk into a room and assess in an instant whether her parents were fighting, and what about. When her father was cheating, her mother confided in her like she was a friend. She spared Elisabeth none of the details.

She was obsessed with being thin and beautiful and, most important, young. She had her daughters using antiaging cream when they were in middle school. She went on fad diets and made them join her. She fasted and encouraged them to do the same. She praised them for being skinny and chastised them when they didn't look their best. She made a game out of the three of them looking in a mirror, taking turns pointing out their imperfections.

"No one is going to tell you when you look like shit," their mother said. "A woman has to be her own worst critic."

Any talk of bodies now made Elisabeth uncomfortable. But in this respect, she thought the damage done to her had been minimal, considering. She had been lucky enough to have teachers who told her she was smart, who encouraged her intellect. Her godfather was a journalist. He saw in her the hallmarks of a writer.

Charlotte, on the other hand, emerged from their mother's care an almost entirely superficial creature. She was naturally thin and pretty, but on top of that she spent hours each morning doing her hair and applying makeup. It surprised no one when she gained a following on Instagram as a self-described "influencer," which involved posting photos of herself in bathing suits on various Caribbean islands.

Their parents divorced when Elisabeth was eight and Charlotte was five. Their mother ran off the day the papers were signed, leaving her daughters in the care of a nanny—and their father, though they rarely saw him. When their mother returned six months later, she and their father had somehow gotten back together. They never explained how or why. They got along almost too well for a while, before things returned to the way they'd always been.

When Elisabeth was a junior in high school, they lived apart for a year. One day, toward the end of that period, she said something to her mother about the two of them having separated, and her mother said, "What gives you the idea that we're separated?"

"Dad living in the beach house was one indication," Elisabeth said, angry, confused.

"You'll understand when you're older," her mother said, an oft-repeated statement that irked Elisabeth because she sensed it wasn't true, yet by definition could not refute it.

Her parents were together again by the time she graduated, holding hands as they watched her accept her diploma.

Almost two decades passed, time enough for her to stop worrying whether their marriage would survive. They had not grown happier or less truculent with age, but they were old now. She figured they had gotten breaking up out of their systems. Then, two years ago, her parents split again. Her father found someone almost immediately on a business trip to Arizona, and moved to Tucson to be with her. He went to some lengths to expedite the divorce, making Elisabeth and Charlotte wonder if he planned to marry this new woman, whom neither of them had met.

The news of her parents' latest breakup still hadn't sunk in. They told her, and Elisabeth put the information away in a box, determined not to let it derail her. She was trying to get pregnant at the time, which consumed so much emotional energy.

Finally, it worked. Then came the bomb drop of a new baby.

In Brooklyn, they lived in an old Italian neighborhood. Every year on the Fourth of July, men set off fireworks on their corner. The noise shook the building; rockets ricocheted off their bedroom windows and twice cracked them down the middle. They never wanted to be the annoying gentrifiers who complained about tradition, so for years, they said nothing.

When Gil was around six weeks old, the fireworks began, and for the first time in his life he seemed scared. His face scrunched up. He sobbed into Elisabeth's shirt. Her protector instincts kicked in. She called the police, even though the cops in their precinct were the brothers and cousins of the guys outside the window. When the officer asked for her name and number, she provided them without thinking.

"You gave them your name?" Andrew said when she hung up.

Two days later, late to the pediatrician, they hustled up the block to the car they had purchased hours before she went into labor.

Andrew pressed the automatic-lock fob, but the doors didn't open.

He tried to unlock the driver's side with the key, but it wouldn't work either.

"Holy shit," he said. "They did that thing where they fill the locks so you can't get in."

"That's a thing?" she said.

Andrew rattled the door handles.

Elisabeth pulled out her phone.

"What are you doing?" he said.

"Googling to see if that's a thing."

"It's a thing," he said.

"Retribution," she said. "For calling the police on them."

"I told you you shouldn't have given your name," he said, shaking his head. Then, "Oh."

"Oh what?"

Andrew blinked. "This isn't our car."

As soon as they had established a hint of a routine, a bit of normalcy, they moved here, a whole new kind of discord.

"Who wants to try some homemade lager?" George said.

It wasn't a question. He was already pulling a brown growler from the fridge.

He filled the glasses preset at the dinner table.

"Those were for water," Faye said, her voice tinged with irritation.

"The Pilgrims never drank water," George said. "Did you know that? Only beer. Even the kids."

"Yes, and most of them were dead by thirty-five." Faye looked at Andrew. "Your father makes beer now. He got a kit in the mail, and he thinks he's Sam Adams."

Elisabeth took a seat at the table, gave the beer a try. She couldn't tell if it was good or disgusting. She took another sip. Faye started talking about coupons. Elisabeth drank until the glass was empty.

"Delicious, right?" George said, refilling it.

She nodded. Already, she felt that lovely blurring of edges, the slight disassociation of self from everyone else in the room. When she was young and got tipsy, all she wanted to do was kiss someone. Now she wanted to take a nap.

"How's the venture going, son?" George asked.

The venture.

That's how he referred to it, every time.

George was a devoted father. If he thought Andrew's idea was a bad one, he didn't let on. But he never called it what it was, which made her wonder.

What it was, was a grill. A solar-powered grill.

Elisabeth had been there when Andrew came up with the idea a decade ago. It was early in their relationship, their first weekend away. They'd gone to Florida for the wedding of his college friend. At the rehearsal dinner, a beach barbecue, everyone stood around admiring the sunset, eating steak and burgers, guzzling the bride's signature cocktail, which tasted like fruit punch but was about eighty percent rum.

That's when Andrew said, "Why are there no solar-powered grills?"

When no one responded, he went on, "Think about it. It's genius. Nobody barbecues in the rain. And with solar you'd avoid that gross charcoal taste, which is, of course, the taste of cancer."

"Eww," said Charlie, the groom. He looked down at his plate.

The burgers were slightly burnt. Elisabeth hoped no one thought that was what had inspired Andrew's comment.

His friends Joel and Ethan nodded.

"That's fucking brilliant," Joel said.

Ethan narrowed his eyes, deep in thought. "I like it."

"We should do it," Andrew said.

The others agreed. Elisabeth wondered if their enthusiasm was genuine. People did barbecue on rainy days, didn't they? And wasn't that charcoal taste the whole point of grilling?

She decided it didn't matter. They were all bombed by that point.

The next morning, lying in the hotel bed, heavy curtains pulled closed, Andrew whispered, "I was up all night thinking about the grill."

It took her a moment to figure out what he meant.

"Do you not think it's a good idea?" he said.

"It's interesting," she said.

"I mean, Joel said it's brilliant."

Joel is a personal injury attorney, she wanted to say, but did not.

Elisabeth was trying to assess whether her hangover was moderate or severe. She needed coffee.

Andrew's intensity for the grill lasted as long as the weekend away. He didn't mention it again for months, until a dinner party at Nomi's, when a colleague of hers claimed his father invented superglue but had never secured a patent, and so got screwed out of millions. Everyone told the story of something they'd thought of. Nomi's husband, Brian, swore he invented TiVo back when he was in middle school.

"He brings it up every time I want to record something," Nomi said.

Andrew explained the grill, going so far as to sketch it out on a napkin—it would resemble a papasan chair, covered in reflective panels that used the heat of the sun to cook food. The food would be placed in a pan that sat on a tripod in the middle of the contraption.

Elisabeth tried to picture a suburban family in a backyard, standing around the thing, drinking beers, waiting for their burgers to be done.

"I need to find an engineer to help me figure out the best curvature for the panels," Andrew said. "That's the key."

"Damn, Andrew," Nomi teased. "You're not messing around."

Elisabeth didn't know until then that he'd thought it through. She was certain she registered disappointment on Andrew's face when no one jumped to declare his idea the best one of all.

That napkin sketch ended up on their refrigerator in Brooklyn. Every time it caught her eye, Elisabeth wondered if Andrew pictured it hanging in a frame behind his desk one day, after he'd made it big.

The grill came up again here and there over the years, half joke, half something else. A stack of books appeared on his side of the bed: The *Solar Electricity Handbook*. And *Off the Grid: Solar at Home*. And *Photovoltaic Design and Installation for Dummies*, which seemed like an oxymoron. Elisabeth never saw Andrew read any of them. At some point, she noticed they were gone.

Five years ago, Andrew left a job at a big consulting firm and took a slight pay cut to go work at a midlevel firm that focused on restaurants. Elisabeth hoped it would make him happier, having a hand in that world. But in a way, it was worse than before. He was close to the people who were doing what he wanted to do, but he wasn't one of them.

He kept the job for three years. They were trying for a baby. That had become their focus. Hers, at least.

Then one night in bed, Andrew said he couldn't breathe.

It scared her. It wasn't like him.

"What's going on?" she said.

Andrew said he was worried he was going to be stuck in a job he loathed for the rest of his life.

"I feel like I'm dying every morning on the way to work," he said. "I wish I was brave enough to take a risk."

"Maybe you should," she said. "Life's too short to have a job you hate."

"You're right," he said. "I should do it."

"Do what?"

"The grill. I mentioned the idea in this meeting last week with the owners of a restaurant group, a potential new client. One of the guys *got* it, you know? I could tell. I think I could get him on board as an early investor, maybe. He said he'd love to see a prototype once I have it."

Elisabeth realized then that she hadn't meant what she said. Having a job you hated was at least half of what it was to be an adult. Andrew was usually practical and reliable and steady. She loved that about him, depended on it.

"This is my dream," he said. "I'd be an inventor in the food space. I'm sure I could come up with more ideas if I had the time. Do you know about the guy who invented the Clog-B-Gone? It's just a piece of plastic that pulls out all the hair that's stuck in a drain. He made twenty-five million in the first year. Imagine if the grill did half that. We'd be set. My parents would be set."

He looked at her with the most hopeful eyes.

"But what would we do about money in the meantime?" she said.

"I have it figured out. I'll stay on at work on a contract basis for the next six months. I'll use that time to get started on developing the grill and to apply for grants and financing for the following year. And not that I'm anticipating it, but we have that money in savings if we ever really need it, right?"

She paused. "Right."

They hadn't merged their finances when they married, only came up with a loose arrangement—he would pay for the day-to-day, and, with her advances, the royalties, and the sale of movie rights from her first book, she would build their savings. For their future child, for college and retirement.

"Are you sure you're okay with this?" he said. "I know it sounds crazy. But I have a feeling now's the time."

That was the moment to voice her reservations, to tell him the truth. But Elisabeth couldn't do it. He had never discouraged her as long as she'd known him.

When George's business imploded, Andrew said he never would have left his job had he known his parents were about to be so strapped. He said he wanted more than anything to help them. Elisabeth assumed he was thinking about the savings account, that he wanted her to offer it up.

"Maybe I'm being overly simplistic," he said when she didn't. "They'd probably resent that. They might never be able to pay us back."

She wanted to say that of course they should offer Faye and George the money. But she couldn't. The money was gone.

Andrew's fellowship had been the deciding factor in them

leaving Brooklyn. He wanted to be closer to his parents so he could at least help them around the house, spend time with them, take George fishing. He applied, and Elisabeth agreed that if he got the fellowship, they could go. She never thought it would happen.

Despite her doubts, she was proud of him for making it this far. Amazed, actually. But then again, anyone with a truly great idea would have taken it to Stanford, or Harvard, or someplace. She could only imagine what the competition had been at the hippie college, where they called the engineering department Greengineering.

The department had a modest fund devoted to innovation, given each year to a promising amateur inventor working on some aspect of eco-friendly technology. The winner got a team of student workers and an adviser. Andrew had a year to make a prototype and get someone to license it. He had no plan for what would happen after that.

As with all her other shortcomings, Elisabeth blamed her inability to believe in him on her mother. She had had no model of what a devoted wife was supposed to look like.

Down through history there were stories of women who stood by men with *ventures*. These women were ultimately rewarded for their faith, for their willingness to live without vacations or home renovations or date nights, all in the service of the Great Idea. The wife who believed ended up rich beyond her dreams, with hobby pursuits like running an eponymous charity or buying the local bookstore in her favorite resort town.

The great man's battle cry: "None of it would have been possible without *her*."

Elisabeth wondered about the failed men, the ones no one talked about. Did their failures have to do with a lack of belief on their wives' parts, or were success stories written after the fact?

Did Steve Jobs's wife secretly get furious at all that tinkering in the garage and wish he'd go sell insurance with her brother until, poof, he struck gold, and then she could say she knew it, she knew it, she had always known.

"Are you making much progress, sweetheart?" Faye asked Andrew now.

Elisabeth looked at her husband.

"It's coming together," he said.

He took a bite of the stroganoff to discourage further questions.

In the early days after they moved, Andrew never stopped talking about his work. One night he came home and announced that a student on his team had calculated that the solar-powered grill had the potential to cook meat three times faster than a charcoal grill. Another night, he had a child's Christmas-morning grin on his face because he had learned there would be focus groups.

But lately, Andrew had no updates. Maybe he went to work and stared at the Internet all day, which Elisabeth figured was what most people did, and which would be fine with her if he had any sort of job security.

"How about you, Lizzy?" George said. "Has a new book idea come to you yet?"

"Not quite," she said.

She regretted telling him that she couldn't figure out what to write about next. George now saw it as yet another way into talking about his favorite subject.

Elisabeth knew what would follow.

"*The Hollow Tree,*" George said. "I'm telling you. It's bestseller material. You'd win a Pulitzer Prize."

"Dad, stop," Andrew said. "I beg of you."

In most respects, he had endless tolerance for his parents. At present, the Hollow Tree was the one exception. It wasn't that anything George said was untrue, but they all recoiled from it because, Elisabeth thought, of the intensity of his delivery. It seemed unhealthy. Not something to be encouraged. Faye said he'd take any excuse to talk about it, no matter whose company he was in. She preferred for Elisabeth and Andrew to change the subject whenever it came up, which it did, every time they saw him.

Last weekend, George had rambled on for half an hour about the importance of subscribing to the local newspaper. He said they needed to get the *Gazette* if they cared about supporting journalism.

"Elisabeth is a journalist," Andrew said.

"Yes," George said. "And?"

"We'll subscribe to the *Gazette* eventually," Andrew said. "It's not exactly top of mind, Dad. We pay for the *Times* online and I can barely manage to read that every day."

Actually, they didn't pay for the *Times*. Of course, they saw themselves as the kind of people who would and should and did, but in reality they still used the free login she'd always used at work, out of laziness more than anything.

Elisabeth felt guilty enough without the reminders from George. When they still lived in the city, they got food delivered almost every night for dinner, even after she read an article about how the website they ordered from was killing restaurants. She always meant to tip in cash, because the article said it was the only way to be sure the delivery guy got the money. But many nights, she didn't have any small bills, so she just added the tip online and hoped for the best, giving the man who arrived at her door an extra-wide smile as she took the warm paper bag from his hands.

Lately, she bought Gil's clothes and toys online, because there were no good stores nearby, and the few places selling organic baby items downtown were too expensive. Elisabeth justified this by reminding herself that she rarely got food delivered anymore, since the only delivery options here were pizza and Chinese.

She could think of plenty of other things they did right. They didn't drive an SUV or eat red meat very often. They recycled. They tried their best to be good. If they didn't have the time to attend protests with George, or sit around chronicling the ills of the world, well, that was normal. George, in his newfound zeal, was fond of saying, "People should be *doing* something and most of them aren't." It was impossible not to feel like he was referring, at least in part, to them.

Now George repeated himself. "How about it, Lizzy? *The Hollow Tree: An Exposé of American Greed*—it sounds big to me."

"Maybe you're right, George," she said. "It could be a big book."

"She's humoring me, but I'll take it," George said.

"I think you should write it," Elisabeth said. "It's your idea."

"I'm not a writer," he said. "You are. Here's a whole chapter for you. 'Commerce: The End of the Mom-and-Pop Shop.' You know the Dead Mall over in Dexter?"

Elisabeth shook her head.

"It's this enormous shopping center, maybe what, fifteen minutes from here? Andrew and his buddies hung out there all the time in high school. It's officially called the Shops at Evergreen Plaza. Years ago, that place was considered the height of sophistication. Now it's mostly empty."

No one replied, but George went on, undeterred.

"I got to thinking about that because, at my discussion group on Sunday, we had a presentation from Hal Donahue, who owns the shoe store downtown. They're going out of business after sixty years. He told us that a while back, customers started coming in, having him get three or four pairs of shoes for them, or their kids, to try on. Then right in front of Hal, they'd go on their phones to see if they could find them cheaper online. You know what Hal said? He said, 'Good luck to them. Is Amazon going to sponsor a Little League team and a parade float on the Fourth of July?' Great question, I thought. People can't live without all that."

"We couldn't live without Amazon," Andrew said.

Elisabeth shot him a look. *Why?*

Andrew never would have admitted it to any of their friends back in Brooklyn. Everyone claimed to be done with Amazon; you had to. Though Elisabeth had seen the packages on doorsteps all over their old neighborhood every evening when she arrived home from work.

"What do you buy there?" George said now.

"Everything," Andrew said. "Mostly stuff for the baby. We have a recurring order set up for diapers, wipes, formula. Free delivery. You should try it. It's so much more convenient than driving to the store, only to find that half the time they don't even have what you need."

"You choose convenience at the expense of humanity," George said.

Faye clucked her tongue at him.

Andrew shrugged. "I'll worry about humanity once my kid starts sleeping through the night."

A low blow, Elisabeth thought, especially considering Andrew never got up in the middle of the night. She gave George an encouraging smile.

"Tell Lizzy about the toaster," he said to Faye.

"What about it?"

"This morning, our new toaster crapped out for no reason," George said. "We bought it a month ago. The one we got rid of was a wedding gift. It still worked fine. But there's no one we can complain to. The store says it's the manufacturer's problem. The manufacturer doesn't answer the phone. You go around in circles until you give up." He smacked his hand against the table for emphasis. "Boom. The Hollow Tree."

"They don't make 'em like they used to," Andrew said.

"I know you're making fun of me, but that statement is one hundred percent correct. The world has gone to shit," George said. "And yet most people are too comfortable to care. We used to think Big Brother would come along and steal everything from us against our will. But now we just hand it to him with a smile."

"You sound like the college kids at my work," Andrew said.

"Good," George said. "I'm glad the young people get it. Gives me hope. They're the ones who will suffer the most if things don't change."

"They're self-identified socialists," Andrew said.

George shrugged.

Looked at one way, he was practically a socialist himself these days. He wanted to dismantle the evils of capitalism. To halt progress in its tracks so that everyone might be equal. Looked at another way, he was almost conservative. George was the only person Elisabeth knew who wasn't in the least bit excited about Obama.

"He keeps saying small business, that's the answer," George had said recently. "How'd that work out for me, huh? Or for you, Lizzy, with your unpaid maternity leave. It's basically this administration's way of saying, without saying it, that none of the real jobs are coming back—manufacturing in this country is dead—so you'd better invent your own industry. But you won't have a job that gives you health insurance, or a pension, or any kind of protection."

Tonight, when Elisabeth asked him which candidate she

should vote for in the upcoming state senate election, George just sighed.

"It doesn't matter," he said. "They're all crooked. They're not coming to save us, Lizzy. We'll have to save ourselves."

When they got home, Andrew said, "My dad seemed even more off the rails than usual with the Hollow Tree stuff tonight."

"He's working out his frustrations," she said. "Just go with it."

Elisabeth had had another beer with dinner, and eaten only a few bites, sneaking the rest to the dog when Faye wasn't looking. The alcohol mixed with her usual exhaustion made her eyelids feel heavy.

"My parents are getting old," Andrew said. "It makes me sad. See, this is why Gil needs a brother."

"You romanticize siblings," she said. "Look at Charlotte and me. We have nothing in common. The only thing we ever talk about is what a disaster our parents are."

"Exactly. That right there. Having a person in the world who knows what it's like to have your parents. Someone to commiserate with. That's what I'm talking about."

"You want Gil to have someone to commiserate with about us."

"Absolutely," he said.

"You know, even if we wanted one, I don't think we could afford to have another kid," she said. "They're expensive. Nomi was telling me that she's looking at pre-K programs that cost thirty thousand a year."

Andrew didn't respond. She wondered if he'd taken that last comment as a slight about how little he was earning. She hadn't meant for him to feel that way. Or maybe she had. Maybe she was being defensive because Charlotte was on her mind and she never thought about Charlotte without thinking about money.

When Elisabeth was twenty-three and Charlotte was twenty, they made a pact: they would never again take one dollar from their father.

This had required sacrifice, especially early on. Elisabeth started waiting tables to supplement her magazine salary, which she had previously spent on clothes and purses. But it was worth it. She was free of him.

From the time she and Charlotte were kids, their father had bribed them into keeping his secrets and accepting his horrid behavior. Elisabeth still remembered the pattern on the sofas in the breezy hotel lobby where he left them with a box of crayons while he went upstairs with some woman, and returned an hour later with a fifty-dollar bill for each of them.

When he lost his temper and punched another father who dared steal his parking spot at Charlotte's fourth-grade ballet recital, he made up for it by buying Charlotte a purebred Havanese puppy. When he showed up reeking of gin, with a woman he introduced as "a colleague," to pick Elisabeth up from a friend's birthday party, he took Elisabeth to Arden Fair the next day for a shopping spree.

He used money as both carrot and stick, threatening to withhold it when he didn't agree with a choice one of them had made. He said he would pay for Elisabeth's education only if she attended a school ranked in the top ten in the country, since otherwise there was no point. He refused to let Charlotte study dance.

"Dance isn't something you study," he said. "It's just something you do."

This led to Charlotte majoring in marketing and ultimately dropping out to go live in Mexico City with a boyfriend she met on spring break.

Their mother would say, *He only wants the best for you,* and it was true, but *the best* was however he defined it.

Their father was at once a charming man and a vicious narcissist with a gift for making his victims forget the pain he'd caused. It worked on their mother. There was nothing a diamond bracelet or a last-minute getaway couldn't smooth over with her.

But fourteen years ago, he did something to Elisabeth that she could not forgive.

Charlotte was living in New York then too. She was at Elisabeth's apartment the day he showed up at the door to make amends. It was meant to be a grand gesture. He'd had to fly across the country.

Elisabeth was in tears when he walked in. When she saw him, every nerve in her body flared.

"Sweetheart," he said. "Cheer up. I know it seems like the sky is falling, but trust me, you'll forget all about this in a week. Know how I know?"

Elisabeth turned her face away from him, wanting to scream.

"Charlotte," he said. "You'll want to hear this too."

"Not now, Daddy," Charlotte said.

But he barreled on, as usual.

"I've arranged for you two to have unlimited use of my brother's house in Southampton for the summer," he said. "We worked out a good deal. Five bedrooms, on the beach, you can bring all your friends. Now, I know you're thinking, But how will we get there? The train is such a hassle. Well, girls. Your new Mercedes convertible is parked outside. Who wants to take it for a spin?"

Elisabeth looked up at him. She'd been awake and crying for forty-eight hours. Her eyeballs ached.

"Get out," she said. "Just go away."

She was disgusted by him, but by herself as well. It had come to this because she had been so easy to buy off.

When he didn't move to leave, she said, "Everything you touch gets twisted. You think you can just meddle in other people's lives whenever you feel like it. Well, I'm done with you."

The look on his face suggested that they were only negotiating; that he thought this was a game.

"Okay then," he said. "Char, I guess this is good news for you. You just went from sharing a new car to having it all to yourself. That is, until Elisabeth stops pouting."

Elisabeth wanted to punch him.

Charlotte was his favorite, and she adored their father. So Elisabeth was shocked when she said, "No, Daddy. You went too far this time. Elisabeth's right. We're done."

He looked stunned. He opened his mouth to speak, but then turned and walked out instead.

After a long pause, Elisabeth met her sister's eye. The two of them had never been close. They were too different. But in that moment, she felt the kind of sisterly devotion she had always wanted as a kid.

"Thank you," she said.

"He deserves it," Charlotte said. "Everything you said is true."

Charlotte was drinking champagne on rich old guys' yachts at fifteen. She traveled the world with all kinds of inappropriate men on their father's dime. He let her do it. Better to have her out of his hair. She seemed to be having fun, but Elisabeth saw then that it had been a performance. Charlotte knew as well as she did what his behavior had done to them.

After their father walked out, neither of them spoke to him for three years. Not until he had a mild heart attack and their mother convinced them he was dying.

To this day, they refused to accept his financial help. Money was power, and their father would have none over them.

Charlotte now lived in a condo on the beach in Turks and Caicos. She taught yoga three days a week at a five-star resort. And she had her Instagram account—she was fond of reminding

Elisabeth that she was a verified user, with seventy-five thousand followers.

"There's no way she lives off that," Andrew had said, many times. "It's impossible. Your dad must be sending her money."

"I know for sure that he isn't," Elisabeth said, though she did not elaborate.

For a long time, Charlotte was supported by her fiancé, Matthew, a finance guy who, like their father, made all his money in shady real estate deals. Three years ago, she called off the wedding. She moved to Turks and Caicos, got on Instagram.

"How many bikinis does she *have?*" Andrew said at the time.

In every picture, Charlotte wore a different bathing suit. She paired the photos with some inspirational nonsense she had written about dreams and destiny and manifesting her truth.

But clearly, Charlotte knew what she was doing. Whenever they spoke to her, she told them about the skin-care companies and high-end sandal brands that sent her free samples, which she promoted in kind. A boutique hotel chain with properties all over the Caribbean sponsored her stays, putting her up in lavish rooms, where she posed half naked in the window, gazing at the ocean through sheer, flowing curtains.

Still, as Andrew often pointed out, it remained unclear how Charlotte paid her bills. Until the day she called Elisabeth in tears and said, "Don't hate me, but I've got to call Daddy. I'm broke. Not just broke, actually. I'm majorly in debt."

"How much debt?" Elisabeth said.

"Two fifty."

"Two hundred and fifty thousand dollars?"

"Getting my business off the ground wasn't cheap, okay? The camera, the clothes, the flights, the blowouts. But it's all about to pay off. Soon I'm going to make twice as much as I owe in one lump sum."

Elisabeth had never heard her sister refer to what she did as a business before.

"How?" she asked.

"I wasn't going to tell anyone until it was official," Charlotte said. "But I'm negotiating a huge sponsorship deal with Enthusium."

"What's that?" Elisabeth said.

"Diet pills."

"You're taking diet pills?"

"God no. They're for desperate fat people. I'm like the aspirational after photo."

"But you'll have to say you're taking them."

"Sure. My point is I need the money sooner than the deal is going to go through. I figured what's the harm in asking Daddy for it. It wouldn't even count as taking his money. It would just be a loan. Once I get this sponsorship, I can pay him right back."

"Don't do that," Elisabeth said. "You'll figure it out. If you're this far in debt, what's the harm in waiting another month or two to pay off your credit card bill?"

"It might be longer than a month or two. Amex is sending debt collectors to my door. It's bad. I could lose everything. Gossip travels fast on a small island. Can you imagine what that would do to my brand?"

"Your brand?"

"I need this weight off my shoulders," Charlotte said. "I've made my decision. I thought I should give you a heads-up before I call him."

Elisabeth's heart pounded. She had gone to great lengths to ensure that her father had no control over her. That was for her own sake. But her need for Charlotte to do the same, Elisabeth knew—that was about punishing him. She didn't want to give it up.

"Let me loan you the money," she said.

Charlotte sniffled. "Really?"

Elisabeth wired the full amount to her the next day, already doubting the decision.

The savings account had had just over three hundred thousand in it—whenever she thought of that, Elisabeth had felt a sense of safety and pride that she had done it on her own. She handed almost all of it over to her sister.

To stay calm, she reminded herself that it was a loan. But two years had passed. The sponsorship deal had yet to happen. Every time Elisabeth asked her about it, Charlotte said they were working out the final details.

In her darkest moments, Elisabeth scoured every comment on her sister's social media accounts to try and find some clue that revealed how soon the money was coming.

Meanwhile, Charlotte borrowed even more. Small amounts, mostly, but they added up. Car payments, rent checks. A three-hundred-dollar restaurant bill when some jerk ran out on her without paying after they'd had a fight.

When she agreed to lend her the money, Elisabeth had no idea that Andrew was about to quit his job. His salary had paid for their living expenses, for IVF, and co-op fees. For everything, really. When they first got together, she sold her single-girl apartment and they bought their place in Brooklyn, which turned out to be a great investment. They were able to buy the new house outright with what they sold it for.

But being a person was expensive. Neither of them was earning much of anything at the moment. Elisabeth was stressed about money in a way she hadn't been since she started refusing her father's. The savings account dipped closer to zero with every dinner out, every grocery order, the sort of expenses she never would have thought twice about when Andrew was in his old job.

He had no idea what their life cost. No clue what she had spent over the years on linens and rugs and furniture and dishes, all the details that added up to an appealing home.

They were accustomed to living a certain way. She couldn't give up the organic berries, the cage-free omega-3 eggs, the good coffee, the cruelty-free dish soap that was three times the price of Dawn. Even if she could give them up, if she made drastic changes, Andrew might suspect.

Elisabeth hadn't bought anything nice for herself in ages. When her high-end skin-care products from Bloomingdale's ran out, she replaced them with creams and serums from CVS. She didn't think they worked nearly as well, but it was possible that was in her head. She had an unworn Theory dress hanging on a clothing rack in the laundry room with the tags still on. She was saving it in case of emergency, should she need something new she could no longer afford.

She told her sister they were low on cash. But she added that Charlotte should keep coming to her if she really needed to. Charlotte kept coming.

Elisabeth still hadn't told Andrew about the loan. He thought they had a nest egg to pull from, to keep them safe. She justified this in the following manner: until he asked outright and she had to answer, she had not lied. There was time to fix it.

It was too late now to tell him the truth. He had quit his job, taken a huge risk, believing they had a cushion. He would be terrified, furious, if he knew.

Elisabeth had betrayed him to help her sister. Her sister, who on the day Gil was born had posted to Instagram a photo of herself on the beach at sunset, naked, in child's pose.

Balasana . . . the breath of new life. Today a child came into this world, made of the same stuff as me—the energy extends, the wisdom renews. Did my infancy ever cease? I am my own baby, soft and amazed. I vow to nurture and care for myself, a precious soul meeting the universe, yet again.

"Is she trying to make it seem like *she* had a baby?" Elisabeth had demanded at the time.

"Is she actually wearing no clothes?" Andrew said.

It was another six hours before Charlotte bothered to text them and say congrats.

Even in her moments of deepest regret, Elisabeth remained pleased that sending the money had kept Charlotte on her side in the family war. This was the only thing she really liked about her sister, but it mattered more than everything else combined.

That night, she couldn't sleep.

Andrew snored beside her. She picked up her phone, went straight to BK Mamas.

Someone had asked for recommendations for a coffee shop to write in. A topic she knew well.

Café Harmony is my go-to, Elisabeth responded. *Perfect ambience, best latte in Brooklyn, and they never rush you out.*

She posted her reply, picturing herself there, alone in a rush of bodies.

Mimi Winchester responded right away. *Harmony closed two weeks ago. Try Kelly's on Court.*

Elisabeth had known Mimi a bit in her twenties, when they both worked in magazines. Mimi was a hustler then, but she had married a hedge-fund guy and now only wrote an article every six months or so, usually a puff piece about a cosmetics line or clothing company run by one of her friends. She would post a link on BK Mamas saying something like *Just for funsies!*

Once, Mimi had come upon Elisabeth sitting alone on a bench

in Carroll Park. Elisabeth was shaking a can of formula, pouring the thick grayish liquid into a bottle for Gil, who was crying in the stroller.

"Oh my gosh, you adopted? That's so admirable!" Mimi said.

Elisabeth was almost certain she wasn't trying to be awful. It just had not occurred to her that a biological mother would do anything but breastfeed.

She wanted to say every mean thing she'd ever thought about Mimi then.

She had hoped the pettiest parts of her, all her foolish insecurities, would somehow be erased by motherhood. At first, she thought it had happened. But they returned when Gil was eight weeks old, like so many uninvited guests.

Café Harmony had closed, and Mimi needed her to know. Why should something as small as that unnerve her? But it did. Elisabeth felt like she'd had her hand slapped.

4

Sam

AT THE END OF EVERY HALLWAY in the dorms was a short flight of stairs that led to four rooms—two large doubles on either side. These were called the platforms. Only seniors were allowed to live in platform rooms, and only they got invited to platform preparties on Friday nights.

Tonight, their platform was hosting. Isabella had made sangria in the recycling bin ahead of time. The too-sweet smell of it filled the room.

Hosting was supposed to be a big deal, but Sam hadn't given it a moment's thought. Clive's flight from London was due in at ten.

Isabella had offered to let Sam take her car to the airport, but it was too nice. It made Sam nervous. Instead she had begged Steph, who managed the basketball team, to let her use the beat-up van they took to away games. Sam had never driven a van, but this she had not mentioned when she made the request.

All week, she had been nervous and excited in equal parts. Her palms hadn't stopped sweating since Tuesday. Her stomach was a mess. It was impossible to imagine Clive here, among her friends. As Isabella had put it, "You simply cannot bring a six-foot-five British man into the dining hall without raising eyebrows."

Sam didn't want to be a topic of conversation. And yet, she couldn't wait to see him. She had missed him so much.

After dinner, Isabella did her makeup for her, and flat-ironed her hair.

Then it was Sam's turn to help Isabella.

It was a comfort, having something to take her mind off Clive for a minute.

Sam opened the mini-fridge and pulled out a vial of clear liquid. She filled a syringe.

"Ready?" she said.

"Ready."

Isabella held up the hem of her blue tank top with one hand and tipped back a tequila shot with the other. Sam poked the needle straight into her taut abdomen, as if throwing a dart.

Isabella winced—from the drink or the pain, Sam wasn't sure.

She counted to five, pulled out the needle, and dabbed an alcohol swab over the drop of blood that bubbled up.

The process had been a shock the first time they did it three weeks ago, the two of them screaming, bouncing around the room for several minutes beforehand.

Finally, Sam had said, "We have to get it together. Trust me. I can do this. My mother's a nurse."

Isabella was selling her eggs to a couple who had advertised in the student paper. They wanted a donor with brown hair and blue eyes, and a grade point average of 3.7 or higher. Isabella had all three, though if they had requested transcripts, they might have noticed that most of her classes were taken in the film department.

She would never meet the couple. The transaction was handled through an agency. Isabella had to provide pictures from various stages of her life.

Sam heard her on the phone.

"Mommy, can you email me some photos from when I was a baby? It's for a class project thingy."

Sam didn't understand why she was doing it. Isabella was wealthier than anyone she'd ever met.

"I'm not rich, my parents are," Isabella often said, which made no sense.

Sam suggested a campus job if she wanted to earn extra money. Isabella seemed aghast. "It would take me a year to make what I'm making in less than a month. Besides, this isn't only about the money. I'm doing it to give back. To share something I have, that someone else needs. Like giving blood. But a much bigger sacrifice, obviously."

Isabella told anyone who would listen how selfless she was being.

The two of them were randomly assigned to be roommates their first year. Early on, they couldn't stand each other. But by the time they were deciding who to live with sophomore year, they stayed together by choice. Sam had once thought of her as just an annoying drama queen, but now Isabella was *her* annoying drama queen.

Perhaps she was donating her eggs for the same reason she did most things. Whenever possible, Isabella needed to be engaged in something exciting, extreme, that superseded the rhythm of her ordinary life. Sam never pointed this out. Their friendship was built on a foundation of mutual acceptance. They supported each other's decisions, no matter how stupid. So Sam didn't say that if all went according to plan, a baby would exist who was one-half Isabella's.

Isabella, in turn, didn't question Sam's relationship with Clive. Other friends made it clear that they thought it was odd. Either by asking too many questions, or by never mentioning Clive at all.

Isabella was voluntarily spending the next four nights across the hall in Lexi and Ramona's room. Ramona hardly ever slept at home. Her girlfriend had a single in the vegan house on Reed Street, so Ramona's bed was always free. Still, Isabella was making a sacrifice.

Sam had been counting down to those nights alone with Clive, but now that he was almost here, she thought she'd miss Isabella a little. It was like with Gil. When she was babysitting, Sam only ever wanted to get him down for a nap so she could do schoolwork or watch TV. But as soon as he was asleep, she had the urge to wake him, craving his company.

At eight-fifteen, Isabella stood in the crowded hall, scooping sangria from the recycling bin into red plastic cups, using a coffee mug that said WHAT WOULD BEYONCÉ DO? as a ladle.

She rocked back and forth to the music, eyelids at half-mast. She took a swig of sangria straight from the mug whenever she thought no one was looking.

Sam watched her as she sipped a beer. She kept checking the time, as if she might somehow forget Clive's arrival.

Even just last year, hearing the music coming from such a party, she had wished to be included. But now, it seemed kind of pointless. It was the same thing they had done last Friday, and the Friday before that. At ten-thirty, they would go as a group to the actual party downstairs, never as much fun as the hours spent preparing for it. Tomorrow, they would wake up late, hungover or still slightly drunk, and stumble down to the dining hall for bagels.

After Sam's summer in London, it no longer seemed normal to live in a hall of near-identical rooms, distinguished one from the other only by curtains or a floral bedspread someone's mother had chosen. It felt absurd to be told what she would eat, and when.

Sam could waste an hour wandering around Beekman Market downtown, picking up tiny soaps and silver tubes of overpriced hand cream, mentally decorating a house she didn't have but could picture herself living in with Clive. She never bought anything. Those soaps would look ridiculous in a plastic shower caddy. The hand cream would get used by every person who entered her room, making Sam stressed at the thought of the cost.

The home she imagined was the one in which she had spent the last few weeks nannying. Elisabeth's house. The rooms, light filled and beautifully furnished, had an air of calm that seemed to spring from Elisabeth herself.

Sam had decided not to work in the dining hall this year as she had in years past. In part, because weekend shifts would impede her ability to see Clive. And if she was honest, she wanted to experience college without washing her friends' dinner plates for once.

She had planned to work two full days a week off campus, but Elisabeth needed three. Sam rearranged her schedule. Now her Tuesdays and Wednesdays were booked with classes from 8:00 a.m. until 6:00, but it was worth it. She had never worked for someone like Elisabeth before. Some days she would pour them both a cup of coffee before she left for work and sit and chat for fifteen minutes, like she wasn't paying Sam to watch her child. Elisabeth wanted to know all about Sam's art and her travels and her plans.

While she was there, Sam often pretended the house was hers, and the baby too. She went to the bookcase in Elisabeth's upstairs hall that held copies of each of her books in hardcover, plus several foreign-language editions, and imagined what it would feel like to have accomplished something like that. Sam thought it must be a relief, among other things.

She loved to wash her hands in Elisabeth's downstairs powder room, with the soft white towels and the wallpaper covered in oversize green leaves. The hand soap was peony scented. Sam felt like a slightly better version of herself each time she used it.

She asked Elisabeth where she'd gotten it.

Elisabeth shrugged and said she couldn't remember.

"The drugstore, I think," she said.

That was her—effortless, uncultivated.

Elisabeth was pretty without having to try. She hardly ever wore makeup. She was a wisp of a woman with a boy's slender build, the body Sam had wanted all her life. Of the two of them, Sam looked more likely to have given birth in the last five months. She wished she could be this kind of woman for a day, an hour. The type who didn't have to roll her jeans up over her belly when she sat, or suffer the indignity of bouncing boobs if ever she went for a jog.

Sam had spotted Elisabeth in the wild once, when she and Isabella were downtown. Isabella saw Sam looking and asked, "Who's that?"

"My boss," Sam had said.

"Are you gonna say hi?"

"No."

"She's cute," Isabella said.

"Please don't hit on my boss."

"How old is she? Like Clive's age?"

"No," Sam said. "I don't know. Older than that, I assume. She's married with a kid."

"When my mother was Clive's age, she had an eight-year-old," Isabella said.

"Don't tell me that," Sam said.

Elisabeth's friends sent extravagant gifts. She received a box of truffles from a chocolate shop in Manhattan as a thank-you for introducing a writer she knew to her agent. Once, her best friend sent flowers, cut short and arranged in a glass vase, because Elisabeth was having a bad day. None of it seemed to matter much to her. When a giant box from Williams Sonoma arrived, Elisabeth didn't open it for a week.

Even her ice cubes were the nicest Sam had ever seen. They were exceptionally cube-like, instead of those cloudy half circles that popped out of normal people's refrigerator doors.

On Monday mornings when Sam opened the fridge to get Gil's bottle, there were leftovers from Sunday dinner wrapped in cellophane—roast chicken stuffed with lemons, red potato wedges sprinkled with dill. She envied Elisabeth then most of all.

Before she left for college, her mother bought her something called Dinner For One. It was a box containing four pieces of matching blue china—a dinner plate, a bread plate, a bowl, a cup. In years past, Sam had put the set to use, but now it sat at the back of the closet. Something about it depressed her.

From what she had seen, most people's twenties were much closer to Dinner For One than they were to Sunday Roast Chicken. Roommates seemed so odd, the more she thought of it. Strangers with whom the only thing you had in common was that none of you could afford to live alone. Sam wanted to skip all that and be settled.

Clive talked about moving to the country. A little house with a room upstairs where she could paint. Children, not right away, but someday. It sounded both wonderful and terrifying.

When Sam saw a used pregnancy test in the dorm bathroom, she thought of how nobody here was hoping for a positive result. She wished she had reached that place in life, when the reaction could be what they showed in the commercials: a happy couple jumping up and down.

"Wear my black halter dress!" Isabella shouted at someone, pulling Sam's attention back to the party. "Keep it! I'm serious! It would look amazing on you."

Isabella was already drunk. Giving her stuff away was a tell-tale sign. In a week or two, she would search both their closets, asking if Sam had seen her black halter anywhere.

A bunch of them had pooled their money for pizza. Sam went

to the stack of boxes on her desk, removed two slices of cheese, and put them on a paper plate. She brought it to her roommate.

"Eat," she said.

Isabella took one bite, then another, and then put the plate on the floor.

"Thank you, Mom," she said. "Do you promise to look after me forever?"

"Yes," Sam said.

"Even when you and Clive are married and raising five kids in England and I'm the mistress of some corporate tycoon in Dubai?"

"Even then," Sam said.

They smiled, because, she thought, they both sort of liked the sound of it.

Isabella took Sam's face in her hands. "I love you so much it hurts."

Sam swore she could feel the grease working its way off Isabella's fingertips and straight into her pores.

"Love you too," she said.

By ten, Isabella was fully sobbing.

A normal occurrence after so many drinks, but it irked Sam. This was supposed to be her night to freak out, to be on the receiving end of the pep talk. She needed to leave for the airport soon.

They went into their room and closed the door.

"What's up?" Sam said.

Isabella looked like she was trying to remember.

"I miss Darryl," she said, finally.

"Darryl?"

"Darren."

"The guy you dated senior year of high school?"

71

"We started dating at the end of junior year, Sam. He was the only boy who ever accepted me as I was."

Isabella must have seen something on Sam's face. She added, "I'm serious."

"I believe you," Sam said. "Though the story would be more compelling if you'd remembered his name."

Isabella pursed her lips, deciding whether or not to protest. Then she flung her head back and laughed.

She had cheated on Darren her first Saturday at college. She called him immediately to confess. They broke up by the time orientation ended. As far as Sam knew, they hadn't spoken since.

"I'm gonna call him," Isabella said, taking her phone from her pocket.

"Let's wait on that," Sam said.

"Fine, then I'll call Toby."

A guy she'd met on her junior year abroad, who broke it off with her right before they left and got back together with his ex, raising the question of whether they'd ever broken up in the first place.

One of the drawbacks of a single-sex education was that the pool of men one had, even to think about, was unbearably small. They kept males around and alive in their imaginations far longer than any normal woman would. It was like prison or war in that way.

Before Clive, Sam's only college relationship was with Julian, a sweet but odd guy who worked in the campus library.

He was an aspiring poet working toward a degree in literature at State, where, he took pains to explain, he had chosen to go only because he got a free ride. In addition to his library job, Julian had three internships—one with a translator in New York City, remotely. One at an indie publishing house in town, and one at the three-college literary journal, *Ambit*.

He told her he ran a writers' group; that she ought to come sometime.

"When do you sleep?" Sam asked.

He laughed, but she was genuinely curious.

Sam liked chatting with him in the library. But she was caught off guard when he asked for her number.

"Aww, he likes you," Isabella said at the time.

"I'm not attracted to him," Sam said. "His hair looks like a Brillo pad. He has a wandering eye."

"He's allowed to check out other women," Isabella said. "You're not even interested in him, what do you care?"

"No, his eye literally wanders. Like, drifts to the side."

"Oh."

It turned out Isabella was right. Julian did like her. Sam tried to like him back. They kissed a handful of times. His tongue felt slimy and too large for his mouth. Sam told Isabella that it reminded her of a clam trying to escape its shell. From then on, Isabella referred to Julian as the Mollusk, which amused Sam and made her feel bad at the same time.

They went to dinner, to the movies. He was the kind of guy she should like, and yet. He wrote her a poem for their one-month anniversary. Sam found it revolting. It was too much. When Julian asked what she thought of the poem, she told him it reminded her of T. S. Eliot. She could tell right away he was disappointed. She supposed he wanted only to sound like himself.

Sam told Julian she needed to focus on her studies. For a while, he texted her whenever he got drunk and pleaded with her to reconsider. Sam never responded.

Ever since, when she saw him in the library, she hid. She had previously studied on the main floor, which was flooded with sunlight. But after their time together, she worked in the basement, because she knew he never went down there.

Isabella flopped onto her bed.

She insisted she wanted to get back to the party and make out with Rosie Simmons, a senior who resembled a young Leonardo DiCaprio.

"Later," Sam said.

"Disco nap!" Isabella said.

"Good idea. Take off your shoes, at least," Sam said.

She pulled the trash can close, in case.

Isabella fumbled with the button on her jeans.

"You look like a fourteen-year-old boy trying to get a girl's pants off for the first time," Sam said. "Except they're your own pants."

Isabella moaned.

"I'm too tired," she said. "Can you do it, please?"

"You're annoying," Sam said, but she complied, pulling the jeans down from the ankles. "I need a crowbar for this. Pajama pants?"

Isabella shook her head. A minute later, she lay passed out in her tank top and underwear, looking like an American Apparel ad. Sam took the blanket she kept folded at the end of her own bed and draped it over Isabella's bottom half, not as much for warmth as to avoid the possibility of Clive seeing her impossibly narrow thighs on the off chance she hadn't woken up by the time they returned.

Sam looked in the mirror. Her stomach flipped.

"More lipstick!" Isabella demanded, without opening her eyes.

5

THE VAN SOUNDED LIKE A rocket ship about to launch. Sam clutched the steering wheel. She imagined breaking down on the side of the road in her short sundress, which was inappropriate for both the hour and the season. She had worn it because it was Clive's favorite.

Her heart pounded as she drove along the dark highway. She pictured him, hurtling through the air overhead, about to touch down in America for the first time. Six months ago, she hadn't known he existed, and now he was her person.

At some point sophomore year, Sam's friends started talking about where they planned to spend their junior year abroad, as if it was a foregone conclusion. Sam had never considered the possibility. Lexi applied to a program in Brazil. Ramona wanted to be in Nepal. Shannon's fellowship included an all-expenses-paid year in Paris.

"Come with me, Sam. Your financial aid will transfer, I think," said Isabella, who had already decided on London and didn't need one cent of financial aid.

Sam got excited, looking at the websites of schools in Scotland, Ireland, France. She went to a question-and-answer session at the International Studies Office and took notes. When the woman running it said, "Expect to spend ten to fifteen thousand on top of your usual school costs for the year," Sam closed her notebook. She understood that there was no way she was going.

Her parents had told her to go to a state school, like they did. By the time she was a senior, they would have three kids in college. If Sam wanted more, she would have to pay for it. For reasons she could not articulate then or even now, she wanted more.

Ultimately, her brother and sister stayed closer to home and went to their parents' alma mater. Brendan wasn't sure what he wanted to do yet. Molly wanted to be a teacher. Set against their ambitions, Sam worried that hers seemed indulgent.

She got a small scholarship and a work-study position. She took the rest out in loans, in her name.

"I'm worried you're too young to understand what this means," her father said as he watched her sign the forms. "I'm sorry. I wish we could have done better by you, Sam."

"You've done great by me," she said, and it was true. She hated making him feel otherwise.

Only after she got to college did she realize that she should have considered not just the cost of affording the school, but the cost of living among the kind of people who could easily afford it. Her friends might decide on a whim to go out for sushi if they didn't like what was on offer in the dining hall. Sam wouldn't join them. She knew from experience that Lexi and Isabella would order one of everything, and while she might get miso soup, the cheapest item on the menu, inevitably, when the bill came, someone would say, "Why don't we just split it?"

The summer after sophomore year felt like any other summer. Sam slept in her childhood bedroom with its ballet-slipper wallpaper. She babysat on the weekends. On weekdays, she temped. Her longest gig was at an ad agency called Fleischer Boone. Her main job was to answer the phone and say "Fleischer Boone" in a professional-sounding voice.

Maybe a quarter of the time, it was her twelve-year-old sister, Caitlin, prank-calling her. "Fleischer Boone," Caitlin would yell in an exaggerated southern drawl, before hanging up and doing it again. "Fleischer Boone! Our chicken is finger-lickin'!"

Any spare moments that summer were spent with Maddie, Sam's best friend from high school, who was pre-med at Clemson. They walked the streets of their hometown free of the angst they'd felt before going to college. They were detached, observant. Visitors from a foreign land.

In July, Maddie saw an ad in the *Globe* for cater-waiters, offering twenty dollars an hour. They went to the training together. It was run by identical twin sisters in their fifties, who wore matching outfits. They taught the class how to serve in four styles—normal, fan, butler, and silver service—as well as the correct way to hold and pour champagne.

At home, Sam's father teased her as she set the dinner table. "Not like that, Sam. We're doing fan service tonight."

In August, Sam's college friends left for their study-abroad programs. She kept up with what they were doing through the photos they shared on social media—pictures of stunning architecture and plates of food and selfies taken with new friends. But it didn't hit her that they were gone until she got back to campus. More to the point, that she was alone.

There were girls in the dorm and acquaintances from her classes whom she liked well enough to say hi to, or go to the movies with sometimes. But the college only meant what it did to her because of her friends.

Sam roomed with a girl who had skipped going abroad to play varsity soccer. She hardly ever saw her. The girl left for practice each morning before Sam was awake and ate in the one dining hall that stayed open late for athletes. Sam missed Isabella so much that sometimes she sat in that empty room and pretended she was about to walk through the door.

"The solitude will give you more time to paint," her mother said, and it was true.

Sam spent long hours in the studio. She sometimes went on a Saturday night, when she knew she'd have the place to herself. But she would have traded that for Isabella any day.

Sam babysat a lot that year. She worked twice as many shifts in the dining hall as she had her first two years. She prepped meals, power-washed dirty dishes, took buckets of composted slop down to the gardens behind the stables that housed the horses some girls brought with them from home.

She had always loved Maria and Delmi, the Salvadoran women who worked full-time in the kitchen. If she hadn't had their familiar faces in her life while her friends were gone, Sam wasn't sure how she would have managed.

They had both worked at the college longer than Sam had been alive. But she tended to think of the kitchen as belonging to Maria.

Delmi had no end of friends who worked in other dorms, who stopped by throughout the day, whispering to one another in Spanish. She worked hard but was always happy to stop what she was doing and chat. Sam had once come upon her alone in the kitchen softly singing a Bon Jovi song into her cell phone in an attempt to win concert tickets from a local radio station.

Maria commanded authority in a way Delmi did not. Any outsider wandering in—a delivery guy with a cart full of boxes, a student worker from another dorm—instinctively approached her with their questions. Maria was petite and full of energy, a coiled spring. She had a pretty face and shiny brown hair and ripped upper arms. She always went above and beyond. She organized the pantry and alphabetized the recipe cards. She memorized the names of all the new students right away each September.

Sam's mother liked to commend people who were particularly good at their jobs. Waiters, doctors, customer-service reps.

"It doesn't matter what the job is," she had told her children on many occasions. "It's how well you do it that matters. I see it at the hospital all the time. Might be an orderly or a surgeon—some people just give their work their all. It makes life better for everyone around them."

Sam told Maria this once, shyly. She said Maria made her think of it.

Of all the student workers in the kitchen, Sam had always been Maria's pet. When she was working there her first year and started crying from homesickness, Maria hugged her and fed her cookies and made her laugh. She did the same when Sam's grandmother died sophomore year. She asked Sam to bring back a rose from the funeral and had it pressed into rosary beads. When Sam passed the one math prerequisite she was forced to take to qualify for Latin honors, Maria presented her with a homemade cheesecake as a reward.

At the start of Sam's junior year, when Maria introduced her to the newest member of the kitchen staff, the girl looked Sam up and down and said, "I know who you are. You're Auntie Maria's little favorite."

"Sam, meet Gabriela, my charming niece," Maria said, rolling her eyes.

Gabriela looked like Maria, but taller. She wore a diamond stud in her nose. Sam soon learned that she was twenty-three and had a baby, Josefine, a chubby one-year-old whose photograph Maria taped next to the weekly menu posted above the salad bar.

The photo was supposed to serve as a reminder to Gabriela. Maria was constantly telling her to watch her tongue, to take a deep breath before speaking.

All the student workers in the kitchen found her intimidating. Including Sam, at first. Gabriela made no secret of the fact that she didn't have time for the stupidity of college girls who lived like slobs, assuming someone else would be there to clean up their messes.

Every day at lunch and dinner, Gabriela neatly filled the metal squares in the salad bar—the large one that held the greens, the four at the end containing different kinds of dressing, and the smaller compartments for things like sliced cucumbers, tomatoes, radishes, croutons, shaved carrots. Ten minutes into any meal, it was all a jumble. Gabriela would come out of the kitchen scowling and fix it so that no one would complain that there was tuna in the cottage cheese or Creamy Ranch in the Low-Fat Italian. Then the next wave of diners would mess it up, and she'd reemerge. Sisyphus pushing the boulder uphill only to watch it roll down again.

Sam shared her frustrations.

When a senior from Connecticut left a puddle of Diet Coke on the floor under the soda dispenser, and Gabriela said, "Do these college girls wipe their own asses, or do they pay someone to do that too?" Sam silently thrilled at the comment.

When a transfer student asked, a bit rudely, for Gabriela to bring her some salt, she responded, "You've got legs in those yoga pants. Get it yourself."

Sam burst out laughing then. Gabriela looked at her, as if seeing Sam for the first time. She smiled.

"Am I wrong?" she said as they walked back into the kitchen.

"No," Sam said. "You say all the things out loud that I wish I could say. Gabriela, you're my hero."

"You can call me Gaby," she said.

Overhearing this, Delmi and Maria both made a noise of astonishment and then laughed at their shared reaction.

"What?" Gaby said.

From then on, Gaby and Sam chatted and joked through their

shifts. Maria would tell them to get back to work, but always with a grin on her face. She liked that they were friends.

"Sam's a good one," Maria said once to her niece.

The comment filled Sam with pride.

Gaby wasn't a substitute for her real friends, exactly. The two of them didn't connect as easily; they didn't like the same music or have much in common. Gaby was busy—she had a second job a few nights a week in the kitchen of a restaurant near where she lived, and otherwise had to get home to her daughter. But most Fridays after work, they walked downtown together to deposit their paychecks. They window-shopped and got coffee and talked. It was nice to have someone to do those things with.

Gaby said what she thought, and seemed not to care whether anyone liked her. Sam found this slightly terrifying and completely appealing. She sensed a sadness in Gaby too, which Gaby never talked about, but it came through when she mentioned that a lot of her friends had bailed when she had a kid. And when she told Sam that she hadn't gone to college right away after high school; hadn't seen the point. She worked retail; she worked in restaurants. At twenty, when most people were nearly done with school, Gaby enrolled at the local community college. She wanted to study bookkeeping, which was what her mother did. She worked days, went to school at night. But after three semesters, she got pregnant, and that was that. Something had to give.

Gaby loved her daughter fiercely. She found her mother annoying and controlling and hard to live with, but she was grateful that she had taken them in and that she helped so much with the baby, as did a cousin who took care of Josie while Gaby worked.

Gaby told Sam all kinds of secrets about the kitchen staff she never would have guessed. She told her Tina, a woman who had left abruptly midway through Sam's first year, was only forty-five, even though she looked sixty; that she had been married four times; and that she had custody of her three grandkids because her daughter was a heroin addict. She told her Delmi's husband had had an affair with some woman from their church, and Delmi had taken him back but now distrusted any female between the ages of sixteen and ninety who so much as looked at him.

Whenever there was a lull in their conversation, Gaby and Sam seemed to fill it by making fun of the students at the college. If there was something uncomfortable about this, Sam pushed it off. Of course, she was one of the students. But if Gaby saw her that way, she never would have chosen Sam to confide in.

One afternoon, as they scooped three hundred perfect spheres of chicken salad into chafing dishes, Sam told Gaby how Lexi used to ask her to set aside popular menu items for her when she was coming late to lunch, even though it hadn't bothered Sam at the time. She told her how once Isabella, feet up on a chair after dinner, looked at her dirty plate and said, "Sam, would you mind? Since you're going to the kitchen anyway?"

"I would have smacked her," Gaby said.

Sam went on to say that Isabella had grown up with a mother who didn't work, and yet the family employed a cook, a nanny, a maid.

"She's just used to a ridiculous level of pampering," Sam said. "Before she got to college, she'd never done laundry. I actually had to teach her."

"This place is such a joke," Gaby said. "Did you see that bullshit banner they hung across the college gates that says *Celebrate Diversity*? I laughed out loud."

In a way, Sam thought, the college was pretty diverse.

Walking onto this campus had been a revelation for her—the transmen, the butch lesbians with shaved heads, the student in her studio art class who raised a hand and said confidently, "Please refer to me as *they*, not *she*."

There were a lot of international students too.

Sam considered saying, *"My friend Shannon is black and my friend Lexi is Korean and my friend Rosa is from the Philippines. Her dad's a diplomat."*

But she knew that somehow the fact of her providing these examples would only prove Gaby's point.

Instead, she told Gaby how Shannon was part of an elite program for African American scholars, and though it was an honor, Shannon said she sometimes felt tokenized on campus. She had been asked to participate in last year's admissions brochure. When Sam said, "That's so cool that they picked you," Shannon just looked at her and said, "Gee, I wonder why."

There was also the fact that the college celebrated diversity, but no one ever mentioned the women, mostly women of color, doing the work to prepare the food, to make the place beautiful, so the students could grow and learn and thrive. The housekeeping staff was almost entirely black, while black students made up just four percent of the student body. They studied historic inequality in their classes, they read about racial and economic injustice, and still they were expected to ignore this uncomfortable truth, to live with it.

One night in November, Gaby invited Sam to a party off campus. It was the first time she'd ever been to the home of someone not connected to the college, other than babysitting. The house was a small ranch on a cul-de-sac. There were a dozen cars parked out front.

They danced and took a lot of shots. Sam flirted with an extremely good-looking firefighter named Trevor, an acquaintance of Gaby's from high school. At the end of the night, Sam made out with someone she thought was him, until Gaby told her Trevor had left half an hour ago.

"Who was that then?" Sam said, gesturing toward the guy whose tongue had been in her mouth moments earlier.

Gaby shrugged. She shook her head and laughed.

Sam went home for Christmas, and the whole time, she dreaded the return to school. Winters in this part of the world were particularly dreary. Especially without Isabella there to make them ramen in the hot pot, without Lexi's hot chocolate spiked with cinnamon and rum. It felt like she was just running the clock until her friends returned.

A tiny ball of resentment formed in her. Why had it been so easy for the rest of them to go?

At the end of January, Isabella told Sam over Skype, "My parents said I can have a ticket to anywhere in the world for my birthday."

"That's so great," Sam said.

She hoped her expression disguised her true feelings. She wished Isabella had told her in a text.

"I chose London," Isabella said.

"You live in London," Sam said.

"I know. It's for you."

"What? No way," Sam said. "That's too much."

"You'll come for ten days, over spring break. Which also happens to be my birthday week. You'll stay with me."

Sam's mother told her to accept.

"You've been so miserable," she said.

"No, I haven't," Sam said.

But the fact that she had the blessing of her mother, who had instructed her never to be indebted, especially to friends, was the push Sam needed.

On the plane, she asked for a gin and tonic just to see what would happen. The flight attendant brought her one without batting an eye. Sam had two more after that. She watched a romantic comedy and stared out the window at the clouds, vowing that she would never become the kind of person who found this anything less than astounding.

Isabella picked her up at Heathrow in a chauffeured car. She had developed a slight British accent and had begun using words like *snog* and *cheers* in casual conversation.

For the next two days, Isabella showed her London. She had spent so much time there with her parents over the years that the bellmen at the Four Seasons knew her by name. They went to tea at Brown's. They toured Buckingham Palace and were certain they saw Kate Middleton going up a staircase, even as they knew it was probably not her. They walked through the Harrods Food Halls and looked at clothes neither of them would ever actually wear. They bought jeans at Top Shop. They went to a bar with bottle service. Isabella put down her American Express before the bill had even arrived.

On Isabella's birthday, Shannon came from Paris for the party. She looked thin. She told them the college provided all the students on her program a daily food allowance but that she skipped lunch most days and saved the money for the future purchase of Chanel sunglasses. She seemed more sophisticated than she was the last time Sam saw her. Shannon was so studious. At the college, she'd worn her old high school track pants to class most days. Now she had on flattering black jeans and a pair of boots made by some designer Isabella recognized on sight. The three of them drank champagne Isabella's father had sent while they got ready. They had dinner with Isabella's new boyfriend, Toby, who was on a year abroad from Georgetown.

"It's pretty serious, you guys," Isabella whispered when he went to the bathroom. "We share a Netflix account."

Shannon met Sam's eye and shook her head, amused.

The party was at a bar called the Zoo in the middle of Leicester Square. There were at least a hundred people there to celebrate Isabella. Sam wondered how she'd had time to make this many friends since August.

Isabella led her around by the hand. She kept telling everyone, "Sam is my birthday present!"

Isabella ordered them each a drink called the GTV. When Sam asked what was in it, Isabella looked shocked by her ignorance.

"Gin, tequila, and vodka," she said.

"God," Sam said.

She drank half, then told Isabella she had to pee.

"I'll come!" Isabella said.

"That's okay," Sam said. "I'll be right back."

As happy as she was to see her, Sam had forgotten how exhausting Isabella could be, how much energy she required.

The bathroom line was thirty women deep. Sam remembered seeing a McDonald's across the road. She ducked out of the bar without telling anyone and went straight there.

On the way back, she looked up at the ornate buildings and wondered how old they were. It was her first time in a foreign country, her first time traveling alone without her family. Sam felt buoyant, happy, in a way she hadn't in months.

She was lost in thought when suddenly she slammed into something solid. A man.

"Jack the Ripper?" he said.

"Excuse me?"

Sam looked up. He was tall and very English, with a crooked grin and spiky hair. Definitely older, though she couldn't say how old. Twenty-five, maybe?

"You here for the ten o'clock Jack the Ripper tour?"

"No," she said. "I was just going to that bar over there."

"Ahh. Well then, that must have sounded odd. You on holiday?"

"Yes."

He handed her a pamphlet.

"Best walking-tour company in the city," he said. "That's not according to me. That's according to *Time Out* magazine."

"Thanks," Sam said.

She scanned the offerings.

"Ooh," she said. "The Blitz: London Turned Crimson."

He laughed. "I have literally never heard anyone point that walk out," he said. "Did you not see the Harry Potter walk? The *Downton Abbey* tour, where we take you to Lady Edith's office and you get to press the keys on her typewriter?"

Sam shrugged. "I'm weird."

"Clearly," he said, appreciative. "I'm Clive, by the way."

"Sam."

She tried to assess whether he was flirting with her. Guys this handsome didn't, usually. Perhaps one's level of attractiveness got inflated overseas, the same way you had to be careful to remember that one pound did not convert to a dollar, but was instead worth a dollar and a half.

"Seems no one's turning up for this thing," he said. "And I've got to be back here in an hour for Ghosts of Victorian London anyway. Fancy a fifty-nine-minute stroll?"

So then, yes. He was flirting.

Sam was not so tipsy as to be blind to the question of whether this was an odd choice, going for a stroll with a stranger instead of back to the party she was supposed to be at. But he was so cute. It would make a good story. And she loved the idea of an hour in London that Isabella hadn't planned, that was only hers.

Clive pointed out interesting things as they went along, as though he couldn't help himself.

"Saint Paul's," he said. "Designed by Sir Christopher Wren in 1675."

And, "Here's City Hall, where the young brides get showered in rice each afternoon at two."

"You know I'm not paying you, right?" Sam teased.

He showed her the remains of the Globe Theatre. A ship anchored in the Thames, a replica of the one Sir Francis Drake sailed around the world four centuries ago. He led her through narrow alleyways that he said had inspired Dickens.

"How do you know all this?" she said.

"I've got a good head for memorizing facts," he said. "And when I can't remember something, I just make it up."

She smiled, trying to discern whether he was serious.

"No, you don't," she said. "Were you a history major in college?"

"College is for people who need to be told how to think," he said. "I've just been around awhile."

Sam felt a flicker of disappointment, and then told herself she was being ridiculous. She was not going to marry the walking-tour guide whose first words to her were *Jack the Ripper*. She needed just to enjoy the hour.

"I did half a year at uni," he said then. "But I had this professor who wouldn't accept what I was saying one day in class. Didn't like being challenged by me. He told me to stop talking. So I walked out and never went back."

The proud way in which he said it made clear that Clive felt he had gotten one over on the guy, when, really, hadn't he only succeeded at robbing himself of an education?

He led her into a tiny, quaint pub, where he knew the bartender.

Clive ordered himself a pint, and a half-pint for her. Sam wasn't sure what to make of that. They sat down at a table in the corner. Underneath his jacket, he wore a fitted red T-shirt over jeans. His upper arms were more muscular than she'd imagined.

He told her he'd grown up in a small town three hours north and lived in Spain for several years. When he lost his job there, an office job, he returned to England.

They compared their favorite novels. When Sam admitted she had never read Ian McEwan, he pulled a book from his backpack and handed it to her.

"His newest," Clive said.

"Are you still reading this?" she said.

"Doesn't matter. You need it more."

He pronounced *matter* without the *t*'s.

The book was wrapped in cellophane.

"A library book?" she said. "But what if you never see me again? You'll get a fine."

"I like to live on the edge," he said.

He leaned in and kissed her. Sam felt an electric charge shoot through her body. After he pulled away, it was like she had completed a yoga class, then chugged half a bottle of white wine on a beach. She felt calm, subdued. She had never in her life been kissed like that.

"Whoa," she said.

He laughed.

When it was time for them to part ways, Sam felt genuine disappointment. She considered tagging along on his next tour, but as if to rid her of this terrible idea, Isabella texted: *Where did you goooooo?*

"It was lovely to share a drink with you," Clive said. "Shame you're only here a week."

"Ten days," Sam replied.

She asked if he had a pen, and wrote her phone number on the back of one of his pamphlets.

Sam tucked it into his jacket pocket.

Isabella was ecstatic when Sam told her the story. She wanted all the details.

"I love that this happened on my birthday," she said. "So was he hot?"

"Oh yes."

"Good accent? Plummy?"

"I have no idea what that means," Sam said.

"What does he do?"

"He gives walking tours."

"I know, but what else? Where is he hoping to take that?"

"Nowhere, I don't think."

Sam recalled, then, Clive saying that he preferred giving night tours so he could sleep until noon.

"But like, maybe he's a comedian or an actor and he does it to pay the bills," Isabella said. "Or maybe he wants to write a memoir about it. Or maybe he runs the company. Does he run the company?"

"No, his friend does. Clive said the guy plans to make a walking-tour app for every major city in Europe."

"That sounds cool," Isabella said. "The friend's job, I mean."

Forty-eight hours passed without a call.

Every time Sam thought of how she'd given him her number, she wanted to die. She replayed their conversation in her head. *It was lovely to share a drink with you*, he'd said. Which meant, of course, *Goodbye forever*. He hadn't asked for her number or offered her his.

But then, there was the Ian McEwan.

Maybe he could just tell she was the kind of person who was incapable of being in possession of a library book without returning it.

When Clive finally called, he said, "I was looking for change for the bus, and what did I find but your number."

"Is that your way of saying you can't stop thinking of me?" Sam said.

He laughed.

They chatted for a bit, but then abruptly, Clive said he had to go, without making any plans.

Sam didn't tell Isabella, but after they hung up, feeling bereft that that was all, she texted him: *I still have your book.*

He texted back a few hours later: *Dinner tomorrow?*

"Make him sweat," Isabella said. "Give it a couple days."

Sam waited as long as she could to reply. Seventeen minutes.

She arrived to the restaurant early, wearing a black top and her new jeans, which Isabella said made her butt look amazing.

Clive was outside, reading a paperback. He had on the shirt he wore the night they met.

He kissed her hello, that kiss like a tranquilizer, and then led her inside, down a hallway and into a low-ceilinged room, packed full of people, all talking at once.

They got seated in a booth. Without asking her opinion, he ordered a bottle of wine and several dishes.

He told her about the legends who had once sat between these walls—Dickens and Twain and G. K. Chesterton.

When Sam said she'd never heard of that last one, Clive shook his head.

"What are they teaching you over there in America?" he said.

Later, Clive ordered something called spotted dick for dessert, raising an eyebrow at her, as if she'd come up with the name herself.

When the bill arrived, he said, "Do you have this phrase in America—*going Dutch*?"

An unpleasant sensation ran through her.

Was she being sexist? Why should it bother her that he didn't offer to pay? But if she had known, she would have suggested someplace cheaper. Sam put down her debit card, mentally calculating where she could cut that money from her budget.

Clive came around to her side of the booth. He slid toward her until their legs were touching. Something chemical overtook every bit of sense in her head. Sam wanted to jump on top of him. To somehow crawl inside him.

"Here's a question," he said. "How old are you?"

"How old do you think?"

"Twenty-six?" he said.

He sounded both hopeful and doubtful.

"How old are you?" she said.

"Thirty-two."

Sam was stunned. She couldn't date a thirty-two-year-old. Her youngest aunt was thirty-two.

"I'm twenty."

"Christ," he said. "To be honest, I hesitated to ask you out because I had a feeling you were young. But not *that* young."

"What do we do now?" she said.

"The smart thing to do would be to part as friends," he said.

They had sex that night. In the morning while he slept, she looked at him. He was quite possibly the handsomest man she'd ever been this close to. Sam had liked him a lot before the sex, but now she felt addicted. She wondered if every woman felt this way, after.

She had only slept with two other people. She lost her virginity to her high school boyfriend, Sanjeev, after much discussion and careful consideration. They left for college still together, but he broke up with her in October of that first year. Sam, in turn, got drunk and went to bed with some rando she met at a party, just to punish Sanjeev, who wouldn't have cared even if he knew, but anyway.

Sex with Clive was something entirely different. He knew what to do. His confidence, his assuredness, were intoxicating.

Sam got out of bed to use the bathroom and tiptoed around the apartment. In the living room, books were stacked on the mantel, on the floor, on every inch of the coffee table. She looked at the spines. Names she recognized but had never read. Borges. Pynchon. Kafka. Amis.

Sam sat on the sofa. She imagined herself living there.

She climbed back into bed beside him.

"You're too old for me," she said when Clive opened his eyes.

"Am I?"

"I can't imagine dating someone in their thirties."

"Good thing you're going," he said. "If you weren't, I'd make a case for myself."

"What would it be?"

"You're clearly older than your years. Maybe I'm a tad immature and we meet in the middle. Something like that."

"Sounds like a recipe for disaster," she said.

They spent every night together until it was time for her to go home.

For the rest of junior year, they talked over Skype at least three times a day. They brought their laptops into bed and fell asleep that way. She was still up doing schoolwork for hours after he dozed off. Sam watched him sleeping and felt a longing she'd never known before. She showed up to work in the kitchen each morning, and Gaby would grin at her, all bleary-eyed, and say, "Oh, you've got it bad, don't you?"

When Clive told Sam he loved her, this man she had met five times, it felt natural to say it back. When he suggested she come live with him for the summer, Sam knew she would go, even as she heard herself saying, "There's no way I could."

"Why not?" he said. "My flatmate's gone until the end of July."

"I couldn't work," she said.

"We'd find you something," he said. "Just say yes. It'll be brilliant."

Since childhood, Sam had been an overthinker. She had always done the responsible thing, fearing that anything less would mess up her life. But this wasn't her life. It was only a summer.

Her mother was furious. Beneath that fury, Sam could tell, was fear. "If you go, you'll never come back," she said. "You need to finish school first."

"I'll come back," Sam said.

"We don't even know this person," her mother said. "And you're going to live with him?"

Sam felt sorry for her. Three years earlier, her parents had the power to forbid her from bringing Sanjeev into her bedroom and closing the door, or going to a party before they'd talked to the host's parents. Now it was up to Sam whether to cross an ocean and move in with someone.

"We won't be living together. Not like that," she said. "His roommate will be gone and it's a two-bedroom, so—"

She let her mother fill in the blank.

Clive shared the ground-floor apartment in Walthamstow with an old friend called Ian, whose Midlands accent Sam could only understand approximately forty percent of the time. Ian was in Ibiza for the first month Sam lived there. In his absence, they played house, cooking dinner and dancing in the kitchen; walking around naked; snuggling on the sofa, trading sections of the *Guardian*.

He showed her his favorite British comedies on his laptop: *Peep Show* and *Spaced* and *The Inbetweeners*. When Clive hugged her, his chin rested perfectly on the top of her head.

They had a small walled garden out back. A previous tenant had planted thyme and oregano. Sam watered them and picked off the best shoots, feeling more adult than she ever had before. She wondered if a person with one life could go somewhere new and just start another. Once, a neighbor rang the bell and said, "This magazine came to my house in the post, but I think it belongs to your husband."

Sam was amazed. The woman had clearly seen them together and assumed they were married. A year ago, a neighbor back home had mistaken her for her sister Caitlin, who was twelve at the time.

It was impossible to separate her feelings for Clive from her feelings about the city itself. Sam was in love with both. Walthamstow was as far from Isabella's London as could be. For the first time, Sam felt like she belonged somewhere that Isabella didn't even know existed, instead of the other way around.

There was an outdoor market on the high street, rows of tents bursting with fruit and vegetables, dresses and handbags, tins of nuts and spices the size of a drum. In a single block, she might see women in burkas, women in saris, women in ripped jeans, all mixed in together. She might stand still and hear a half-dozen languages spoken at once.

Carrying out otherwise mundane tasks in a foreign country felt like an achievement. Small victories like catching the right train or learning the funny names of things in the grocery store: *Rocket. Aubergine. Fairy cakes.*

Sam went to every museum. She was in awe of the city. She felt like an infant, discovering the world. She sometimes went on Clive's walking tours and pretended to be a flirty stranger.

Sam took photographs and then, alone back at the house, painted from them on blank postcards. She had never been the type who could set up an easel in public and go for it while strangers watched over her shoulder.

She painted an old church in Hampstead, boarded up, blackened by dirt and decay, the hands on the clock out front rusted and unmoving. She painted the homeless men sleeping beneath the overhang, their stuffed red shopping bags in a line against the door. She painted a proper British woman in a fur coat and hat, walking a beagle with a flowered umbrella in its mouth. She painted the window of a chocolate shop, and the double-decker buses on Oxford Street.

She sent all her paintings home to her mother and father.

Three weeks after Sam arrived in London, a friend of Clive's got her a temp job in a legal office in Covent Garden. She was filling in for someone's secretary who was out with a cold. It was only a one-day assignment, but Clive's friend said if Sam did well, it might lead to more.

The day consisted of sitting at the sick woman's desk, looking at framed photographs of her children, and answering the phone.

Saint John Foster's office. No, I'm sorry. He's not in.

Saint John Foster's office. May I take your name and number?

The guy in the next cubicle waited until after lunch to pop his head up and say, *FYI—it's pronounced* Sinjin.

Sam told Clive the story when she got home. They both kept bursting into laughter at random moments for the rest of the night.

Someone else Clive knew set Sam up with an interview at a nannying agency.

She filled out a long application, checking *no* on questions such as *Have you ever shaken a baby in frustration?* And *Do you enjoy fire?*

The interviewer mentioned a family up the road. They were from Toronto, and only in the country two more months for the father's job. They had eighteen-month-old twin boys. The mother was about to give birth again any day, and their nanny had just quit with no warning.

"The mum is a bit . . . difficult," the interviewer said.

She had frizzy hair, the color of an eggplant, and was eating a little bag of prawn-flavored potato chips, which Sam found revolting.

"Let me rephrase that. The mum is overwhelmed. Would you be free to meet them tomorrow?"

Sam said she would.

The twins hid behind their mother's legs when she answered the door the next morning.

"Allison," the woman said, extending her hand.

Sam shook it and, as she did so, noticed the carpets. She wondered how Allison managed to keep them so white.

They went into a living room full of white furniture.

Within minutes, Sam was down on the floor with both boys, playing blocks. Allison sat in an armchair, watching. Her belly was so perfectly round and she was otherwise so slim that it looked like she might reach under her shirt at any moment and pull out a basketball.

"Back in Canada, I led a department of fifty people," she said. "Yet I find it impossible to manage these two on my own."

Sam gave her a sympathetic look and wondered why she had chosen to have a third. "It's a difficult age," she said. She had noticed that mothers said this about every age.

"Thank you for saying that," Allison said. "Sometimes I feel like I'm losing my mind. I'm not naturally a kid person. Like what you're doing—making a tower of those blocks. It would never occur to me. Anyway. Your role would be primarily to watch the twins. I'll keep the new baby with me most of the time. I don't let them have sugar, other than some fruit. I prefer they not get dirty outside, because—"

"Because everything here is white," Sam said, as if she thought this was perfectly sensible.

"Exactly," Allison said. She sounded relieved.

Sam was pondering whether she even wanted the position when Allison said, "As for pay," and named an hourly rate that was almost twice what she had made temping the previous summer.

The job provided a rhythm to her days. It made Sam feel like she actually lived in London, as opposed to just visiting. She turned her key in the front door each morning and saw the twins in the kitchen down the hall, in their high chairs, awaiting breakfast. They always ate the same thing: a slice of toast with cheddar cheese, and a slice of toast with jam, cut into squares and split evenly between them.

When Clive's roommate, Ian, came home at the end of July, it occurred to Sam that she and Clive had never spent time together in the company of others.

The apartment looked different to her with Ian in it. He kept an ashtray, half full of cigarette butts, on the coffee table. He liked to bring in stray cats.

"Not only cats, mind you," Clive said. "He brought a fox in here once."

"A *baby* fox," Ian said, as if that made all the difference.

The place smelled like cigarettes and men. The carpet throughout was orange shag. The kitchen was cramped, the sink full of dishes. Clive and Ian had a routine in which each of them played a record for the other, choosing the next song based on a word or theme in the one that came before. They could keep at it all night, Sam sitting there with a tight smile, wishing Ian would go to bed, feeling like a killjoy.

When Clive's friends came over, she grew bashful. Some of them were married; a few had even had time to get divorced. They had careers in advertising or publicity or IT. One guy was a pharmacist. Sam suspected them all of seeing her as a twit, and to her great annoyance, she sort of acted like one in their presence, staying mute most of the time.

She loved Clive's brother Miles and his wife, Nicola, and their two kids. Nicola was the kind of woman who liked other women instinctively. She told Sam, "I'm so happy to have another girl around!" She emailed links to sales happening in London, with messages saying *Wish I could come!*

But they lived way out in the country. Sam and Clive didn't see them much.

Clive's mother terrified her. She was nearly an old lady. Her hands were wrinkled, her hair pure white. The way she stared at Sam made her flush with guilt, like perhaps she had a camera hooked up in Clive's bedroom and knew everything they had done in there.

But when they were alone, it was magic.

Clive showed her London, the parts tourists never got to see. They hiked through the Epping Forest. It was a short journey from the chicken takeaways and frozen-food shops and discarded mattresses in their neighborhood, and yet it felt like escaping to a dreamland.

They walked hand in hand along the canals of Little Venice,

Clive pointing out the white stucco mansions where Annie Lennox and Paul McCartney and Sigmund Freud had once lived. He took her picture in front of a houseboat owned by Richard Branson. On another boat, a floating café, they stopped for tea and scones.

He took her to Lisbon and Dubrovnik and Berlin. Cities where they could get a cheap hotel room, or stay in spare bedrooms, with friends of his, or friends of friends. Sam sometimes suggested more traditional destinations—Paris, Rome. But as Clive explained it, those places were overpriced and tired.

"You'll see the Eiffel Tower up close and it will look just like it did in the five thousand pictures you've seen," he said.

Every day, Sam paused to consider the astonishing state of her life.

Clive loved her paintings, hung them all over the apartment.

He brought her to all the galleries. Her favorite was Matilda Grey in Mayfair, a space dedicated to the work of women.

"This is my happy place," Sam told him. They returned again and again.

Once, while Clive was at work, and Sam was talking to Isabella over Skype, Isabella said, "Isn't there *anything* wrong with him? Usually we do a good amount of bitching about the guys we date, but Clive doesn't seem to do anything wrong ever."

"He doesn't," Sam said.

She thought then of what she'd found, but it didn't seem worth mentioning. And really, it was her own fault for snooping. This had been Sam's bad habit ever since she was seven and read *Harriet the Spy*. As a kid, she got in trouble multiple times for reading her sister Molly's diary. In the extremely rare event that she was left home alone, Sam would go through her mother's dresser drawers. There, she had found an old black-and-white copy of *The Joy of Sex*, complete with ten pages of photographs of naked men and women in various poses. She smuggled the book into school, to the horror and delight of her friends.

One evening, when he didn't know she was looking, Sam watched Clive sort through the mail, scowl at a large brown envelope, and then shove it on the top shelf of his closet. She didn't say anything, but instead went to look at it later while he was out at the store. He hadn't opened it yet. The return address said *Clerk of Courts*. Maybe he owed money—she'd heard him complain to Ian about how broke he was. She recalled a time when his nephew, Freddy, said, "Daddy says Uncle Clive made a whopper of a mistake when he—" only to have Nicola clap a hand over his mouth.

Sam couldn't stop thinking about what the envelope contained. Each time she checked, Clive still hadn't opened it. By the time she resolved to steam it open, like in an old movie, the envelope was gone.

Soon after, she looked at Clive's emails for clues. She didn't find much. She was reminded that he signed every message with the words *Stay Gold*, which for some reason made her uneasy. He'd long ago started signing emails to her with *Love*, and so she had blocked this out.

There was a folder titled "Laura," but it contained no messages. Sam was up late pondering this.

She had asked Clive about previous relationships. He told her he had never been involved in anything serious.

"What about you?" he said.

Sam told him about Sanjeev, how they were together for three years, how she got along with his sisters and parents and sometimes missed them.

"But that wasn't serious," Clive said. "You were in high school."

He said it like it was a hundred years ago, when, really, it was three.

First thing the next morning after coming across the "Laura" folder, Sam said, while they were still in bed, "Laura is a nice name. I always thought I'd maybe name a daughter that one day. Laura. It's pretty, right? Like Laura Linney."

She thought he might say, *I used to have a girlfriend by that name*. Or that his expression would give something away.

But Clive only said, "I have no idea who Laura Linney is, but sure," before wrapping her in a hug and kissing her all over her face as she screamed in delight.

They had sex every day, at least once. It seemed to smooth over any tensions, any doubts in her mind.

Sam and Clive ate dinner in the park most evenings. They might pack salad and cheese sandwiches and a bottle of cheap white wine, but still it seemed romantic to sit on a blanket in the grass, side by side.

She tried not to think about leaving. The idea of it seemed impossible. That she should return to her life at school without him there beside her in bed each night; without waking up in the morning to the sound of him whistling in the shower. The smell of Clive's skin was enough to make her want to cry if she imagined herself no longer knowing it. When Sam talked to her friends about plans for next year, she could tell that none of them expected her and Clive to continue together. It made her want to hold on even tighter. She thought of her mother's warning that she would never return. Part of her wanted to stay.

One night toward the end of the summer, watching Clive make a funny face as he bit into a baguette, Sam began to cry.

"I don't know what I'm going to do without you," she said.

"Then marry me," he said. "And you won't have to find out."

Sam laughed through her tears. "My mother would kill me if I didn't go back and finish school."

"That's nine months," he said. "You'll go and you'll finish, we'll visit each other, and then you'll come back here, and we'll get married. What do you say?"

All this time, her life had been going in a certain direction. But she saw now that it didn't have to stay that way. Things could change. Things ought to change.

"Okay," she said, feeling elated, and a bit ill.

He kissed her, and rolled her onto the blanket.

The following Saturday, Clive told Sam he was taking her ring shopping. She pictured the two of them in a jewelry shop, everyone wondering what they were doing together. She pictured Clive wincing at the price tags, as he did sometimes when he read a dinner menu in a restaurant.

"Flying back and forth to see one another for a year is going to be expensive," she said. "Maybe we should hold off on a ring and save our money. I don't even care about a ring, to be honest."

Clive smiled. "So practical," he said. "All right. But there will be a ring one day. I promise you that."

Sam felt relieved that there would be no ring for now. She chose not to spend too much time wondering why.

From then on, whenever Clive introduced her to anyone, it was as his fiancée. She told her friends that they were kind of engaged. She didn't dare tell her parents, which seemed like a bad sign. But Sam never voiced her doubts to Clive. She left London with the understanding that the separation was temporary.

They had made promises, but back at home, her real life had resumed, poking holes in the fantasy. The problem was Clive had been in his real life all along. Sam loved him. She did. But sometimes she could project herself into the future, see herself married to someone more appropriate. Or was that her fear? Other people's voices in her head? Everyone said to go with your gut, but when Sam tunneled down and listened, she couldn't hear anything one way or the other.

6

B Y THE TIME CLIVE TEXTED to say his plane had landed,
Sam was at the international arrivals gate feeling like she
might throw up.

When she saw him, she was nervous, unable to think of how
to stand, or what to say.

"Babe!" he yelled, coming over and kissing her right away,
which was appropriate, and yet Sam felt shy and awkward, like
this was the first meeting of two strangers entering into an
arranged marriage.

"How was the flight?" she said stiffly, willing herself to act
normal.

"Fine," he said. He gave her a curious look. "You all right?"

"Yeah," she said. "I'm so glad you're here."

When they reached the van it was somehow understood that
they should climb into the last row and have sex, right there in
the crowded parking garage. His bare butt and pale legs on the
blue vinyl seat, pants at his ankles. Sam straddled him in her summer dress, with a full view through the rear window of travelers
coming and going.

After that, she felt better. They lay down together for a bit,
and she told him about the party, about Isabella's meltdown over
a guy whose name she had forgotten.

On the drive back, he pointed out everything that was different from the UK, just as she had done when she first went there.

Clive told her about the book he'd started on the plane, a history of the Labour Party. Sam tried to follow along, but she didn't know any of the backstory or who the players were. He was so smart. He liked nature documentaries and never went anywhere without a book in his hand. Clive made her wonder about the American education system. He was better read than any college graduate she knew.

Sam sometimes lied to make Clive sound better. His résumé did not reflect *him*.

When they reached the dorm, she heard the party raging in the dining hall and hurried Clive upstairs.

The platform hallway was empty, strewn with red plastic cups and paper plates. Sam felt relieved. They wouldn't be bombarded by a wall of nosy drunk girls, like she'd feared. Not tonight, at least.

The recycling bin lay on its side. A thin trickle of sangria had made its way to the outer edge, and onto the green carpet.

Sam opened the door to her room. Isabella was gone, her bed neatly made.

"I recognize this place," Clive said.

Sam was confused, but then she remembered their video chats.

"I've never seen this half of the room before," he said.

She had imagined them going for a walk, though there wasn't much to see. Clive said he was exhausted. They lay down in bed and he held her. He fell asleep right away.

Sam stayed in his arms, breathing in his familiar soapy scent, amazed that he was actually here.

Usually at this hour, she'd be wondering what he was doing. Sleeping, most likely. If it was a Saturday, Clive would be out at a club, dancing with friends. When they lived together, Sam had never joined in these outings. He often came home at four or five in the morning. Once she had asked his roommate, Ian, how they managed to stay up so late. *Ecstasy, my darling,* Ian said. Then, seeing the look on her face, he added, *Sorry. I forget what an innocent you are.*

Sometimes Sam looked at online reviews for the walking-tour company and searched for mentions of Clive, though afterward she always regretted it.

My girlfriends and I have done the Haunted London tour three times, mostly because of the hottie guide, one woman had written.

Another wrote: *We did the Highgate Village walk on Sunday. Small group size. Interesting look at an area I knew nothing about. My husband said the sexy tour guide played it fast and loose with the facts, but I think he's just jealous.*

Sam got up and went to her desk. She switched on the lamp and started reading her art history assignment. This was nice, she told herself. This was what she wanted. Clive was here, and she was living her regular life, with him in it.

She tried to focus on the book. They were to read three hundred fifty dense pages over the weekend, which seemed impossible, but Sam knew that, somehow, she would get it done.

Before college, she had attended public school. Teachers usually liked her because she was well behaved and required nothing of them. She was a good student, without having to try. And she was known for her paintings, which always won a blue ribbon at the school art fair.

In ninth grade, her best friend, Maddie, had entered one of Sam's paintings—a picture of sailboats at a marina on Cape Cod—into a competition for young artists, sponsored by the New England Arts League. Sam won. She got to go to the governor's mansion. She received a check for three hundred dollars. She loved Maddie so much in that moment. Sam never would have entered on her own. From then on, she took painting seriously.

Once, she had dreamed of actually being a painter someday. But she knew now that she wasn't good enough, because of the way her professors and peers regarded her work.

"Competent but not strikingly original" was how one instructor described her final project sophomore year. During a critique, a classmate said of one of Sam's paintings, "There's something a little, I don't know—hotel room—about it."

Sam liked to paint landscapes and portraits and bowls of fruit. There was nothing edgy about her work, which somehow felt embarrassing. But then, there was nothing edgy about *her*.

Academics too were a struggle when she first got to college. She hadn't anticipated that. After Sam received the first and only C of her life, she realized she would have to work harder if she wanted to keep up with girls who had attended New England prep schools and spent their summer vacations touring Europe.

She found that, with some effort, she enjoyed academic work and was good at it. Since arriving here, she had never missed a class. Her first year, she calculated what she would eventually owe in student loans and divided the amount by the number of credits needed to graduate, and then divided that by the number of times each class met. When she wanted to skip History of European Decorative Arts, 1400–1800 or The Making of Modern Visual Culture, Sam reminded herself that this would be fifty-seven dollars thrown down a deep dark hole.

Her friend Shannon got her interested in the markers of academic excellence—dean's list and Latin honors and Phi Beta Kappa. Things Sam had never given any thought to before, but now wanted to achieve no matter the cost. She sometimes felt like she and Shannon were competing, but in a healthy way. As Isabella put it, they were both destined to prevail in the nerd Olympics, it was only a question of who would win silver and who would win gold.

Isabella and Lexi periodically took an entire day off from classes. *Mental health day!* Isabella would declare, switching on the TV from her bed.

Lexi was adopted from Korea when she was a year old. Her mother was her father's fourth wife. Lexi was her mother's only child and her father's fifth. They were divorced by the time she started kindergarten. From then on, she and her mother lived in a two-story luxury condo in Chicago overlooking Lake Michigan. Lexi attended an all-girls high school that cost as much as their college.

"Everyone was either a shoplifter or a bulimic," Lexi said once. "It was so dumb."

Sam wondered which category Lexi had belonged to.

Isabella was the fourth generation of women in her family to attend the college. She bragged that she would have gotten in even if she had walked into the library and set it on fire during her campus interview. A chair in the French department was endowed in her grandmother's name. (Sam wasn't sure what this meant. If there was an actual chair with a plaque on it somewhere. She figured it had to be more than that, but didn't want to ask.)

Sam had gotten in, she assumed, based on her essay. It was about President Washington—Shirley Washington, president of the college. Even when she wrote it, Sam knew the topic was a risk, bordering on sycophantic. But what she wrote was true: When Sam was in high school, President Washington had given a speech that went viral online. She talked about how she was the first in her family to attend college, how there should be no barriers to entry, how all women deserved a first-rate education, regardless of race, age, or ability to pay. When Sam saw the speech, it awakened something in her.

Once she was on campus, Sam learned that she wasn't alone in her love. President Washington was a celebrity. A smile from her, a hello spoken in passing, were things a person held on to and talked about for weeks. When she addressed the student body in Driscoll Hall, they chanted her name: *Shir-ley! Shir-ley! Shir-ley!* They stomped their feet, and it seemed like the balcony might collapse beneath the weight of their enthusiasm.

Sam tried to read now, but she couldn't follow the words on the page. She kept looking over at Clive, as if to be certain he was actually there.

Lately, she had been struggling against the sensation that her life here was second to her real life with him. But now he was here, and Sam felt strange. She needed air.

She went down the back stairs and through the dining hall to get outside. The room smelled like sweat and Axe body spray. Music pounded through her. She felt as if she'd landed here from another world entirely.

Tables and chairs had been stacked against walls to make space for a dance floor, which was full of underclasswomen from all over campus flirting with guys who claimed to go to State, though half of them were most likely still in high school.

Sam didn't see any of her friends in the crowd. They were probably off in a corner, talking among themselves. Two or three years ago, a couple of them might have flirted, tried to meet someone, but they knew well enough now that there was no one here to meet. If a guy tried to engage one of them, the others tightened the circle.

Two bros leaned against a table, debating something, shoving each other every so often, sloshing beer onto the floor. When Sam got close, she saw that the short one in the brown jacket was dragging the sharp point of a bottle opener back and forth across the tabletop, carving a straight line into the wood.

"Do you mind?" she said. "People live here."

He looked up at her. He slid the opener into his pocket.

"Sorry," he said.

Sam was surprised at how direct she'd been. Impressed, even. She couldn't wait to tell Gaby about the exchange.

Her friends on the kitchen staff would be the ones to have to deal with the mess in the morning. Maria often said she had raised two boys, but nothing had prepared her for how disgusting a bunch of college girls could be. After every Saturday night party, there were pools of vomit on the dining hall floor.

Each spring, there was an all-campus food fight in the quad. Nobody seemed to wonder who cleaned up afterward, but it was them, Sam's friends, and the dining and housekeeping staffs of other dorms. She always went out and tried to help, though they shooed her away.

Gaby, Maria, and Delmi lived in Weaverville, a town thirty miles up the highway, that Sam had heard of but never been to. They took an hour-long bus ride to campus each day. Working an early morning shift, exhausted or hungover or both, Sam had always been careful not to complain. She had only had to climb out of bed, wash her face, and stumble downstairs to get to work.

When she first worked with them, the women talked mostly among themselves, ignoring the student workers in the kitchen other than to tell them what to do. For some reason, Sam wanted in on their conversation. At one point, she listened as they whispered about Delmi's brother, who'd been injured on a construction site.

She blurted out, "My dad works in construction too, building houses."

Actually, he was a contractor.

Sam added, "I'm the first person in my family to ever go to school at a place like this."

She knew what she was doing. She was trying to say *I am one of you, not one of them.* A slightly desperate move, but it seemed to work. After that, they included her. They let her keep her frozen daiquiri mix and chicken nuggets in the industrial freezer, and even gave her a key so she could get her stuff out whenever she liked.

At the end of each week, when they emptied the refrigerators, Maria wrapped up any decent-looking leftovers so she and Delmi could take them home. Sometimes there would be a third foil-wrapped parcel on the counter for Sam.

"I saved you some of your favorite," Maria would say, squeezing her hand.

Sam sat on the stoop, ignoring the crowds coming and going from the party.

Ramona's Volvo was parked out front. Sam recognized it by the slightly askew OBAMA '08 bumper sticker. It was entirely possible Ramona herself had put it there, even though she could neither drive nor vote in 2008.

All of Sam's friends regretted not being born four years sooner, so that they might have been a part of that historic night. Sam was fifteen when Obama was elected. She remembered hearing horns honking, voices cheering, on their quiet suburban street. Shannon said it was the first time she ever saw her father cry. To have a president who looked like him, he said, was one of the great surprises of his life. He hadn't thought it possible until it happened.

In 2012, they went to vote as a group. They took pictures in front of the school gymnasium where they cast their first ballots, lined up shoulder to shoulder like high school seniors before the prom. It was somewhat exciting, but it lacked the drama of the previous election. They had paid vague attention to the polls. They knew already who the winner would be.

Sam thought of texting Isabella now to come outside and talk. Isabella always had good things to say about Clive, which Sam knew was entirely for her benefit. When Sam asked if she thought she was rushing into things by agreeing to marry him, Isabella said, "On the one hand, definitely. On the other hand, six months together when you've lived together for part of the time is different than just six months. Cohabitation is like dog years."

Sam didn't text her. She was almost positive that, soon enough, she would feel normal again. She didn't want Isabella to have a bad story about Clive to file away and offer up as proof of something later on. Besides, Isabella would try to drag her into the party, and that felt like a betrayal of Clive somehow.

After ten minutes or so, she felt a familiar desire to be with him. It was a feeling she was used to having to endure. But this time, for once, Clive was right upstairs.

When she got to her room, he was awake. Lying in bed with his arm flexed, his head resting on his fist, waiting for her. He gave her a familiar grin.

A pulse of desire went through her.

"Where'd you go off to?" he said.

"Just needed a little air. I thought you'd be passed out till morning."

"Nope. I've got my second wind. Let's take that walk you promised me."

Sam smiled. "Yeah?"

"Yeah."

They walked downtown, holding hands, laughing. Every business was shut besides the fancy Italian restaurant and Lanchard's, a dive bar where local guys hung around shooting pool, watching ESPN, eating bowls of cold popcorn, and smoking in the bathroom. Sam and her friends went there often, but only because some of them weren't twenty-one yet, and the doorman accepted even the worst fake IDs.

She and Clive sat on a bench outside the post office, talking, huddled together, his arm around her shoulder. It was just like it had always been when they were alone. Sam felt drunk with love.

When they got home, they brushed their teeth together, each with an arm wrapped around the other's waist, as ridiculous as that was. They had sex in her bed, then watched an old episode of *Frasier* and ate the package of chocolate digestives he'd brought.

When the credits ran at the end of the show, Clive said, "Oh! I have something for you."

He got out of bed, still naked, reached into his suitcase, and pulled out a little hardcover book with a print of roses across the front.

"Not what I was looking for, but this is also for you," he said. "Spotted it at my mum's house, and I figured you'd probably never read it, but that you'd love it. It's a nearly perfect novel."

He handed the book to her.

Sam read the title. *Angel* by Elizabeth Taylor.

Just as she was opening her mouth to ask the question, Clive said, with a hint of condescension, "No, not that Elizabeth Taylor."

"Obviously," she said.

"That name was a curse for the poor woman," he went on. "Had she married someone else and had some other name, she might not have ended up one of the most underrated writers of all time."

Sam considered this strange form of bad luck as Clive continued to rummage around in the suitcase.

Finally, he found a cardboard tube, and took from it two pieces of rolled-up construction paper.

"From Freddy and Sophie," he said.

She had drawn a rainbow and he had drawn a bird, and they had both written the words *I LOVE YOU, AUNTIE SAM*.

"I miss them," Sam said.

Twice over the summer, Clive's brother and sister-in-law had come to visit them in London with the kids for a weekend. Nicola and Miles went off on their own for one night each time, and Sam and Clive took Freddy and Sophie to the toy store and out for dinner. Unlike many other people in their families, the children had no judgment about Sam and Clive as a couple. He was so good with them. Sam could easily picture a whole, happy life with him in those moments.

"I'm going to tape these up first thing," she said. "Let's FaceTime them tomorrow, yeah?"

"Sure thing, babe," he said.

Sam fell asleep soon after, more content than she'd been in weeks.

She awoke the next morning to the unmistakable sound of some-one trying to be quiet. She heard drawers open and shut and opened her eyes to see Isabella, rifling around in her dresser.

"Sorry!" she whispered. "I'll be out in a sec. Trying to find my headphones. You haven't seen them, have you?"

"No," Sam said. She pulled the comforter over Clive's bare back.

Of course, she knew that Isabella would need access to the room sometimes, but still she was annoyed—headphones hardly seemed essential.

"How was the first night?" Isabella said, whispering, but loudly. A stage whisper.

"Good. How was yours?"

"The usual. Lexi split a bottle of Goldschläger with some frat boy and ended up puking these beautiful gold flakes."

"Hmm," Sam said.

Clive stirred beside her.

She willed him to stay asleep. But instead he woke up fully and said, "Hello there."

"Hiya," Isabella said. "Welcome to America!"

"Thanks."

They had spent very little time together in London. A week after Sam arrived for the summer, Isabella went home. Isabella and Clive had never quite clicked, but they tried to be nice to each other for her sake.

Clive reached his arm down to the floor and scooped up his boxer briefs, then shimmied into them under the covers.

Sam felt like there was something indecent about it. She wished Isabella had knocked before coming in, or that Clive would have had the good sense to pretend to be asleep until she left.

When he stood and said, "I'll just pop to the loo," Sam blurted out, "Wear pants!"

He gave her a funny look. "Did you think I was going to go wandering pantsless down the hall?"

Clive found his jeans and T-shirt from the night before slung over a chair. He put them on and left the room, whistling.

Isabella said, "He's got a really good body for an old guy."

Sam threw a pillow at her.

She was totally naked under the comforter. She held it up to her chin. Her friends here were all so casual about nudity. Isabella would spend entire mornings sitting around in just panties and a bra, like some man's fantasy of what a college girl did in her spare time.

"Should I wait for you two for breakfast?" Isabella said.

"No," Sam said quickly, deciding on the spot that there was

no way she was taking him into the dining hall if she could help it.

Isabella shrugged. "Okay, see you later."

For a moment, Sam was alone. She looked out the window, down at the cars whizzing along Main Street. She felt certain that every one of those drivers had themselves figured out in a way she never would. How was it possible to be happy with someone one minute, and mortified the next? To feel at once like a woman, and like a stupid kid? Would it ever get better?

Yes, she reminded herself. When she was no longer living here, in this in-between place. When they could be together again for real.

When Clive came back, she said, "I was thinking breakfast in bed could be fun."

"Mmm," he said, nodding approvingly.

"I'll go down to the dining hall and get us each a plate. You want a bagel? Eggs? French toast? Potatoes? Bacon?"

"All of the above," he said. "But first, there's something else I'd like to do in your bed."

"Oh," Sam said. She pushed the comforter onto the floor. "By all means. Have at it."

Over the course of the weekend that followed, Sam thought often of a line from one of Gil's picture books: *The walls became the world all around.*

They never left her room. They spent Saturday and Sunday in bed, with hardly any clothes on, just talking and watching movies on TV and touching at all times, as if to make up for the days and weeks they'd been forced to spend apart.

They ordered Chinese delivery on Saturday night. Otherwise, Sam went to the dining hall at mealtimes, before it got crowded, and filled a Tupperware with enough food for them both.

The women in the kitchen made fun of her when she ducked in to grab coffee on Sunday morning, holding a container heaped with toast and fruit and eggs.

On the other side of the door, students could get coffee from a machine by pressing a button, but it was watered down, bitter. Sam had gotten used to drinking the good coffee they brought from home and brewed for themselves, back when she worked the early morning shift. She still drank it most days.

"Looks like you're working up an appetite," Gaby said, nodding toward Sam's plate.

"Let us see him!" Delmi said. "Are you keeping the man tied up, like he's your prisoner?"

"Kinky," Gaby said.

The older women didn't laugh. Perhaps they thought it was inappropriate, or maybe they just didn't get the joke.

"I want all the details," Gaby said, quieter now so that only Sam could hear. "Come on. I live in my mother's spare bedroom with a toddler. Let me live vicariously!"

Sam laughed. "We're just—reading a lot."

Gaby smirked. "Right."

Sam thought their dorm-room hideaway was romantic, at first. But by the third day, the room smelled like sex and pizza. Clive's open suitcase and dirty clothes seemed to take up every available inch of space on the floor. She kept climbing and tripping over his things. There was a stack of dishes by the door, which she kept forgetting to bring downstairs, as if by magical thinking she might summon someone from room service to come pick them up.

On Monday morning, Sam surveyed the room and said, "Why don't we go out and do something?"

Elisabeth had given her the day off when she heard Clive would be visiting.

They decided on a hike. She packed a picnic in the dining hall just before lunch, filling her backpack with sandwiches and cookies wrapped in paper napkins. She added two shiny red apples.

Gaby looked on, arms crossed, that same smirk on her face.

"Shut up," Sam said.

"What? I said nothing. You're a growing girl, you need nourishment. Did you remember to pack the lunch essentials—plastic forks? Salt and pepper packets? Condoms?"

"Gaby!" Sam said.

It amazed her that she could do things in bed with Clive that an hour later she was too embarrassed to even acknowledge to her friend. Isabella would pump her for details, and Sam would probably oblige, but she knew she would blush the whole time.

Sam and Clive took the thirty-minute bus ride to Mount Huntington. It was an easy hike, just an hour to the top. She walked behind him, noting the way the muscles in his calves bulged whenever he took a step. She liked his long, skinny legs.

He had to go back to London later that night.

From the top of the mountain, she could see the whole valley below. They sat and talked about next year, what it would be like to wake up together every morning. In the distance, Sam saw the college and the town around it. A cluster of brick buildings and paved roads, surrounded by green trees, some of them beginning to show signs of turning, of the coming fall.

After Clive was gone, Isabella said, "I feel like I haven't seen you in a week."

"I know," Sam said.

"Last night a bunch of us were watching TV in the living room. Everyone was asking where you were. I told them you were busy being in love upstairs. They all thought you'd gone home for a funeral or something. None of them even knew Clive was here."

Sam laughed.

"Why'd you stay holed up the whole time?" Isabella said. "Were you trying to hide him?"

"Why would I do that?" Sam said.

She wondered if it was exactly what she'd done.

7

Elisabeth

ELISABETH DIDN'T WANT TO GO to book club, but
Andrew insisted.

"You'll feel happier here once you've made friends,"
he said. "I can hold down the fort. I'll have my mom come over
and keep me company."

Stephanie Preston lived three houses away. It was harder to
come up with an excuse not to attend than it was just to go. Elisabeth supposed it was nice that they had invited her. The five
women around her age on the block were a group. Established
long before she arrived. They even had a name for themselves.
The Laurels.

It wasn't a group Elisabeth particularly wanted to be part of,
and yet.

"I think I'll fake sick," she said.

She stood in the front hall with her hummus plate in one hand
and a tote bag slung over her shoulder, containing her wallet,
phone, book, keys, and breast pump. Andrew and the baby looked
so cozy on the sofa. She wanted to nestle in beside them.

"If you stay home, you'll have to spend an entire evening with
my mother. Think of it that way," he said.

Right on cue, Faye came in the front door, loaded down with
plastic bags.

A case of diet soda and a package of Hershey bars poked out.

"You brought us groceries," Elisabeth said.

"These are mine," Faye said. "George says I can't shop at Costco anymore. He says bulk shopping hurts the little guy. We had a blowout fight about it. I need to hide some things in the fridge in your garage."

"Okay," Andrew said, like there was nothing unusual about the request.

"I don't understand how that works," Elisabeth said.

"Like this," Faye said. "I bought a twenty-pack of butter. I'll come over whenever I need a new stick, and I'll tell George I got it at Gibson's grocery, and paid a premium."

Elisabeth tried to catch Andrew's eye to convey that he should shut this down. Otherwise, Faye would have an excuse to drop in on them whenever she pleased. But Andrew was wiping spit-up off of Gil's chin.

He wouldn't have told Faye no even if he had seen her expression.

As the mother of a son, Elisabeth finally grasped why things between her and Faye had always been somewhat strained.

"When Andrew was six, he said he was going to marry me," Faye told her when they called his parents on the night they got engaged. In response, Elisabeth had only managed to say, "My goodness."

It had never occurred to her that she might have a boy. Even after a blood test confirmed it, she still could only imagine a smaller version of herself—a mercurial girl, who loved all the girlie things she once did. Elisabeth couldn't help but feel disappointed. She googled *Can you take a boy to the* Nutcracker? *Do boys read Laura Ingalls Wilder?*

But as soon as she saw Gil, she understood.

Arriving at Stephanie's house, Elisabeth smiled at a pretty strawberry blonde at the door, waiting to be let in. She wore jeans and a Burberry trench coat, and she held a tray covered in tinfoil.

"We haven't met," she said. "I'm Gwen Hynes."

"Elisabeth Ronson. My husband and I moved into the white house over there two months ago. Which house is yours? I thought I'd met everyone on the block."

The women had come to meet her as a group, the Saturday after she and Andrew moved in. They brought cookies one of them had made and a bottle of wine. They were full of good information—about the local public pool and how to get free trash stickers at town hall, and whom to call if they needed an electrician, a handyman, painters. They were nice enough, but Elisabeth felt like they were sizing her up.

Now Gwen leaned in close and whispered, "I live four blocks away. My admission into the Laurel Street book club was controversial."

Her tone seemed to suggest that she was both joking and telling the truth.

"Elisabeth Ronson," she went on. "I recognize your name. You write for the *Times*."

"Used to. Yes."

"I loved your book."

She had written two, but there was never a need to ask which of them someone was referring to. Her first, an examination of the real and alleged feuds between actresses in old Hollywood, took off. There was a movie deal, coverage in all the right places.

Her second, a history of the diet industry in America, came out the same week as half a dozen huge books, including the one that went on to win the Pulitzer that year. It just got buried. Nobody read it besides Nomi, Andrew, George, and about seventeen strangers.

People regularly came up to her at cocktail parties and praised her first book, then said they were dying for her to write another.

"I did," Elisabeth would say. "It came out two years ago."

Privately, she thought her second book was the best thing she'd ever written. Her agent, Amelia, said she agreed, and that all writers were subject to the randomness of the marketplace. It was meant to be comforting, but Elisabeth thought that if she wasn't supposed to take responsibility for the failure of the second book, then the success of the first one might have also been a fluke.

Now, to Gwen, she said only, "Thanks. That's nice of you to say."

"My next-door neighbor teaches narrative nonfiction at the college," Gwen said. "Would you mind if I let her know you're living here now? I'm sure she'd love to have you speak to her class."

"I'd be happy to."

The door swung open, and there stood Stephanie in bright red lipstick, her hair blown out big. She wore tight black stretch pants and three-inch leopard-print heels. All Elisabeth could think of was Olivia Newton-John in the last scene of *Grease*.

Instead of hello, Stephanie said, "Wine!"

They followed her to the kitchen, where she filled two goblets that looked like they belonged at a Renaissance fair.

Stephanie handed one to each of them.

"Stephanie, it's a Wednesday," Gwen said with a laugh.

"Chuck's away and the kids are at my mother's," Stephanie said. "Let's party. The girls are in here."

As she led them into the living room, Stephanie asked Gwen how her weekend in Vermont had been.

"Nice," Gwen said. "Quiet. We traipsed around in nature and

had a couple of dinners out, and slept in on Sunday. We've both been working so hard, it was great to decompress."

"Sleeping in. Dinners out," Stephanie said. "I think I remember what that was like. Elisabeth, Gwen is the only one in the book group smart enough not to have procreated, in case these sound like foreign concepts to you too."

Gwen smiled tightly. Elisabeth thought she recognized the expression. It was one she herself had made plenty in recent years.

"Gwen, Elisabeth has a new baby," Stephanie said. "He's adorable. What's his name again?"

"Gilbert," Elisabeth said, wanting to change the subject for Gwen's sake.

"That's right. Gilbert." Stephanie sounded as if she still wasn't sure.

Elisabeth and Gwen laid down their offerings on the coffee table, which was already crowded with food no one had touched. A tray heaped with cheese slices and crackers arranged in the shape of a fan. A bowl of onion dip, its smooth brown surface undisturbed, but for a curlicue where the mixing spoon had been lifted out. There were potato chips; blue corn chips; salsa; pigs in a blanket; bruschetta. No rhyme or reason to any of it.

A small white powder puff of a dog kept jumping up on its hind legs and sniffing around the edges of things, making it all that much less appetizing.

Melody, Karen, and Pam were packed onto the love seat. Debbie, the doughy stay-at-home mom who lived directly across the street from Elisabeth, sat to their right, in an upholstered chair pulled in from the dining room.

"We just started our discussion," Stephanie said as she perched on the arm of the love seat.

Elisabeth was embarrassed to see that she was the only one who had brought her copy of *The Group*. She took the empty chair beside Debbie. Gwen took the only other available seat, a bench several feet away.

"Pam," Stephanie said. "You were saying something about the title."

"I thought it was misleading," Pam said. "I guess I thought they'd be more like us. More like an actual group."

"They were a group in college," Melody said. "Then they grew apart. It's realistic, right? How many of us are still close to our college besties?"

Besties, Elisabeth thought, trying to push down her disdain.

She thought of Nomi. They hadn't grown apart, had they? Their degree of closeness at any given moment tended to depend on circumstance—they drifted when Nomi went to Pennsylvania for grad school, came back together when she got a job in New York. Nomi met Brian before Elisabeth met Andrew, and there was a brief period when they didn't speak as much as they once had. But then they were both coupled up, both getting married. They had things in common again. Motherhood had bonded them more than anything. Through it all, there was a connection that felt far from circumstantial and could not fray with distance. At least this was what she hoped.

"I found most of the characters so unlikable," Pam said. "Who would want to be friends with someone who has an affair with a married man and then helps him commit his wife to an asylum?"

"I don't think we're meant to think of them as our friends," Gwen said.

Debbie seemed to take this as agreement with her point.

"Blame Melody. She picked it," she said. Then, to Elisabeth, "Melody's the brainy one."

Melody shrugged, *guilty as charged*. "Sue me, I'm an English major," she said.

No, you're a forty-two-year-old realtor, Elisabeth thought.

"She always picks some serious book that the rest of us skipped in high school," Debbie went on. "Be glad you weren't here for *Rebecca*."

Gwen got up from her seat. "I'm going to grab a drink," she said. "Anyone want anything?"

They all shook their heads. Elisabeth noticed Gwen hadn't touched her wine.

"Why don't we go around and each say one nice thing about the book?" Stephanie said.

"As Mary McCarthy turns in her grave," Gwen whispered as she passed on her way to the kitchen, her long scarf brushing Elisabeth's arm.

Elisabeth wanted to follow her, but suspected that might be an odd thing to do.

"I think it would make a good movie," Karen said.

"You say that about every book," said Melody.

"I do not."

"Karen, did you even read it?"

"I read half."

"I liked the writing," Debbie said. "But it was confusing. I couldn't get past the names. I'm sorry, but they were so goofy. Dottie and Polly and Priss."

If only all parents were sophisticated enough to choose a name like Debbie.

A few years back, a distant cousin of Andrew's had skied into a tree and suffered a brain injury. Afterward, she couldn't stop herself from saying out loud whatever came into her head. This sort of thing would be ruinous were it to happen to Elisabeth. No one in her life, with the exception of the baby, would be able to stand her if they knew what she was thinking.

Gwen came back in then, holding a can of seltzer.

A sharp beep emitted from a video baby monitor Debbie

clutched in one hand. She held a glass of Chardonnay in the other. At first, Elisabeth thought the monitor was for Stephanie's kids, upstairs. The screen showed the ghostly black-and-white figures of two bodies lying side by side. But Stephanie had said the kids were at her mother's.

"Are those your kids?" Elisabeth asked.

Debbie nodded. "No reason to pay a sitter when I'm across the street, right? Craig gets home from poker around eight. He'll babysit after that."

Elisabeth made eye contact with Gwen.

She wished she could talk only to her. From that brief exchange on the front stoop, that whispered comment, she was positive the two of them would be friends.

"Debbie, you have to remember *The Group* was written in the thirties," Melody said.

"Actually, it was written in the fifties, about the thirties," Gwen said. "It has such a delicious, detached quality. I love it."

"I guess I prefer something more modern," Debbie said. "Something we can relate to. Like *Fifty Shades*."

"But it sheds so much light on the present," Gwen said. "On all that *hasn't* changed."

"Like what?" Debbie said, perplexed.

Elisabeth wished she had the guts to say, *Like there are still women who, when their husband is in charge of the kids, will say he's babysitting.*

One scene in the book made her cry. A character wants to nurse her newborn son, but the hospital staff and her husband insist upon formula as the normal course of things. The character is made to lie in her hospital bed listening to her baby wail in a room down the hall. She's tortured by the sound.

Now the recommendations were flipped, the pressures reversed, but still so much was forced on a mother.

"Among other things," Gwen said. "There's the great stuff about women in the workplace, some of which felt grossly contemporary to me. Not to mention, the reminder that we're always just a voting cycle away from a return to back-alley abortions."

Debbie looked horrified. "Gwen."

"Ladies," Stephanie said. "It's only a book. It doesn't matter. Agree to disagree. Here's something much more interesting: Joan Walker saw Tim Bauer's car parked in the lot at the Motel Six in Dexter on Tuesday. In the middle of the day. She recognized the plates."

"No."

"Yes."

"I thought Joan worked at the high school on Tuesdays."

"She got laid off."

"Again?"

"Yes. Janet was all too happy to rub that in her face."

Six minutes. That was all the time they were going to spend talking about the novel Elisabeth had stayed up reading, even though she was exhausted, so that she would sound intelligent when they discussed it.

For the next two hours, they conversed with fervor about the secrets of women she didn't know. Debbie appointed herself Elisabeth's translator.

"Janet is Stephanie's sister-in-law," she whispered. "They don't get along."

"Joan's daughter had a problem with drugs. It was so sad. She's doing better now, though. She sells mineral makeup on the Internet. Joan says she makes a fortune."

Elisabeth wanted to say, *Thank you, but really, I don't care.*

Would these be her people now?

Stephanie refilled every wineglass as soon as it was halfway empty. Elisabeth put her hand over the top of hers after the second pour. The rest of them were bombed, minus Gwen, who only ever drank water as far as Elisabeth saw. Eventually, Stephanie cleared away the untouched hors d'oeuvres and replaced them with dessert—chocolate-covered strawberries, cookies, and cupcakes and brownies, none of which anyone ate.

"How are things at your house, Elisabeth?" Melody asked.

Elisabeth wasn't sure what to say. So few words had been directed at her tonight that, like some electronic device, she was still switched on but had gone into sleep mode.

"They're—good," she said.

"All unpacked?"

"Yes, finally."

She had unpacked immediately upon moving in, but that seemed annoying to admit. Elisabeth was good at unpacking, good at anything finite that required no real deliberation.

"No trouble with water in the basement?" Melody said.

"No."

"We haven't had much rain since they moved in," Pam pointed out. "Wait until the snow starts. That's the real test."

"It must be a huge change," Melody said. "Where did you live in the city?"

"Brooklyn. Carroll Gardens."

"Did you own or rent?"

"We owned."

"That's a pricey area, isn't it?"

"We got a great deal on our place," Elisabeth said, trying to sound breezy.

The conversation was beginning to feel like an interrogation.

"You owned in Brooklyn before it got super hot?" Melody said. She threw her head back. "Why can't I be one of those people who make genius real estate decisions?"

Elisabeth felt proud of herself, though she said, "We just got lucky, buying when we did."

"Maybe your luck will rub off on us, and Laurel Street will

shoot up in value soon," Melody said. "We were so glad when you bought that house. For the longest time, I thought no one ever would."

"Why?" Elisabeth said. "Is it haunted?"

She was joking, but they all looked down into their laps.

"Mrs. Dillon's mother did die there, and it was a terrible death, but no. I doubt it's haunted," Melody said. "It's just that they were lazy. They didn't take care of things. I remember walking into the open house, and there was this huge crack in the wall right there in the entryway. I pointed it out to Maureen, the listing agent. We're old friends. I said, 'Maureen, that's structural.' And she said no, it wasn't, it was a crack in the paint. I said, 'I've been doing this for fifteen years, I know what I'm looking at.' So then Maureen looked at me and whispered, 'Suckers from the city seeking *charm*. That's my only hope.'"

"Melody!" Stephanie said.

"What? I'm teasing. It's such a nice house. The pride of the block. You got it inspected, didn't you?"

"Where did you grow up, Elisabeth?" Stephanie said.

"California. Sacramento."

"Are your folks still out there?"

She didn't feel like telling the whole story, so she just said yes.

"That must be hard, being apart from your mom when you have a new baby," Stephanie said.

Something she felt like talking about even less.

"Speaking of," Elisabeth said. "I hope this isn't too much information, but I should go home and nurse. I'm very—full."

"We've all been there," Stephanie said. "Isn't it the worst? But don't leave. I have an old pump you can use around here somewhere."

"I brought mine."

Elisabeth regretted the words as soon as they were out of her mouth.

She excused herself to go to the bathroom.

She had to pass through the kitchen to get there. The word EAT was spelled out on the wall in giant red metal letters. Perhaps Stephanie needed a regular reminder of what the room was for.

Elisabeth pinched her own wrist. *Banana*. She sounded obnoxious, even to herself.

Oh, but those women were awful.

In the bathroom, she set up the yellow pump on the counter, plugged it into the wall, slid the cups into two slits in her bra, and turned it on.

She stood against the sink and listened to the slurping sound of the machine as it extracted her milk.

She texted Nomi. *I'm in hell*.

Elisabeth waited for a reply, but none came. Even though she knew Nomi was probably putting the kids to bed, Elisabeth pictured her out for dinner with fabulous new friends.

At least she could sit in here alone for twenty minutes.

She wished she had thought to record the conversation, or that she had brought a pen and paper to take notes. Maybe there was a book in all this. The pitfalls of trying to make friends in middle age, or suburban moms who drink too much.

It was her way of drawing a line between them and herself, playing the observer so she didn't have to care whether or not she fit in. She'd been doing it all her life. Andrew said she was like this because she was a writer, but he had that backward; she was a writer because she was like this.

When she got back to the living room, they were shouting over one another.

"The wine bar?"

"We go there all the time. The point is to shake things up."

"Margaritas at La Paloma?"

"Closes at ten."

"Lanchard's," Stephanie said.

"Eww, that place is nasty. Your feet stick to the floor."

"It's fun," Stephanie said. "Plus, it's where the construction crews go to drink after work. Nothing wrong with some eye candy."

Gwen pulled on her trench coat with an enthusiasm that surprised Elisabeth. She hadn't taken her for the stick-to-the-floor, eye-candy type.

"I've got to run," Gwen said. "We leave for Hong Kong tomorrow and I still have tons to do."

"Hong Kong?" Elisabeth said.

"I'm going for work," Gwen said. "My husband is tagging along."

"What do you do?"

"I teach East Asian studies at the college, but I'm on sabbatical this year. I'm also a photographer, so that's what this trip is about."

"How long will you be gone?"

"Three months."

Elisabeth felt crestfallen. Maybe she could walk Gwen home, at least. Test her hunch that the two of them might be friends.

When they moved here, she had imagined that the women in her neighborhood would be academics. Elisabeth fell in love with the house and didn't worry about the rest. So much was up to chance. Somehow they had landed on a block full of upwardly mobile townies, plus Karen, who was from Minnesota and married to a professor, but still fit in like she had lived here all her life. Had Elisabeth and Andrew bought four blocks away, she might have lived next door to Gwen, and two doors down from Gwen's friend, who taught narrative nonfiction. Elisabeth saw that other version of herself strolling along Main Street on the way to lunch with her new neighbors, and felt actual sadness over the loss.

"I should get going too," she said. "I need to relieve Andrew. He's been texting me every second."

A lie, but the Laurels nodded knowingly.

"The best thing for him is to have this time with the baby so he knows he can do it," Stephanie said.

"She's right," Debbie said. "I never did that, and to this day Craig calls me every ten minutes when he's home alone with them. 'Deb, where do we keep the Band-Aids?' 'Deb, where's the little spoons?'"

Stephanie sighed. "As my mother always says, there are only two kinds of people in the world: women and children."

Elisabeth promised them she would nip in the bud this problem that she didn't actually have.

Everyone made their way into coats and out onto the lawn. Gwen had managed to slip off without notice. Elisabeth envied her to an unhealthy degree.

It was a warm, balmy night, probably the last of its kind until spring.

They ambled down the sidewalk.

When they reached her house, Elisabeth said, "Thanks for everything. That was so much fun."

The porch light went on. Andrew appeared at the door.

"Let your wife come out with us," yelled Stephanie, as if Elisabeth was the life of the party, even though they'd barely spoken to her all night. "Can't you spare her this once?"

"Go!" Andrew said, too eager. The baby was asleep. His mother's car wasn't in the driveway. He was probably loving having time alone to watch sports or porn or videos of golden retrievers jumping into swimming pools.

"Are you sure?" Elisabeth said. She gave him a look, which she hoped made clear that this was an opportunity for him to be her hero, or for her to murder him when she got home, depending.

"Have fun," he said.

When they reached the corner, Stephanie said, "By the way, I can't stay late, guys, I have to go to Hong Kong tomorrow."

The rest of them cackled.

"It's like, we get it, Gwen, you're important," Debbie said. "You went to Yale. Big whoop, so did I."

Debbie went to Yale?

"She's one of those selfish, childless people," Pam said.

"Pam!" Karen said.

"What? There's something unnatural about a woman who doesn't want kids. We all know that."

"Would you want to have kids with Christopher?" Debbie said.

"You guys, our new friend is going to think we're awful," Karen said, looking at Elisabeth. "The thing is, Gwen can be a show-off. Her husband works with mine at the college. Different departments, but they're both on some committee, and we seem to get thrown together at these boring faculty events. So that's why we have to include her in book club. Her husband—he's an acquired taste."

"He'll hit on you within five minutes of saying hello," Debbie said.

High school never ended. It just took on different shapes, new casts of characters. Elisabeth had only recovered from the real thing when she went away to college and met her best friend, the person who understood her better than anyone.

She missed Nomi more than she had since the day she left Brooklyn.

They had to walk through campus to get to town. Elisabeth noted a small group of college girls standing at the bus stop, wearing basically nothing. She wondered where they were going dressed like that in the middle of the week. They had on far too much makeup, and shoes they couldn't walk in. They looked like overgrown toddlers, unsure of their footing. Sometimes she was so glad to be old.

Pam hooked her arm through Elisabeth's, in a show of forced intimacy.

"Tell us about your husband. He's—an inventor? I think that's what someone told me. Is that right?"

"Yes," Elisabeth said. "He was a consultant until recently, but he's had this idea in mind for years, and he decided to go for it."

She tried to sound enthusiastic.

"What's the idea?" Karen said.

"It's a solar-powered grill."

She expected them to ask her to explain, as most people did when the grill came up.

But Melody exclaimed, "He was on *Shark Tank*!"

"No," Elisabeth said.

"Yes! I remember the solar-powered grill. It had a clever name. Fun Sun? Bun Sun?"

"That wasn't him."

Melody frowned. "Oh."

They reached the edge of town, and Stephanie tripped in the crosswalk, teetering into a food-delivery guy in his twenties. Stephanie grabbed hold of him to steady herself, then said out loud, "Debbie, feel this arm, it's like a hunk of marble."

The kid appeared to be as horrified as Elisabeth felt.

When they got to Lanchard's and sat down at the bar, the Laurels were so loud and rude and annoying that people kept giving them dirty looks, and Elisabeth had the urge to shout, *I'm not with these women!*

She glanced around the room. There, at a table in the corner with half a dozen other girls, was Sam.

Elisabeth's relief upon seeing her was perhaps out of proportion with how close they were. Sam had only been watching Gil for a month. Still, Elisabeth was fond of her.

The sight of Sam felt like being rescued.

On Sam's first day, Elisabeth had purposely scheduled a therapy session at ten so she would be forced to leave the house. But it felt too soon to go to the office space she had rented as a place to write. After therapy, she went to the campus art museum. Standing in front of a painting of what looked like a blood-splattered mermaid, she began to panic. What had she been thinking leaving her precious child with a stranger, a virtual child herself?

She nearly jumped when a wrinkled woman with white hair touched her elbow and whispered, "How old is your baby?"

Was she a mind reader? Had Elisabeth hallucinated her?

"The way you're swaying," the woman said.

Elisabeth realized that she was moving her hips left and then right, left and then right.

"All new mothers do it, even when the baby isn't there," the woman said. "Like when you get off a boat and still feel it rocking."

She didn't sound judgmental. But Elisabeth imagined she was wondering why the mother of an infant was alone in a third-rate art museum on a Monday.

"Have a good day," she said, and walked straight home.

The closer she got, the faster she moved. Her nipples pricked with pain. Sam wasn't expecting her. She might have stuck the baby in the crib and gone off to study in another room, headphones blocking the sound of his cries. Or maybe she was shooting up in the basement. Elisabeth's urge to protect Gil was so primal that, by the time she entered the house and poked her head into the living room, she was already picturing her hands around Sam's throat.

They were on a blanket on the floor. The baby on his back, staring up at Sam, cooing as she talked sweetly to him.

Sam noticed Elisabeth and said, "Hi there."

"I left my laptop," Elisabeth said. "I'm so out of it."

She went up to her room, closed the door, and slept for the next three hours.

Since that day, she had rarely gotten any meaningful work done. She left the house after Sam arrived and went downtown. Sometimes she ran errands. Sometimes she read in a coffee shop. Sometimes she walked to her office space and jotted down ideas, and sometimes she went intending to do so, but ended up falling asleep on the floor.

But after that first day, Elisabeth never worried about Gil when he was in Sam's care. She recognized this for the gift it was.

Now, at the bar, Elisabeth was drawn to Sam's side. She needed the company of someone familiar, someone she actually liked. The thought entered her mind that her babysitter was out at a bar on a Wednesday, and was supposed to work tomorrow. But Elisabeth couldn't exactly judge when she herself was here.

"Hey," Elisabeth said when she reached her.

A pretty brunette next to Sam smiled up.

"Hi! I'm Isabella!" There was a pause before she added, "The roommate."

"Of course," Elisabeth said, though she didn't think Sam had ever mentioned her by name.

"Have you guys been here long?"

"Long enough," Sam said.

"Sam was in her pajamas sketching a picture of her grand-mother an hour ago. We had to drag her out," Isabella said.

"It's for a class," Sam said, defensive. "This senior showcase thing. I wasn't just like sitting there, drawing my grandmother."

"Her fiancé left on Monday night and she's still moping," Isabella said.

Fiancé. Sam had never called him that, had she?

"Right," Elisabeth said. "How was his visit?"

"Great," Sam said, sounding forlorn. "Too short."

Sam's roommate said, "Can I ask you a question? I hope this doesn't sound rude, but—we only come here because our friend Shannon is a genius who skipped two grades and is only nineteen. Why would anyone over the age of twenty-one come in here by choice?"

Sam looked mortified.

Elisabeth laughed.

"I have no idea," she said.

Sam stood then, and turned her back to Isabella and the other girls so that she was only talking to Elisabeth.

"Sorry about my roommate, she's a little drunk," she said.

Sam eyed the Laurels, laughing uproariously, guzzling white wine at the bar.

"I've never seen anyone here order anything but beer," she said. "I didn't even know they served wine."

"It's entirely possible those women travel with Chardonnay in their purses," Elisabeth said. "They're my—friends. Book club? Neighbors. I sort of got dragged here against my will."

"Me too," Sam said.

"Actually, I think I'm going to head home," Elisabeth said. "I can barely keep my eyes open."

"Okay," Sam said. "It was good to see you."

Elisabeth paused, then said, "Want to walk back with me? It's nice out."

"Sure," Sam said. "I'd love to."

"I don't want to take you away from your friends if you're not ready."

"I'm ready."

Elisabeth said a quick goodbye to the Laurels.

"That's my babysitter," she whispered. "She's really drunk. I think I need to get her home."

"Oh, aren't you sweet," Stephanie said. "Come back when you're done, okay?"

"I will," Elisabeth lied.

Walking out to the sidewalk, she felt like herself for the first time all night.

"Confession," she said. "I just used you as my excuse for leaving. I owe you one."

Sam smiled.

"Andrew's home with the baby?" she asked.

"Yup. His first time alone," Elisabeth said. "Well, actually, he wasn't alone. My mother-in-law came over."

"It must be nice having family nearby to help."

"Yeah," Elisabeth said. "To be honest, she's not very helpful, though. If anything, we moved here to help them, though we're supposed to act like it's the reverse. My father-in-law lost his business a couple years ago, and since then, things haven't been right with him. He's the greatest guy, but something's off. Something other than the fact that they are basically penniless now. He's mad at the world. He wants us all to change our lives and rebel against the system."

"Oh," Sam said, and looked confused.

For all that they had chatted in the last month, they rarely spoke about themselves or their families. They talked about Sam's schoolwork and the news and celebrities, and the baby. Safe subjects.

Now wasn't the time to get into George and the Hollow Tree;

the fact that Faye was secretly shopping at Costco to avoid a lecture or that George had recently written half a dozen angry letters after seeing a guy on the evening news whose three Saint Bernards died from eating dog food contaminated with salmonella.

"Millions of cans were recalled," George shouted, getting worked up. "Imagine if that was Duke. The tenth recall of its kind in six months, and no one's gonna do anything. Corporate greed wins again."

Corporate greed was his favorite catch-all term. He wrote Elisabeth a long email about it, including a link to a story about developers who were buying up farmland in the area and building cheap houses no one wanted.

Elisabeth always felt guilty by association when George mentioned corporate greed. Andrew had spent close to twenty years working in corporate America. And though she rarely felt protective of her father, there was something innate, not chosen, about the way in which she recoiled from the reminder that he was in real estate; he was precisely the sort of person George considered responsible for the downfall of America.

No, she would say none of this to Sam.

Elisabeth tried to think up some other story to tell about her in-laws.

"Faye, my mother-in-law, wanted Gilbert to be named for her father. Norman. She just went ahead and called him Normy for a month after he was born. When I told Andrew to tell her to quit it, she said, 'What? It's a nickname.' So. That's what we're dealing with there."

"Clive's sister-in-law wanted to name her daughter Trinket," Sam said.

Elisabeth wrinkled her nose. "No. Did she do it?"

"They went with Sophie in the end."

Elisabeth circled back around then to something Sam's room-mate had said at the bar.

"Wait a second. You and Clive are engaged?"

"Sort of," Sam said. "I mean, yes. But technically, no."

"Sounds complicated."

"I agreed to marry him, but sometimes I have my doubts. Not about Clive, just . . . ." She trailed off. "I can't believe I said that. But it's normal, isn't it? Everyone gets cold feet."

Elisabeth nodded. She could tell already, without knowing the details, that Sam would never marry the guy. But she would wrestle with the decision as if it was a decision that required wrestling for some untold amount of time. The only question was how long Sam would torture herself trying to make up her mind.

"Sorry," Sam said. "I don't mean to bore you with this."

"It's not boring," Elisabeth said. "What's he like? Does he make you happy?"

"Yes. I've never been so happy as when we're together. He's the best man I've ever met."

That word, *man*. It made Elisabeth wonder.

"How old is Clive?" she said.

"Thirty-three."

"And you're what? Twenty-one?"

"I know it sounds like a big age difference. But our rela-tionship is the furthest thing from the typical slimy-older-guy, dumb-younger-girl scenario. I pursued him, for one thing. When we met, I thought he was much younger than he is; he thought I was older. It's not like either of us was seeking out—"

Elisabeth put up her hands. "Not judging. I've dated older guys. Just don't rush yourself. You'll know what's right when you know."

"Thanks," Sam said. She looked grateful, even though Elisa-beth hadn't said anything profound. It felt good to ignore her own problems and focus on someone else's. Especially someone this young, for whom bromides could pass as wisdom.

"What does he do for a living?" Elisabeth said.

"He gives walking tours," Sam said. "Well, actually, he runs the business. He has this idea for an app he's working on."

"Sounds great."

"I do love him," Sam said, but she sounded defeated. "I think things will be better when we're settled. Like you."

Elisabeth both envied and felt sorry for her that she was naïve enough to see marriage as an ending, an achievement, instead of the start of something so much harder and more complicated than what came before.

"The big secret of adulthood is that you never feel settled," Elisabeth said. "Just unsettled in new ways. Your twenties are about getting the things you want—the career, the man. Your thirties are about figuring out what to do with that stuff once you've got it."

Ten years ago, all the women she knew dreamed of meeting someone and getting married. Now Elisabeth didn't have a friend who hadn't fantasized about divorce. One spoke of moving uptown, living alone, getting a small dog. Another clung to the idea of marrying someone better looking the second time around, a man who earned more and never farted in bed. They agreed that shared custody would be hard, but it would also mean entire days and nights without children to care for. These notions got them through the reality of being partnered, just as thoughts of being partnered had once buoyed them through singlehood.

A young girl who looked sixteen, but had to be older, ran past them in tears. Another girl followed, yelling, "Lily! Please! He's an asshole. His tattoo isn't even spelled right."

Elisabeth and Sam locked eyes and laughed.

"I don't belong here anymore," Sam said.

"I know the feeling," Elisabeth replied before she had time to think better of it.

"I used to," Sam said. "But this past summer, I lived with Clive, I worked in London. Not to be the clichéd girl who went abroad and feels like she came back a different person, but—that's basically what happened. It's so juvenile here. I've outgrown it. What about you? Why don't you belong?"

Elisabeth shook her head. "I guess I need to get used to it. Where we lived before, I had friends. Every weekend was something to look forward to. Now I only get excited about new episodes of *The Dividers* on Sunday nights."

"I love that show," Sam said. "We don't have cable in the dorms, but my mom records it for me and I binge-watch whenever I'm home. My friend Maddie, my best friend from high school, she's in med school in Manhattan. She got me into it."

"Do you think about going to the city after graduation?" Elisabeth said.

"I used to, kind of. Maddie and I always talked about it. But I don't know. It's cool, but I get overwhelmed there."

"You'd get used to that. There's no better place for a young creative person."

Sam nodded. "But it's so expensive. I'd probably have to live in a cardboard box."

"Everyone feels that way in the beginning," Elisabeth said. "Believe me, if I could figure it out, you can. You're ten times smarter than I was at your age." She paused. "I hate thinking about money, don't you? I prefer to pretend it doesn't exist."

"But *how* did you figure it out?" Sam said.

"I had four roommates at first," Elisabeth said. "In a two-bedroom across from a fire station. All our furniture was stuff we dragged in from the curb. This was before bedbugs. It was the best."

"My mom thinks I should go there too, and live with Maddie and work at a museum," Sam said. "She has no clue how competitive those jobs are. It's like she believes I could walk in off the street and they'd hire me."

"I might be able to help you," Elisabeth said. "I know some people in the art world."

"Thank you. That's so nice. But. I know it sounds dumb, but there's also Clive to consider."

Elisabeth nodded. "Right. So then, you'd move to London?"

"He'd like me to."

"What about you? Are you into the idea?"

"In some ways, yes."

"What would you do over there?"

"My absolute dream job that I'll never get would be to work at the Matilda Grey gallery."

"Why do you think you can't get it?"

"Because I applied and they said no."

Elisabeth smiled. "How is that possible? How could they not want you?"

"I'm not a UK citizen and I don't have any special abilities. They were nice about it. The woman said she'd hire me in a minute if it wasn't for that. But if I want to work in London, it will have to be off the books, as a nanny or something. Unless Clive and I get married." This last part she said in an almost embarrassed way. "I do hear what you're saying about New York City. I'm sure it's great."

Elisabeth sighed. "Maybe I'm romanticizing. I miss it. I didn't think I would."

She was Sam's age, a college senior, when she first visited Manhattan on her own, without her parents dragging her to Tavern on the Green and Radio City Music Hall. A girl from her dorm, Siobhan something, invited Elisabeth when they ran into each other early one Sunday morning. Siobhan's art class was taking a three-hour bus ride to the Met and back. There were plenty of empty seats. Elisabeth went along. She and Siobhan ditched the group and spent the afternoon roaming around the Upper East Side. They ended up at a coffee shop on Third Avenue stuffed full of faded couches and antique chairs. People sat reading the paper, chatting across tables. The two girls watched them, finding it all extraordinary.

"Imagine if this was your life," Siobhan said.

A year later, taking a stroll from her new apartment on Eighty-sixth Street, Elisabeth realized that coffee shop was three blocks from where she lived. It made the city seem intimate, familiar.

She hadn't thought of Siobhan in years. As you made your way through life, there were people who stuck, the ones who stayed around forever and whom you came to need as much as you needed water or air. Others were meant to keep you company for a time. In the moment, you rarely knew which would be which.

She didn't want Sam to miss out on the city. But then, the city had changed. When Elisabeth started as an editorial assistant, the world of her bosses was one of expensed lunches and clothes; hired drivers who waited outside the building all day in case an editor should want to go somewhere. Now there was none of that. What would have once been a five-thousand-word article was assigned at eight hundred words. Elisabeth got paid the same per word as she did when she started in the business fifteen years ago. Meanwhile, the cost of living in the city had exploded.

When she was six months pregnant with Gil, she went to see Patti Smith give a reading in Brooklyn Bridge Park. The sun was setting behind her, a stunning backdrop of rippling dark water, glass buildings, and pink sky, the bridge lit up for the night.

During the question-and-answer period at the end, a boy

raised his hand and asked what advice Patti had for young artists starting out in New York.

"Move to Detroit," she said.

They parted ways outside Sam's dorm. Elisabeth felt light. She was happy that she didn't have to go in there, that she was on her way home to her lovely house, her family. She could remember what it felt like to have nothing figured out. Life was better on this side of things. *Settled*, as Sam had put it.

At home, she stepped into the front hall and looked up to see the crack in the wall. Melody was right; it was indeed huge. Elisabeth had never noticed, but now she would, and every time she would wonder if it was a sign that the entire house might one day fall down on top of them.

She shut off the light, tiptoed upstairs and into their room. Andrew was sitting up in bed in the dark, looking at his phone. He gave her a wave.

She peered down at the baby asleep in the bassinet.

His face was a kaleidoscope. Turn him this way and he resembled her grandmother; that way and she swore he was her father-in-law. When he smiled, he looked like Andrew. Elisabeth caught her reflection in the mirror once and thought, I see my son in that woman. His face somehow more familiar than her own.

She changed into sweats and climbed into bed.

"How was it?" Andrew whispered.

"Ridiculous."

Her phone lit up with an incoming text.

Thanks for the walk and the chat. See you tomorrow morning!

On a whim, Elisabeth typed back, *Do you want to come over and watch* The Dividers *with me on Sunday? Join us for dinner beforehand?*

Sure! Sam replied.

"Nomi?" Andrew said.

"No. Sam."

"Sam who?"

"Sam the babysitter. We ran into each other tonight. Turns out she loves *The Dividers*. I was asking if she wants to come over and watch it this weekend."

"Hmm," he said. "Is that weird?"

"She doesn't have cable."

Elisabeth paused, thinking over what he'd said. "Is it weird?"

"I'm not sure."

There was a moment of silence, a look in Andrew's eye that she thought she could read.

They had not yet attempted sex since the baby was born. Elisabeth's doctor gave her the all clear at her six-week postnatal appointment, but it seemed too soon. A survey of her friends revealed that none of them had done it until their babies were somewhere between four and six months old. Elisabeth took this as permission to not even think about sex until the five-month mark, which was now, but it could wait a bit longer.

"Someone died in this house," she said.

Andrew's face was blank.

"Does that not freak you out?"

"The house is ninety years old. I'd assume someone died in most houses that age."

"But this was recent. It was a horrible death."

"What happened?"

"I don't know."

He smiled at her, bemused, then looked back at his phone. She glanced at the screen, something sports related.

Out of habit, Elisabeth looked at her own phone.

The first thing that appeared when she clicked on the BK

Mamas page was a close-up picture of a toddler's cheek, covered in oozing red bumps.

Is this eczema or ringworm??? the poster had asked. Forty-nine people replied.

Elisabeth clicked away, wishing to rid her mind of the image. Elsewhere on Facebook, several of her writer friends had posted photos from a book party in Brooklyn the night before. All the usual smiling faces. Elisabeth had slipped out of that world without making a ripple.

She went to her sister's Instagram, hoping to see the words that could solve her biggest problem: *Sponsored post.*

But the latest was just another photograph of Charlotte lying on a surfboard in a green bikini, paddling out to sea, head held high, hair hanging in damp waves over her impossibly toned upper arms.

> *"IF . . . If I never danced until dawn. If I had never tasted my true love's kiss—or the sting of his betrayal. If I did not greet my fears with freedom . . . then I would never have known such abundance. The lustre of it all. My lustrous hair is a road map of where I've been and who I'm becoming. Not a straight line, but an exquisite tangle. Lustre hair care products with SPF 35 are my new go-to, guys. Highly recommend. Sending love and lustre from the shores of Bathsheba Beach."*

Elisabeth sighed.

Lustre. There was no such word.

Even more irritating was Charlotte's insistence on putting quotation marks around half the things she wrote. Elisabeth had tried to explain that this made it look like she was quoting herself.

Charlotte said, "But I am quoting myself. Someday I might do a book of my quotations."

Had a diet pill company Elisabeth had never heard of really offered her sister half a million dollars to promote their product? Had there ever even been a sponsorship deal? As recently as a month ago, Charlotte had said her lawyer was ironing out final details on the contract. But what if the whole thing had been a lie?

Elisabeth shook her head, as if to empty it of the thought. That wasn't a path she could go down tonight.

She closed the tab. A moment later, she opened a new one.

She googled *Sun Bun* and then *Bun Sun* and finally *solar powered, Sun Bun*.

There it was—the Sun Fun 5000 by Solar Tech.

TURNS OUT THERE IS SOMETHING NEW UNDER THE SUN! Our solar-powered cooker heats up five times faster than charcoal! As featured on Shark Tank.

Elisabeth felt a heaviness sink from her chest down into her gut.

There was a photograph of a smiling young woman at the bottom of the page.

Dr. Noreen Brigham invented the Sun Fun while on a Fulbright scholarship in the Himalayas, working with nomads on solutions for energy poverty. She received her doctorate from Harvard University and was named to the Forbes 40 Under 40 innovators list in 2011.

Andrew had once said an invention was only as good as the story behind it. She thought of the night he came up with his idea. How did drunk guys at a wedding compare to nomads in the Himalayas?

Elisabeth looked over at him. She felt like she was about to tell him someone he loved had died.

"Honey. Do you know about this?"

She handed him the phone.

Andrew glanced at the screen.

"I think I've seen it," he said.

"And it's not a problem?"

"No. See? It says right there. That's a solar-powered cooker. Mine's a grill."

"Sure. But aren't they the same thing? A device for cooking outside, using solar?"

"That folds up. It's portable. You can take it camping or whatever. Mine is meant to replace the family grill. It's a more solid piece of equipment."

So the Sun Fun was the same as his invention, but portable. And where his heated up three times faster than a charcoal grill, this one worked five times faster. And unlike his, it already existed.

"It's fine," Andrew said. "The R-and-D guys I've talked to know all about the competition. They're not concerned. Trust me."

Elisabeth didn't trust him, not on this. That was the problem.

She was about to put the phone down when Nomi replied to her text from earlier.

Book club was a bust?

It had been hours since Elisabeth reached out, lonely in the bathroom at Stephanie's house. She knew her frustration was about Andrew and the Laurels, but she suddenly felt irrationally angry about Nomi's silence. Nomi wouldn't set a date to come visit. She never asked about the house.

Book club was soul-destroying, she wrote. *Where were you??*

Uhh . . . right here where I usually am. You're the one who moved away, remember?

A minute later, Nomi added a winking emoji to make clear that it was a joke, but Elisabeth knew it wasn't, not entirely. Nomi was right. What did she expect?

She took a deep breath.

How was your night? she wrote.

I asked Brian to get a vasectomy and he said no, because what if his second wife wants kids. To which I said, fair point. So nothing accomplished there.

Nomi and Brian both had a cool frankness about them. She was the executive director of a national nonprofit that focused on educating girls in the Third World. He worked in politics. They were tough, assertive, blunt. They could be almost cruel to each other at times, and it was fine, because each of them knew the other could take it.

If Brian had decided, shortly before the birth of their first child, to leave his job and become an inventor, Nomi would have said, *You're an idiot. No.* That would have been the end of it.

Elisabeth and Andrew's marriage was nothing like theirs. Andrew was sensitive. In both senses of the word. There were so many things she couldn't say. Her people only had two speeds: contentedness and sledgehammer. Elisabeth had never learned how to argue without chipping off a piece of the other person. She didn't want to do that to Andrew. So sometimes she kept things from him, things she only told Nomi or Violet, or both.

I'm worried about Sam, she typed.

I told you the young ones are a nightmare, Nomi replied. *They have no fear. The girl I have on the weekends comes late, and walks in with coffee from Blue Bottle, as if to point out that she could have arrived on time if she wanted to. Then she can't be bothered to throw the cup away. Leaves it on my kitchen table when she goes.*

Ha, Elisabeth wrote. *But wait, no. I meant I'm worried about Sam's relationship. She told me tonight that her boyfriend is 33. He's way too old for her. Oh, and they're sort of engaged.*

A long moment followed, in which she conjured up the face Nomi was making.

Finally, Elisabeth wrote, *What?*

Nomi replied: *I didn't even know Angela was married for the first three months she worked for us. Be careful. She's not your friend, she's your employee.*

I know! Elisabeth wrote back. *Of course.*

8

Sam

THE NEXT THREE SUNDAYS in a row, Sam went to Elisabeth's house for dinner.

When Elisabeth invited her, Sam had felt a fluttering. It reminded her of the first and only time her middle school crush said her name out loud, in the course of asking to borrow a pencil.

"I bet it's a trick to get you to babysit for free," Isabella said.

But each time, Gilbert was in bed when she arrived. If he cried out and she stood to get him, Elisabeth would say, "You're not on the clock, Sam. You're our guest," before leaving the room to tend to the baby herself.

There was music playing whenever Sam got there, something she wouldn't think to listen to, and yet it was just right—the Beach Boys or Patsy Cline or Otis Redding. When Sam got back to the dorm, she'd play that album over and over for the rest of the week.

It was only the three of them, but they made it special. Place mats and tea candles on the dining room table, small silver bowls of kale chips and Brazil nuts set out on the kitchen island. Simple fresh-cut flowers; like white tulips or yellow roses, with no filler. The flowers would still be there when Sam came to work the next day, but they'd be gone before they had a chance to wilt or turn the water all swampy, as had happened the one time Clive sent her an arrangement.

Sam couldn't recall her parents ever hosting a dinner party. Only big family gatherings, with sandwich platters and a Crock-Pot full of her mother's meatballs. Her relatives sat all over the house, wherever they could find a spot. They ate off paper plates, with paper napkins in colors coordinated to the occasion.

Her parents threw a neighborhood cookout once or twice a summer, with too much food—afterward, the family ate burnt hot dogs and steak and macaroni salad for a week. At home, entertaining guests was about filling bellies and making sure the house was presentable: the toilets flushed, the toys put away.

Sam wondered how Andrew and Elisabeth managed to make everything perfect. The house was spotless, but she never saw them clean. When she rang the doorbell on a Sunday, they had usually just gotten back from taking a long walk or a drive to the antique shops in Grantville. It almost seemed as if they'd forgotten she was coming but were glad to see her and fully prepared to host on zero notice. She couldn't imagine them frantic, screaming at each other five minutes before she arrived to get in the shower already or hide the pile of laundry on the stairs.

Andrew did the cooking. Sam and Elisabeth sat at the counter, drinking wine that was probably ten times nicer than anything Sam drank in the normal course of things, though she couldn't tell the difference. Their red-wine glasses were stemless. White, Andrew said, required a stem. It bothered him when a restaurant got this backward, as white wine in a stemless glass was inappropriately warmed by the hands of the person drinking it.

"I like white in a stemless glass," Elisabeth said. "What do you prefer, Sam? Stemless or stem?"

"Not sure I have a preference."

You never saw an actual wineglass in the dorms. Now Sam considered buying one. It was impossible to feel sophisticated while drinking from a red plastic cup.

Over dinner, they chatted with ease, discussing politics and movies and books. Andrew pointed out which items he bought at the farmers market behind the post office. Every family Sam had ever babysat for in this town was crazy for the farmers market. Never before in her life had she encountered such enthusiasm about buying vegetables.

She told them about the painting class she was taking this semester, how they were supposed to paint the same tomato week after week. It had started off firm and plump and shiny red, and was now wrinkled, sprouting mold.

"Is it a commentary on the brutality of the aging process?" Elisabeth said.

"I think it's just a tomato," Sam said.

They laughed.

She felt a thrill when she made them laugh.

"See, this is why no one in the department likes me," Sam said. "I don't have an artist's brain. I just like painting pretty pictures."

"You sell yourself short," Elisabeth said.

"I agree," Andrew said.

Sam studied their interactions. They were sometimes affectionate, but never in a gross way. Once, when "You're My Best Friend" by Queen started playing, he placed his hand on the small of her back, and she smiled at him, a very private smile, before turning to Sam and saying sheepishly, "Our song."

Andrew was a compact man, slim, and not much taller than Elisabeth. His brown hair was cut neatly, like the boys Sam remembered from Sunday school. Elisabeth, she thought of as stylish, cool. Andrew was more dad-like. He wore oxford shirts and loafers while hanging around the house.

Elisabeth and Andrew laughed at one another's stories and respectfully considered each other's arguments. They went out of their way to be kind to one another. He made her coffee every morning and brought it to her in bed. She was forever mentioning how his shirt made his eyes look even bluer than usual, things like that. This intrigued Sam.

Her own parents never fought, but they regarded each other like sturdy furniture—useful, reliable, there.

While doing her reading for class one morning, she underlined a passage in Edith Wharton: *Ours was a robust passion that could give an open-eyed account of itself, and not a beautiful madness shrinking away from the proof.*

That was them, Andrew and Elisabeth. It was, Sam realized, what she wanted for herself. She knew people looked at what she and Clive had and saw a beautiful madness. Madness, anyway.

Sam and Clive had no shared frame of reference. She remembered a night last summer when his friends came over to their flat to play Celebrity. Sam didn't know who any of the clues were—Patsy Palmer and Nigel Havers and Cilla Black. The rest of them laughed uproariously at the string of impressions, none of which made sense to her.

She hated them in that moment, even Clive. She hated their smugness, as if no one had ever had a group of friends before.

Wanting her to feel included, she supposed, their flatmate, Ian, and his girlfriend, Chevy, insisted Sam try acting out one of the answers. She pulled a slip of paper from a hat and looked at it. Who the hell was Terry Wogan?

"Sorry, I've never heard of this person," she said, flustered. "Someone else should do this. I'll mess it up."

"You're so young," Chevy said, adoringly.

"No, she's just American," Clive said.

But really, it was both.

The best part of dinner at Andrew and Elisabeth's was what happened afterward. In the den upstairs, Sam and Elisabeth were finally alone and free to get into things. They curled their bare feet under their bodies, facing each other on the couch. They talked not about culture and current events, as it seemed one had to in front of men, but about friends and ex-boyfriends and their families.

Elisabeth had a sister who lived in the Caribbean. "A bit of a wild child," she said. "A free spirit, I guess you could say. She has this enormous Instagram following."

(Later, back at the dorm, Sam and Isabella found the page. Elisabeth's sister was hot. In the most recent image, she stood on a paddleboard in turquoise water, wearing a black bikini with a confusing number of straps. *Mantra for Today: Be Here Now. Tortola, you leave me breathless with your beauty. Thank you Stella Maris Hotels for making every journey unforgettable.* Isabella said, "Do you think she's breathless because that bathing suit is so tight?")

Elisabeth mentioned one night that she was semi-estranged from her parents, but she didn't provide details. This surprised Sam. She could usually sense when someone came from an unstable family. The college was full of such girls. Elisabeth didn't give off their sort of energy.

Being semi-estranged sounded impossible, like being semi-pregnant. Sam wondered, but did not ask, what exactly this meant. She never forgot that Elisabeth was her employer. She liked the casual nature of their relationship, but she was careful to let Elisabeth set the boundaries.

She thought about it a lot, though. What it would be like to have a baby and not speak to your parents. Or semi—not speak to them, anyway.

When she eventually gave birth, Sam imagined her family would be there every second. Her mother and sisters in the delivery room, her brother and dad pacing outside the door. Afterward, her cousins and aunts and uncles would crowd around in the hospital room, as it had always been in their family. Set against that, Elisabeth and Andrew seemed so alone in the world.

Every so often, Elisabeth would share some telling detail. She told Sam that her mother was obsessed with being thin, that she prided herself on weighing not an ounce more than she had on her wedding day.

"When my sister and I were in middle school, high school, she'd have all three of us go on a diet and compete to see who could lose the most weight."

"But you're so thin to begin with," Sam said.

"I know. So is my sister. The whole thing really messed her up."

Elisabeth remembered everything Sam told her. She never failed to follow up on even the most trivial matters.

"What did Hailey say when Isabella confronted her about stealing the shampoo?" she once asked, with genuine interest.

Sam asked how long she and Andrew were together before they got married.

"Six years," Elisabeth said. "I was in no rush. We probably never would have done it if Andrew hadn't forced the issue."

"Really?"

"I'm sure we'd be *together*. But—marriage. I never thought it was for me. We eloped. My mother-in-law hated that, but she was relieved that we'd no longer be living in sin."

"I sometimes picture a big wedding, with all my younger cousins as flower girls, in pink poufy dresses, and me with this long veil," Sam said. "But then when I think about the people involved—Clive waiting at the end of the aisle, our mothers sitting on either side—it all seems highly embarrassing."

"I tend to break out in hives at weddings," Elisabeth said. "True story."

Wherever a conversation led them, they stopped speaking at exactly 8:59. From 9:00 to 10:00 they watched *The Dividers* in silence. Had Elisabeth talked during the show, Sam would have done the same, but she liked that they didn't. If a particularly shocking plot twist occurred, they might turn to each other with wide eyes for a second before looking back at the screen, but that was all. When the closing credits rolled, Elisabeth stretched, stood up, and said, "It's late. I should let you get back," and Sam went home.

"What makes them think you want to hang out with your bosses at the weekend?" Clive said on the phone one Monday morning. "It's like they think they own you because they pay you."

"It's not like that," Sam said. "We're more like friends."

"Hmm," he said.

"Last night we were watching TV and Elisabeth's cell phone rang, and she answered it and said she couldn't talk because her friend Sam was over."

In the moment, it made Sam feel kind of proud, though she felt dumb recounting it, holding it up as evidence of something.

"But it's all on her terms," Clive said.

"Of course it is. What am I going to do, invite them to dinner in the dining hall? 'Hey, guys! Come on over. It's tuna noodle casserole night.'"

Sam knew what he was afraid of, but she also knew that he had no reason to be.

"Once you meet her, you'll understand," she said.

Her first year away at college, Sam missed suburban living rooms, the stuffed cupboards of middle-aged people. She missed kids. She started babysitting for the Walkers. They lived on a farm ten miles outside of town and had two moms, Jessica and Ann, who played more stereotypical gender roles than any straight couple Sam knew. Jessica had given birth to their three children, ages four, two, and one. A stay-at-home mom who did everything around the house, she was the disciplinarian. Ann was a doctor. She worked long hours. When she came home, she did things that made Jessica angry, like reaching into her coat pocket to pull out handfuls of gummy bears and giving them to the kids after they had already brushed their teeth.

Jessica often complained to Sam about it.

At the time, Sam was not yet over her high school boyfriend and spent many evenings staring at his screen name on Gchat, willing him to contact her. She was not exactly an expert on marriage. Still, she offered feedback when Jessica asked. Jessica hugged her after, saying, "What would I do without you?"

But it was Jessica who refused to let Ann drive her home the night it snowed and Sam's clunky old Cutlass got stuck in the mud outside their house. They didn't have a driveway. They parked in what was basically a field. The same thing had happened twice before, and both times, Ann had pushed her free while Sam sat in the driver's seat with her foot on the gas.

The night of the snowstorm, they were hosting five lesbian couples and their children for dinner. Jessica was in a tizzy. She said she couldn't spare Ann for as long as it would take to give Sam a push, and certainly not long enough to drive her home and get back.

She said, "I'm sorry, Sam, but why do you drive that thing? It's not safe. Call a cab and we'll pay for it."

Sam called and went outside and walked down the steep hill that led to their property. The hill dropped right onto a dark country road. Soon, several pairs of headlights slowed as they approached, but all of them turned in front of her. The dinner guests.

She waited and waited. The snow picked up. She wondered if the cabdriver had gotten lost, or decided not to go out in this weather. Sam hadn't brought her cell phone, since there was no service out here.

Rage bubbled up in her chest. She wanted to cry, but remembered a story her brother told her about a guy he knew whose eyelids had frozen shut. Sam wasn't sure whether Brendan had made the story up, but she wasn't willing to risk it.

She waited until she couldn't feel her toes inside her boots. When she ran her hand over her hair, it was caked in snow.

Sam told herself she would sooner freeze to death than ask Ann and Jessica for help. But eventually, she had no choice but to hike back up the slick hill and knock at their kitchen door.

The looks on everyone's faces when they saw her there.

"Sam?" Ann said. "What on earth?"

It turned out she had been waiting in the snow for an hour and a half.

Dinner was winding down by then. The table was set with coffee cups and dessert plates, most of which had a bite or two of chocolate cake left on them. One of the visiting couples drove her home. The next morning, her RA took her back to dig out the car. Sam didn't announce herself, and the Walkers didn't come outside. She never spoke to them again.

Sam had cared for many people's children. She was used to being treated like family when it suited them, and the hired help when it did not. But Elisabeth wasn't that way. Elisabeth considered her an equal. It was what Sam needed now. A real adult in her life to call a friend.

Sam called her parents' house one Sunday at the usual time. After two rings, she heard a new outgoing voicemail message recorded by her sister Caitlin.

You've reached the O'Connells. We're not home right now. We will probably cry when we learn that we missed this call, so please leave a message at the beep. Tell us everything. Do not leave out a single detail.

Strange, Sam thought.

The line went silent. She couldn't remember if she'd heard a beep.

"Hi, Mom," she said. "Umm. I was calling to—"

Suddenly, the sound of Caitlin's laughter broke through.

"Sam, it's me. I was kidding."

Sam groaned. "Put Mom on."

Her mother sounded pleased when Sam told her Elisabeth and Andrew had started inviting her to Sunday dinners. She insisted Sam not go empty-handed, that she bring them flowers, at least. Sam understood the sentiment, but felt certain this would be awkward. She wouldn't know where to get flowers, other than the Stop & Shop on the outskirts of town, where there were always a few wilting arrangements in a refrigerated case. She would no doubt ruin everything by bringing them baby's breath or something equally objectionable.

Lilies are only suitable for a memorial service, Elisabeth had said once, and Sam cringed, thinking of how much she liked lilies and hadn't realized until that moment that she shouldn't.

"Clive suggested I bring them something too," she told her mother, even though it wasn't true, because it never hurt to frame Clive in a positive light. Her mother sometimes asked how he was doing, but she did so in such a pinched tone that Sam could tell she didn't want an answer. Sam's father never mentioned Clive at all.

Her family hadn't met him yet. Sam's mom asked her not to tell her siblings how old Clive was. She hadn't told Clive that.

Her brother, Brendan, had been with his girlfriend Katie since eighth grade. Katie fit so seamlessly into their family that an outsider observing them might think she was a cousin. Brendan and Katie's future was clearly drawn. They would marry, have two kids, buy a house in their hometown.

This was what Sam's parents wanted for all their children. Sam was a pleaser, a good girl. She didn't want to upset them. She wished they could understand that her being with Clive was not a form of rebellion. She had simply fallen in love.

On Fridays, Elisabeth saw her shrink at ten and went to Pilates at two-thirty. Sam didn't know what she did in between, but she never came home before four. Other days of the week, Elisabeth might pop in and out, keeping Sam on her toes. If Gil was napping, Sam would wash all but one dirty dish, which she saved as a prop, to scrub when Elisabeth came through the door, giving the appearance that she was doing something other than sitting on the sofa, reading back issues of *The New Yorker*.

But on Fridays, she was unsupervised. On Fridays, Sam and Gil had their own routine. She hadn't mentioned it to Elisabeth.

The second Friday in October, as usual, Sam filled two bottles with formula. She dressed the baby in his puffy red coat and soft fleece shoes, and strapped him into the stroller.

She left a note, in case: *Gone for a walk!*

Then she locked the door with the spare key Elisabeth had given her, and they were off.

Laurel Street was a pretty, tree-lined block. Black SUVs sat in most of the driveways, imposing as sentinels, guarding big houses in shades of white and gray. The modern mother would not be caught dead in a minivan. Though when you thought about it, an SUV was just a boxy version of the same. Sam once said as much to Elisabeth, who said, "Exactly. Andrew tried to talk me into getting one. But there is no way."

Through the slats of backyard fences, Sam could make out signs of life. A fat Labrador lay on its side in the sun. A grandmother pushed a toddler on a swing. On front lawns, bicycles were tossed down and strollers left abandoned, for naptime or to catch a ringing telephone. The kind of people who lived here had no fear that when they came out again, these objects would be gone.

Foss-Lanford Hall stood at the farthest edge of campus, a five-minute walk from Elisabeth's house. All Sam had to do was go to the end of Laurel, turn right on Main, then travel onward for two blocks until she reached the tall hedge that separated the college from the world. On one side was a yellow Victorian with a swing on the front porch; on the other, the plain brick building that housed Sam and a hundred of her peers.

No visitor to Foss-Lanford was ever so adored as Gil. In a matter of weeks, he had become the communal baby, a mascot of sorts. Sometimes Sam left him with someone while she ran to write a note on a friend's whiteboard or grab coffee downstairs. Occasionally, when she returned, her room was empty. But she never worried. She knew Gil was safe in the arms of some besotted young woman.

Isabella burst into tears when she held him. Shannon would say, "I'm sorry, young man, but I am not a baby person," before picking Gil up, and refusing to give him back.

Now, like most Fridays, Sam pushed the stroller down the long corridor that led to the dining hall. The women who worked there, all of them mothers, loved Gil most and knew best what to do with him.

Sam passed through the empty dining room, footsteps echoing on the linoleum. The floors had been swept clean. The wooden tables gleamed.

She could hear Maria laughing.

Sam pushed Gil's stroller toward the sound, and through the swinging doors that led to the kitchen.

It was at least ten degrees warmer on the other side. The windows were covered in steam. Delmi kept plants on the high windowsills—a cascading jade; an array of succulents; aloe that resembled long fingers, which the women cracked open when their hands bled from washing dishes in winter. At the center of all that green, a painted statue of the Virgin Mary peeked out from behind the leaves.

Sam saw them before they saw her. Delmi was at the counter, chopping heaps of peppers and onions. Maria and Gaby stood side by side at the island in the center of the room, breading chicken breasts. Maria dunked each one into a huge silver bowl of raw eggs, then handed it to Gaby, who rolled it in a mountain of breadcrumbs and laid it flat on a cookie sheet.

They talked, as they did all day, every day, rapid-fire and without looking up at one another.

"He should have been fired by now," Delmi said.

"He's doing just what they want him to," said Maria. "He's playing the role of the bad guy. He'll probably get promoted."

"That asshole should try living off twelve bucks an hour," Gaby said. "See how he likes it."

"Gabriela!" Maria said. "Watch your mouth!"

Still, Maria laughed. She had tears in her eyes from laughing.

"What asshole?" Sam said.

They all looked up.

The room fell silent.

She felt for the first time like she had barged in on them.

Then they adjusted, relaxed.

Delmi unstrapped Gil from the stroller and took him in her arms. She was his favorite. She made a funny face he loved, filling her cheeks with air, then pretending to pop them. Gil laughed every time she did it, and Delmi was happy to do it again and again.

"I have treats for you," she said in a singsong voice, carrying him into the pantry.

She returned a moment later, placed the corner of a saltine on his tongue, and let it dissolve there like a communion wafer.

"Who were you talking about? Who's the asshole?" Sam said, her nosiness getting the better of her.

She had never heard either of the older women swear. Doing so in front of them felt illicit, even if she was just repeating Gaby.

"The head of RADS," Gaby said. "You know. Barney."

RADS stood for Residence and Dining Services. Though Sam had technically worked in the department her first three years of school, she couldn't have named the person in charge until last year, when Barney Reardon took the job.

Gaby had told Sam everything. How Barney was hired to cut the budget and did so by cutting their pay, when the kitchen staff hadn't gotten a raise in eight years as it was. How the new health insurance plan was useless.

Ironically, Gaby said, she had only left her better-paying restaurant job because she had no benefits and Maria had convinced her that, with the baby, she needed decent insurance. She'd had some complications after Josie was born. Super high blood pressure that landed her back in the hospital twice. She was supposed to follow up with a specialist, but she still hadn't.

"What would be the point of even knowing if I need surgery or whatever," Gaby had said at the time. "A five-thousand-dollar deductible. Who has five thousand dollars to pay a doctor before getting any coverage?"

Sam shook her head, though she had only a vague idea of what the word *deductible* meant. She was still on her parents' insurance and had never had to deal with the specifics.

Maria and Delmi had never once complained to Sam about anything. When Gaby came along, it was a revelation.

Now, when Gaby said Barney Reardon's name, Maria clucked her tongue, bringing the conversation to an end.

Delmi plopped Gil in the stroller with a new cracker.

"Okay, *chiquito*. That's a good boy."

Maria said, "Sam. Get the cookie dough out of the fridge and scoop it onto some parchment, will you? We're behind."

It was kind of ridiculous, how much it meant to her to be asked. To feel like she still belonged among them.

That afternoon, Isabella and Sam laid Gil down on Isabella's bed with a couple of toys and played with him while they watched TV. Ramona, Shannon, and Lexi all came by to see him. Gil beamed at each visitor, as if he'd been expecting them.

As Sam was leaving the dorm a few hours later, she saw Gaby coming out of the ladies' room by the front door. She was dressed to go home, in jeans and high-heeled boots. Her long hair hung at her shoulders.

"Hi, Gil!" Gaby called. She moaned. "Seeing him makes me miss Josie so much. By the way. Her birthday party is gonna be the second Saturday in November, at my house. Can you come?"

"Of course!" Sam said. She made a mental note to write this down.

"Great, I'll text you the address."

"I miss our Friday paycheck walks," Sam said. "I feel like I don't even know what's going on with you."

"I know. You've been busy," Gaby said.

It was true, but it felt like an accusation.

"Sorry," Sam said. "This nannying job has made my weeks so full."

"And the boyfriend," Gaby teased.

"Yeah. That too."

"I miss having you in the kitchen. The other student workers don't even look at me. I'm not sure they know I speak English," Gaby said. "Or maybe they're just scared of me."

"That sounds more likely," Sam said.

They laughed.

"What was going on earlier, in the kitchen?" Sam said. "That whole thing about Barney Reardon."

"My aunt was pissed at me for telling you who we were talking about," Gaby said.

"Why?"

"She doesn't think it's right to discuss our issues with the college in front of a student."

"It's not just some student," Sam said. "It's me."

"I know, but Maria has her opinions on how things should be done." Gaby paused, like she was considering whether or not to obey her aunt's wishes. Then she said, "You know how only three dining halls on campus stay open June through August?"

"No," Sam said.

During the school year, the college prided itself on offering dining in almost every dorm, so that students could eat where they lived, an approximation of home. Sam had never considered what happened in the summer.

"Well, they do," Gaby went on. "Three dining halls, down from fifteen. Everyone scrambles to get a job in one of them. If you don't, this cheap-ass place lays you off for the summer and rehires you at the start of the school year. Three months without pay or benefits."

"Professors get paid for the summer months, don't they?" Sam said.

"I mean, I think so," Gaby said. "They must. Anyway. This morning Barney announced that, next summer, only one dining hall is gonna stay open. So, even fewer jobs. My aunt is freaking out. She's too nice. She and my mom. They want to help everyone. They send money home to so many relatives, money they don't even have."

On one of their Friday walks last year, Gaby had filled in the gaps in what Sam knew of Maria's story.

Along with her sister, Gaby's mother, Maria came to America from El Salvador as a teenager, after her brother and father were murdered. She married an American, a guy in the military, whom Gaby described as a total scumbag.

Soon after they divorced, left alone with two young children, Maria fell in love with someone else. Like her, he was from El Salvador. They married. Through Maria, he got his citizenship. Then one day he told her he had never loved her. He had a family in Texas. A wife and kids. He only wanted his papers. He left, and Maria never heard from him again. Technically, they were still married. She saw no need to divorce because, from then on, she considered herself done with men.

It was hard for Sam to imagine Maria this way, as assertive and happy as she now seemed. She wondered where all those dark memories were stored. It was a bit like hearing stories of her grandfather going to war. Sam couldn't imagine the old man in the armchair dodging bullets, even as she knew that he had.

Sam had once cried in Maria's arms because her sisters had the flu and couldn't come for Family Weekend. Maria had allowed this, had comforted her as if it was a problem worth mentioning.

Gaby told Sam that her mother and Maria were considered the lucky ones in their family. Their undocumented cousins, newer arrivals to this country, boarded vans before dawn each morning and were transported to local farms, where they worked for less than minimum wage, fourteen-hour days, seven days a week, with no overtime pay.

This was why, Gaby said, Maria was careful never to complain.

"At the end of the school year last year, after Barney had cut everyone's pay, Maria was so worried about making ends meet that she went through the trash all over campus, collecting things students left behind," Gaby said now. "Do you know how humiliating that was for her? These girls, the things they throw away—"

"I know," Sam said.

In the final days of her sophomore year, she had acquired a cast-off mini-fridge, a rug, and a pair of lamps that her mother deemed nice enough to put in the family room at home.

"Even in the kitchen, they told us to throw away an almost-new blender, boxes of dishes, a six-hundred-dollar mixer that worked perfectly fine."

Sam nodded. The school periodically replaced such things, long before they needed replacing.

"Maria sold all that crap, to pay some bills," Gaby said. "Not that she got much for it. But still, she felt so bad, so embarrassed. You know she prides herself on being professional. Everything on the up-and-up. I told her that's her right. She has to survive."

"Of course," Sam said.

"It's even worse for poor Delmi. At least Maria's sons, my cousins, they contribute. Delmi's kids are, like, thirtysomething and they all live off her. She can't even make rent at this point."

"What about you?" Sam said. "Are you okay?"

"I'm fine," Gaby said. "This job is just temporary for me. Hopefully soon I'll have enough saved so that me and Josie can move out of my mom's. And then eventually, I'll get around to finishing school."

Gaby's words made Sam feel guilty. She had wondered many times what it must be like for Gaby, having to serve three meals a day to college girls whose lives were so much easier than her own.

Gaby looked past her. She said, "The princess wants you."

Sam turned her head to see Isabella on the stairs.

Isabella paused halfway down.

"You forgot your phone," she said, dangling it over the railing.

"She can't be bothered to do those last few steps," Gaby said softly, as if narrating a nature film. "The princess is tired. Maybe her maid could come and carry her the rest of the way."

Sam didn't think Isabella could hear her. But still.

She looked from one friend to the other. She regretted, now, the things she'd said about Isabella when she was gone. Sam had inadvertently made Gaby despise her, when she had only been trying to say that Isabella was lovable in spite of her entitlement. Hadn't that been her point?

Isabella didn't like Gaby either. She seemed intimidated that Sam should have a friend she didn't know. She watched Gaby's expressions in the dining hall and said, "What flew up her ass?"

Sam was happy not to be working in the kitchen this year. She got to sleep later. Caring for Gil was so much easier than that job had been. But she felt bad eating with her friends as Gaby worked. Especially when Isabella put her feet on the table, or left a pile of crumbs when she was done, further convincing Gaby that every bad thing she believed about her was true.

Sam and Gil walked in the front door at ten to five, later than usual. Elisabeth's car pulled into the driveway soon after.

When she came in, she was on the phone, talking fast. "I feel like I'm closing in on something interesting," Elisabeth said.

She looked at Sam and rolled her eyes.

"Frankly, I need the money," Elisabeth said. "I can't tell you how much I need it. Long story. A bad investment."

Without a word exchanged between them, Elisabeth took Gil

from Sam, placed him in his bouncy seat, reached into her wallet, and pulled out the week's pay in cash.

"Yes, totally," she said into the phone. "I've been thinking the same thing."

Thank you, she mouthed to Sam, giving her the bills.

Sam put on her coat and kissed Gil on the cheek. "Bye-bye," she said, shaking his fat hand.

She waved at Elisabeth, who, in turn, placed her palm over the cell phone's receiver and whispered, "Are you coming for dinner on Sunday?"

"I'd love that," Sam whispered back.

"Great. See you then."

Elisabeth raised her voice and resumed talking enthusiastically to whoever was on the other end of the line.

When Sam was working, she let herself in each morning at Elisabeth's request. But when she joined them for dinner, she rang the bell.

That Sunday, Elisabeth answered the door with Gil in her arms.

"He refuses to go down," she said. "I hope he's not getting sick."

"Poor peanut," Sam said.

"Guess who had his first solid food today?" Elisabeth said. "The pediatrician said to wait until he's six months and, even then, just purees to start. But Andrew was eating a cracker, and Gil plucked it out of his hand and ate it, like he'd done it a million times. Can you believe that?"

Sam thought of all the saltines she had seen him eat. Delmi was a mother of five, so sure of herself, that it had never occurred to Sam that Gil was too young.

She had watched a child take his first steps while babysitting on a Friday night in high school, and never mentioned it to the parents.

In London, she sometimes took the twins to the park and let them dig in the dark earth, against their mother's wishes. They had no shovels to dig with, so she let them use silver soup spoons. At first, they freaked out when their hands got dirty, holding their palms up in alarm. Her last week before leaving, Tom found a slug in the dirt and dropped it into his mouth. Sam felt almost proud. She felt like Mary Poppins at the end of the movie. Her work here was done; she could float away.

"A cracker!" was all she said now. "Aren't you a big boy?"

Elisabeth kissed Gil.

"This one is an old soul, Sam. He knows things. I swear."

9

Elisabeth

HALLOWEEN FELL ON A FRIDAY.

Elisabeth had never had trick-or-treaters before. It was the sort of thing she daydreamed about when she imagined owning a house. In a fit of excitement, she bought a dozen bags of candy two weeks in advance. She and Andrew had since devoured the contents of three of them.

Now she stood, shaking what remained into two wooden salad bowls. She tossed the candy with her hands as Sam looked on from her seat at the kitchen island. Gil was in Sam's lap, dressed as a mouse. Their neighbor Pam had offered Elisabeth the costume, a hand-me-down worn by her two kids. It was a one-piece gray fleece suit, with a tail and a hood that had oversize floppy pink ears sewn on. Elisabeth and Sam could not resist putting Gil in it first thing that morning, and adding black eyeliner whiskers to his cheeks.

"We don't want all the good candy on top, and the boring stuff at the bottom," Elisabeth said now. "I've got to mix it so the kids see a variety of options."

"You don't have any boring stuff," Sam said. "I always wondered about those people who give out Raisinets. Do they, like, hate children?"

In fifteen minutes, Sam would go home. Weekends now were the opposite of what they used to be—Elisabeth dreaded the days without Sam's company, the long stretches with no childcare. She accomplished nothing on the weekends. The only part she looked forward to were Sunday nights, chatting with Sam on the sofa upstairs. Those were often the only real conversations she had all week. By the time Monday morning arrived, she practically threw Gil into Sam's arms, starving for a bit of freedom.

She told Nomi that this made her feel like a terrible mother.

All mothers hate weekends, Nomi said. *TGIM!*

Elisabeth's phone buzzed on the counter. A text from Faye: *Pic of G in his costume, please! Bad day over here—another letter from the bank about the house . . . Nana needs a pick-me-up.*

Elisabeth sent Faye a few of the roughly one hundred photos she'd taken earlier, pushing down the feeling that she was responsible for her mother-in-law's predicament. She imagined Faye sending a message like that and wondering why Elisabeth didn't just say, *Let us help you.*

She flipped the phone over so she couldn't see the screen.

"What are you up to tonight?" she asked Sam.

"Costume party at State. Isabella and I are going as those creepy twins from *The Shining*. But, like, a sexy version. Her idea."

"That sounds fun."

"Ehh, it'll be like every other party, but with less clothing. I kind of hate Halloween. It's such a sexist holiday."

"Hmm," Elisabeth said. This had never occurred to her.

Years ago, Andrew invited her to a Halloween party, their fourth or fifth date. They ended up sneaking off to the roof with a bottle of wine and talking. They lost track of time. When they finally came back downstairs, the party was over. The hosts had gone to bed.

Tonight, he would probably insist on working once he got home. He was putting together an application for a conference in

Denver, where, if chosen, he would get to present his invention to potential investors.

Elisabeth would be alone with the baby, answering the door, smiling at all the witches and goblins and ghosts. She had been looking forward to it, but now it seemed depressing. Back in Brooklyn, Nomi was taking her kids to the Park Slope parade with friends, and then to a big group dinner at a new restaurant on Fourth Avenue.

"Isabella is picking me up here at five," Sam said. "We're going to get our nails done. Or, I should say, she is. I'm tagging along because the place has free kombucha."

For an instant, Elisabeth felt hurt that they hadn't invited her.

She told herself to get a grip. She hadn't slept more than two or three hours at a stretch for the last week. It made her thinking cloudy, her instincts strange.

Just before five, the doorbell rang.

Elisabeth felt a ridiculous surge of delight.

"First customers," she said.

She went to the door with the candy. Sam followed, holding Gilbert.

Sam's roommate stood on the other side of the door, wearing flip-flops and jeans and a black peacoat.

"Trick or treat," she said. She reached into the bowl and pulled out a mini Snickers.

"Isabella," Sam said. "I told you to wait outside."

"I know, but I have to pee."

"Elisabeth, you remember Isabella," Sam said.

"Hi!" Isabella said. "Hey, do you mind if I use your bathroom real quick?"

She seemed so comfortable in her skin. Elisabeth couldn't remember ever feeling that way, certainly not at that age.

"So?" Isabella said. "The bathroom?"

Elisabeth hadn't invited her in.

"Oh!" she said. "Right. It's down the hall there."

Isabella went in and closed the door, and Sam whispered, "I'm sorry. She's just like that. I can't control her."

"Why are you sorry?" Elisabeth said. "It's fine."

They returned to their spots in the kitchen. Elisabeth pulled her wallet from her purse and handed Sam her week's pay. Doing so always made her think of how little she'd accomplished, how she didn't have much to show for those hours of childcare.

They both acted sheepish during the exchange, every time. Sam didn't feel like an employee. Giving her that thin stack of bills each Friday was the only reminder that she was.

Nomi had asked over text if Sam did Gil's laundry or made baby food.

It's part of a nanny's job, she wrote.

Elisabeth replied, *I could never ask Sam to do that kind of stuff.*

To which Nomi responded with the eye-roll emoji.

Nomi had a team of people under her at work. She knew how to be the boss. Elisabeth had never had so much as an assistant. She didn't even like to be home when the cleaning lady came every other Saturday morning. It felt wrong, drinking coffee in her bathrobe while some woman whose last name she didn't know scrubbed her toilet. She had hated the way her own mother talked to housekeepers and gardeners and nannies, with that air of superiority.

In Brooklyn, for years, Elisabeth watched black nannies care for white children and thought there was something problematic about the whole arrangement. She swore she would never take part in it. Much of parenthood was doing, saying, and being things you once swore you'd never do, say, or be. But what Elisabeth had with Sam made her feel above all that.

Isabella found them in the kitchen. "This neighborhood is adorable," she said.

"I know, right?" Sam said. "While we spend our night trying not to get roofied by frat boys dressed as pirates, you'll be here enjoying all the cute trick-or-treaters."

"You make the party sound like so much fun," Elisabeth said.

"These things bore me," Sam said. "And they're disgusting when you think of it."

"Please note: they didn't bore her when she was unattached and allowed to make out at parties," Isabella said.

"What do you mean they're disgusting?" Elisabeth said.

Sam sighed. "We follow certain rules—never go to the bathroom without a friend, don't let your girlfriends leave with anyone if they seem too drunk. Don't accept a drink that you didn't see poured."

"That seems sensible," Elisabeth said.

"I wish instead of all that we refused to go to parties where it's pretty likely somewhere in the building a girl with an inferior protection plan is getting raped."

"Way to suck the fun out of it," Isabella said.

"So why do you go?" Elisabeth said.

"Because if I don't, this one will give me hell."

"She spends most of her free time talking to a boyfriend in a different time zone," Isabella said. "It's tragic. This is our senior year."

"See what I mean?" Sam said. "Okay, let's go start the fun."

"Stay awhile if you want," Elisabeth said. "Or do you have an appointment for the nails?"

"It's a walk-in place," Isabella said.

"How about a glass of wine then?"

"Sure!" Isabella answered before Sam could say anything.

Elisabeth tried to read Sam's expression.

"Only if you want to," she said. "Don't let me keep you."

Sam smiled. "A glass of wine sounds great."

Elisabeth opened a good bottle of Cabernet that a former coworker of Andrew's had given him as a farewell gift. She poured three glasses, filling them almost to the top.

"Cheers," they said, clinking the glasses together. "Happy Halloween!"

Isabella took a gulp of wine, then unbuttoned her coat. She was rail thin, but she had a paunch. She looked four or five months pregnant. A beer belly? Elisabeth wondered. She had met Isabella at that bar, briefly, but hadn't noticed it. She had been sitting down then, though.

A hard knock at the front door ushered in forty minutes of trick-or-treaters, a blur of kids in costume, trailed by parents, many of them in costume too. After the fifth family in a row dressed in a *Star Wars* motif, Isabella said what Elisabeth was thinking: "These moms want to show that they've still got it, so they go as Princess Leia and make the kids be stormtroopers. Do those kids even know what stormtroopers are?"

Elisabeth poured more wine and put out a plate of cheese and crackers to counterbalance the candy they'd eaten. Her face seemed to vibrate from the sugar.

"When I first lived in the city," she said, "I worked at a women's magazine. I lived in a fifth-floor walk-up with four roommates and spent my days doing expense reports, but I got to go to Heidi Klum's Halloween party. My boss was sick, so she gave me her invitation."

"Tell me everything," Isabella said.

"Heidi was dressed as Lady Godiva. She rode in on a horse."

"I hope I have a story as good as that one next Halloween," Isabella said. "When I'm no longer living here in Boringsville. Or hauling around this gut." She put both hands on her stomach.

Elisabeth wasn't sure what to say.

"I don't usually look like this," Isabella said. "I'm donating my eggs and I'm on all these drugs to make them huge. When I walk, I can feel them swishing around in there. It's disgusting."

Before Elisabeth could formulate a question, Isabella said, "Gotta pee again. BRB," and was gone.

Elisabeth looked at Sam. "She's—"

"I know," Sam said. "It's crazy."

"Is she desperate for the cash?"

"No. She says she's worried about money, but I have no idea why."

"No one ever thinks they have enough money," Elisabeth said.

"She has enough. Believe me. Her dad's the president of a bank or something."

"Has anybody tried to talk her out of it?"

"Once Isabella makes up her mind, you kind of have to let her go and hope she figures it out on her own," Sam said.

"She's giving herself shots every day?"

"No. I do them."

Elisabeth felt herself flash from friend to angry mother. Who would ask a girl this age to sell her eggs? Why had Sam gone along, and never even mentioned it to her?

When Isabella came back, asking whether they thought Heidi Klum had had work done, Elisabeth said, "Don't do it."

Isabella blinked. "Do what?"

"Don't sell your eggs."

"I have to. I signed a contract."

"That doesn't matter."

"It doesn't?"

"No."

Whoever had the eggs had the rights. Elisabeth remembered

that much from her research. You couldn't force someone to give you a part of her own body, no matter what she had promised.

"Last month, I was taking progesterone, estrogen, Gonal-F, Menopur," Isabella said. "Those are the names of the drugs."

"I know," Elisabeth said. "I did IVF to have Gil."

"You did?" Sam said.

"So you know," Isabella said. "It was only supposed to take a month. I started in September, but I guess the doctor got the drug combination wrong because there weren't as many follicles as they were hoping. So this month, they increased the dosages, and boom—I'm huge."

"Hyperstimulation," Elisabeth said. "They gave you too much medication this time."

"But everything is looking good," Isabella said. "I'll get paid twice what we originally agreed to, since it's gone on so long. It's almost over. I'll do the egg retrieval on Tuesday."

"They put you under for that," Elisabeth said.

"I know. Thank God."

So blasé. Elisabeth wanted to shake her.

"Have you told your parents?"

"Of course not."

"This is a huge deal," she said. "You will have a child out there somewhere."

"It's not my child, it's my egg," Isabella said, as if Elisabeth had missed something. "And this couple seems adorable. Kim and Tim. Their names rhyme. How cute is that? I want to help them. They deserve it."

Elisabeth looked to Sam, but Sam only shrugged.

"Please think about it," she said. "You're going to regret this one day. It's not worth the money, I'm telling you."

Isabella seemed like the type who could laugh anything off. But just for a moment, Elisabeth thought she saw something cross the girl's face. An understanding of what she'd said. She hoped she had gotten through.

"How long did you have to do IVF for?" Sam asked quietly.

"A year."

"Was it awful?"

"It was both really bad and not that bad," Elisabeth said. "Those months when it didn't work after I basically made it my full-time job were awful. I did so many ridiculous things to make it happen."

"Like what?" Sam asked.

On top of all the shots, she had a daily regimen, culled from the advice of doctors, friends, and random women in online forums, of meditation, baby aspirin, iron supplements, bone broth, pomegranate juice, six cups of red raspberry leaf tea, followed by six cups of nettle tea. There was the acupuncturist who took a gentle, spa-like approach to enhancing her fertility. And the one who said the more pain the better, shooting electrical currents into her abdomen through thick needles. At Faye's urging, on a work trip to Montreal, Elisabeth hiked to the top of Mount Royal to procure oil from Saint Joseph's Oratory, which she rubbed onto her belly each night, even though she was an atheist.

She looked at Sam and Isabella, unaware of the desperation that could take hold if you waited too long. How did you tell girls like this that there was something called a vaginal steam and it cost three hundred dollars, which you were beyond willing to pay, in the hopes that it might be the magic bullet? The answer was you didn't tell them. They weren't ready for that kind of information.

Elisabeth had once gone for a Mayan abdominal massage. She was embarrassed by her disappointment upon learning on arrival that the masseuse's name was Rochelle Moskowitz. For the price, she'd been hoping for an actual Mayan. The massage itself was not at all relaxing. Rochelle was running behind that day, so they started fifteen minutes late. Rochelle instructed Elisabeth to envision a nest of feathers and rocks. But all she could think about was that she was going to be late for dinner with her coworker Pearl.

When Rochelle Moskowitz said, "Do you want to meet your girlfriend now?" Elisabeth replied, "Yes." Amazed that this woman had somehow read her mind.

Rochelle took Elisabeth's hand and rubbed it along her pubic bone. Apparently by *your girlfriend*, she had meant *your uterus*.

"You guys are at the age where a woman's body is supposed to make babies," she told Isabella and Sam. "I'm at the age where a lot of women actually do it. But that doesn't mean you should sell your eggs. This stuff is so emotionally and morally fraught, even when it's your own children you're carrying."

"How so?" Isabella said.

"Like in my case, I have two extra embryos. I don't want any more kids. But I wanted one child so badly that I promised Andrew if we did IVF, I wouldn't leave any embryos behind. He was raised Catholic; I don't know if that's why he's so determined. He says it's because he's an only child. He knows what that feels like. He wants Gil to have a sibling."

What was she doing? She shouldn't have shared that. Andrew would be mortified if he knew.

"What else do you two have on tap for the weekend?" she said, trying to steer the conversation back to a neutral place.

"A friend's birthday tomorrow night," Isabella said. "And a party in our dorm on Sunday because there's no class on Monday. It's Lucretia Chesnutt Day."

"What's that?"

"Lucretia Chesnutt was the first African American woman to

graduate from the college," Sam said. "The school honors her on her birthday every year. There are panels and lectures and guest speakers, all on the topic of diversity."

She sounded proud.

"Do you want the day off from here, so you can go?" Elisabeth said, silently praying the answer would be no.

"Nah," Sam said. "It's okay. Thanks, though."

"Are you sure?"

"No one goes to the panels," Isabella said. "We usually go to the mall."

"I've gone to the panels," Sam said.

"I'm not into it," Isabella said. "Like, look at us. We are all about inclusion! One day a year."

"It's not just one day," Sam said. "What about the fellows?"

"Right," Isabella said. "The college has this program for black first-generation college students who got amazing grades in high school. The Lucretia Chesnutt fellows. They're all totally brilliant. They get a free ride. But the way the school trots them out on special occasions—it's weird."

"I think it's inspiring," Sam said.

Isabella rolled her eyes, and Elisabeth understood that she was not as earnest, as pure, as Sam was.

"A fellowship for geniuses doesn't address actual, structural problems," Isabella said. "School inequality, access to test prep. Only the most elite kids get singled out. What about everyone else at a bad high school? Don't they deserve a shot?"

"I feel like you stole that opinion from Shannon," Sam said. Then, to Elisabeth, "Our friend Shannon is one of the fellows."

Elisabeth nodded. "Ahh."

"You can't steal an opinion," Isabella said. "I agree with Shannon is more like it."

"Why shouldn't someone who excels academically be rewarded for it?" Sam said. "I didn't grow up around the kind of people who went to schools like this one. I didn't have an SAT tutor like you and Lexi. If I hadn't seen President Washington's speech online, I would never have applied."

Sam looked at Elisabeth. "President Washington gives this incredible lecture called 'If Women Ran the World.' It's on YouTube. I've watched it like a hundred times."

"Sam has a major crush on President Washington if you couldn't tell," Isabella said.

It was both touching and absurd, how they referred to her that way, as if she were the actual president.

"And what does she suggest would happen if women ran the world?" Elisabeth said.

"That it would be better in every way," Sam said.

Elisabeth snorted.

"You don't think so?"

"I think it all comes down to power. And the individual. Women are every bit as capable of being evil and corrupt as men are. They just haven't had as much opportunity to show it, historically speaking."

"But you're a feminist, right?" Sam said.

"I don't even know what that word means anymore. They use it to sell soap now."

Both girls stared at her. Elisabeth felt like the biggest cynic who had ever lived.

"Yes, though. I'm a feminist. Of course," she said. "I should stop talking. Sleep deprivation has left me with no filter."

She turned to Isabella. "Gil's going through a bad patch. They call them Wonder Weeks. The baby is up all night and a total disaster, but allegedly by the end of it, he's mastered new skills. Though I think that might just be something they tell mothers so we don't go insane."

"Doesn't your husband ever get up with him?" Isabella said.

"Iz," Sam said.

"We switch off at bedtime and in the morning, but in the middle of the night, Andrew doesn't wake up. He doesn't hear the baby crying. I have no idea how that's possible, but that's what he says."

"What if you didn't hear him crying either?" Isabella said.

"But I do. I even wake up somehow knowing he's *about* to cry."

"But what if you gave it a minute? Didn't jump up. What would happen?"

Elisabeth didn't think she could lie there and listen to Gil cry until the sound grew loud enough to rouse her husband, but she smiled at the suggestion.

The back door opened then. Andrew stepped into the kitchen.

They started giggling like ten-year-old girls at a slumber party.

"What?" he said. "Aww, look at the mouse."

Andrew lifted Gil from his bouncy seat atop the counter.

"Is it safe to have this here?" he said.

Few things annoyed her more than when he walked in and immediately critiqued some baby-related decision she had made in his absence.

A response came quickly to mind, but Elisabeth chose not to say it out loud.

Andrew looked into the bowls of candy. Only a handful of Tootsie Rolls and Milk Duds remained. She should have thought to save him some.

"The trick-or-treaters cleaned us out," she said.

Elisabeth saw him eye the mountain of silvery wrappers on the counter, next to the empty wine bottle.

"Huh," he said.

"Oh wow. It's six-fifteen," Sam said. "We better get going before the nail place closes."

Elisabeth went with them to the front door.

"Thanks for keeping me company," she said. "Have fun tonight."

Isabella hugged her goodbye, a move that surprised her.

"Think about my advice, please," Elisabeth said.

"Okay," Isabella said. "And you think about mine." She cast a glance in the general direction of Andrew.

Elisabeth watched them cross the lawn to Isabella's car, a blue Audi.

Across the street, Debbie had installed an inflatable black cat in front of her house. It was maybe ten feet long and taller than the tops of her first-floor windows. There were fake cobwebs on the bushes, and orange flashing lights wrapped around the columns on her porch. Tonight, she had added eight jack-o'-lanterns, two on each step, and a sound machine that let out a terrifying laugh every time someone passed by. Elisabeth had never seen anyone go so all out for Halloween. God help them at Christmas.

She had gone inside Debbie's house last week, for book club. They were discussing *Breakfast at Tiffany's*, which they had selected because it was shorter than *The Secret History*, and there was a movie version they could watch if, as Karen put it, they needed a break from reading.

It was a tamer affair than the first meeting Elisabeth attended, since nobody's husband was away. They sat around Debbie's dining room table eating crudités and baba ghanoush and drinking bad wine. Every so often, one of Debbie's children wandered in and shook the television remote in her direction, which meant they wanted her to come change the channel.

At some point, Elisabeth asked, "Have any of you heard from Gwen?"

They shook their heads.

"That reminds me," Karen said. "Josh says she forced Christopher to go along with her to Hong Kong because he got into some hot water with a student of his."

"He's such a creep," Stephanie said.

"Tell us more," Debbie said. "Details!"

"Yes!" the rest of them shouted.

They were reveling in it.

Elisabeth wished she hadn't raised the subject. She wondered if what the Laurels were saying was true. She couldn't picture Gwen with a guy like that.

"That's all I know," Karen said. "Josh swore me to secrecy, so don't tell anybody."

You just told everyone, Elisabeth thought but did not say.

As she was closing her front door now, she saw a woman her age dressed as Princess Leia—a brown wig, a tight white dress with a slit up to her crotch, tall white leather boots underneath. She was walking a dog in a Yoda costume.

Elisabeth remembered what Isabella had said earlier.

She went back toward the kitchen, smiling, thinking that she ought to tell Andrew.

"Do you still want to make burgers?" she said before she realized he was holding up the empty wine bottle.

"How was this?" he said.

"Fine."

"This is a hundred-dollar Cabernet," he said.

"No. A hundred dollars?"

"Yeah."

She could tell he was annoyed, even as he made it sound like it was just something to say.

"I'm sorry," she said. "Were you saving it for something?"

"No, but—it's one thing when it's just Sam, a glass at dinner, but should you be getting these kids drunk? Are they even twenty-one?"

"Nobody was drunk," she said.

"Really? The way you were all laughing when I came in, it kind of sounded like you were."

"That was the sound of people enjoying themselves, Andrew," she said. "Sorry if it offended you."

She took the baby from him and went upstairs.

The doorbell rang three more times, but neither of them answered.

Elisabeth gave Gil his bath and put him to bed. Then she went into the upstairs den and switched on the TV. She wanted dinner, but she was stubborn. After that exchange, Andrew would need to come to her.

She couldn't stop thinking about Isabella. She had to find a way to talk her out of it. She imagined the woman who was expecting the eggs, who might not get them now because of her. Elisabeth wondered who she was, where she lived, how long she'd been trying.

She herself had spent her late twenties and early thirties debating whether she even wanted children. For years, Elisabeth hoped for a burst of estrogen that would drown out her fears and turn her baby crazy. In the end, she didn't know what the best answer was, but she could do simple math. The thing about choosing not to was that the door closed eventually. The thing about choosing to was that the door would never close.

How many choices had she made in her life to avoid having regrets later on?

The deliberation lasted so long that she somehow convinced herself it would be the hardest part. Everyone around her was pregnant, or had recently been pregnant, or both. Nomi had Alex by then, and was trying for a second.

Elisabeth woke one morning to a photo of three home pregnancy tests on her phone, above the words: *It's faint, but I think I see a double line. Do you??? Or is it a pee line? (The top two tests are mine. I made Brian pee on the bottom one as a control.)*

"Nomi thinks she's pregnant again, but she can't decide if it's a second line or a pee line," Elisabeth said.

She showed Andrew the picture.

"What's a pee line?" he replied.

Elisabeth felt actual excitement upon taking her last birth control pill. An unfamiliar calm settled over her. For the first time, nothing could penetrate. It wasn't just about her anymore. She felt like she was rolled in layers of tissue paper and Bubble Wrap. A precious and fragile object.

Her first miscarriage was upsetting, but she knew lots of people who'd had one. The second made her scared to try again, for fear that another loss might destroy her. After the third, Elisabeth's OB suggested testing, which revealed chromosomal issues. She referred them to an endocrinologist on the Upper East Side.

There was usually a two-month wait to see him, but his secretary said Elisabeth was in luck—she called on a Wednesday, and he'd had a cancellation for that Friday.

"We are so lucky," she kept telling Andrew.

What you consider luck can change fast, she thought.

The doctor said if they did IVF, they could test the embryos, only put in the healthy ones.

"You're thirty-five, not twenty-five," he reminded her three times in ten minutes, as if she might have forgotten.

Even though it was a consultation, Elisabeth was swept into a room for an ultrasound immediately after he finished his sales pitch.

"Are we doing this?" she asked Andrew. "Should I be having an ultrasound?"

A few minutes later, she was having it.

"Your uterine lining is thin," the doctor said, moving the wand around inside her. "Your lining is the Holiday Inn, okay? I am looking for the Four Seasons. Don't worry, we can thicken it."

He started naming things, like items on a grocery list. *Progesterone injections. Viagra suppositories.*

She and Andrew both had blood work, sitting in two cubicles, facing each other. The worst date they'd ever been on. Afterward, they went for beers at an Irish bar across from the hospital. She wondered how many dire conversations had played out between those walls.

She had dinner with Nomi that night, at a Thai place on Smith Street.

Elisabeth had the folder the doctor had given her tucked beneath one arm. She put it on the table between them.

Nomi ordered the drunken noodles with extra tofu. She was eight weeks pregnant, a vegetarian, trying to get as much protein as possible.

When Elisabeth opened the folder, and said she was sorry to burden her with it, Nomi said, "Bad news isn't catching."

Because she was such a good friend, Nomi asked how Elisabeth felt about her being pregnant. Elisabeth told her she never wanted to be that person, jealous of her friends. But she was jealous—of Nomi, of their friend Lauren, who just had her third healthy child by accident and without incident.

At home, she went deep with the online searches to find out what IVF would entail. The doctor had told them already, but Elisabeth wanted to see it written out, all in one place. *You will be injected with four different kinds of hormones a day, you will have blood work and a transvaginal ultrasound every day or two, and after two weeks of this, you will be sedated and have surgery to extract your overgrown eggs. Meanwhile, in another room, your husband will ejaculate into a cup.*

This seemed to sum up everything there was to the problem of woman versus man.

In the middle of the night, she googled.

Does IVF cause cancer? Possibly. Maybe. What doesn't?

She grew obsessed with the idea that children born through IVF looked abnormal. She emailed herself images of babies, success stories from various fertility sites. In the morning, she showed them to Andrew and asked, "Do these look like real kids to you?"

Once, she googled *Do IVF babies*— and the search results autofilled the rest with *have a soul?*, which sent her down a Catholic fertility message board rabbit hole.

A woman on another board said if you tried IVF six times, statistically speaking, you would most likely succeed. Elisabeth thought if she had to try six times, she would run away. She'd go off the grid, become a hermit.

But then, you never knew. Before all this, she hadn't understood IVF, period, those people so hungry to make a child in their own image. *Why wouldn't they adopt?* she had said. *We would adopt if it ever came to that.*

She confessed her message board addiction to friends over drinks. It turned out they were all on the boards for something. The shared interest could be anything—everyone in the group enjoyed cooking, or they were all lawyers, or they had attended the same private girls' school thirty years ago. This was where women met now. Where they told one another their secrets.

Elisabeth's friend Amy was on the message boards because she hated her stepkids. She wasn't expecting to feel that way. Her coworker Maisy was on a board for married women pondering lesbian affairs. They would never post. But they lurked and lurked. None of them read books anymore.

When Nomi went in for an ultrasound at nine weeks, there was no heartbeat. She had to take a drug to force herself to miscarry what was left inside her. She was nervous, as the women online reported a great deal of pain and bloodshed. One woman said she wanted to warn others: *You might see the baby's eyes.*

Elisabeth went to Nomi's apartment and played race cars with Alex, her three-year-old. Nomi felt crampy. The drug could take four days to work fully. The doctor gave her twenty pills and said he hoped she wouldn't need them all.

Elisabeth made them lunch, then put Nomi and Alex down for a nap.

Back at home, she tried to write. But she was distracted. In the next two days, she would visit Nomi twice more as this baby, or this idea of a baby, left her body. She would go to the organic children's store on Court Street and buy three precious outfits for friends who had just had babies, or were about to. She would order the hormones that, starting next month, Andrew would inject her with nightly, in the hopes of making a baby of their own.

Elisabeth was three weeks into it, bloated and hormonal, at the annual holiday party at her agent's office. She had been feeling Scrooge-like all day, but this event usually cheered her. Afterward, a bunch of them went to a bar. They sat around a table, drinking whiskey. A former *Times* colleague of hers commented that a mystery writer in her fifties had just been chastising a young hipster novelist for riding a bicycle without a helmet, and now the mystery writer was outside smoking.

"We are all allowed one deadly vice," the hipster said.

A while later, an intern from the agency pulled a chair up beside Elisabeth and said she loved her books. In the next breath, the girl was telling her that she rescued French bulldogs, a breed so sickly that they can only mate via artificial insemination.

"If you can't get pregnant on your own, that's the universe telling you you weren't meant to procreate," the girl said. She sipped her beer.

It was so piercing, the feeling.

She wasn't talking about you, Elisabeth told herself. She smiled back.

Her friends had gone off the pill, charted their basal body temperature. They wanted it. But still, a lot of them wept when they got a positive test. They weren't ready. They didn't think it would happen so fast. This was one more thing the whole IVF experience had robbed her of—the right to be ambivalent. Why would you subject yourself to all that if you were not sure? But she wasn't. She wondered how many others in that fluorescent-lit waiting room felt the same way.

Andrew took it in stride, as he did most things. He appeared to, anyway. They laughed through the shots and the sad early mornings waiting for blood draws, even though she had read that couples who went through IVF without success almost always divorced. At first, Elisabeth felt a bit smug about how well they were bearing up. But then came the losses. They didn't seem to hit him like they did her, and it was infuriating. The more they happened, the more hormones they pumped into her, the more she saw how this could pull two people apart.

She almost gave up several times, but doing IVF was like having a gambling addiction. The suspicion that the next time might be *the* time kept her coming back.

It was like gambling in another way too. The money they poured into it was twice what they'd agreed to spend. There was a dollar amount, a line they would not cross, but then they crossed it, and crossed the second line they drew, and the third.

She knew people who had taken out bank loans to pay for IVF. The clinic handed out a pamphlet for an IVF-specific credit card.

After a year, the process felt so separate from parenthood that Elisabeth questioned whether she even wanted a baby, or if she just wanted to win. But then, riding home on a not-very-crowded F train one afternoon, she sat across from an exceptionally cute infant in a bear hat.

"How old?" the man sitting beside the baby asked.

"Six months," the mother said.

They both grinned. Elisabeth did too, as did the woman two seats down, and a young guy looking up from his newspaper. They were all hopelessly in love with the baby. It even made them like one another.

As much as they collectively knew about how hard it is to be human, she thought then that they must also know something deeper about how special it is, how beautiful. Why else would they react with such joy to the existence of one of their own, starting out?

Elisabeth was four months pregnant with Gil before she believed it. She kept saying, *If I'm pregnant*, and Andrew and Nomi would say, *You are*.

Nomi was pregnant again too by then, due any day.

Now Elisabeth could finally be on the good message boards, the ones where stupid women fretted about baby names. They sent lists to one another, perfect strangers, for opinions. She took a screenshot once, and texted it to Andrew. The post said *Help!!! I can't decide. I'm thinking Max or Lucas or Sebastian or Harry or Thor.*

"What are the names of the boys in Alex's class?" she asked Nomi.

Nomi listed them off on her fingers. "Jax. Zev. Kip. Cruz. Dune. Bo. Blue."

Elisabeth frowned. "Those aren't even names, they're just sounds."

When she was eight months along, Nomi added her to the BK Mamas group, a Brooklyn rite of passage. Nomi said it was great for getting cheap secondhand baby gear, much of it barely, if ever, used. But the real appeal was the conversation, the drama, the lunacy.

"What is there to get dramatic about?" Elisabeth asked.

"You'll see," Nomi said.

Gil was born on a perfect day, the sky pure blue.

Elisabeth could usually count on herself to have the wrong reaction to major life events, so she was grateful for the bliss she felt and the knowledge that, for once, she had gotten what she wanted, and it was better than she dreamed.

The love was an astonishment. Every time she looked at him, she felt a shock of wonder at how close she had come to never knowing it.

Andrew knocked on the closed door of the den.

Elisabeth got up from the couch and let him in. He held a plate in each hand. He had made cheeseburgers, with caramelized onions and avocado and sweet potato fries, her favorite.

They sat down.

He put the plates on the table and took hold of the remote.

"That smells amazing," she said.

"I'm sorry," he said. "I had a shitty day at work. I forget sometimes, what it must be like for you, on your own all day."

"It's okay. I'm sorry about the wine."

"What are you watching?"

The show had just switched over from one she liked, about bargain hunting for beach homes, to one she despised so much it made her angry whenever it came on.

Luxury Tiny Houses.

"You can change the channel," she said.

"Why? I know you secretly love this show," he said. "Be proud. Do you."

An off-screen voice said, *This one-hundred-fifty-square-foot jewel outside Indianapolis is a steal at only eighty-five thousand dollars.*

"Can't you get an actual house outside Indianapolis for that amount?" she said.

Bob and Alice bought this antique trunk at an estate sale. It now functions as a stylish litter box for their four cats, and a seating area when guests come over.

"Please," she said. "I'm begging you. Make it stop."

She reached to grab the remote from his hand, and Andrew pulled her in close for a kiss. Elisabeth fell into him.

They lay together as he flipped through the channels.

"I love you a lot, you know," he said.

"I love you too."

At two-forty in the morning, Elisabeth woke up. A moment later, Gil began to wail.

She shot up in bed, but then she slowly lay back down and closed her eyes. She started counting in her head. She got to ninety-eight before Andrew stirred.

She listened to his footsteps as he padded over to the baby.

"What's up, buddy? You need a bottle?" he said.

He wasn't keeping his voice down. She didn't open her eyes. She could feel him standing there, looking at her.

Then she heard the hall light switch on, and the sound of Andrew's whispers as he carried Gil downstairs.

Elisabeth rolled over and sank into the pillows, a smile blooming on her face.

10

Sam

ELISABETH WAS CLEARLY PISSED when Andrew accepted a wedding invitation from a guy at work he barely knew without asking her first.

The groom had met his bride three months ago, on a website called GeekLove.

"It's a potluck," Elisabeth said, revolted. "A potluck wedding."

Sam thought that sounded kind of nice, but she kept the thought to herself.

Even more annoying to Elisabeth was Andrew having asked his parents to babysit.

"Would you do me the biggest favor and watch Gil at their house?" Elisabeth asked. "I don't trust them alone with him. I'll tell them I'd already asked you and you need the money, so I didn't want to cancel on you, but that, really, they're in charge."

"Okay."

"But, Sam," Elisabeth said. "Really, you're in charge."

This was how Sam came to find herself at Andrew's parents' house at one o'clock on a Saturday afternoon.

Andrew and Elisabeth dropped Sam and Gil off on their way to the wedding.

"My mother will want to do everything," Andrew said in the car. "So this should be an easy day for you."

Elisabeth met Sam's eye in the rearview mirror and shook her head.

For an hour after Andrew and Elisabeth left, she sat with the grandparents, watching Gil roll around on a blanket on the living room floor. A large black dog with white patches beneath his eyes kept sniffing the baby and licking his face. When Sam made a noise to indicate that she wasn't sure about this, Andrew's mother, Faye, said, "He's harmless."

Sam knew Elisabeth wouldn't like it, but who was she to argue with the grandmother?

There were Thanksgiving decorations everywhere. Stalks of dried yellow and red corn hung on the front door. On the coffee table, on top of a giant lace doily, a wicker cornucopia spilled forth with Hershey's Kisses. It was the dead opposite of the way Elisabeth decorated. Her house did not change with the seasons. She would never be the sort of woman who wore earrings in the shape of Christmas ornaments, or a sweater with a pumpkin on it.

Faye was that sort of woman. She taught elementary school and seemed to delight in Gil's every gurgle. At first, watching her with him, Sam thought Elisabeth had underestimated Faye. But when it came time for a diaper change and a bottle, Faye said, "I've got a million chores to do, so we'll leave you to it."

They'd set up the Pack 'n Play in the spare bedroom. Sam brought the baby in and closed the door.

She heard Faye complaining about her presence a few minutes later.

"We raised her husband, but she doesn't trust us to watch his son for four hours. Tell me how that makes sense," she hissed.

George, Andrew's dad, shushed her.

Sam wasn't sure what to do. If Faye had made a move to take care of Gil, she wouldn't have stopped her. As it was, Sam changed him, gave him a bottle, sang to him for five minutes, and he was out. Exhausted, she supposed, from the attention and the change of scenery. Sam placed him in the playpen and went to leave the room, but then she thought better of it. What was she going to do out there? She sat on the edge of the bed, a bed that probably never got used. It sagged and squeaked when she put her weight on it.

Sam scrolled through her phone, but that soon became boring. Her father and brother had exchanged fourteen texts about the Patriots. They'd included the whole family, even though no one else replied, or cared about football.

She had the novel Clive had given her in her purse. *Angel.* Clive kept asking if she had started it yet, which she hadn't. Once, Elisabeth spotted the book peeking out of Sam's bag and exclaimed over how much she loved it. Sam heard herself telling a lie, the words stolen from Clive: "Me too. It's one of my favorites. It's so unfair that, because of her name, Elizabeth Taylor never really got the recognition she deserved."

"Totally," Elisabeth said. "I've always thought that!"

Sam had brought along some reading for class, but she had left her book bag out in George and Faye's front hall with her coat. She wasn't in the mood anyway. Two days ago, Shannon had come running into Sam's room to show her the letter she'd received, alerting her that she'd been selected for Phi Beta Kappa. Shannon assumed Sam had gotten one too. Sam tried to hide her disappointment. She went to her adviser's office and asked why she hadn't been picked. Her GPA was as high as Shannon's and she had taken all the classes she thought were needed. He told her it probably had to do with fulfilling more requirements and said he'd look into it.

There was at all times this pressure to be the best, to have everything figured out. Sam admired Elisabeth's laid-back attitude about such things. She aspired to be more like her. Elisabeth spoke of waitressing to support her writing career in the early days and made it sound fun. The things that weighed on Sam—her loans, her job prospects—were all hurdles Elisabeth had cleared, and now she assured Sam that she could do the same.

When the pressure got to be too much, Sam took solace in Clive's plan for the two of them. She pictured the country house he described. She pictured herself baking bread from scratch. She never admitted either of these things to anyone but him.

Sam looked around the room now. A clear plastic dry-cleaning bag full of dark suits hung on the back of the door. The floral wallpaper was peeling in the corners.

One of her professors had said he feared for the future of art because this generation didn't know how to *look*. They didn't take notice of their surroundings—of light, shape, space. Ever since, Sam was determined to prove him wrong.

Today she had been surprised on arrival, pleasantly so, that this was the sort of house Andrew grew up in. Seeing a person's childhood home gave you more insight into him than days of conversation ever could.

Sam was raised in a house like this—perfectly nice, but not fancy or done up. It didn't get great light. The beige carpets were old and stained in places. The furniture didn't match. Faye and George had a leather La-Z-Boy recliner and an overstuffed paisley sofa in the living room, and the biggest TV she had ever seen.

This guest room doubled as an office. A heavy wooden desk too big for the space had been jammed in by the window, with a spare kitchen chair pulled up to it. On top were several dozen overstuffed folders, stacked in haphazard piles. There were Post-it notes all over the wall behind.

Sam got a familiar, tingling feeling in her stomach. The sensation that always preceded snooping. She felt herself pulled toward the desk, listening as she walked, to determine if anyone was outside the door.

She had been trying to cut back, though she still sometimes checked out what Isabella was looking at on her laptop in the minutes after she left the room to shower. Isabella treated Google like a Magic 8 Ball. A couple weeks ago, after her conversation with Elisabeth about it, Sam saw that she had googled *Will I regret selling my eggs?*

Whatever Isabella found must have convinced her that Elisabeth was right, because after she came out of the shower, she asked Sam to go for a walk. Isabella poured them each a mug of tequila, the only booze they had on hand. She gathered up her needles and hormones in a shopping bag and flung the whole thing into the pond when they passed, without so much as slowing down.

(The fertility clinic sent a bill for two thousand dollars, stating that, since Isabella had canceled the deal, she was now responsible for her medical expenses. Isabella called her father. "Daddy, I need two grand. No, you don't want to know what for.")

Babysitting had always presented the best snooping opportunities. People tidied their houses the first few times a new sitter came, but once they were used to her, they'd leave everything out in the open. Pills. Bills. Angry letters. Lingerie.

Sam vowed not to snoop at Elisabeth's house. She had twice walked into the master bedroom, only to turn right back around. But she hadn't been able to stop herself from looking inside the plain brown paper bag she found under the bathroom sink when she opened the cabinet to get more toilet paper. The bag contained ten maxipads, each as thick as her thumb; a can of antiseptic numbing spray; and four pairs of giant disposable underwear, all of which she recognized as the accessories a woman required after giving birth. It seemed impossible that someone as elegant as Elisabeth could be subjected to such degradation. But Sam reasoned that, much like death, bringing a baby into the world was a great equalizer.

She had seen it all in London. Not hidden in a brown paper bag, but spread out on the dining room table. Here, she arrived months after everything was cleaned up and in order. There, she was right in the midst of it as it happened.

The day Allison's baby was born, Sam showed up for work and found the twins, eighteen months old, sitting on the stoop in their pajamas. She led them inside. Allison's husband, Joe, was in the kitchen, looking confused, gazing down at the box of Weetabix in his hands like he half expected it to explode.

The husband was a moron in that case. But even in the best of these situations, she had gleaned, men were useless. As soon as Allison was back from the hospital, the doula and the night nurse rolled in. Sam had never seen her in less than a turtleneck and chinos, but thirty seconds after meeting the doula, Allison was unbuttoning her shirt in the kitchen and placing her nipples into shot glasses of warm salt water, which the woman held in each hand.

Sam nearly said something when she saw the doula follow Allison into the bathroom. She wanted to warn her that Allison was not the type, that if she went in there, she'd be fired on the spot. But it happened too fast. The bathroom door swung open, then shut, giving Sam just long enough to see Allison's bare knees.

She was on the toilet.

Dear God.

Sam pressed her ear to the door.

"This is a frozen maxipad soaked in witch hazel," the doula said. "Stick it in your knickers. It will help with the pain."

"You're a miracle," Allison purred. "I bled a lot just now. Here, have a look. Is this normal? Did I pop a stitch?"

The doula fed her watermelon and parsley to reduce the swelling on her ankles. Allison swallowed each bite like an obedient child.

The doula provided tips for what to do with the baby too, and these Sam tried to memorize. Stick a pinkie finger facing upward in a newborn's mouth, and he'd stop crying. Swaddle him tight and he'd sleep three times as long.

Now, in George and Faye's guest room, Sam lifted the cover of a green file folder. It contained an assortment of news stories— some clipped from actual papers, others printed out from online. She scanned the headlines:

A DRIVER'S SUICIDE REVEALS THE DARK SIDE OF THE GIG ECONOMY.

GNAWING AWAY AT HEALTH CARE.

MIDDLE-CLASS FAMILIES INCREASINGLY LOOK TO COMMUNITY COLLEGE.

THE END OF THE AMERICAN DREAM.

Each article was highlighted and underlined, with handwritten notes in the margins.

The folder beneath that one held only a yellow legal pad, every line filled. At the top of the first page were the words *MY STORY (for Lizzy)*.

Sam started reading:

NOTES ON THE HOLLOW TREE: The idea that while America might seem to be progressing as ever before, in fact, all the support of decades past is gone.

You've heard all this by now in bits and pieces. But I

wanted to get it down on paper, in one place. In case you ever take me up on writing the book . . .

The thing I should say to start with is this—ever since I was a teenager, my favorite thing to do in the world was drive.

Most guys in my position would have given up the actual driving part a long time ago. Not me. When the company was still alive, I ran a staff meeting on Thursdays, stopping on the way to pick up coffee and doughnuts. But outside that one hour a week, I was driving. I ate my meals in the car, logging a good twelve hours a day at least. I loved it.

But let me back up. For a while after high school, I worked in the paper plant like everyone else I knew. When the plant closed, I was twenty-eight, four years married, with a two-year-old kid. After that, I drove a cab, among other jobs—stock boy at Elmer's hardware, seasonal work making Christmas deliveries for the post office, you name it. I was a moving man, a summer janitor at the middle school, and sometimes an electrician. (I had no formal training, but luckily no one ever asked.)

I split the cab with three other guys. It was white and smelled like someone else's cigarettes. One day when I'm thirty-one, I pick up two women at the airport, dressed in black, clearly coming from the city. (No offense.) They were bone thin and they left their sunglasses on when they got in, even though it was raining. One of them barked an address at me, without saying so much as hello, and for the rest of the ride they pretended I wasn't there, like the car was driving itself.

"The cabs here are gross," one of them said. "Have they never heard of a car service? Town Cars. Your name on a sign. A guy to carry your bags. Decent air-conditioning. How hard is that."

They were bad tippers, but I have to credit them with giving me the idea that would keep our family afloat for the next thirty-five years. I saved up, buying one Lincoln, used. I had business cards printed with our home phone number, and asked the nicer hotels and restaurants for fifty miles around if I could leave a stack at the front desk.

I made Faye answer the phone in the kitchen, "Riley's Car Service. We'll get you there." You can imagine how much she loved that.

After a couple years, it started to pay off. I had accounts, entire companies, who worked exclusively with me. I rented that small storefront in town. I bought more cars, and hired help. From then on, I had at least four guys driving for me, a part-time bookkeeper, and a girl who answered the phones.

You know how the story ends. Two and a half years ago, I'm on an airport run. I pull up to the curb outside Terminal B and see Rocky, one of my guys, on his day off. He's wearing jeans, standing by the open trunk of his own car, an old Toyota. I honked the horn and waved, then pulled up alongside him. I made a joke about him taking a busman's holiday.

Then I noticed the couple in the back seat. I watched them climb out. The guy pulled two suitcases from the trunk, and handed Rocky some cash.

I wondered: Were they friends of his? Cousins? If so, why were they giving him cash?

I thought it over and I figured it was probably for gas.

I didn't think about it again until I ran into Rocky at the car wash a few days later.

He said to me, "Listen, boss. I know you know what I'm up to. I hope you know I never used the Lincoln for that."

Never used the Lincoln for what? By then, I'd forgotten all about the airport.

My mind wandered straight to drug deals, bank robberies. I asked what he was talking about. He got this look on his face, and said, "I'm driving for Uber on my days off."

I said, "What the hell is Uber?"

After Rocky filled me in, I told him it was fine. I didn't care if my guys had other jobs on the side. And this Uber, some online thing where a driver could be anyone, no permits, no experience, just a guy in jeans driving his own car? I couldn't see that taking off with the sort of clientele we served.

I told Rocky Uber had nothing to do with me.

He seemed surprised. He thanked me for being cool about it. He said he made good money doing it, too good to pass up.

"How much?" I asked.

It was three dollars more per hour than I paid.

A few months later, by the time I had to fire all my guys and the bookkeeper and the girl who answered the phones, Uber wasn't paying their drivers shit anymore. (Pardon my French.) But passengers had gone nuts for the convenience, and now they refused to do it any other way.

As you know, I kept the company going in name only for a while. Pathetic. I was the only driver, and even so, my days were maybe half booked at best.

That's when Faye suggested I start driving for Uber myself. If you can't beat 'em, join 'em, that kind of thing.

I'll admit to you, I was mad at her for saying it, even though I'd already had the same thought.

More time passed. No money to show for it. So I gave in.

My first day driving for Uber, my very first customer was Victor Winslow, the head of an insurance company based in Albany. Victor lives on the West Coast. He contracted with me fifteen years ago to be the company's official transportation in the area. I gave him a great deal. I made sure to drive him myself when he came to town.

"George," Victor said when he saw me. "This is a treat."

"Isn't it," I said.

I didn't say another word after that.

In the Uber, I do everything as nice as I did when I was driving for myself—the suit, the mints, all of it. Watching in the rearview mirror while Victor chugged two bottles of Poland Spring, I had to hold tight to the steering wheel to keep from punching him.

At the end of every Uber ride, I'm supposed to give the passenger a star rating between one and five and, if I want, a brief explanation of that rating. The passenger does the same for me. If a passenger gets a low rating, it's harder to get picked up.

Here's what I wrote for my pal Victor Winslow. *One Star—AVOID. Passenger was intoxicated and belligerent.*

At this, Sam laughed out loud.

The baby stirred, but a moment later, he was still.

As she turned back to the legal pad, she heard a soft knock at the door.

Sam closed the folder and returned to the bed. She was sitting there, staring at the wall, when George opened the door a crack and whispered, "You want some lunch?"

She looked at him.

"Sure," she said. "I'll set up the baby monitor and be right out."

"Meet me in the kitchen. Turkey and Swiss okay?"

"Sounds great," she said.

Sam found him at the kitchen counter, spreading yellow mustard and mayonnaise onto slices of wheat bread. News radio played in the background.

"Gil sure does love you," he said.

"He's such a good baby," she said.

"He is. But you've got a way with him. I can tell. I'll bet you come from a big family."

"I'm the oldest of four," she said.

"Faye had four in her family too," he said.

"Where is Faye?"

"She's off with the realtor, talking about ways to spruce this place up for cheap. Did Andrew and Elisabeth tell you we're selling?"

"No," she said.

She wondered if it had to do with him losing his job. She remembered now how Elisabeth had said once that George and Faye were penniless. What exactly did that mean?

"Just after Turkey Day, this old place will be on the market," he said. "It hasn't hit me yet, but Faye says it's happening. Nothing's selling around here, though, so we'll have to wait and see."

He brought their sandwiches to the table.

"You want a soda?" he said.

"I'm fine without," Sam said. "Thanks."

George opened a large bag of potato chips and set it down between them. He sat across from her.

He asked where she grew up and what she was studying and what her dad did for a living.

"Samantha O'Connell," he said. "A good Irish Catholic, I'm assuming."

She hadn't been to Mass for three years, other than on Christmas. But Sam said yes.

"We raised Andrew in the Church. He made his communion and confirmation and all that. Are you religious?"

"Not really," she said.

"No, neither is he."

"But my parents are. I have a lot of respect for religion."

There were people, lots of them, most of them maybe, whose personalities were fixed, who seemed as though they'd act the same in front of their own brother or the president. Sam envied them. She had always been a chameleon, programmed to change as needed in order to be liked. Had George presented himself as lapsed, she would have listed all the reasons why she never went to church anymore.

"That's good," George said. Then he shook his head and said, "Sorry for the third degree. I used to run a car service. I talked to my passengers all day long. I asked people everything about themselves. I could tell right away if someone didn't feel like talking, and I respected that. But most wanted to chat, at least. Spill their guts to me sometimes too."

"I'd love that job," she said, before wondering if it sounded silly or condescending.

"I still drive people around, but not as much as I used to."

She nodded. She thought he sounded wistful, but it was possible she was making it up.

"What's it like, going to an all girls' school?" he said. "How do you meet a decent guy when you go to a school like that? I can just feel Faye telling me to mind my business."

Isabella would have corrected him: *It's not a girls' school, it's a women's college*.

Sam said, "I have a boyfriend, but he lives in London."

"London, England?"

"Yup."

"How do you make that work?"

He really seemed to want to know. Something about this endeared him to her.

"It's hard," she said. "I miss him a lot. But we talk on the phone. We write letters."

"Letters!" George said. "That's refreshing."

"He's better about it than I am. We talk over Skype and Snapchat, mostly. And we see each other in person more than you'd think. His sister-in-law works for an airline, so she gets us good deals. He visited me here in early October. He'll be back again for Valentine's Day. In between, I'll see him in London, during winter break."

It made her feel kind of fancy, saying it. In years past, her friends went somewhere exotic over school vacations. Sam never went anywhere but home. Her first year here, when everyone returned from winter break with a tan, Sam wondered how it was possible that so many of her fellow students were from Florida.

Isabella sometimes met up with her friends from boarding school for a long weekend away. She had admitted more than once to Sam that she didn't actually like them much. They could be mean and shallow. They had never been there for her in a crisis. "You're probably the first real friend I ever had," Isabella said.

Still, her boarding school classmates had travel budgets similar to hers, and so they continued to meet up, at hotels Sam's parents could never afford, let alone Sam herself.

"The cab ride from the airport to campus isn't cheap," George said now. "You have a car?"

"No. I used to. Bessie. She was a seventeen-year-old Cutlass Supreme, previously owned by my great-aunt Dot."

"A Cutlass Supreme, that's no joke," George said.

"My mom always said it was like driving a Sherman tank. You should have seen me parallel park that thing. I got so good at it. But Bessie died officially last summer on my brother's watch."

"Oh no."

"I cried," Sam said. "Anyway. When Clive visited last time, I borrowed a friend's van to pick him up."

"I'll tell you what. Whenever he comes back, I'll pick him up and drop him off in the Town Car, free of charge."

"No," she said.

"For my grandson's best friend? Of course I will."

Sam grinned. "Thank you. That's so nice."

A voice on the radio was talking about the nation's crippling levels of student loan debt. She introduced Randy, a man in his thirties who still lived with his parents because of it.

"Hope you're not caught up in that mess," George said.

"The crippling-debt part, yes," Sam said. "The living-with-my-parents part, no. They've got a strict policy that once we move out, no one's allowed to move back in."

"Smart parents," George said.

He shook his head. "It's hard to know how anyone makes it anymore. The odds are against the people, I can tell you that."

Sam recalled the humiliated look on her father's face when they discussed her college loans, the way he said, "I wish we could have done better by you."

"I know what you mean," she said now.

"I'm glad Gil's got an influence like you in his life," George said. "Has Elisabeth ever mentioned the Hollow Tree to you?"

The words were familiar. Sam had to think a second. Then she remembered: she had seen them written on George's notepad.

"No," she said. "I don't think so."

The sandwiches were finished. George stood and cleared their plates. He pulled two Klondike bars from the freezer, and handed one to her.

"It's this pet theory of mine," he said.

She could tell he wanted her to insist that he go on.

"Tell me about it," she said.

Sam unwrapped the foil and bit into the ice-cream bar. The thin chocolate shell gave a satisfying crack against her teeth.

"I could give you a million examples," he said. "I collect them. You might have seen all my folders in the office."

She wondered if he knew what she'd been up to in there. If this was his way of telling her.

Sam didn't respond, only leaned in to show that she was interested.

George began to rattle off the evidence.

"Faye got a bill for some blood work. Six grand. It was a mix-up with the insurance, but she has since wasted weeks of her life trying to clear it up, waiting on hold, never reaching a real person, getting nowhere. Her sister called here all upset one day because she'd gone to the bank to apply for a mortgage, and the loan officer said those things could be tricky with low-income applicants. Betsy was so mad. 'Low income,' she said. 'When did I stop being middle class? And why did no one tell me about it?' My brother got fired from his job as a prison guard when the state decided to privatize the jails. Then he was hired back, with less pay and without his pension."

This reminded Sam of her friends in the dining hall. She almost said so, but George wasn't done.

He told her he talked to the Mexican kids who worked at the car wash a lot. One day, one of the regulars wasn't around, and George asked after him. The others said he'd gotten sick from the fumes. He had no sick leave or workers' comp. Those kids made half the minimum wage, which was somehow legal, the thinking being that customers would make up for it in tips, which they didn't.

A few months ago, George said, he started attending a discussion group made up of concerned local citizens.

"It's helped me," he said. "These guys get it. After my business went under, I felt like a failure. But then I started to see the patterns. Now I know that the failure is much bigger than me. They want us to think it's our own problem. To feel like shit about ourselves. Then we won't fight back."

Sam felt her face grow hot at a memory from childhood: She, Brendan, and Molly in the back seat of their mother's station wagon, on the way to pick up their father at the train. From the driver's seat, their mother said, "You three need to be extra good and quiet on the ride home. Dad got a pink slip today."

It was one of those moments when the adult was too caught up in her own concerns to translate. They didn't know what a pink slip was, only, from her manner, that it was bad. When their father got in the car, he wasn't his usual playful self. He sat, stone still and silent. Sam found it terrifying. They all did. Molly started to cry, and Brendan gave her the meanest look to shut her up.

The next morning, their father didn't get out of bed. Their mother said they weren't allowed to tell their cousins what had happened.

"Did Dad do something wrong?" Brendan asked.

"Of course not," their mother said.

Sam understood why he had asked. There was so much shame in the air.

"I like your theory," she told George. "So you have a whole discussion group dedicated to talking about this?"

"Technically, discussion group isn't about the Hollow Tree. These guys have been getting together for years to talk. But it does all seem to come back around to the Hollow Tree sooner or later."

"It sounds fascinating."

"You should come next time. Us geezers would get a real kick out of having some young blood in the mix."

"Sure," Sam said. "I'd love to."

"Our next meeting is a week from tomorrow," George said. "I'll pick you up."

In the car on the way home, Elisabeth said the wedding had been a disaster. They didn't have enough chairs. They didn't think to buy ice; the drinks were lukewarm. During his toast, the groom's father forgot the bride's name.

"And oh my God, Sam, Andrew didn't think it was worth warning me beforehand that they are *goths*."

"They're not goths," he said. "They just wear black all the time."

"To their wedding?" Elisabeth said.

"Okay, the fishnet tights and the bride's headpiece were a surprise," he said. "Was that supposed to be—a dead bird?"

Elisabeth and Andrew laughed.

"Was that supposed to be a dead bird?" Elisabeth repeated. "File under: questions no one should have to ask on your wedding day."

"Fair point," Andrew said.

"When their marriage ends in two years, do you think we get that serving platter back?" she said.

"That's kind of a shitty thing to say," Andrew said, a slight edge in his voice.

"I was kidding."

Sam exchanged a wide-eyed look with the baby.

"Anyway, at least the cake was good," Elisabeth said. "I had two pieces. I'll be going for a run as soon as we get home."

Sam told them about the conversation she'd had with George, and how he invited her to his discussion group.

"Oh my God, that's insane," Elisabeth said. "Obviously, you do not have to go. Andrew, tell her."

"I'll tell my dad you're not going," he said. "I'm sorry he tried to suck you in."

"I want to go," Sam said. "I thought all the Hollow Tree stuff was interesting."

Elisabeth swiveled her head to look at her. "You did?"

"Yeah. You two don't agree with him?"

"Of course I agree—the Man is bad, the little guy gets screwed over," Elisabeth said. She sounded bored. "That's kind of a tale as old as time."

That wasn't what George had said exactly. Sam thought there was more to it than that.

"It's just that he's suddenly realized something about injustice and he wants everyone, all of us, to care as much as he does. If you're not taking to the streets or going to his discussion group, you're complicit," Elisabeth said. "When actually, it's a lot more complicated than that."

They fell silent. Sam thought about George. She thought again of how the Hollow Tree applied to all the stories Gaby had told her about Barney Reardon.

She was about to raise this with Elisabeth and Andrew when, with sickening clarity, she remembered: today was the second Saturday in November. She had forgotten about the birthday party for Gaby's daughter.

How could she have forgotten, when these past few weeks, it

seemed to be all that Gaby and Maria talked about? Should they hire a clown, or were clowns, as Gaby argued, just too creepy? Homemade cake or bakery cake? Pink balloons or purple? (In the end, they went with both.)

Maria showed everyone a picture on her phone of the pink dress she bought for Josie to wear, and a pink party hat with the number 2 on it in glitter.

Sam went to text Gaby right away, and realized as she did so that the last three messages in the thread had been sent by Gaby, with no response from her.

The first said *You around?* The second must have arrived right after Gaby invited her to the party. It contained Gaby's address. The third was a long story about some guy Gaby had gone on two dates with. Sam vaguely recalled seeing the text come in late at night and skimming it while she was talking to Clive, reminding herself to respond in the morning. But she had been so busy. Lately, a thought like that just came and went.

Now she typed: *OMG, just realized today was Josie's party. I had to work. I am SO sorry I missed it. How did it go? Send pics!*

Sam could tell Gaby had read the text. She kept looking down at her phone to see if she had replied. No response. No response. Sam turned the ringer up.

Elisabeth and Andrew thanked her over and over when they dropped her in front of the dorm.

"You're the greatest," Elisabeth said. "I don't know what we'd do without you."

Sam wanted to say, *No, I'm not, I'm an asshole*, but she just smiled and said, "Anytime."

She had planned to get in bed and watch the Judy Garland movie marathon on Turner Classics. She told Isabella about it before leaving that morning, and Isabella replied, "You rebel, you. I hate to miss it, but Lexi and I have that concert at State."

They had invited Sam, but the tickets were seventy bucks.

"I'll cover yours. It will be an early Christmas present," Isabella said.

Sam wished it was acceptable to say yes to an offer like that. Instead, she took comfort in the thought of having their room to herself for the night.

But when she opened the door, three guys with gelled hair sat on her bed, and there was Isabella at her desk, in the lap of a fourth, whom she'd met the week before.

The stripper's assistant.

They had only referred to him that way since. Sam could not remember his real name. He worked as a bouncer at a bar near State. On Thursday night, he showed up at a birthday party in the living room of their dorm, along with a male stripper, who was covered in camouflage body paint. Twenty of them sat in a circle, drinking vodka and screaming when the stripper got too close. He stood in the middle, gyrating to "Born in the U.S.A.," pulling off articles of clothing until all that remained was a G-string printed with the American flag. Despite this spectacle, many of the women in the room were watching the hot guy who stood in the doorway, arms crossed, wearing a gray T-shirt and jeans.

Isabella ended up inviting him to their room for a drink after. He said he didn't drink on the job, but he'd love a cup of tea. She made him one in her hot pot, and for the next two hours, he sat there sipping chamomile and telling them his life story.

His friend the stripper, he said, had recently been beaten up by some customer's angry boyfriend, and now he didn't want to go anywhere without backup. He couldn't stop stripping. He needed the money to get his online degree in criminal justice.

"Aren't those degrees like a fraud?" Isabella said.

The stripper's assistant shrugged in such a way that Sam wondered if he knew what *fraud* meant.

She and Isabella continued drinking vodka. When Isabella started licking the guy's ear, Sam took a pillow and went to sleep across the hall in Ramona and Lexi's room.

The stripper's assistant wasn't someone she had expected to see again. But here he was, with, Sam saw now, a huge bottle of beer duct-taped to each of his hands. They all had bottles taped to them like that.

"Sam," Isabella said. "Have you ever played Edward Forty-hands? Play with us!"

Sam stood still in the doorway.

"Can you not sit on my bed, please?" she said.

"She seems fun," one of the guys said.

"Shut up," Isabella said. "It's her room."

Sam missed Clive. She wanted to be in their flat in London, curled up on the couch beside him, watching TV.

"I thought you were going to that concert," she said.

"Lexi's too hungover," Isabella said. "And I don't feel like a crowd. Oh shit. Your movie marathon. I forgot. Can you watch it downstairs in the living room? We ordered pizza."

Sam stepped backward into the hall, then slammed the door. She stood there for a few moments, heart thudding in her chest. Inside her room, someone whispered something and they all laughed. For an instant, she despised Isabella.

It wasn't Isabella's fault, though. Their living situation was unnatural. Sam couldn't stand it anymore. She thought of George, with his piles of paper, his discussion group. She couldn't wait to go and be among people who lived beyond this bubble.

A text message from Gaby arrived then.

Don't worry about it.

Sam stared at the screen, hoping Gaby would say more. But she didn't.

Sam felt horrible. She typed out a long, rambling excuse and then deleted it. She responded instead with just a heart.

She went outside and walked down Main, to Laurel. She stood there for twenty minutes, until she saw Elisabeth's porch light go on, and then her small frame, in shadow, coming down the stairs, breaking into a run.

It was maybe forty-five seconds until she got to the corner. Elisabeth passed Sam at first, then turned right back.

"Hey!" she called. "Where are you off to?"

"Hi," Sam said, attempting nonchalance. "I decided to take a walk."

Then, for no good reason, she started to cry.

"Sam!" Elisabeth said, hugging her. "What happened?"

"Nothing. It's silly."

"Stay here," Elisabeth said. "I'll be right back. Let me take you to dinner."

"No," Sam said. "You were going for a run. I don't want to disrupt your plans."

Though Elisabeth's offer was precisely what she wanted.

"We can try that Italian place, Casa Roma," Elisabeth said. "It's supposed to be good, right? Have you been?"

"Never."

Casa Roma was the kind of restaurant one only went to with visiting parents.

"This is so nice of you," Sam said. "Are you sure?"

"Yes. Andrew could use a little alone time with Gil. And I could stand to go out for once."

An hour later, they had finished a bottle of wine and decided to order two more glasses to have with their entrées.

"Much more responsible than a second bottle," Elisabeth said.

"When I was a kid, we were never allowed to order a drink in a restaurant," Sam said. "I still feel so indulgent whenever I do it, even if it's just a Coke. I expect my mother to pop out from behind a curtain and yell, 'You're having water!'"

Elisabeth smiled. "Oh yes, I remember that too."

Sam got chicken Parmesan. It was the most delicious thing she had ever tasted.

She took a giant bite, just as Elisabeth asked, "Is Clive your first love?"

Sam shook her head, mouth full. After she swallowed, she said, "Sanjeev. My high school boyfriend. When he broke it off with me I thought I would die. I mean that literally. I lay on the floor in a ball. I didn't eat for days. No other life event has ever made me not eat."

The last time she saw him was right before she visited Isabella in London. Sam had only recently stopped thinking of him every day then, and there he was, emailing to see if she'd like to meet for dinner. She found that she didn't like him as much as she used to—he bragged a lot, and his hair had gotten too shaggy. But at the end of the night, he hugged her. He smelled the same. She got into her car and cried. Meeting Clive had released her from all that.

"I almost envy that feeling now," Elisabeth said. "I've been through it. I know it's the worst. But there is something kind of great about the extremity of the despair. Feeling *that* strongly about love."

"So I guess Andrew wasn't your first love?" Sam said.

She twirled spaghetti around her fork, then wondered if it was childish to do so. She felt happy, sophisticated, having this conversation at a candlelit table covered in white linen.

"No, no, no," Elisabeth said. "The first was Jacob. I was wild about him. I thought we'd spend the rest of our lives together."

"What happened?" Sam said.

"My father slept with his mother."

Sam was stunned. She might have had a hundred guesses and never come up with that.

"Jacob left me over it. The whole thing ended his parents' marriage. It was dark."

"Oh God," Sam said.

"His mother thought my father was going to marry her. That's why she confessed everything to her husband. When my father dropped her, she tried to kill herself. Jacob didn't want anything to do with me after that."

"How awful."

"It was. We were living together by then."

"Did your mom find out about the affair?"

"She knew. Just part of my parents' sick games. When I stopped speaking to my father because of it, my mother told me not to be selfish, that it had nothing to do with me."

"That is horrible," Sam said. "I'm so sorry."

"He'd always been a philanderer. But that one, I have to believe, was just for the purpose of breaking us up. My father hated Jacob. He wanted him gone. And my father has to get his way."

"Why did he hate him?"

"Jacob was a musician. Covered in tattoos. Long hair, the works. Not up to my parents' standards. That's the kind of guy I used to go for."

"When you met Andrew, were your parents elated? He seems like the type parents love."

Sam wondered if this was why Elisabeth had chosen him, but Elisabeth shook her head.

"It wasn't until after Andrew and I eloped that I even told them about him. If anything, them liking him might have worked against him. But I was ready. For a nice, stable guy who treated me well and was smart and kind and steady. You'll see. Your friends will lose their taste for bad boys in a few years. It gets old."

"Did your father ever apologize?"

"God no, he's incapable. My sister, Charlotte, is the one family member who fully understood and acknowledged how screwed up it was. She didn't speak to our father either, during those three years we weren't talking. Then he had a heart attack. That ended the standoff. But Charlotte and I still keep our parents at arm's length, even now. There are ways my father would love to use to get back in our good graces, but neither of us will let him."

So this was what she meant by *semi-estranged*.

"I don't think my parents like Clive very much," Sam said. "They don't believe we'll be able to live, with my being just out of school and him doing what he does."

"Andrew and I were in the same boat when we met," Elisabeth said. "Totally on our own. But we made it work. You will too, Sam, if it's what you want."

Sam took such comfort in her advice, coming, as it did, from experience. It was like she was in the presence of an older, wiser version of herself. She could tell Elisabeth liked giving her advice too, being the voice of reason.

When the bill came, Elisabeth wouldn't let Sam near it.

"I can't believe how cheap this place is," she said. "Compared to restaurants in the city, it's like nothing."

George's discussion group met in the quiet commercial center of the town where he and Faye lived. Every third storefront was boarded up. A veterinarian's office was gone, and a bookstore. A hot pink poster board was taped to a plate-glass window under a sign that read DONAHUE'S SHOES.

Thank you for six wonderful decades, someone had written by hand. *It was our pleasure to serve you.*

"We fought hard for that one," George said as they passed. "We got a group together to protest online shopping. There was even a one-day boycott. We got over fifty signatures from people agreeing to take part. But poor Hal, eventually he had no choice but to close."

Next door to where the shoe store had been was Lindy's Bakery. George pushed the door open. A bell jingled overhead.

Inside, there were four small tables, three of which were empty.

Three old guys and a heavyset woman in an apron sat at the fourth table, white coffee cups in front of them.

"I'd like to introduce a special guest," George said. "Everyone, meet Sam—she's here to bring our average age down to a hundred and two. Sam, this is Herbert Benson, Diego Ramirez, Jim Brewer, and Miss Lindy Rose, proprietor of this fine establishment."

Sam had pictured a crowd of fifteen or twenty people. A podium and rows of chairs. But these three men were it. Plus, maybe, Lindy. Sam couldn't tell if she was part of the group or taking a load off because business was slow.

They had passed a Starbucks on the way here, and George said, "I'll never understand how a place so devoid of charm got to be so popular."

Lindy's Bakery was not at all charming. It had Styrofoam ceiling tiles, a linoleum floor, and a small glass case beside the register that contained exactly one sticky bun, one jelly doughnut, and three rolls.

"Coffee, you two?" Lindy said, rising from her seat.

"Sure, thank you," Sam said.

"Decaf for me," George said.

They sat with the others and exchanged pleasantries for a few minutes. Diego read the schedule of discussion topics for the day: Herbert was to give a report on teacher salaries in the local public schools. Then they would talk about two articles Jim had photocopied from the newspaper.

"And before we go, let's talk about the demonstration at City Hall the week after next," Diego said. "I finally got that youngster from the *Gazette* on the phone. He said he'll try to be there."

The rest of them nodded in appreciation.

"He'll try," Diego continued. "Because he's so important. Two years out of State and the kid thinks he's Jimmy Breslin."

"Sam, you should know, we never get many people at our demonstrations," Herbert said. "Us, a couple of the wives, and a handful of friends and neighbors, if we're lucky. But still, it's a contribution."

"Do you post about them online?" she asked. "Like on Facebook or something?"

The men stared back. None of them were on Facebook.

"I could make a page," Sam said. "And then local people and businesses could share it on their pages."

"Lindy, you got a Facebook page?" Herbert yelled, startling Sam.

"Of course I do!" came a voice from the back.

They talked for two hours. Some of it was interesting, though Sam faded out for long stretches, only tuning back in when one of them raised his voice to make a point.

At the end, as everyone was putting on their coats, Jim asked if she would come again next week. Sam said yes, even as she mentally listed better ways to use the time: studying, napping, hanging out with her friends.

"We're having a guest speaker," Jim said. "To warn you, it might get kind of intense."

Over the course of the next week, Sam wondered who the speaker would be. She asked Elisabeth if she knew. Elisabeth said she had no idea what went on at George's meetings.

George picked Sam up again the following Sunday. She liked their time in the car together. In some strange way, he reminded her of home. He drove the twenty minutes to get her and take her to Lindy's, three blocks from where he started. George would drive her back too. It was a lot of extra time in the car, but he said he didn't mind.

"Faye's not used to having me home so much," he said. "It's good for her to have the run of the house for a bit."

The guest speaker turned out to be a well-dressed woman in a pantsuit, with a patterned scarf around her neck and a neatly cropped bob. She spoke calmly, assertively about the problem of drug use in their community and the fact that public officials weren't doing enough to help. Sam listened, riveted, as the woman described how pharmaceutical companies had gotten rich off prescribing the meds that led to opioid addiction, which had stolen so many young lives.

Sam was not expecting what came next. The woman passed around a photograph of a smiling, pretty blonde blowing out the candles on a cake.

"My daughter Julia," she said. "That was her last birthday. She was thirty-one."

She went on to talk about her daughter—who rode horses and rescued dogs and loved country music. How she got addicted to pain pills after a car accident. How the accident didn't kill her, but the pills did.

When the woman was done talking, Sam surprised herself by being the first to respond.

"My uncle Pete, my mom's youngest brother, got hooked on OxyContin a few years ago," she said. "He took it for back pain, but then he just couldn't get off it. He's such a good guy. The last person you'd suspect of being an addict. He has three kids."

It was the sort of thing her parents would say not to tell anyone outside the family, but Sam felt safe here. She thought of what George had told her about blaming the individual when, really, the blame lay with some larger entity.

"It can happen to anyone," the woman said, nodding.

"I'm so sorry about your daughter," Sam said.

George nodded like a proud parent.

"We'll be demonstrating outside the city council hearing for increased funding next week," Jim said. "We should each pledge to recruit one or two people to come. Sam, could you post about it online, like you said?"

She told him she would.

She added the event to the Facebook pages of all the surrounding towns. She asked the student paper to put it on their website on the Local Listings page. The more asks she made, the more she wanted to impress the old guys by bringing out as many people as possible. She printed up actual flyers and hung them on trees and in classrooms, on the bulletin boards at College Hall and the post office. She sent emails requesting the help of the Feminist Alliance, the Campus Democrats, and the Dial Tones, the school's second most popular a cappella group.

Sam wondered if any of them would come. She didn't want to disappoint George.

Students at the college were always staging walkouts and protests.

Arriving to Martin Hall for her British poetry class one Tuesday, Sam found dozens of people streaming from the building.

"Is it a fire drill?" she asked one of them.

"No," the girl said. "It's a walkout."

"A walkout for what?" Sam asked.

The girl shrugged. "I have no idea."

A former secretary of state had given the commencement address last year. Half the graduating students stood up and turned their backs when she took the stage. Sam had never been certain why, exactly.

In the past three months, Sam had marched alongside her fellow students three times—twice when young black men were killed by police officers in faraway states, and once to demand global action against climate change.

But off-campus protests were another matter. Students from the college rarely intermingled with the people who lived in the surrounding area.

On their way to the demonstration, Sam said, "I haven't gotten as big a response as I'd hoped."

"That's all right," George said. "You tried, that's the important thing. Our group is lucky to have you."

In the end, twenty-three people, eleven of them students from the college, arrived at City Hall. One of the students was Isabella, who had come only because Sam promised they'd go for beers at the local dive bar after, but even so, she found it inspiring. Those eleven students had traveled twenty miles to be there. They had come because of her.

The mother of the young woman who died was there, with the familiar photograph printed on her T-shirt—in the picture, the light of the birthday candles against her daughter's cheeks made her look like an angel.

Three members of the Dial Tones sang Joan Baez.

Lindy brought bagels.

George seemed happy. He said it was a good showing. Sam wondered if it bothered him that Faye wasn't there.

Andrew stopped by for a short while on his way home from work, but said he needed to get back to help Elisabeth.

"She wanted to be here, but—the baby," he said.

Sam recalled Elisabeth saying once, "Having a baby is the greatest excuse in the world for bowing out of things you don't want to do."

She watched Andrew walk to his car.

Diego tapped Sam on the shoulder then and said, "This is the reporter I told you about. Benjamin Ross. Sam is the youngest member of our group."

Sam smiled as she turned toward him.

Benjamin Ross was almost handsome. Black, wavy hair; olive skin; a black leather jacket. He had all the components, but there was something off. Maybe it was the smirk on his face, the know-it-all look he gave her before he'd even said a word.

"I hear you're responsible for this great turnout," he said.

Sam couldn't tell if he was being sarcastic.

"How did you end up in the discussion group?" he said. He smiled now.

"I babysit for George Riley's grandson."

"Right," he said. "Those guys are a trip. They have a new story idea for me every week. Whether I like it or not."

Sam wondered how old he was. Not much older than her—Diego had said he graduated two years ago. He had the confidence of someone much older.

Benjamin asked what she was studying, and where. He asked where she was from. But he didn't seem to care about any of the answers. He kept looking past her, as if waiting for someone better to come along.

Sam didn't like him, and yet she had never been so attracted to anybody, not since meeting Clive. Was that even possible, to be attracted to someone you sensed was loathsome? She saw Isabella, talking to Jim and Herbert. Sam wished she could consult her.

Benjamin asked what she was doing after graduation, but only as a means of telling her that he was in the process of applying to grad school. Hoping for Northwestern.

He was, at least on paper, the kind of person everyone in her life would have loved to see her with. The right age, the right job, the correct amount of ambition. It would all be so simple. Sam imagined herself telling relatives at Christmas, *I'm applying for jobs in Chicago right now. We'll be there while Ben gets his master's.*

A moment later, the real Benjamin said, "Well, nice to meet you," and walked off, toward a fast-moving guy in a suit.

The demonstration was a success. The city council voted in their favor.

Afterward, George's discussion group took Sam and Isabella for a steak dinner to celebrate. The restaurant was dark, with blood-red walls and high-backed leather chairs. The place exuded masculinity in a way nothing in Sam's daily life did.

It was there, sitting next to George, feeling energized and inspired, that she brought up her friends in the dining hall and told him about all they'd had to deal with since that terrible man, Barney Reardon, took over as their boss.

"They are the best people in the world. You'd love them," Sam said. "They're like us. I want to do something to help. It dawned on me today that students at the college are always protesting awful things that are happening at a distance. But we could take action to change the lives of women we see every day. Why wouldn't we do that?"

"I like your thinking," George said. "You should talk to them about the most effective ways for you to advocate on their behalf. I'm sure having a student faction on their side would be useful. You can demand things that maybe they can't."

"I bet President Washington has no clue what's been happening to them," Sam said.

"President Washington?"

"The president of the college. She grew up in public housing. She's all about equality and diversity and empowering women on campus. That shouldn't only apply to the students, right? We could stage a teach-in outside her office. Or maybe get people to sign a petition."

"Sure," George said.

Sam had committed President Washington's famous speech to memory. She ran lines from it in her head, as if saying a prayer.

If women ran the world, no child would be hungry.

If women ran the world, we would listen when others speak, aware that the solution usually comes by doing just that.

If women ran the world, we would shine a light on the truth, as hard as it may sometimes be to bear it.

Sam had a vision—President Washington offering Gaby a full scholarship, Gaby giving a speech at her graduation, thanking Sam for putting it all in motion.

She had never had a conversation with President Washington, and yet Sam felt like she knew her. Passing by her red-brick mansion in the middle of campus gave Sam a peaceful feeling, like a grown-up was present, watching over them all.

At breakfast the next morning, still in pajamas, Sam told Gaby about the protest, and about her idea.

Gaby wore her apron over jeans. She was in the process of refilling pitchers of juice.

"I am absolutely positive President Washington would be on your side," Sam said.

"Why? She works for the company, not us," Gaby said.

"What company?" Sam said.

"The college."

Sam had never thought of the place in that way.

"I know this could make a difference," she said. "Trust me. We can't let some guy come in and treat women this way and get away with it. Barney Reardon needs to be held accountable."

"You're crazy," Gaby said, but with a smile that put Sam at ease.

Gaby had acted cool toward her since Josie's birthday. She told Maria Sam had missed the party because she was sick. When Sam thanked her for doing so, Gaby said, "I did it to spare my aunt's feelings, not yours."

Sam had tried to make up for it. She bought the baby a nice present—a pink-and-purple tent that folded up to almost nothing. She invited Gaby out for lunch so they could finally catch up. They laughed their way through the meal, Gaby telling Sam about a disastrous date she'd been on with a guy she met at her restaurant job; Sam telling Gaby about how she had started hanging out with a bunch of old men.

She thought now that Gaby had forgiven her, and it was a relief. Sam couldn't bear for anyone to be mad at her, especially someone like Gaby, who wouldn't hide her anger or pretend things were fine, the way most women did.

A student approached the buffet, groggy-eyed. She poured orange juice from a pitcher Gaby had just filled into one of the short glasses that reminded Sam of summer camp. The girl held the pitcher in one hand, the glass in the other.

Sam knew the exact weight of that pitcher when it was full. She almost said something, but before she could, the girl had lost control, the pitcher twisting her wrist so that the glass overflowed.

"Dammit," Gaby said under her breath.

"I'm so sorry," the girl said.

She fumbled around, then grabbed a stack of cocktail napkins from the buffet and started dropping them over the mess. Each small square dissolved into the puddle.

"No, not like that," Gaby said. "Just—leave it."

She took a rag from her pocket and began sopping up the juice. The girl walked off toward a table of others, her face gone red.

"Oh my God, could someone please teach these girls some common sense? I swear every last one admitted to this school is an imbecile," Gaby said.

It was the sort of thing they might have remarked to one another a year ago in the course of working a shift together, but something in her tone seemed meaner than usual. *Every last one.* Sam wondered if Gaby was still mad about her missing the party. She wanted to ask, but instead pretended to laugh. Then they were laughing together, and that felt good, even if the reason for their laughter was unkind.

"So will you float my idea about talking to President Washington to Maria?" Sam said. "If she says yes, I'm sure Delmi will agree. And then Delmi can convince all her friends to get on board."

Gaby rolled her eyes. "Maria would never agree to something like that."

"Why do you say that?"

"She's resigned to the way things are, I guess. She'd say you don't make demands when you know you're replaceable," Gaby said. "That's just how it is."

Sam didn't agree. Gaby was assuming the worst, as usual.

"I can see those wheels turning in your head, Sam," Gaby said. "Consider that Maria's first cousin works at a dairy where his job is to inseminate cows. Compared to that, this place is paradise."

Sam grimaced.

"Hey. I'm done tonight at seven if you want to grab a beer," Gaby said.

"I wish I could, but I talk to Clive at seven every weeknight now. It's like a ritual. Any later, and he's basically a zombie the next day."

Gaby turned prickly. "Got it."

"I know," Sam said. "I'm sorry."

She had seen the same expression from Isabella, from Lexi, from Shannon. None of them understood why she would sacrifice a night with friends for a phone chat with her long-distance boyfriend. Clive, meanwhile, pouted on the rare occasion when she wasn't there to answer his call, or when he proposed a date for a visit that overlapped with exams or a weekend when Sam had other plans. It seemed like no matter what she did, someone felt neglected. Sam was expected to be two places at once, to split herself in half.

There were also Sunday dinners at Elisabeth's, and discussion group with George, which her friends understood even less. Last year, Sam had spent so many nights and weekends alone, looking for something to do. This year, she needed more hours in the day. It seemed that life was always like that. Too much to do, or not enough, but never the perfect amount.

Other places where she ought to have been, she simply wasn't. She hadn't called her grandparents in weeks, even though her mother said, "They'd love to hear from you," every time they talked.

"Tomorrow I'm off at four and I have an hour before I have to leave for the restaurant," Gaby said.

"Ugh, I'm supposed to do something with Isabella," Sam said. "Sorry. We're like ships passing in the night lately."

"It's fine," Gaby said. "I won't bother to ask again. Since you're the one with the crazy schedule, why don't you tell me when you have some free time."

Sam tried to push away the guilt this brought on in her.

"I will," she said. "Soon."

At dinner on Sunday night, Elisabeth didn't ask about the demonstration.

They talked about other things. The death of Mike Nichols; how much they had all loved *The Graduate*.

Andrew had made an apple tart for dessert. As he sliced it, Sam started talking about Gaby.

"My friend I met working my old campus job," she said. "She has a two-year-old daughter."

"She's a student at the college and she has a two-year-old?" Elisabeth said.

"No, no, she just works there."

Sam told them all the things she'd told George about the women in the dining hall, and how she was trying to think up ways to help them.

"You have a heart of gold, Sam," Elisabeth said.

"You know what their situation makes me think of, right?" Sam said.

"What?"

"The Hollow Tree! It's a perfect example."

"Oh my God," Elisabeth said. "George has really gotten to you."

"My dad says it was thanks to you that they had such a crowd at City Hall," Andrew said. "He thinks we should clone you."

"Yes, because she humors his rantings about the end of the world as we know it," Elisabeth said. "Please know that you don't have to do that for our sake, Sam. Babysitting George isn't part of your job description."

Sam wasn't sure how to respond. She thought they were far beyond job descriptions by now.

Elisabeth

O N HER LAST DAY OF WORK before the semester ended, Sam arrived with a Christmas present for Gil in a silver gift bag. Only then did Elisabeth realize she should have gotten something for Sam. She spent half the day looking for the perfect thing, even though she had sworn to herself that she would write no matter what.

She wondered if any male writer was ever waylaid by such a task. Perhaps more of them ought to be. She often thought that equality between the sexes should be achieved by men growing more thoughtful and attentive, rather than women becoming less so.

Elisabeth went into several shops downtown. She decided against scented candles, earrings, and a gift card for a massage. With each additional stop, the truth about what lay ahead grew clearer—five weeks without childcare, five weeks without Sam.

She settled on a soft, blue cashmere sweater from a boutique on Plum Street. Sam had complained about how cold it was in the dorm; they had no control over the heat. Elisabeth could picture her in this sweater, reading in the lamplight.

She ate a salad for lunch at the new café next to the movie theater and then went to the stationery store for a card. She filled it out, looked at the clock. It was time to go home.

A certain amount of procrastination had always been baked

into her writing process. Until Gil was born, she could work whenever she wanted. Often, it had happened late at night, after everything else on her to-do list. Now, if she didn't do it when Sam was there, she didn't do it at all. Elisabeth told herself that when Sam came back in January, she would somehow become more disciplined.

At the door as Sam was leaving, Elisabeth pressed the gift into her hands and wished her luck with finals.

"Are you stressed?" she asked.

"I'm most nervous about this senior art showcase I'm in at the campus museum," Sam said. "It counts for half my grade in Studio."

"At the museum? That's a big deal," Elisabeth said.

"Not really. It's in the basement."

"When is it? Is it open to the public?"

"Yes. Next Sunday from five to eight," Sam said. "I'd love it if you came, but I wasn't going to mention it. Please don't feel like you have to. I know you guys are busy."

Elisabeth told her they'd be there.

When she closed the door, she felt a strange degree of relief that it was not goodbye.

Elisabeth, Andrew, and Gil arrived at the museum the following Sunday at five-thirty, the baby in a sling on Andrew's chest. The room was full of college girls in groups of three or four or five, drinking red wine from clear plastic cups. Elisabeth didn't know what it was about them that she found intimidating, but as soon as she saw the crowd, she said, "I need a drink."

Two men wearing tweed jackets and an older woman in a flowing black cardigan huddled by a folding table, on which sat several bottles of wine.

Elisabeth went straight over and filled two cups.

She said hello to the professors.

They seemed baffled by her presence.

"Hello," the woman said, as if it were a question, the way people used to answer the telephone.

Returning to Andrew, Elisabeth whispered, "Are we the only outsiders here?"

"It would appear so, yes."

"Have you seen Sam?"

"No."

Over his shoulder stood a lanky girl in a blue peasant skirt. She was topless, long dishwater hair covering her breasts. She held a small paper plate of crackers and chatted with two other girls as if there was nothing out of the ordinary.

"Andrew," Elisabeth said, glancing toward her.

He looked over, then back at Elisabeth, eyes wide.

A girl with a septum piercing stared at them as if to say, *You got a problem with that?*

Elisabeth took her husband by the arm. "Come on, let's look at the art."

They passed several black-and-white photos of a zaftig woman with dark lips and eyebrows. There were paintings of flowers, O'Keeffe rip-offs, or perhaps they were meant as homage.

One student had pinned Ziploc bags of varying sizes to a corkboard—the largest bag contained long red strands of hair, cut from the artist's own head; another held fine clippings collected from her razor; another still, a few unmistakably coarse tufts of pubic hair.

"Moving on," Andrew said.

They turned a corner to see a painting of a woman on a porch, looking out at the ocean in the distance. It was so different from everything else on display. Classic, old-fashioned.

Elisabeth's first thought was that it was beautiful. It reminded her of Cassatt. Her second was that this must be Sam's. A glance at the placard taped to the wall confirmed it.

She stepped back.

"She's good."

Andrew laughed.

"What?"

"You sounded shocked when you said that."

"No. I mean, she's really good. Don't you think?"

He looked closer at the painting. "It's pretty."

Elisabeth felt a hand on her shoulder. She turned to see Sam in jeans and a green sweater. Beside her was Isabella, a bright red Santa hat on her head.

"I'm so sorry you got here before me," Sam said as they hugged hello. "Isabella got us locked out of our dorm room, and I was wearing sweats and no shoes. It took the maintenance guy an hour to come pick the lock."

"Sam," Elisabeth said. "You're so talented. I had no idea. I thought you'd be good, but—you're great."

"You don't have to say that," Sam said, sounding bashful.

"I mean it. I'd love to buy this," Elisabeth said. "Is it for sale?"

Andrew gave her a look. She wished she could freeze time and explain that she was only trying to convince Sam of her sincerity, and besides, it wasn't likely to cost very much.

"That's so sweet," Sam said. "Honestly, I'd just give it to you. But I made this for my mom for Christmas. It's based off a photo of my grandmother taken down the Cape when I was little. She passed away a couple years back."

"Is that a family beach house?" Elisabeth asked.

She tried to remember if Sam had ever mentioned one.

"I wish," Sam said. "That's the hotel where my cousin got married."

"Your mom's going to love it," Andrew said. "What a thoughtful gift."

"Maybe I could convince you to let me commission something after winter break," Elisabeth said.

"Sure," Sam said.

"A picture of Gil, even."

"I'd love that."

"Hey, what's up with the girl who forgot her shirt?" Andrew whispered.

Sam looked over. "That's her thing. She's going topless this entire year to prove—Izzy, what's she trying to prove again?"

Isabella rolled her eyes. "Who knows. If someone had to make it her thing, you'd hope it would be a girl with better tits."

"Ignore her," Sam said.

Isabella grinned. She plopped the Santa hat on Gil's head and he gave her a huge smile. Sam snapped a picture with her phone.

Later that night, she texted it to Elisabeth with a heart, and the words, *Thank you for being there.*

It would be a month before they saw each other again. Sam would take the bus home to Boston and spend two weeks there, then fly to London to see Clive the day after Christmas.

Elisabeth got into a funk thinking about it, and about the larger sadness it foretold. In a few months, Sam would be gone for good, and then whom would she talk to, what would she do here?

Have a great break, she texted back.

As a rule, Elisabeth and Andrew kept images of Gil off the Internet, for reasons of privacy and pedophiles and other dangers they didn't know about but knew enough to fear. Faye had never understood this. Andrew had to threaten not to send her any photos if she shared even one on social media.

But the photo of Gil in the Santa hat was so irresistibly cute. The day after the art show, unable to help herself, Elisabeth posted it to Facebook.

Soon after, her mother posted the same shot to her own page, with the words *Best Christmas present this family ever got!* As if she'd been there when the picture was taken, or had anything whatsoever to do with it, when she had not yet met her grandchild and he was seven months old.

Two days later, she announced over email that she was going to Aspen alone for the holidays.

Festive! Elisabeth wrote back. *Have fun.*

Within twenty minutes, her father called and asked if he could come spend Christmas with them at the new house. Her parents no longer spoke to each other, but they remained in a mind-meld. They often asked her the same question at the same moment over text, or emailed the same video clip from the previous night's episode of *60 Minutes*.

Elisabeth told her father yes, though she had been planning to avoid her family. They did not normally get together for the holidays. They lived across the country, which provided an excellent excuse. Before she got married, Elisabeth spent Thanksgiving and Christmas in the city, with friends. Half the people she knew there might as well have been orphans. But she suspected that marriage and children would draw her parents back to her. Which was one reason why neither had ever appealed much.

"We can't wait to see the baby," her father said before they hung up the phone.

"We?"

"Me and Gloria."

"Why is she coming? Not that she isn't welcome. But—doesn't she want to spend Christmas with her own kids?"

"Not particularly."

A week passed. Her mother wrote to say she was having second thoughts about Aspen.

It's time for me to meet my grandson already.

Elisabeth hesitated before responding. She wanted to know what was behind the change of heart. Probably her mother had realized all her friends would be with their grandchildren, and she didn't want to be the odd man out. Or maybe she had somehow intuited that Elisabeth's father was coming.

Despite everything, an ancient childhood urge to protect her mother crept in.

Elisabeth called her father and explained the situation.

"So I'm thinking Gloria probably shouldn't come," she said.

"Why not?"

"Because, as I just told you, Mom will be here."

"Your mother won't mind having Gloria around."

"I think she might."

"She's a big girl. She'll deal."

After they hung up, she texted her mother: *You're totally welcome, but just so you know: Dad will be here . . . he's bringing his girlfriend. I'm sorry, I couldn't talk him out of it, you know how he is . . .*

It annoyed her to be in between them yet again. Especially because she didn't really want either of them to come.

Her mother replied immediately: *I look forward to seeing them both.*

Her mother, who once threw a plate of chicken at her father's head during dinner when he chewed too loudly; who told Elisabeth the day she turned sixteen that she had never loved her husband, had only married him for his looks and his money.

Fine, but I'm not going to tolerate anything but perfect behavior from everyone. This is Gil's first Christmas.

Elisabeth was trying to sound tough.

Scout's honor, her mother wrote back.

For once in her life, she felt that she was in control of her family. A grandchild was currency. Something they wanted, which only she possessed.

Still, she sent her sister, Charlotte, an email with the subject line: *YOU ARE COMING TO MY HOUSE FOR CHRIST-MAS.* In the body, Elisabeth wrote: *Mom and Dad will both be here. I need moral support. This is not optional.* She added a smiley face so as not to sound too demanding. But within minutes, she sent a follow-up: *P.S. I'm dead serious. Do not even attempt to pretend this went to your spam folder.*

It was the least Charlotte could do after everything Elisabeth had done for her.

By dinnertime, she hadn't replied.

Elisabeth thought of every SOS her sister had sent over the past few years, expecting an immediate response. She had always delivered.

She was irritable while they ate and, afterward, watching TV. Annoyed about her family's intrusion into their life, and even more so about the sliver of stupid hope in her that maybe this time would be different.

"What's up?" Andrew said as they brushed their teeth before bed.

"I'm dreading this family visit. What was I thinking, telling them they can come? I told my sister she has to swear to come too, upon pain of death."

"Why?"

"Safety in numbers? Misery loves company? Something like that."

"Sounds fun," he said, his words garbled.

Andrew had worked up a foam of toothpaste. It dribbled from between his lips as he brushed.

He shook his head like a dog after a bath, spitting the foam into the sink and pulling something from his mouth.

"What's that?" she said.

He held it up to the light.

"A bristle from my new toothbrush came out while I was brushing."

"God," she said.

"I could have swallowed it."

He narrowed his eyes in mock indignation. "Hollow fucking Tree," he said, throwing the toothbrush on the counter with such force that it bounced twice and landed on the floor.

"You're awful," she said.

They laughed.

In bed that night, Elisabeth tried to count backward from one hundred, but each time, her thoughts intruded before she reached the high eighties.

She got up and checked on the baby. They had moved him into his own room, which made her happy and wistful in equal parts. She slept better now, but she would never again experience those first, all-consuming weeks and months.

As Gil grew older, more solid, Andrew seemed to find his footing as a dad. He was more involved. There were more things the two of them could do together. They had games and routines of their own that Elisabeth had nothing to do with. She had started leaving Gil with Andrew on the occasional Saturday while she tried to work. This too felt bittersweet.

Recently, her agent had said it was past time to tell her publisher what she planned to write next. Elisabeth proposed a book on Title IX and the history of women in sports, based on the last series of articles she'd been assigned before the baby was born.

She had already done most of the research and the interviews. It could be a short book, something to bridge the gap between her pre-Gil self and whatever version of her was coming next.

She had no particular interest in sports, but she thought the women's individual journeys were compelling. Had it not been for a change in federal law, they might never have played high school soccer or basketball, or had the chance to go to college on an athletic scholarship.

Elisabeth pitched the idea, and her agent and editor seemed encouraging, if underwhelmed.

"Try it," her agent said. "Why not?"

Elisabeth returned to bed now and shut her eyes, but still, sleep would not come.

She remembered her old middle-of-the-night companions, the BK Mamas. It had been a while since she looked at the Facebook page—weeks? A month? In part, this was because Gil now slept through the night. Maybe it also had something to do with Sam. Elisabeth had someone to keep her company, to talk to her about the baby as much as she wanted.

But mostly, she stopped looking because things there had started getting strange. The page was like that: it tended to go in cycles. A month or so of true kindness and support—a woman gave a stranger's sister a kidney once; someone was always collecting clothes and toys and gear for refugee families or Christmas gifts for kids in shelters. Everyone gave generously. But then, inevitably, they'd start fighting, and that would be the tone for a while.

When last she looked, a flurry of passive aggression burst forth because a woman asked for advice about whether or not to stop nursing her three-month-old.

I've been diagnosed with D-MER, a condition that causes me to have suicidal thoughts when my milk lets down. (Yes, this is an actual thing.) Is it okay to stop nursing?? Will I regret it?

A few people told her to go for the formula and never look back, that her mental health was paramount. But others, in their subtle way, encouraged her to keep on.

Poor Momma! That sounds miserable. Thank goodness the letdown only lasts a second. Hang in there!

Breast is best, but do what you gotta do. ☺

One mother was clear in her disdain for the idea. Elisabeth almost appreciated this, set against the approach of the others: *Yes, you'll regret it. When your sweet baby becomes an obese toddler thanks to your reliance on Big Food.*

In another instance, someone posted a photograph of a man in Cobble Hill Park, holding a camera.

Beware this pervert! she wrote. *I spotted him this morning surreptitiously taking pictures of two little girls on the playground.*

Someone else commented that she had seen him doing the same thing in the past, and all hell broke loose. In a matter of hours, the guy's picture was on every mommy blog and message board in the city.

The next day, the original poster wrote a brief mea culpa: *I have since learned that the man whose photo I shared yesterday is the father of those children he was photographing, so I am deleting my previous post.*

That was it. No apology for smearing the guy, no collective horror over what they'd done to him.

Despite swearing off the group after that, Elisabeth thought to herself now that there was no harm in taking a look, just this once.

The post of the moment, added after midnight, was from a woman who wrote that her husband was out of town on business, and there was a live mouse squealing and writhing around on a glue trap in her kitchen. It had managed to pull up a single leg, but the detached foot was stuck to the pad, along with the other foot, still attached to the mouse.

I know some of you rave about TaskMaster, that site where you can book someone by the hour to move stuff/build furniture/ run errands/whatever. Is it reasonable to reserve someone for an hour right now to come deal with this?? If I give a huge tip???

Elisabeth put the phone down.

She woke the next morning feeling relaxed. Friday. Sam arriving soon.

Then Elisabeth remembered—no Sam today. No Sam for the rest of the month.

Andrew left early for work.

The baby was crabby. He could sit now, but still couldn't crawl, and it frustrated him. He whined half the time. Elisabeth hated the sound. She felt awful for him. She placed him on his hands and knees, holding his stomach a few inches off the ground.

"You're almost there," she said. "You can do it."

She played him some Raffi and gave him a wooden spoon to bang against a pot. Gil stuck the spoon in his mouth.

At nine o'clock, she looked at her phone. Only an hour had passed since Andrew went to work. It felt like days. Elisabeth considered breaking her own rule and watching TV in front of Gil. But after flipping through the channels twice and finding nothing of interest, she decided it wasn't worth the guilt.

At nine-fifteen, while filling a bottle with formula, she realized she had forgotten to cancel therapy.

"Shit," she said.

Violet wouldn't let her back out this late. She would make Elisabeth pay for the session either way.

She and Gil were still in their pajamas. Elisabeth plopped him in the center of her bed with three board books while she hurried to get dressed. When he started to cry, she added her cell phone to the pile of enticements.

She put Gil in a fleece jumpsuit with a smiling elephant printed on the butt. She gathered diapers, bottles, toys, a change of clothes, the stroller. Maybe she would take him out to lunch after, make a day of it.

Gil cried in the car, all the way to town. She wondered if he was teething. Faye had said to rub whiskey on his gums when the time came. This struck Elisabeth as something for which the authorities might come and take your child away, but she said she would keep it in mind.

The public lot was full. She circled the small downtown four times before she spotted a tight space at a meter. Elisabeth squeezed into it, ignoring that her bumper was touching the car in front of her and the one behind.

She unfolded the stroller like an accordion on the sidewalk, then lifted the baby from his car seat and placed him inside, tucking a thick blanket over him.

Her appointment should have started six minutes ago. Violet would act put out, she was certain.

Elisabeth rushed the three blocks to her office. As she crossed Calvin Street, a Hispanic woman coming in the other direction looked at the baby and exclaimed, as if she knew him.

"Chiquito!"

She made a face, puffing out her cheeks as far as they could go, then pretending to pop them.

Gil laughed.

Elisabeth gave the woman a strange smile, and kept walking. She scanned her memory. She felt certain she had never seen her before.

Violet answered the door to her office with a disappointed look on her face. Then she noticed the baby and brightened.

"Who do we have here?"

"Sorry. The sitter called in sick at the last minute."

Elisabeth figured this small white lie would engender sympathy, and perhaps get her points for showing up at all.

Gil had fallen asleep. She wheeled his stroller toward the couch, hoping he wouldn't remember this. His mother, dragging him along to her shrink.

"So," Elisabeth said as she sat down.

"So," Violet said. She smiled without showing her teeth. She always waited for Elisabeth to go first.

"I guess I'm stressed about the holidays, like everyone," she said. "My parents are both coming to our house, which is definitely a bad idea. My father's bringing a date. It's not what I would have wanted for Gil, for his first Christmas."

"What would you have wanted?"

"For the three of us to be left alone, I guess. Or not even that. A completely different family? No Christmas at all? I don't do well with holidays."

"Do you have any happy memories of holidays when you were a child?" Violet asked.

"No." Elisabeth paused. "Did I ever tell you about my fear of houses? When my first friend got married and bought a house, I went to visit her. After she and her husband went to bed, I was sitting alone in their living room and I had a panic attack. I kept thinking of things they talked about that day—a new washing machine, a cookout they were planning. I couldn't wait to get back to my New York apartment, and my not-real life."

"Why do you call it not real?"

"In the city, you somehow always feel like things are in flux. My babysitter, Sam, she talks all the time about wanting to feel settled. I find being settled unnerving. The stillness is harder than I thought it would be."

Violet nodded. "So you create ways of making things unstill."

"Like what?"

Violet shrugged, as if someone else had said the last words out of her mouth.

Elisabeth nodded toward the baby. "What are you supposed to do when your model is utter shit, and you want better for your own kid? But at the end of the day, you're still yourself."

"That's why you're here," Violet said. "It seems to me like you're doing a great job so far."

"Thank you. I appreciate that. But it's easy to hide your faults from a baby. How do I do it when he's older? Sometimes I think Andrew and I couldn't be more different from our families. Other times, I'm afraid we're doomed to become them."

"How so?"

"A million different ways. I think of what my mother did when I was a kid, confiding in me about my father's affairs. Needing me to indulge her every insecurity. A child shouldn't be so aware of her mother's demons. A child shouldn't know her mother has demons at all. Is that right?"

Violet, annoyingly, did not respond.

When Elisabeth was up late with Gil, when he got the cradle cap, when he had a particularly revolting diaper situation, she thought of how her parents must have cared for her in these same ways. What did you owe the person who made such sacrifices on your behalf, sacrifices you would never remember?

As Elisabeth pictured things she and Gil would do together when he grew, memories of her own childhood returned—the way her father let her stir milk into his coffee in the mornings;

how her mother sat her down beside her at her dressing table and taught her how to apply lipstick. Her father taking her and Charlotte to the bird sanctuary. Her mother reading them Beatrix Potter. These had been buried beneath what came after.

The bond between parent and child was all-consuming, and yet its power was not cumulative. It had to be remade again and again throughout the course of a lifetime. A mother could do everything right early on, and still, if she failed to renegotiate the terms, all would be lost.

"I look for mothers everywhere," Elisabeth said. She didn't want Violet to think she meant her, so she added, "At least I did in my twenties and early thirties. I wanted someone to show me how to be. But that never happened. Times that are supposed to be about family bonding or celebrations are hard for me. I suck at going on vacation. I'm a ruiner of festive moments."

Violet looked interested for once. "Give me an example."

"I went into a deep depression at a Jimmy Buffett concert one New Year's Eve," Elisabeth said. "We got there and I was fine, and then all of a sudden I started acting like a huge bitch for no reason. Poor Andrew was sitting beside me, not knowing what to say, as oversize yellow balloons with smiley faces painted on them bounced off our heads. We left after three songs. Who does that?"

"You'd be surprised," Violet said, as if patients came in every day complaining of Jimmy Buffett–induced despair. "What about it depressed you?"

"I have no idea."

"Give it a minute. Think."

Elisabeth tried, but she felt like she was making up an answer, not having some kind of epiphany.

"Maybe it was the sense of community. The shared love of Hawaiian shirts and homemade hats and rum drinks. The joy they all exuded. I wish I loved anything half as much as those people loved Jimmy Buffett."

"Community," Violet said. "That makes sense."

"It does."

She scribbled something in her notebook, then looked up. "When was this?"

"Years ago."

"So the feeling of not having a place you belong, it's not new. Not necessarily to do with moving here."

Elisabeth considered this, the rare wise observation on Violet's part.

"I guess that's right," she said. "I was alone a lot as a kid. Inappropriate things happened around me, and I didn't know what to do with them. It's yet another reason why I resent my parents' money. No one feels sorry for a rich girl with terrible parents. In most people's eyes, my problems weren't problems at all."

"How are things with Andrew?" Violet asked.

"Fine. Good. He keeps pushing for a second baby."

"Even though he knows you don't want one."

"He thinks I do secretly want one, but I'm scared."

Violet looked skeptical.

"Maybe he's right," Elisabeth said, feeling suddenly protective of Andrew. "He knows me better than anyone. There was a time I didn't know if I even wanted one. Now I can't imagine life without him. Then again, we got so lucky with Gil. I don't want to tempt fate. Our family's chemistry feels—delicate. A daughter would be especially terrifying. I'd ruin her for sure. Everything is so good. I don't want to jeopardize that."

"You say things are so good. But you and Andrew never tell each other what you mean," Violet said. "He still has no clue about all that money you gave to your sister."

"It was a loan," Elisabeth said.

It felt shameful that Violet, whom she didn't even particularly like, should know this about her, and not Andrew, the person she was closest to in the world.

"Have you thought about couple's counseling?" Violet said, as if it was the first time she had mentioned the idea.

She brought it up at almost every session.

"I can't see either of us doing that," Elisabeth said.

Violet closed her eyes. Annoyed or asleep, it was hard to say.

When the session ended, Gil had just woken up and was chattering away in the stroller.

"Thanks," Elisabeth said as she wrote out a check. "I'll see you next Friday."

"Actually, I won't be here next week," Violet said.

"Taking a vacation?"

There was always this moment at the end. Elisabeth had made herself vulnerable, and now time was up. It was like having someone switch on the lights at an orgy.

Violet seemed uncomfortable with the question. "Yes."

Elisabeth wanted to ask where she was going, the way she would ask any other person who had just told her she was going somewhere. But she knew Violet would consider this boundary crossing.

"Did you ever see that movie *What About Bob*?" Elisabeth said.

"I don't think so."

"Bill Murray? No?"

Whenever Elisabeth asked if she'd seen a movie, or read a novel, or an article on the front page of the Sunday *Times*, Violet said no. Elisabeth wondered if she simply consumed nothing of the culture, which was odd in its own right. Or if telling Elisabeth she had read something would, for Violet, constitute sharing.

Elisabeth called Andrew from the car to discuss.

"How can you be expected to pour your soul out to a person who won't tell you even the most minor details about her life. Is that normal? What do you think?"

Andrew said, "I think therapy is making you worse instead of better."

At home, she found a Christmas card from Sam in the mailbox.

Elisabeth tore it open, baby still in her arms, as if Sam herself might pop out of the envelope.

She wished she had gotten it together to send Sam, or anybody, a card. She knew she was supposed to have one made up with an adorable picture of Gil on the front, the sort of cards she'd been receiving for weeks from friends. But the thought exhausted her.

Elisabeth had the urge to text Sam, but that would be strange, wouldn't it, reaching out to her at home?

She texted Nomi instead: *I hate Christmas.*

Fa la la la la! Nomi wrote back.

12

TWO WEEKS PASSED IN A HAZE of shopping for presents nobody needed and going to parties no one wished to attend.

At Andrew's office gathering, people stood around cubicles, making forced conversation—men and women who spent all day together as it was, and their spouses, who weren't overly interested in knowing one another, plus the student workers from the lab, who were just there for the free beer.

The goth couple whose wedding they had attended in November showed everyone cell-phone pictures of their honeymoon in Reno.

Bowls of pretzels and M&M's sat on the conference room table, like it was a nine-year-old's birthday party.

Elisabeth talked to a junior with a handlebar mustache. He told her he'd grown it to play Ophelia in a gender-blind production of *Hamlet*.

"The director wants us to really lean into it," he said.

She remembered then, Andrew coming home and telling her about it, saying, "I'm probably not smart enough to understand, but can't they just do *Bye Bye Birdie* for once?"

Elisabeth told the kid that she and Andrew couldn't wait to see the show.

"Andrew's the best," he said. "We all love being on his project. He's a really good mentor, you know."

She nodded, though she actually hadn't known until then.

Starting the day after Thanksgiving, whenever Elisabeth ran into any of her neighbors, they mentioned Stephanie Preston's annual holiday bash. Debbie pronounced it *legendary*.

Elisabeth was trying to think of an excuse for why she couldn't go, when Debbie mentioned that Gwen would be there.

"She's back from China," Debbie said. "Her husband, Christopher, have you met him? He came home early, apparently. She ended up cutting her trip short. Probably wise not to leave Christopher home alone too long, if you know what I mean."

Stephanie sent paper invitations with RSVP cards. The postage stamp was a miniature photograph of her kids eating candy canes.

Adults only. Formal attire required.

"So, not my ugly Christmas sweater then?" Andrew said as they got ready.

"I'll pay you a thousand dollars," she said.

Elisabeth wore a royal-blue fitted dress with three-quarter-length sleeves, and nude heels. Taking in her reflection in the bedroom mirror, she felt pleased. She looked almost exactly like her old self, dressed up for a night out. Her hair was getting long, but she was afraid to let anyone around here touch it. Soon they would go back to the city for a visit, and she'd see Zachary, who had been cutting her hair for a decade.

Since Sam was gone and they weren't going far, they'd asked Faye to babysit.

Gil was already in bed when she arrived.

"If he wakes up, call me and we'll come right back," Elisabeth said. "We're only a few houses away."

Faye rolled her eyes.

"Go," she said.

Elisabeth and Andrew descended the front steps and walked to the curb.

"A rare moment alone together," he said.

She smiled, nodded.

Neither of them said anything after that.

They used to sit across from each other in restaurants four or five nights a week, and just talk. Now she struggled to think of something to say that wasn't about Gil. Her thoughts spiraled— were they content? Would they go the distance? Or when Gil was old enough to stop needing them, would they realize there was no *them* anymore?

What constituted a happy marriage?

At Stephanie's house, the front door was cracked open. The sounds of the party drifted outside.

There was a table in the front hall covered with blank name tags and Sharpies. A sign in a plastic frame read WELCOME! PLEASE TAKE OFF YOUR SHOES AND LEAVE THEM AT THE DOOR. YES, WE'RE *THOSE* PEOPLE.

"I'm not taking my shoes off," Elisabeth said. "My toes look awful. This dress will look all wrong with bare feet."

"I support you," Andrew said.

He bent to fill out a name tag, then stuck it to her chest.

Elisabeth looked down at what he'd written: *Yes, I'm THAT person*.

She peeled the sticker off.

They hung their coats on a rack beside the table. The banister leading upstairs was wrapped in fake green garland. A plastic Santa the size of a small child stared at them.

Laughter traveled out from the kitchen.

"We don't have to stay long, right?" she said.

"Really? I was hoping we'd be here all night," he said. "Seriously, though, let's try to have a good time, okay?"

"Yeah," she said.

Stephanie popped into the hallway, in a bright red, skintight dress.

"Get in here, you two," she said.

She glanced at Elisabeth's shoes, but didn't say anything.

They were whisked into separate conversations—Elisabeth into the crowd of women in the kitchen; Andrew into a throng of men seated around the dining room table, talking about sports. There was nothing sadder than men talking about sports. Why did they accept it as their only form of communication with one another?

A bar had been set up on the kitchen island. There were paper napkins printed with Christmas trees, plastic cups, and several open bottles of wine and liquor.

Elisabeth fixed herself a gin and tonic. She said hello to the Laurels, and half a dozen other women who looked like them, whom she hadn't met before.

"What about you? Do you have the Elf on the Shelf?" said a woman wearing jingle-bell earrings.

Elisabeth searched her memory for what that was.

"Her son is too young," Debbie said. "He's just a baby."

"Well, trust me," the woman continued. "That elf will be your best friend in a few years. My kids act like angels when they think he's watching and taking notes for Santa."

Elisabeth remembered now. Her friend Pearl at her old job had told her about this.

The Elf on the Shelf is the perfect introduction to life in a surveillance state was how she'd put it.

"You girls make motherhood so difficult for yourselves," said the one older woman in the group. She wore a black dress, too tight for her sagging midsection. "We never would have dreamed of setting up a doll in a different pose every night to amuse our children. Or as a way to get them to behave. We just threatened to spank them and that was that."

Elisabeth stared at her.

Then Stephanie grabbed her and pulled her over.

"Elisabeth!" she said, drawing out each syllable. She was already drunk. "I'd like you to meet my bestie. My ride or die. My *mom*."

The older woman smiled and rolled her eyes in faux embarrassment. "Hi there. I'm Linda."

Like Stephanie, she seemed extremely proud of herself for no apparent reason.

Elisabeth took a deep breath. She was being judgmental, harsh. She pinched herself. *Banana banana banana.*

"Elisabeth has a brand-new baby," Stephanie said.

"That itty-bitty waist, and you've got a brand-new baby," Linda said, admiringly. "Very impressive."

"He's not brand-new," Elisabeth said. "He's seven months old."

"How are you finding the baby stage? It was my least favorite part of motherhood, if I'm honest," Linda said.

"I love it," Elisabeth said.

"When do you think you'll have another? It's the most fun, having two," Linda said. "Watching that sibling bond happen right in front of your eyes. Though it's true what they say—after the first, your mind is gone for a year. After the second, it's gone for good."

Stephanie and Linda laughed. Elisabeth wondered what their minds had been like to begin with. She wondered why so many people felt it was their job to insist that women have more children, while simultaneously pointing out how terrible it would be when they did. She poured herself more gin.

The doorbell rang.

Stephanie flitted off to greet another guest. Linda launched into a story about a fight that was brewing at her church over whose grandchild would portray Baby Jesus in the Nativity play.

"My friend Judy and I have a quiet campaign going to get her grandson, Dylan, in there. He's an angel. Those blond curls you just want to *eat*."

Elisabeth missed Gil. "My son has those curls," she said.

"You should see this kid they're planning on using," Linda said. "He has a strawberry birthmark and *eczema*."

She said *eczema* as if it were the plague.

As soon as an opportune moment arose, Elisabeth excused herself.

She walked into the living room alone.

Stephanie had two Christmas trees as tall as the ceiling, covered with blinking lights. Why two? An attempt to be as showy as possible?

The Laurels coordinated their outdoor holiday decorations. They all hung big rainbow-colored bulbs on their bushes, and enormous prewired wreaths over their garage doors. But no one told Elisabeth and Andrew, who had purchased tiny white lights online, and a puny wreath from the Boy Scouts when they came door-to-door. Their house looked shabby, half done, compared with the sea of bright colors and lit-up snowmen and the actual sleigh pulled by eight plastic reindeer on Debbie's lawn.

A week ago, the Laurels had invited Elisabeth to a Christmas cookie exchange, which entailed baking ten dozen of one kind of cookie, then meeting at Pam's with nine other women who'd done the same, and mixing and matching until everyone had ten dozen assorted cookies to give as gifts.

It's like a chain letter, but with cookies, she had explained in a text to Nomi. *Given that I have never baked one dozen cookies, let alone ten, I think I'll pass . . .*

When she repeated this to Andrew later, he said, "I know the people around here are a bit much. But you have to admit, they're great neighbors."

It was true that Stephanie's husband had snowblown their

driveway when the first winter storm hit without warning. And when Gil spiked a fever and Elisabeth got home from the store with the Tylenol, a total wreck, Karen happened to be walking by and got her sister, a pediatric nurse, on the phone.

After the cookie exchange, Pam showed up at her house with a pretty tin, and Elisabeth actually gasped upon opening the lid to find twelve perfect cookies—beautifully iced snowmen and presents; chunky rounds bursting with cranberries and white chocolate and nuts. She was glad then that she had not attempted to bring ten dozen slice-and-bakes and pass them off as her grandmother's recipe.

Maybe Andrew was right. Maybe the Laurels weren't as bad as she had originally thought. But despite their small kindnesses, Elisabeth was standing alone in Stephanie's living room right now, hoping none of them would join her. She didn't think she would ever fit in here. She felt melancholy in the midst of everyone else's apparent ease and merriment.

She checked the time. She was wondering whether they could leave yet when she heard voices. She turned to see Gwen with a handsome guy. He had shaggy hair that made him look more boyish than he was, even though it was gray.

Elisabeth was so excited to see her. "Gwen!" she shouted, with a tad too much enthusiasm. "Elisabeth," she reminded her, in case. "We met here. At book club."

"I remember," Gwen said. "The unlikable Mary McCarthy."

"When did you get back from Hong Kong?" Elisabeth asked, even though Debbie had already told her.

"Last week." Gwen put a hand on the man's sleeve. "This is my husband, Christopher. Chris, this is Elisabeth. She and her family moved here from Brooklyn not too long ago."

"I recognize you," Elisabeth said. "Where do I know you from?"

He shrugged. "It's a small town."

She thought he sounded defensive, as if she had accused him of something.

Andrew came in then, looking for her. Elisabeth made introductions.

They moved on to other topics—the trip to China, how quiet this town felt when the students were gone. Elisabeth kept working the thought over, like a piece of spinach stuck between her teeth. Christopher was so familiar.

"What do you do at the college?" she asked him.

"I'm an adjunct right now. I teach in the art department."

"Do you know Sam O'Connell?"

"Sure," Christopher said. "She was one of my best students a couple years back."

Elisabeth felt proud to a degree she was sure wasn't earned.

"She's our babysitter," she said. "Isn't she great?"

"She's a senior now?" he said, without answering her question.

"Yes. Ugh, don't remind me. I'll be lost without her next year. She's like a member of the family at this point. She might move to England to be with her boyfriend after graduation. Go live in the country, that's their plan. But deep down, I think she really wants to work in a gallery."

He didn't reply. It made Elisabeth uneasy. His eyes wandered down to her breasts and then up again, as if someone was pulling a string attached to the top of his head.

She kept talking.

"We can't let her, right? She's too talented. I don't even know why she wants to work in a gallery. She should just paint."

"You've seen one painting," Andrew said.

"No, it's true," Christopher said. "She has natural talent."

"I'm so glad to hear you say that. She doesn't think anyone at the college thinks she's good," Elisabeth said.

"Sam's one of the best in the department at the moment, technically speaking," he said. "Unfortunately, she doesn't take risks. She doesn't have anything new to say."

Annoying. What did he know?

"We saw her final project for the semester," Elisabeth said. "The portrait of her grandmother."

She paused to discern whether he knew what she was referring to, but he gave no indication one way or the other.

"Were you at that art show last Sunday?" she asked.

Maybe that was where she'd seen him.

Christopher let out a sound somewhere between a scoff and a cough. "I wasn't. I try to avoid those things."

Then it clicked.

"I know where I recognize you from," she said. "I was on campus at the start of the school year to hang a flyer, and you were talking to some poor girl whose grandmother had died."

His expression was blank.

"At College Hall. She wanted an extension on a paper," she said.

"You wouldn't believe how many grandmothers die the day a paper is due," he said. "That, and midterms, appear to be the leading causes of death among grandparents, as far as I can tell."

He didn't smile. Gwen laughed, to make it clear that he was trying to be funny.

The look on Andrew's face matched the way Elisabeth felt. It made her want to kiss him. Maybe the definition of a happy marriage was simply not wishing you were married to anyone's husband but your own.

"We should get going before the baby wakes up and my mom decides to give him a cupcake instead of the bottle we left in the fridge," Andrew said.

"Oh no," Gwen said.

"Do you guys have kids?"

It surprised Elisabeth that Andrew would ask that question, the question they themselves hated being asked for so long.

"We don't," Gwen said.

"Smart people," Andrew said. "You probably get to sleep past five a.m. on a Saturday."

She gave him a look. Had he forgotten already?

"Five would constitute sleeping in for me," Christopher said.

"He's a big cyclist," Gwen said. "He sometimes does sixty miles in a day."

"That's—impressive," Elisabeth said.

She wondered if all that cycling might contribute to low sperm count.

They wouldn't be couple friends, that much was clear. But still, she liked Gwen.

"We should get together now that you're back," Elisabeth said.

"I'd love that."

The voices in the kitchen had grown louder. Stephanie's laugh rose to a cackle.

"I suppose I should thank her and say goodbye," Elisabeth said. "But I don't want to go back in there."

"I'll tell her you had to get home to your sitter," Gwen said.

"Bless you."

Gwen followed them to the door and wrote her contact information on a leftover name tag. Elisabeth did the same.

"I'm so happy to run into you again," Gwen said. "This reminds me. My friend would love to have you speak to her class if you're still willing."

"Anytime," Elisabeth said. "Have her email me."

On the walk home, Andrew said she should be careful blabbing about Sam and her plans for next year.

"I got carried away," she said. "The gin. But while we're on the topic of subjects to avoid in casual conversation, don't you remember how hard it was when we were trying and people just assumed we didn't want kids?"

Andrew looked back toward Stephanie's house. "Those two? You sure?"

"She didn't say anything, but I have a feeling."

"They don't seem like the type."

Elisabeth dropped the name tag Gwen had handed her into her purse. It sank to the bottom, drawn down into a stew of loose change and drugstore receipts and linty pacifiers, where it would remain for the next five months.

Charlotte had taken a week to get back to her about the holiday. Finally, she agreed to come if Elisabeth could help with her travel expenses. Elisabeth sent a check for four hundred dollars to help offset the cost of her flight, which Charlotte acknowledged with a text saying *You're the best!* Followed by an emoji of a winky face blowing a kiss.

Let's avoid any money talk in front of Andrew when you get here, okay? she replied. *Things are kind of tense on that front.*

Charlotte's response was a sad face, which Elisabeth took to mean *I'm sorry to hear that.*

Her sister brought conch fritters packed in dry ice. She was so tan, the color of a Barbie. She drank too much on Christmas Eve when the three of them, plus the baby, went out for dinner. Charlotte carried on about how idyllic life on Turks was, while in the same breath mourning the loss of a trust-fund kid turned scuba instructor who went for a night swim and got eaten by wild dogs.

"He was a good friend of Davey's," she said. "It hit him hard."

"Who's Davey?" Elisabeth said.

"Davey," Charlotte said, as if it were obvious, as if Davey were their brother. "I told you about him. He's getting here tomorrow afternoon."

"You didn't tell me you were bringing anyone."

"Will he be joining us for lunch?" Andrew said.

His tone was bright, but Elisabeth could tell he was calculating whether they had enough food.

"Yes," Charlotte said. "He wouldn't miss it. I told him what a great cook you are."

Andrew tried to hide how proud the comment made him.

He blushed, which made Elisabeth smile.

Charlotte was exasperating, but still, they laughed a lot that night. Everyone was in good spirits. They told old stories that Andrew had never heard.

Elisabeth's parents got in late. They had each booked a room at the Hotel Calvin, without consulting her or each other. Around ten, they both texted at the same time to say they'd had a run-in in the lobby while checking in, and wasn't that just their luck?

Elisabeth showed the messages to Charlotte, who rolled her eyes.

"Those two deserve each other," she said. "I don't mean that as a compliment."

"I'm really happy you're here," Elisabeth said.

"Me too," Charlotte said with a smile. She put her arm around Elisabeth's shoulder.

The next morning, Christmas Day, everyone arrived at once.

Elisabeth saw them through the window, getting out of their cars and coming up the walkway. Her in-laws; her father and his girlfriend, who had, surprisingly, a retirement-age hippie vibe about her; Charlotte in black leather pants and a fuzzy white sweater, no coat; and, bringing up the rear, their mother, thinner than ever and impeccably dressed in a skirt-suit and heels, like a member of Congress attending the State of the Union. Elisabeth knew from Charlotte that she had recently gotten Botox, a chin lift, and something called CoolSculpting, which promised to freeze off her nonexistent fat deposits. She was carrying seven shopping bags from Saks.

Elisabeth took a deep breath. It was too much. She had imagined receiving them one at a time. She wanted to hide, but opened the door instead.

"Merry Christmas," they all said, doing their best impersonation of a real family.

They crowded into the front hall. Andrew took everyone's coats. Elisabeth's mother regarded Gil in her arms and said, "Now *there* you are," as if she'd been looking for him all these months. She reached out to hold him, which surprised Elisabeth.

Elisabeth passed the baby over and felt moved in some small way when Gil touched her mother's face and the two of them smiled at each other.

"These are my grandfather's curls," her mother said. "He had blond ringlets in all his childhood photographs. Remember?"

"No," Elisabeth said. She couldn't recall ever seeing a photograph of her great-grandfather.

She wondered for the millionth time why her mother hadn't come sooner. Why she was the rare woman for whom meeting her first grandchild was not a high priority. Now that she was here, she seemed to love him.

Elisabeth's father intruded on the moment.

"Pleasure to meet you, young man," he said, like Gil was the new guy at the office. She half expected him to shake the baby's hand.

"Say hi to Gloria," he said to Elisabeth.

"Sorry, yes, hi," Elisabeth said. "Great to meet you."

It was, in fact, one of the more awkward situations she'd ever been in. Her parents meeting her firstborn child, the two of them in the same small space, but not together anymore. And this woman, a stranger, whom Elisabeth was expected to treat with grace, because she was an adult and the host of this gathering.

She offered them all coffee. When she went to the kitchen to fix it, her father-in-law ducked into the room, put his hands on her shoulders, and whispered, "Courage."

Elisabeth smiled.

"Thanks, George," she said.

They took their places in the living room like actors in a play—her father and Gloria on the sofa, thighs touching; Andrew's parents in matching armchairs, five feet apart. The rest of them sat on chairs pulled in from the dining room, all arranged around Gil, who was seated on a blanket on the floor, their little king. From time to time, one of them scooped him up, unable to resist, and everyone else glowed with jealousy.

Faye played the expert. She said things like, "Don't forget to support his head," and "He loves to be bounced—no, not that hard. Here, like this."

Elisabeth's mother kept sneaking glances at her father and Gloria. She had placed the bags from Saks around her chair as if building a wall between herself and anyone who might wish to do her harm. Eventually, she gave them to their intended recipients. A Burberry scarf for Andrew, leather driving gloves for Elisabeth. Gifts you might buy for someone you wanted to impress but had never met before.

George and Faye handed out scratch-off tickets tucked inside plain white envelopes. It was what they did every year, but now, for the first time, Elisabeth thought it had a whiff of desperation about it. This was precisely what was wrong with Christmas.

It was ridiculous that they felt obliged to spend any amount of money, given the state of their finances.

Her father kept saying, "Let Gloria hold the baby. Gloria hasn't had a turn."

Charlotte rarely looked up from her phone.

They brought Gil gifts meant for a three-year-old—plastic dinosaur figurines, a tricycle. The saving grace was how much he adored their adoration, giving his biggest, flirtiest smile to them all, and laughing when Charlotte reached into one of the Saks bags, pulled out a red bow, and stuck it to his shirt.

When all the packages had been opened, Elisabeth's father said to her mother, "Janey, how's California? I miss it sometimes."

"It's fine," she said. "I'd ask how Arizona is, but, well, it's Arizona."

"You used to beg me to send you to Canyon Ranch."

"For a weekend. But long term? Arizona is where sad old men go to die."

Elisabeth tensed, wondering if this was banter or the start of something. Over the years, watching them, anticipating their moods and moves, had become her addiction. It didn't go away because they were divorced.

But her father chuckled.

"Come visit," he said.

"Oh, Michael," her mother said.

Elisabeth thought there was a hint of warmth behind the words.

She looked from one parent to the other, and for a moment they were a family again. Not that they'd ever been a very good one, but still, it was something.

She had to squeeze her eyes shut to rid herself of this notion.

Her whole life, she had viewed their marriage as somehow above all others, even though it was worse than most. Her parents had cultivated this, acting as if suffering was the proof of a superior union.

It had been one of the great lessons of her life, learning that this was not so. She wondered now if she had learned it at all, or if it was something she knew, but could not fully believe.

"You may have a point about Arizona," he said. "But I suppose I am an old man, after all. We love it, don't we, Gloria?"

"I've been in Tucson since '83," Gloria said. "There hasn't been a morning since that I haven't hiked Sabino Canyon."

"How nice," said Elisabeth's mother, a woman who would no sooner hike than shave her head.

"We eat dinner under the stars almost every night," Gloria went on. "Which reminds me. Andrew, when will we get one of your famous grills? I can't think of a better place for one than Arizona. We have three hundred sunny days a year."

"Are you on the tourism board?" Elisabeth's mother asked. "Are you a paid spokesperson?"

Elisabeth and Charlotte locked eyes.

"We're still working on a prototype," Andrew said. "It will be ready soon, I hope. We've hit a few snags, but we're getting there."

"I read once that two-thirds of all inventors never see any profits," Elisabeth's father said, like it was merely an interesting factoid, nothing to do with them.

Andrew got up to check on the food, which he said would be ready soon.

Elisabeth took Gil into the den upstairs to nurse.

So far, the day had had its strained moments, but it was going better than she'd imagined. She attributed this to Gil. His presence was a balm. One thing everyone could agree on.

Once they had established a peaceful rhythm, Elisabeth closed her eyes.

She had almost drifted off to sleep when a voice said, "You're *still* doing that?"

Her mother.

Elisabeth kept her eyes shut.

"Yup."

"I'm having bad flashbacks just looking at you."

"Then don't look." Elisabeth opened her eyes. "What flashbacks? I didn't think you breastfed."

"Charlotte, no. But I breastfed you forever."

She found that she was happy to be wrong.

"You did?"

"Yes. For like, a month." Her mother paused. "You look wonderful, by the way. Your body just bounced right back."

Elisabeth bristled at this. She didn't respond, but her mother went on talking anyway.

"Of course, that's what usually happens the first time. It's like your body is willing to put up with all that once, but after the second time—forget it. You're a saggy balloon for life."

She lowered her voice to a whisper. "Tell me the truth—do you think your father looks bad? I think he does. That Gloria is positively fat. She must eat a dozen doughnuts while she's hiking every morning."

Elisabeth laughed in spite of herself. She noticed now that her mother had moved on from coffee to a glass of red wine.

It was true that Gloria was larger than she'd imagined. Not fat, really. But not toned and tightened. Not her father's usual type. Her face was weathered, tan and wrinkled from living in the desert for so long. Elisabeth didn't think she had any makeup on. Gloria's gray hair hung down past her shoulders in messy waves that looked like they had never encountered a blow-dryer. Maybe not even a brush.

Elisabeth figured all this probably bothered her mother more than if he had arrived with some gorgeous twenty-five-year-old. His interest in Gloria ran counter to her belief that beauty was all that mattered, that it could keep a woman safe.

"It must be hard for you, seeing Dad with her," Elisabeth said.

Her mother shrugged. "Exclusivity was never a privilege I enjoyed, even when we were married. Though it's true, I never had to spend Christmas with one of his mistresses before."

Elisabeth resisted the urge to say that Gloria wasn't his mistress. She was his partner. They had been together for two years.

"We'd better get back downstairs," she said.

"I'll take my friend, please," her mother said, once again reaching for Gil.

Elisabeth handed him over.

"Why didn't you come sooner to see him?" she said.

"I wasn't invited," her mother said.

"That's not true. You don't need an invitation. You never even expressed an interest."

"Well, I'm here now. Isn't that enough?"

It wasn't, but Elisabeth supposed it had to be.

When they descended the staircase, Charlotte stood in front of the open front door, hugging a guy with long blond dreadlocks. He wore shorts and a short-sleeved polo shirt, as if weather traveled with a person, rather than changing from place to place.

Elisabeth wanted to tell them to stop letting the heat out, or the cold air in, whichever it was.

She said, "You must be Davey. Welcome."

He smiled back.

"Mom, Davey is the mastermind behind all the gorgeous photos of me online," Charlotte said. "He has the patience of a saint."

Davey shrugged. "It's not hard, when your subject is as exquisite as this."

Elisabeth had never considered that there was someone else there, snapping the photo, in those seemingly solitary moments when Charlotte contemplated the meaning of life while standing on a deserted beach in revealing swimwear.

"You're right in time for lunch," Elisabeth said. "Hope you're hungry."

Andrew had made a ham and au gratin potatoes and string beans and rolls. He baked three pies for dessert. Everyone gathered in the dining room, where he had set the table the previous day, as his mother always did at Christmas.

"This looks so pretty," Faye said. "You two have outdone yourselves."

Elisabeth's own mother was staring down at her manicure.

In front of Faye, Elisabeth had often been embarrassed by their relative extravagance. Faye knew how much they'd spent on the bathroom renovation, because she came right out and asked Andrew, and then declared it a fortune. Every time they got a new piece of furniture, Faye asked where it was from, and no matter what the response, she said, "Oof. Pricey." They joked that they could tell her something came from a dumpster and her answer would remain the same.

Now Elisabeth sensed her mother assessing the house and finding it shabby, small. It could fit into a corner of the one she'd grown up in. In a way, she felt proud of this. Her mother had always wanted more than everyone else. Elisabeth was content with less.

"It feels funny, having Christmas somewhere other than our house for the first time since Andrew was born," Faye said. "Come to think of it, we'll never spend a holiday there again."

Her eyes watered.

Elisabeth wanted to say that this probably wasn't the case, but she figured Faye would rather not be reminded that the house had been on the market for three weeks, without a single offer.

"But," Faye said, sitting up straight, "old traditions must give way if new ones are to blossom."

It sounded like something from a fortune cookie.

"We thought it would be nice for the baby to spend his first Christmas at home," Andrew said, like this was news, when they had discussed it ten times already.

"Did you get a Christmas card from your aunt Betsy?" Faye said. "She asked me if you got it when we talked this morning."

"I think so?" Andrew said.

"Our Christmas card this year was a picture of us in front of a cactus, with a Santa hat on top," Gloria said. When no one reacted, she added, "Of the cactus."

Elisabeth had somehow missed that. She wondered if her father was supposed to have sent it, or if they'd been left off the list on purpose.

"Sam sent us a Christmas card," George said. "Wasn't that sweet."

"That's right," Elisabeth said. "She asked me for your address."

"Somebody raised that girl right," George said.

"Who's Sam?" said Elisabeth's father.

"Gil's babysitter," Elisabeth said.

"I heard from her over email two mornings back," George said.

"You did?"

This bugged her for some reason. Elisabeth had been trying to respect Sam's space. She hadn't reached out at all.

"Why are you emailing their babysitter?" Elisabeth's mother said.

"We're in a discussion group together," George said. "A civics thing. It was sort of related to that."

"How so?" said Elisabeth's mother, clearly thinking George

had a more sinister reason for emailing Sam. She looked directly at Faye.

"For a while now, Sam's been wanting to help the women who work in her campus dining hall," George said. "I guess one of them has a small child. And this young woman was more or less denied access to childcare at the college. She told Sam, and now Sam's more fired up than ever to do something."

"I didn't hear about that," Elisabeth said.

"It just happened," George said. "Right when Sam was about to head home for the holiday. She wants to write a letter to the president of the college. She really admires that woman."

"I know," Elisabeth said.

Out of curiosity, after hearing Sam lavish praise upon her, Elisabeth had looked Shirley Washington up online. The woman had been on the board of directors at Goldman Sachs during the financial crisis. She made half a million a year from it. She left in 2009, with seven million in stock, after being on the committee that doled out generous severance packages to criminal bankers. She was not the saint Sam imagined her to be.

Elisabeth was surprised that it hadn't become more of a campus scandal. From the stories published in the *Gazette* at the time, it seemed that alums of the college had demanded that Shirley Washington donate her ill-gotten earnings. But she didn't, nor did she ever publicly comment. Eventually, the story just went away. She gave a speech about the inherent selflessness of women, and the speech went viral. By the time Sam arrived at the college a year later, all signs of outrage had vanished.

"The babysitter is in a civics group with George?" Elisabeth's mother said now, to no one in particular.

"Yes. She's a fellow activist," George said.

"I didn't realize you were one," Elisabeth's father said.

"It's a fairly recent development. Have the kids told you about my theory? The Hollow Tree?"

"Dad," Andrew said, shaking his head. "No."

"What is it?" said Davey, who hadn't said anything since announcing that their house smelled just like his grandmother's.

"Take, for example, my wife, Faye," George said.

"Why me?" Faye said.

George raised a hand. "Let me say my piece. Faye's a grade school teacher, has been for forty years. The first time they did one of those active-shooter drills at the school, she called me crying after. She knew it wasn't real, but she said going through the motions almost killed her. Tell them, Faye."

"Dad, this isn't very Christmasy," Andrew said.

"No, tell us," Davey said.

"We had to practice squeezing into the supply closet and keeping still," Faye said matter-of-factly. "Then the children had to lie on the floor and pretend to be dead. I told them, 'This is how we'll stay safe if someone dangerous brings a gun to school.' They're seven."

"Shit," Davey said.

"Now the school does these drills every three months," George said. "They are as routine a part of Faye's schedule as lice checks or class-picture day. This is our country's solution to the problem of guns. Teachers hiding in a closet with all their kids. My wife as a human shield. Instead of following the money and going after the crooked lobbyists like they should."

"This is why I prefer to live on-island," Charlotte said. "It's a simple way of life. None of the corruption and violence that pollute America. No one we know cares about material things. We live for the authentic experience. Right, Davey?"

"I hadn't thought of it in those terms, but I think that's right," Davey said.

George nodded, but the look on his face said he wasn't buying it. Elisabeth recalled the epic rant he went on some months ago, when they described to him what an influencer was.

"Teaching on the whole is so much worse than it was when Faye started," George said now. "The young ones in her school have master's degrees, but they all work second jobs to get by. Once you could raise a family on a teacher's salary, but not anymore. The state of some of her students is pitiful. Faye has always had to supply a few each year with paper and pencils, but now it's toothbrushes, deodorant, sometimes money for the cafeteria."

"That's messed up," Davey said.

"Yes, it is," George said.

That bit of encouragement was all he needed to keep on.

"Even yesterday, Faye and I were at the grocery store checkout and this woman about our age zipped the bacon past the scanner, and Faye saw that it cost five dollars," he said. "So she said to the woman, 'I thought that was on sale.' The woman seemed offended. She said, 'It is on sale. That's a good price.' When we were walking out of there, what did you say to me, Faye?"

Faye shook her head. "I can't remember."

"You said, 'That used to be a job for teenagers. When did grown women start doing it? And what jobs do teenagers have now?'"

"Yeah," Davey said, nodding. "Hell yeah."

Elisabeth wondered if he was stoned.

"What does that have to do with guns?" Charlotte said.

"It has to do with the state this country is in," George said. "Those are two small examples of hundreds. Thousands. I look through the papers every day and cut out articles about how the average American is getting screwed. You look at them side by side, you start to see a pattern. This morning even, there's a story about people going bankrupt from medical bills on the front page of the *Gazette*. On Christmas Day. There's no end to it."

Elisabeth's father cocked his head to the side. She could tell he was thinking it over. She appreciated this, as she knew George looked up to him, in a way. Despite his many flaws, her father was successful, well educated, worldly.

"You sound a little nuts, George," he said at last.

"Dad!" Elisabeth said.

"Michael!" said both her mother and Gloria.

Poor George looked like he'd been hit from behind. Elisabeth sent him an apologetic smile. For years now, George had been the closest thing she had to a father figure. How dare her father treat him like that?

She thought of how George prominently displayed her two books on the coffee table in his living room, and how, after reading each of them, he had taken the time to write her a long letter detailing his favorite parts. Her father hadn't finished either book and didn't even feel bad about it, just said, *You know me, I like a thick presidential biography and that's about it.*

"George, have you tried the potatoes?" Gloria said. She lifted the serving dish and reached across the table to pass it to him.

Elisabeth watched her father watching Gloria.

The woman wore slacks and a silvery old-lady blouse, but you'd think she was Claudia Schiffer in a negligee the way he stared.

"Gloria is so good at taking care of a man," he said. "On our second date, I went to her place for dinner. She cooked. I'd thrown out my neck doing something or other. She gave me a two-hour massage. Best I've ever had."

Why he would choose this moment to say those words was anyone's guess.

"What did you do on your first date?" Davey asked. A question nobody else cared to hear the answer to.

Her father and Gloria exchanged a revolting look.

"Dinner and dancing," he said. "You know, Davey, women

like to be shown a great time. If you do that for them, they'll make you happy. It's as simple as that."

As if anything could be simple when you were telling the story of your new great love in front of the woman who, until recently, had been your wife for forty years.

"Young men today have no clue what they're doing," he went on. "They send a girl a text message. They can't fathom talking to her and asking her out on a date. You should try it, Davey. You'll have them lining up at the door. Women are starved for romance."

"He's right," Gloria said. "Elisabeth, hon, do you have any butter for these rolls?"

"Oh shoot, I forgot to put it out," Andrew said, rising.

Gloria stood up. "Keep your seat. I'll grab it."

She left the room. Elisabeth's father followed.

"Mom, are you okay?" Charlotte said.

Their mother nodded. "I could use more wine."

"I'll get it," Elisabeth said.

"Bring the bottle, will you?" her mother said.

Elisabeth took her mother's empty glass into the kitchen.

Her father and Gloria were locked in an embrace by the sink. She covered her eyes.

"Oops. Caught in the act." Gloria giggled.

"Dad," Elisabeth said. "Why are you giving Charlotte's boyfriend dating advice?"

"That guy?" her father said. "No way he's her boyfriend. Not her type. Don't you remember Matthew Callanan?"

Even three years later, he held Matthew up as proof that Charlotte was capable of making good choices.

"You mean the Matthew Callanan she left at the altar?"

"Don't exaggerate, Boo. She called it off months before the wedding."

"The invitations had already gone out," she said.

"I still think there's a solid chance those two will get back together," her father said. He laughed and shook his head, as if at an amusing anecdote he didn't feel the need to share.

"Matthew Callanan," he said. "Great kid."

The three of them went back to the dining room, where Faye was telling Davey about something called the new math.

Elisabeth felt sorry for her mother, who was watching her father and Gloria as they took their seats, his hand on the small of her back.

Charlotte was watching too.

Elisabeth met her eye. Her expression, she knew, would be enough to communicate her thoughts. When they were kids, Elisabeth used Charlotte as a sweet and adorable distraction, a buffer she could wedge between their parents when they fought.

"Try the conch, Daddy," Charlotte said, passing a tray of what looked like any other unidentifiable fried thing. "That's considered a delicacy on-island."

Their father took a few pieces with his fingers, ignoring the tongs that rested on the tray.

"I was wondering what the charge for three hundred bucks from Da Seafood Hut on my Amex was," he said. He popped a conch fritter into his mouth.

Elisabeth looked from him to Charlotte, slowly comprehending his meaning.

"Seriously?" she said to her sister.

"What?"

"What do you mean, *what*? You're taking money from him?"

"Who do you think owns that condo on the beach?" their father said.

"I thought it was a rental," Elisabeth said. Her body went rigid with anger. "Didn't you mention the rent, Charlotte?"

Charlotte fixed her face with an innocent look. "I might have said *rent* when I meant *HOA fees,* I don't know."

"Though to be fair, I pay those too," their father said, with a shit-eating grin.

"You have no shame," Elisabeth said. "You drained my bank account. And you didn't even need the money?"

"I told you I'm working on paying you back," Charlotte said. "I've said it a hundred times. But none of you believe in me. Do you? *Elisabeth's the writer, Charlotte can't be a writer too.* Well, guess what. I am. And I'm more successful than you'll ever be."

"What?" Elisabeth said, baffled as to where she should even begin.

"People go online every day to receive my wisdom," Charlotte said.

"They go online every day to hate-read your nonsense posts and to ogle you in a bikini," Elisabeth said. "When will you grow up and take responsibility for yourself?"

"Me?" Charlotte said. "I only came here because you needed someone to referee while you play house."

"Shut up," Elisabeth said. "You're just like them, you know."

"I know," Charlotte said. "At least I know it. You think you're not. That's the sad part."

"When have you sent her money?" Andrew said.

Andrew.

Elisabeth looked at him. His expression was confused, hurt.

"She drained the account?" he said.

"I'd say that's a bit of an exaggeration," Charlotte said. "And I was only worth helping as long as you thought I wasn't getting help from Dad. You were trying to manipulate me. You thought I was stupid."

"That's right, I did," Elisabeth said. "Turns out you're just a monster."

Her father raised his voice. "Elisabeth. Stop attacking her. Yes, I help Charlotte. I'm happy to. I've done the same for you."

"No, you haven't."

"Yes, I have."

"I haven't taken a penny from you since I was twenty-three."

"Be that as it may, you're supported. Who bought you your first apartment?" he said. "I don't recall you paying me back. No, you took that money and bought a better place in Brooklyn. As you should have. Then you sold that, and you took *that* money, and you bought this house. Or, I should say, I bought this house."

Shame coursed through her. Somehow she had never thought of this.

"Face it, Boo," he went on. "Someday I'm going to die, and all that dirty money will go to you whether you like it or not. If it makes you feel better to send Charlotte rent she doesn't need, go ahead. I'll get you back eventually."

Would a normal person perceive the threat in his tone, or would such a person wonder how she could be angry because someone gave her a pile of cash? But her father's money had been a weight around her neck. Elisabeth had been proud and relieved all these years that he couldn't lord it over her anymore, when, really, he could. He did.

She was mortified to be having this conversation in front of George and Faye. They stared down at their food as if they couldn't hear over it. Elisabeth appreciated the gesture so much.

She kept trying to meet Andrew's eye, but he wouldn't look at her. She was furious with herself for not telling him sooner. It was a secret she had managed to keep for two years, and then, in the presence of her family, she had undone it with one offhand remark.

"Honey," she said. "Say something. Please."

Andrew still looked confused. "So, all this time you thought Charlotte wasn't taking his money, *you've* been supporting her?"

"I wouldn't say supporting, exactly," Elisabeth said. "I've helped her for the last couple years while she waited for this sponsorship deal to happen. It was a loan."

"Not that diet pill thing," Davey said. "I talked her out of that months ago."

Everyone was silent for a long while.

Davey's words sank in. *Months ago.* Charlotte had known for that long that she wasn't going to pay Elisabeth back.

She felt sick. She would never see that money again.

Faye dipped her napkin into her water glass and started wiping Gil's face, as if she did this all the time.

"Don't these two make gorgeous babies?" she said, clearly hoping they could change the subject. "I keep asking when they're going to have another."

"Let's not rush it," Elisabeth's mother said.

"Why not?" Elisabeth said, offended, even though she had no intention of having another.

"Motherhood is making you tense," her mother said.

"It is," Charlotte agreed.

"Unbelievable," Elisabeth said. "Of course you'd find a way to turn this back on me."

She wanted to scream at all the members of her immediate family, each for a different reason. She wanted them out of her house.

"You know, I wondered earlier why we don't do holidays together more often," she said, in a manner that would sound calm, happy, if you didn't understand the words, just in case Gil was storing the memory. "But now I remember."

Andrew's chair scraped against the floor.

"I'm going out for a while," he said.

She followed him to the front door.

"I'll come with you," she said. "We should talk."

He just looked at her and shook his head.

Elisabeth returned to the dining room. She said, "It's time for all of you to go."

Andrew came home after an hour, but did not address her.

He took the baby and went upstairs.

Elisabeth started cleaning.

Andrew's pies sat uneaten on the counter. He had spent the night before layering a lattice crust onto the pecan pie. He made leaves out of dough and lined them up like a wreath around the edge. It looked perfect, like a picture from a magazine. The sight of it filled her with regret, despair.

After Gil was in bed, Andrew found her in the kitchen and said, "So."

Elisabeth was grateful for that single syllable, for the broken silence.

"Wasn't there three hundred thousand dollars in that account?" he said.

"Yes."

"You gave it all to her?"

"Almost."

"That money was from your book," Andrew said. "You worked hard for that."

She was amazed that he was thinking of her in this moment. She started to say so.

But Andrew wasn't finished.

"Do you know how difficult it was for me to ask you about taking some of that money for my parents?"

"You never asked me," she said quietly.

Immediately, she thought of her mother saying she hadn't come sooner because she wasn't invited. There were questions that shouldn't require asking.

"Bullshit," he said. "Sorry I never wrote up a formal request, but you knew I wanted it. You made me feel like an asshole for that."

"Andrew, no."

"Yes, you did. Now I understand why. I didn't think we kept things from each other."

"We don't," she said, even though she had.

Andrew inhaled, ran a hand through his hair. He looked like he was trying not to cry.

He had been wronged and she wanted so badly to comfort him.

"I wanted to tell you," she said. "I didn't know how. Sometimes it's just so hard to say certain things to each other, do you know what I mean?"

"Sure," he said. "Like how ever since we've moved here, you've been acting like a terrible snob, like you're better than the whole goddamn world because you lived in Brooklyn?"

"Jesus," she said. "That was kind of mean."

"We're not your parents," he said. "Learn to trust me, will you? Otherwise, what's the point of any of this?"

"Any of what?" she asked.

When Andrew didn't reply, she understood: he meant their life together, all of it.

Andrew said he was tired, that he was going to bed, even though it was only eight o'clock.

"I'll sleep in the den," he said.

"Seriously? Honey, I—"

She saw something flicker in his eye.

"What?" she said.

"When we were doing IVF, you wanted a second baby. Then all of a sudden, you didn't. Is this why? Because you thought you'd have to go on supporting Charlotte? You kept talking about how expensive another kid would be."

"Yes," she said, though it was another lie. What was wrong with her?

She needed Andrew on her side. He had never not been on her side before.

Elisabeth felt terrified, watching him climb the stairs, like he might not come back down.

She wondered what Charlotte was doing now. Elisabeth imagined her in some dive bar, crying to Davey about how unfair it was.

She looked at her Instagram for clues, not that Charlotte would ever share a photo from this place, with its gray skies and suburban houses and fully clothed people.

The latest picture had been posted twenty minutes earlier.

Charlotte in a metallic one-piece, the sides cut out to reveal her abs to such an extent that it was somehow more revealing than a string bikini would have been.

She was laughing, head thrown back in a solid impression of joy. It was nighttime. Behind her was a palm tree, strung with white Christmas lights. The text beneath said: *Merry + Bright xoxo @ Renaissance Island, Aruba.*

Where was Charlotte when she typed those words? In the passenger seat of her weird boyfriend's rental car? When was the picture taken? Elisabeth thought of typing a comment along the lines of *Don't believe her. She's full of shit. She's probably eating her feelings in a Taco Bell parking lot right now.*

Elisabeth took a deep breath. Her eyes landed on a silver gift bag on the kitchen counter. A bottle of wine poked out from the top. It was the present Sam brought on her last day of work.

She thought of Sam, how these rooms were usually theirs, and felt so tranquil.

Elisabeth imagined Sam presenting her mother with the portrait she'd made, her mother bursting into tears at the sight of it. She would be crying at the memory of her own mother, the woman in the painting, only because she was gone; the memories all happy ones.

She pictured Sam in the bosom of her good, solid family on Christmas. Eggnog—but not too much—and homemade cookies, and more cousins than you could count. Elisabeth was long past wishing she could have all that, since there was no point. But now she wished it for Gil.

The thought even made her a bit sad for her own mother, whose father died when she was twelve; her mother went into a psych ward and never came out. She was raised by indifferent relatives, bounced around until she turned eighteen. Treated by all, she had told them, like a burden.

Could Elisabeth blame her mother, without considering what she had been through? Without weighing the sins of the mother who came before her, and the one before that? She didn't want to carry it, but she had no choice. She was made up of women she'd never met. How to escape them and become something new?

She remembered a night, a year ago, when she was pregnant and walking home from a book party, thinking of what kind of mother she would be. She was too like her own mother, she feared, but softer edged. In her mother's stories of a younger self, she was soft too. Maybe Elisabeth needed to try to be the person her mother would have become had her life not been so harsh.

That's what she'd been thinking then.

Now, she looked again at the gift bag on the counter. She went toward it, as if toward the light.

In the morning, she woke up with a headache. She had had too much of Sam's wine before bed. Elisabeth had thought that maybe Andrew would be there when she got upstairs, but he had been serious about sleeping in the den. For the first time ever, they slept in separate rooms under the same roof. There was something so alarming about it. That after ten years, a shift like that could occur.

When she got to the kitchen, Andrew was already there, washing dishes.

"Hi," he said.

She tried to assess his tone. Neutral, she decided.

But when she attempted a joke and said, "I guess the upside of everyone leaving early is that we get to have pie for breakfast," he did not laugh, or even glance up at her.

Elisabeth's eyes landed on the empty French press on the counter, and she knew the anger he felt had not passed. Of course it hadn't.

It was the first morning since they moved here that Andrew hadn't made her coffee. She thought this was the equivalent of another man slapping her across the face.

Another first, then: for once, Elisabeth wished they could be more like her parents had been when she was young. That they could scream and throw things and make vicious accusations and come right up to the edge of disaster, but then turn back.

The cold shoulder, the unknown, felt worse than anything he might say.

13

December 26

1:04 PM

Dear Sam,

Merry Christmas, a day late. Did your mother love the painting? I keep imagining her unwrapping it and bursting into tears. I ran into a professor of yours at a party last week (Christopher . . . something). We were both going on and on about how talented you are.

Hope your family had a great holiday. Ours was a shit show. But after everyone left last night, I finally opened your present for Gil. It was the perfect thing. xx E

P.S. You did NOT have to get that bottle of wine for Andrew and me. You're too sweet. It definitely came in handy last night . . .

December 26

7:49 PM

Hello from Logan Airport!

So sorry to hear about your Christmas. What happened???

Yes, my mom loved the painting. Yes, she cried. Ha ha. I think you must mean Christopher Gillis, and I'm shocked he said nice things about me (or even knows who I am!).

I've had him in class twice, but he never seemed to notice me. He has a reputation for being kind of a creep. There are always rumors about him and some student.

I'm glad you liked the Mozart cube! I hope the wine tasted okay. It's definitely not as nice as what you're used to. I LOVE the sweater you gave me, and I've been wearing it constantly, as my dad is one of those dads who refuses to turn the heat up above 65, even when the temperature is below freezing.

I'll see Clive in just a few hours! I'm excited. Though every time we meet again it's almost like I don't know him. I get all nervous and tongue-tied. Then I get over it. Wish we could somehow fast-forward to the getting over it part.

Sam

December 27
2:01 AM

S—

Drifting off to sleep, but wanted to say quickly—the wine was great! Thanks again! Safe travels. xx E

P.S. I'm jealous of your family. They sound so nice and NORMAL.

December 27
9:37 PM

You're funny. My family IS pretty nice and normal, I guess. Possibly too normal? They just expect everyone to follow a certain script. No one wants to hear about Clive, which makes me feel bad. My cousin brought some guy she's been dating for three weeks home for Christmas, and everyone was falling all over him because he goes to Notre Dame.

Clive wanted us to spend Christmas together, but I couldn't picture him at my parents' house, opening presents in the morning with the rest of us. And I didn't want to be apart from my family.

I wish I cared less what they think/what people think of me in general. My sister Caitlin is thirteen and she's so much more confident than I will ever be. She still climbs into my mother's lap, without worrying what anyone will say. She does that, AND she dyed the tips of her hair hot pink. She's an amazing artist. Much better than I am.

I made it to England! Clive's family has an annual Boxing Day celebration at his mother's house in the country. This year they pushed it back a day so I could attend, which was nice, but I wished they hadn't, as I would have rather spent my first full day here alone with him.

During lunch, I tried to cut into an undercooked carrot and sent it shooting across his mother's dining room! She definitely saw, as did Clive, and his brother. The worst part was no one said anything. I want to die just thinking about it.

Our niece and nephew, Freddy and Sophie, make everything better. I know they're not technically my niece and nephew yet, but they call me Auntie Sam. When I'm here, we spend as much time together as we can. They're family now. It amazes me that you can go somewhere new and a whole life will grow up around you.

Hope you've recovered some from Christmas,
Sam

December 28
7:18 AM

I laughed out loud while reading about the flying carrot. Then I remembered it hours later, and started laughing all over again. No one said anything?? It would have been so much better if somebody made a joke! Dying to know: Did you retrieve the carrot, or leave it there?

They say in-laws and money are the two things couples fight about most. I myself am currently embroiled in battles on both fronts. Aren't relationships fun? xx E

P.S. I somehow doubt your 13-year-old sister is a better artist than you are. You're too modest.

December 31
10:04 AM

Definitely just left the carrot. It's probably still there, on the rug beside the china cabinet, a monument to my awkwardness.

Happy New Year to you guys! Clive and I are having dinner at our favorite Indian place, and then we're supposed to meet up with his friends at a club. (Ugh. He thinks they are my friends too, and that they'll all be dying to see me. False, but sweet of him, I guess.) Today we walked around the city, and had so much fun. I love London. Didn't realize how much I missed it.

January 4
4:51 PM

Hi there,

Happy New Year! Counting down the days until you get back. Gil is a madman right now. Sam, he's crawling. He is into EVERYTHING. I've called Poison Control twice in the past three days. (He ate some diaper cream, and then a handful of Miracle-Gro from that potted plant in the living room.) Soon I think they'll be able to recognize me by my voice.

I took him to the art museum yesterday. They had this

gorgeous collection of Madonna and Child paintings. It got me thinking that this could be a great project for the piece I want to commission from you. Featuring Gil as the child. And maybe, if you don't think it's too strange, YOU as the Madonna. You have that gorgeous curvy figure that I am sadly lacking. Since you worked off of a photo for the piece you made for your mom, I thought maybe I could snap some shots of you holding Gil in that classic pose. Also, what if the finished Madonna looks like a blend of the two of us, you and me? It feels fitting, since we've cared for this baby together in his first year of life. Andrew thinks it's super bizarre of me to ask you this, but you're an artist, so I think you'll get it. Let me know. xx E

January 5
2:19 PM

I love that idea. Let's do it! Also. Exciting news. I was in Waterstone's yesterday and they had a copy of your first book. The UK edition! I had to buy it, of course. I told the guy at the checkout that I know you, ha! I have read 100 pages and I'm hooked. You're so talented. Now I feel proud knowing that while I'm at your house reading *Where's Spot?* for the fourteenth time in a row to your adorable baby, you're writing your next masterpiece.

Going to keep reading until Clive gets home from work. I just woke up from an afternoon nap. At school, I nap every day. Usually right before dinner. It's the best. I appreciate it so much now because I won't be able to do it much longer. Soon I'll have a job, and adult responsibilities. I feel like I have to savor my freedom, since I know it can't last.

January 6
7:02 AM

Ahh yes, I know that feeling. When I was pregnant with Gil, my doctor's office was a few blocks from Central Park. After every appointment, I'd go there and sit on a bench by the sailboat pond and marvel at how no one in the world knew or cared where I was. A few more months and I would never be truly unaccountable again.

Thanks for the kind words, but Sam, this is an order—never ever pay for one of my books. I will give you copies if you want them. Don't be too proud of me, either. That masterpiece-in-progress you mentioned is usually a blank page. Still waiting for my brain to return in full. I wonder if it ever will . . . xx E

January 12
5:57 AM

Hi Elisabeth,

I hope you don't mind, but I'm sitting here crying, the only one in the flat awake, and I've decided you're the best person to ask about this. None of my friends have the life experience to understand. I was up all night. I'm so upset. At dinner last night, Clive asked if I wanted to start thinking about where in the city we should live next fall. I sort of clammed up, and then I felt bad. I felt all this pressure barreling down on me, even though this IS what I want. Then, later, I got an email from school letting me know that I'm being considered for Phi Beta Kappa, but in order to be eligible, I need to take a classical language class. Latin or ancient Greek! I thought I'd met all my requirements already. So I was stressing out, because language classes at the college meet EVERY DAY. Which would mean there'd be no way I could visit Clive for a long weekend next semester. (Don't worry, it wouldn't affect my work schedule—language classes meet early in the morning!) That started a fight between Clive and me. He said I'm achievement obsessed, that it's very American of me, and kind of silly, to want this title. He told me not to be so swotty, whatever that means. He's probably right. I don't even know why I want it.

How did you know Andrew was the one? That you were ready to cut off all other possibilities in order to pursue that relationship fully? Feel free to ignore me if this is too personal a question, or if you're too busy. Thanks for any words of wisdom. Sam

P.S. Give Gil a kiss for me. I can't believe he's crawling!

January 12
1:19 AM

Dear Sam,

Good thing I'm an insomniac and can thus reply instantaneously. I've had so many nights like the one you've just been through. Wish I could give you a hug. We are both the sort of people, I think, who always want to do the right thing. But in matters of the heart, it's not always clear what the right thing is. How did I know A was the one? I'm not totally sure I did, but I was at that point in my life when I was ready to make the leap. So much of this stuff is about timing, which sounds dreadfully practical, but it's true. Has to be the right guy AND the right time. Does that make sense? I know how painful these things can be, but you have so much ahead of you, truly. I'm here if you want to talk, anytime. xx E

P.S. PBK is a huge deal. I'm proud of you. You're so close.

January 16
10:08 AM

Dear Elisabeth,

Sorry I took a few days to respond. Our Internet here went out, so I had to wait until I could sneak off to the library. Things are better. Clive and I had a big talk. He totally gets it. I feel ready to make the leap, as you said. I guess no one can ever feel 100% sure, can they? I promised Clive that I will move back to London for good as soon as I have my diploma. We can work out the details then. We picked out dish towels for our future place today at this cool shop called Kitschen Sink. (I'm excited about dish towels! Could I be a bigger nerd?)

I told my adviser that I'm not going to take the extra language class. I don't care that much about Phi Beta Kappa. There wouldn't be any guarantee that I'd get it, even if I did take the class. I feel a huge sense of relief now that that's settled.

Please give my love to Andrew and to George, and especially to Gil. I miss him! I hope he remembers me when I get back. Can't wait to see you all.

Love, Sam

14

Sam

THE ARRIVAL OF A PACKAGE in the campus mail was signified by a bright green slip of paper in your mailbox. To claim it, you had to wait in line at the window and present the green slip to the student working on the other side. Despite all knowledge to the contrary, whenever Sam twisted her mailbox key and opened the door to find such a notice, she imagined the package would be something incredible, life altering. Before meeting Clive, she dreamed of flowers from her ex-boyfriend, and a card begging her to take him back. Now she pictured Clive surprising her with an extravagant gift he could never afford—a designer dress; a first-class ticket on a flight to Morocco, leaving that afternoon.

She always opened a package as soon as she reached the post office lobby, unable to wait for the privacy of her room. Inevitably, it contained something underwhelming, like a jumbo bag of cough drops her grandmother bought two-for-one at Walgreens, sending one to Sam and the other to her brother.

On Valentine's Day, before she even opened her eyes, Sam told herself not to expect anything. Clive was arriving on Wednesday, four days from now. It would make no sense for him to have something delivered today. Anyway, he thought Valentine's Day was a manufactured holiday, designed to put money in the pockets of florists and greeting card companies.

He sent her two or three love letters a week. Since they shared their day-to-day on the telephone and over Skype, the letters were mostly declarations of how much he adored her and missed her, coupled with detailed descriptions of what he'd like to do to her were she standing in front of him. Reading them, Sam felt a rush, and yet she could not help playing out a fantasy in which she died prematurely and her grieving mother discovered the words Clive had written, causing her to die also, of mortification.

Sam kept the letters stacked in the drawer of her nightstand, the blue airmail stickers in the upper-left corner giving her a boost whenever she saw them.

But there would be no letter today, if she knew Clive. He had strong opinions. When it came to Valentine's Day, he said he refused to participate in anything that cynical masquerading as romance.

Today, Sam told herself, would be a Saturday like any other. In the morning, she went to the art building to work. In the dining hall at lunch, there were heart-shaped sugar cookies dyed a pale pink and a giant bowl of conversation hearts. When Sam went upstairs after she ate, she found that Isabella had placed three of them on her pillow:

OH BABY
HOT STUFF
CRAZY 4 U

In the afternoon, she procrastinated; she watched TV.

She avoided the mail until five, when her curiosity got the best of her.

On the off chance Clive *had* sent something, she didn't want to miss it, not mention it, and potentially hurt his feelings.

Sam felt a burst of elation upon seeing a green slip in her box, like she had unwrapped a Wonka bar to find a Golden Ticket. The line at the window was twice as long as usual. She watched each student present her slip and walk off with a vase of red roses or a large box wrapped in brown paper.

There was a charge in the air, not unlike the one that emerged in grade school when a second-tier holiday like this rolled around. All those silent expectations knocking up against one another, creating a new kind of energy. It was the case even though campus on this day could be divided into the small faction of women who had dates in town and the far greater number who would be attending *The Vagina Monologues*. Sam had agreed to babysit.

To pass the time in line, she read the notices on the classifieds board. A new club called Knitting for Social Justice was meeting every Tuesday in Reynolds House; a Take Back the Night vigil would be held on the quad this coming Thursday. There were index cards tacked up by people seeking rides to New York City or Philadelphia or to the airport. Sam was grateful that George had offered to take her to get Clive on Wednesday.

One notice stood out from the rest. It was printed on neon-orange paper, and at the top were the words WAKE UP. Sam made eye contact with the woman behind her in line, to indicate that she'd be right back. She went closer, so she could read the smaller print on the page. It was a letter to the student body, signed by seventy-five adjunct professors from various departments, warning that if working conditions didn't improve, they would soon boycott.

Apparently only tenured professors were making more than minimum wage and receiving benefits. Sam thought of all the instructors she'd had here. She couldn't say who had tenure and who didn't. Except for a few old guys who definitely had it and, as a result, completely phoned it in in the classroom.

She thought right away of the Hollow Tree. She snapped a picture of the letter with her phone to show George the next time they met.

Elisabeth and Andrew believed George was abnormally obsessed with the Hollow Tree, but Sam agreed with him that once you started looking, you saw examples of it everywhere. And as George said, the terrible treatment was never going to stop until the people demanded it.

It was what had inspired Sam to write a plea of her own.

On the last day of the semester, just before she went home, Sam found Gaby crying to Maria in the dining hall. Gaby wiped the tears away when she saw Sam there, but when Sam asked if she was okay, Gaby told her that the cousin who watched her daughter while she worked had found a job and couldn't take care of Josie anymore.

"Day care is so expensive," Gaby said. "I'll never be able to move out of my mother's place if I have to pay for it."

"What about the College Children's Center?" Sam said. "My friend Rosa works there part-time. It's supposed to be really good."

Maria and Gaby gave her identical looks.

"What?" Sam said.

"That's not for support staff, it's for professors," Maria said.

"Are you sure?" Sam said.

"Technically it's open to everyone. But the place costs a fortune," Gaby said.

"I thought it was free if you worked here," Sam said.

She remembered an English professor who talked about it once in class, how she had chosen to take her position because the college was so family-friendly.

"Uhh, no," Gaby said. "It's only free to professors who are full-time."

"So it's free for the highest-paid people and no one else?" Sam said.

"Exactly. Plus, it opens for the day at eight, no early drop-off. But everyone in housekeeping and dining has to be at work by six-thirty. Get it? That's not by accident."

"Maybe I could help you in the mornings," Sam said, even as she cringed at the thought of being up that early. "I could watch Josie from the time you get here and walk her to the Children's Center when it opens."

"No," Maria said. "She'll figure something out."

The more Sam thought of the situation, the angrier it made her. She kept recalling the sight of Gaby, usually so tough and composed, reduced to tears. There had to be something she could do.

On the bus ride home for Christmas break, an idea came to her. Sam searched for a notebook in her bag and couldn't find one. The only paper she had was the novel Clive had given her, *Angel*, which she had been carrying around for weeks and still hadn't read. Sam sketched out the first draft of a letter to President Washington inside the back cover. She imagined sending it to the editors of the college paper, asking them to print it.

By the time her dad and her sister Caitlin arrived to pick her up at South Station, she had talked herself out of it. But a week later, Gaby was still on her mind. Sam emailed George and told him what had happened, and that she wanted to do something, a letter to the paper, maybe. George wrote back right away. He suggested that she wait until the start of the semester, and then circulate her letter, getting as many student signatures as possible.

On the plane to London, Sam tried to read *Angel* and found herself reading what she'd written instead. It was actually pretty good. She made adjustments, crossing out bits about Gaby that seemed too personal, trying to shorten and strengthen her sentences.

When she read it to Clive and asked if she was being too harsh, he said, "I don't think you're being harsh enough. Don't hold back. Let her know you're watching."

One day, while Clive was out giving a tour of the Tower of London, she texted Gaby. *Have you figured out day care for Josie yet?*

Gaby replied, *Ugh, yes. So expensive.*

Sam logged on to her laptop and cued up President Washington's speech, the one that made her apply to the college in the first place. When her face loaded on the screen, it was like seeing a friend, or a beloved wise aunt.

If women ran the world, they wouldn't be afraid to speak truth to power, she said. *If women ran the world, they would use power not for personal gain, but to lift up the voices of the powerless.*

By the time the video ended, Sam was certain that not only should she send the letter, but that President Washington would want her to. She understood why George had suggested getting signatures. But there wasn't time. And George didn't know her peer group—everyone would have input, changes, ideas. It wouldn't be as easy as just asking them to add their names.

Sam fiddled with the letter over the course of that day and the next. She stayed up working until three in the morning. In the end, she included everything: How Barney Reardon had decreased their pay, had made their insurance worse to the point where they couldn't even afford to use it. How the kitchen staff kept the whole college running, and yet were treated as less than. She wrote about these women who worked more than full-time having to take food home to feed their families, having to sell students' trash to keep their lights on. She wrote that it was massively unfair for an institution to brag about being family-friendly while ignoring some people's children and embracing others'.

When it was finally done, Sam emailed the letter right away, before she lost her nerve. She didn't sign her name in the end. She even went so far as to create a fake email account. She received a message back from an editor the next morning, saying the *Collegian* would be running the letter in February, when school was back in session.

At some point each day now, Sam checked. The month was half over and the letter had yet to appear. Whenever she saw her friends in the kitchen, she felt a rush of excitement, as if she were planning a surprise party that they would soon find out about. She imagined students picketing on their behalf, demanding change.

Sam resumed her place in the post office line.

The package turned out to be from her father.

She should have known. Every year since she could remember, he had given her a Disney princess valentine. He still did it now, in an ironic way. This year's card, like all of them, was hot pink. Belle on the front wearing a yellow ball gown, holding a book, beneath the words *Daughter: Someday You'll Be Anything You Want!*

Her father had also sent a large red satin box of chocolates, heart shaped, with a flimsy fake flower attached.

Sam typed out a text to Isabella: *Not even a card from Clive* ☹.

Instead of hitting send, though, she deleted it, watching the letters disappear one by one as she tapped her finger on the screen.

She took a picture of the card and sent it to the group text she had with her siblings. There was a separate thread that included their parents, but this one was reserved for making fun of or otherwise discussing them behind their backs.

A text came back from her brother, Brendan, not to the group. Only to her.

Mom let it slip that Dad hasn't had a single new project since August. She is freaking out. She's taking all these extra shifts and basically working around the clock. I'm worried.

Their father's business was unpredictable. Good years, and bad. The bad ones never got easier or less surprising when they came.

Caitlin was too young for this sort of information. Sam wasn't sure why Brendan hadn't included Molly, why he chose to single her out with the news. Because she was the oldest, she supposed.

Oh no, she wrote back.

We need to help, he wrote.

How?

Maybe we should each set a little money aside in case things don't get better soon.

Sam would never say what she was thinking out loud. It made her feel like a selfish jerk. But—why was this their job? All her friends had their parents' fortunes thrown at them. The idea of having to help their parents, reversing those roles, never would have occurred to any of them. Why, in her family, was it always about not having enough?

Her second thought was of her father, and the fact that he had thought of her even in a stressful moment, and sent his usual valentine as if nothing was wrong. He would never burden her with his struggles. Nor, she knew, would he ever accept a penny from his children.

She hoped Brendan was overreacting.

Okay, she texted back. *I'll try. Let me know if you hear more.*

Sam texted her dad then. *Love you, Daddy. Thanks for the card and the candy. Happy Valentine's Day! Miss you.*

She put her phone in her bag.

She was due at Elisabeth's in forty minutes. An awkward amount of time. If she went back to the dorm, she would end up chatting in the hall, accomplishing nothing. She went to the library instead.

Once inside the heavy front door, Sam saw Julian, the Mollusk, with whom she'd had that brief semi-romance two years ago. He probably didn't think of her anymore. He was leaning against the circulation desk, talking to some girl.

But still, Sam ducked into the stairwell to avoid him.

On the wall hung a poster for an upcoming job fair. GRADUA-TION IS THREE MONTHS AWAY! THEN WHAT???

She knew the date, but still this shocked her. Three months until college was over.

Before winter break, few of her friends had jobs lined up for next year. Isabella had interned at J.P. Morgan the previous summer and was offered a job there in the fall. But most of them didn't know what they would do next.

While she was home over break, most people, hearing that Sam was a senior, only had that one question. It had become exhausting. It was like the way someone might ask a child what he planned to be for Halloween because it was October and then, in December, ask what he wanted for Christmas.

Recruiters had flooded the campus in recent weeks. Lexi had two offers from book publishers, one in marketing, one in editorial; Shannon accepted a position with a start-up in San Francisco. Several friends had begun to hear back from graduate programs. Suddenly it seemed like only Sam was without a plan.

She went to a résumé workshop at the Career Development Office, expecting the woman there to be impressed, imagining that she might say, *I know of a great position for you!*

The woman's only feedback was that Sam should use a clearer font and not include her GPA.

"But my GPA is the only impressive thing about me," Sam said.

"It's not considered mature or professional to include one's GPA," the woman said, sounding robotic, as if she'd said it a thousand times before, which she probably had.

Sam wondered then why she'd been made to care so much about a number no one would ever know.

"It's an extremely competitive job market," the woman said. "It's important to do things the right way."

In that moment, Sam sank deep into the dream of marrying Clive and moving to the country and not needing to compete at all. She looked at the woman, so smug, and thought with pleasure that there was another way, which she knew nothing about.

Now, red heart-shaped box tucked under one arm, Sam took the stairs straight to the library's basement. It was empty, as usual. She selected a carrel in a corner and unzipped her backpack, pulling out her copy of *Villette*.

The box of chocolates sat on the desk in front of her. Sam looked away. She switched on the lamp and opened the book. But she had no willpower. Before she read a word, she lifted the lid. Inside was a guide to what each chocolate contained.

She would eat one piece now, and one after dinner. The rest she would offer to her friends.

Sam began with the best: a ganache-filled square, soft and easy in her mouth, melting quickly away. There were two others of the same variety. She ate them before moving on to the caramels, jaw aching as she chewed each one like a savage. Next, she nibbled the three flat crispy disks stacked inside a single ruffled wax-paper cup. Then the coconut, which she only half liked.

When the box contained nothing but undesirables—two chocolates with gooey pink centers and a foil-wrapped cherry—Sam sat back, breathed in. It would be better to leave them. At least then she could say she hadn't eaten the entire thing.

On the other hand, maybe it was best to take the whole heart down at once and start with a clean slate tomorrow.

Sam ate the last few pieces, leaving part of a pink fluffy one, in a nod to restraint. On her way out of the library, she threw the heart-shaped box in the trash.

She immediately felt remorseful. When she was a child and her father gave her a box like that, she saw it as a thing of beauty and treated it as sacred. She kept those boxes on display in her bedroom, lined up side by side on the top shelf of her bookcase.

She could see them now—red and pink, foil wrapped or satin, but for one, her favorite, which was covered in a soft fabric printed with daisies. Sam thought she might cry. She wished more than anything to be that child again. Someone for whom all decisions were made, and love was background noise; uneventful, absolute.

Elisabeth wore an emerald-green wrap dress and tall black boots. Her hair, which was usually pulled back, had been blown out and fell in soft waves at her shoulders.

"You look pretty," Sam said.

They stood in the front hall. Elisabeth fastened the back onto a gold earring in the shape of a knot. Sam thought it seemed too preppy for her. She usually wore silver, something dangly and antique.

Elisabeth acted embarrassed by the compliment.

"I don't even know why we're going out," she said. "A prix fixe dinner. Valentine's Day is such a scam."

"That's what Clive says."

Elisabeth widened her eyes. "Oh! What did he get you?"

Sam was saved from having to answer by Andrew, coming down the stairs in a crisp white oxford shirt and navy pants.

"Baby's fast asleep. We ordered you pizza," he said. "It's in there on the counter whenever you want it."

Sam felt ill from all the chocolate. She wondered if pizza would make it better or worse.

When they were gone, she spotted a blue gift box on the table in the hall. It contained another box inside, this one covered in velvet. Sam lifted it out and opened the hinge. Empty.

The gold earrings. Andrew must have given them to Elisabeth tonight.

There was a card beneath the box. Sam slipped it out of its envelope. The card was made to look old, like a greeting from Victorian times: Cupid shooting a red heart from his bow, and the words *I Love You* floating above on a white banner.

Inside, Andrew had only written *Love, A.*

Ever since she got back from winter break, Sam had sensed that something was off with Andrew. She had joined them for Sunday dinner the past two weekends. Both times, he barely spoke a word to Elisabeth. To Sam, he was his usual friendly self. But it almost seemed as if he couldn't see his wife across the table. She'd make a comment or praise his cooking, and Andrew wouldn't look up.

Tonight things seemed more normal between him and Elisabeth. She thought so, anyway.

Sam went to the kitchen and put two slices of pizza on a plate. She ate them in quick succession, standing in front of the window that looked out on the backyard, even though it was too dark to see anything.

Clive called her cell at seven.

"I'm off to bed," he said. "I started packing tonight. I can't wait to see you."

"Me too," Sam said.

She had last seen him in London over winter break. A good trip overall, except that he kept pressuring her to decide things she didn't feel ready to decide. In the end, she felt bad about this. She wanted to be with him. That was all that mattered.

But now Sam was worried about the weekend in New York City, which had seemed like a good idea at the time.

The moment she announced a problem, Elisabeth wanted to solve it. When Sam said casually, in the course of a conversation about Clive's upcoming visit, that she wished she could take him somewhere instead of being stuck on campus the entire time, Elisabeth said, "We're going to the city the weekend after he gets here. Come with us! We can give you guys a ride."

She suggested that they leave on Saturday morning. In exchange for the ride, Sam and Clive would watch Gil that first night, and then they'd all do their own thing until Monday evening, at which point they would drive back. Two weeks ago, Sam thought it sounded like fun, and Clive said he was game.

But now the thought of them in the car for all those hours made her nervous. What would they talk about? What would they think of him?

Over break, she and Elisabeth had exchanged so many emails, said things that they probably wouldn't have if they were in the same room. It had brought them closer, and yet when Sam thought of some of the things she'd said about Clive, she winced.

She kept thinking about a weekend last summer, when the two of them went to Liverpool and stayed in a house borrowed from friends of Clive's who were on vacation in Amsterdam. Hand in hand, they walked through Sefton Park, where, Clive said, in springtime, so many daffodils bloomed that they completely obscured the grass. They ate meat pies and walked to the Beatles museum, where Sam bought a postcard to send home to her dad. They pretended that house was their own, lying on the couch in their underwear, making dinner together in the sleek kitchen, all marble and steel. She wanted to return to that moment, that feeling, now.

Sam unloaded the dishwasher, and then went upstairs. She checked on Gil even though she could tell from the video monitor that he was asleep. She straightened the den, stacking magazines into a neat pile, folding the soft knitted blanket someone had tossed down on the ottoman.

She was watching her third episode of *The Office* when Isabella texted a photo of an enormous bicep tattooed with the letter *I* in what looked like calligraphy.

V-Day with the stripper's assistant! she wrote.

What is that? Sam replied.

He got my initial tattooed on him!

Why???

Because he loooooves me? Because we had tequila shots and the tattoo parlor was having a sale?

Of all the things a person might buy because it was on sale, a tattoo had to be the dumbest.

Sam wondered if Isabella would bring him back to the dorm again tonight. Their first meeting had been three months ago. Since then, they hadn't seen each other, besides that one time when he came over with his gross friends. They exchanged dirty text messages a few times a week. Valentine's Day seemed a strange choice for their first real date, but then the entire situation was strange.

When Sam scrolled through Instagram on her phone later, she saw that Isabella had posted the bicep picture. Everyone was demanding to know whose arm that was. Sam knew Isabella must be lapping up the attention.

Andrew and Elisabeth got home after ten. Elisabeth seemed tipsy. She kept giggling. She was talking faster than usual. She hugged Sam good night.

Halfway back to the dorm, Sam reached into her purse for her keys, and her hand landed on a foil pack of birth control pills, reminding her that she had forgotten to take one at the usual time, after dinner.

She popped the day's pill from the package. As she lifted it to her mouth, it fell onto the sidewalk. Sam got down on her knees and felt around. The sky was so dark, it seemed like the middle of the night. The three closest streetlights had been burned out for weeks.

She took off her gloves. She turned on the flashlight on her phone and held it, hand shaking, over the concrete. No sign of the pill. She said a Hail Mary in her head, and then another, running her hand through the patch of dead grass that separated the sidewalk from the street. The earth was frozen, hard to the touch.

Finally, she felt something small and solid. She managed to roll the pill under her finger so that, by the time she picked it up, it was smeared with dirt. She imagined all the things it might have come into contact with—a dog might have just peed there, and she'd never know.

Sam swallowed the pill down, overcome with relief.

When she had returned from England at the end of August, her parents threw her a big welcome-home party. The morning of, Sam woke up and vomited all over her bedsheets. It was too late to cancel. Her mother quarantined her in her bedroom and put the guests in the backyard. She alternated between ferrying food and drinks to them, and checking on Sam.

At some point, she called the pediatrician.

"Dr. Bloom is on the phone," her mother said. "She's asking if you ate anything funny."

"Not that I can think of."

"She says no," her mother said into the phone. "Hold on. Any changes to your routine? New medications? No, right?"

"I started taking the pill about a month ago," Sam said.

She hadn't thought this would come as a shock. But her mother's expression told her otherwise. She left the room and slammed the door, and didn't come back until the last guest had gone home.

The following days, before she returned to campus, were hard. Sam kept bumping up against her parents, like they didn't know how to be in one another's presence anymore. She missed

Clive. She couldn't believe she had lived with him, talked about marriage, and yet here she was, sleeping in her childhood bedroom, surrounded by dolls and snow globes. She wondered if her mother was thinking of how she had encouraged Sam's original trip to London, the one during which she met Clive, and wishing she hadn't.

To cheer her up, Sam's father pressed all the paintings she'd sent home to him into an album.

Your memories, he said.

Sam had cried, flipping through. Each picture of her former life was like a dead butterfly, wings pinned to the page.

On Tuesday night, Sam set her alarm so that she was up early the next day, an hour before the morning rush in the bathroom. She spent a long time in the shower, shaving her legs and underarms, an activity she skipped most of the time. She used something called a ten-minute hair mask that Isabella said was the best product money could buy and exfoliated her entire body with a cocoa-butter scrub she had spotted in someone's shower caddy a week ago and determined to borrow for Clive's arrival.

Afterward, Sam put on makeup for the first time since she returned from London last month. She blew out her hair. She wore a dress he liked, black, printed with purple and orange flowers. It pulled her in at the waist and landed just above her knee.

Once she was ready, she went downstairs. There were only a few students in the dining hall. In half an hour, the room would be packed, voices echoing against the high ceiling. But now there was a hush. The ones who ate this early ate alone, reading thick textbooks or staring at their phones.

Sam passed the buffet. The scrambled eggs hadn't been touched. The tower of shiny green apples was as yet undisturbed.

She pushed the swinging door into the kitchen, where Maria, Delmi, and Gaby were at work.

Maria opened her eyes wide.

"Check out the movie star," she said.

She spun Sam around in a circle.

The others oohed approvingly.

"Good dress," Gaby said.

"Thanks," Sam said.

She went to the pantry where the coffee maker lived. She poured herself a cup.

Maria followed her. She licked the palm of her hand and rubbed it against Sam's hair.

"There," she said. "A piece was sticking up. Listen, we got a request for workers for a big alumnae dinner, the Thursday before graduation. Pays time and a half. Gaby's doing it. Should I sign you up?"

"Sure," Sam said. "Thanks."

After sophomore year, she stuck around when the spring semester ended to earn extra money. She waited tables at reunion dinners each night and helped make sandwiches and snickerdoodles for the senior brown-bag picnic out on the soccer field. The recently vacated dorm rooms were occupied by old ladies in flannel nightgowns who wanted to chat with her while they applied eye cream in front of the bathroom mirror. This was supposed to be a perk of the reunion experience, getting to stay in your former dorm. Sam had witnessed two women in Eileen Fisher, fighting over who got the single on the fourth floor that both of them had once occupied.

The women's presence in the rooms where she was so used to seeing her fellow dorm mates had creeped her out. It was as if all her friends had aged fifty years and only she remained young.

"Sam," Maria said now. "The dinner? It's at President Washington's house."

Sam gasped. "I love her."

"I know you do. That's why I thought of you."

"I've always wanted to go inside her house."

By then, Sam thought, the school paper would have published her letter. Maybe President Washington would know who she was.

Sam and Maria went back out to the kitchen and joined the others.

"What time does his flight get in?" Gaby said.

"Nine."

"And where will the Princess go while he's here? Did she get a room at the Ritz?"

"She goes across the hall, to our friends' room," Sam said. "It's actually so nice of her."

Sam wished Gaby and Isabella could like each other. Maybe they just needed to get to know one another. She should make a plan to hang out with both of them some night soon, after Clive was gone.

"Sam," Delmi said. "Are you still pretending you have a boyfriend?"

It was a joke she'd started back in October, after Clive visited the first time and Sam didn't introduce them. After he left, they teased her—*Is there even a Clive, really? Is he your imaginary Clive?*

Sam sipped her coffee as Gaby showed her a video on her phone of Josie dancing to Taylor Swift.

"We have to introduce her to Gil soon," Sam said. "I have a feeling they'll hit it off. Who knows? Maybe they'll get married."

"Maybe so," Gaby said.

"Gil better look out," Maria said. "Josie's a fireball. She's got a temper like her mama."

"It's true," Gaby said. She sounded proud.

She had only once mentioned Josie's father to Sam. He was

a guy she met working in a restaurant. They dated casually for a few months, and then Gaby realized she was pregnant.

"I didn't tell him," she said. "He was about to move to Michigan. He would have been a shitty dad. Fun guy to party with, but to have a kid with? No thanks."

Sam wondered about this sometimes. She wondered if and when Josie would ask about him, and what Gaby would say. She wondered if Gaby had ever considered having an abortion, but didn't think it was her place to ask. Like Maria, Gaby wore a small gold cross on a chain around her neck. Sam never asked about that either.

At five to eight, she rinsed her cup and put it in the dishwasher, the first of hundreds to be washed that day.

"You'd better bring him here as soon as you get back from the airport," Delmi said. "Otherwise, I might have to tell everyone at dinner the sad story of your invisible friend."

Sam grinned.

"All right," she said. "Okay."

There were muffins cooling in tins on the countertop. Sam pulled two of them out by their paper liners, using the tips of her fingers.

"See you later," she said.

She was waiting inside the front door of Foss-Lanford when George pulled up to take her to the airport, five minutes ahead of schedule.

"You clean up nice," he said as she got into the passenger seat.

"Thanks."

"Ol' '55" played on the car radio, one of her father's favorite songs.

Sam handed George a muffin.

"Fresh from the oven," she said.

"I didn't realize dorm rooms had ovens," he said.

"Ha ha. Courtesy of my friends in the dining hall."

George took a bite.

"Now, that is delicious," he said. "How are your friends doing, anyway? They've been on my mind. Are you still wanting to do something on their behalf?"

"Yes," she said, but she didn't elaborate. Sam planned to surprise George with a copy of her letter when it ran in the paper. She would include a note, telling him how much he had inspired her.

"There's something I'd like to bring up at our next discussion group," George said. "Don't let me forget. I was talking to a man at church on Sunday. This poor bastard lost his job and his insurance along with it. Then his wife got diagnosed with Parkinson's. The bills have just about sunk them."

"That's awful," she said.

"In general, I think it's better for our group to talk big picture as opposed to individual stories," George said. "But in this case, maybe we can help."

"Are you thinking crowdfunding?" Sam said.

"Yes," George said. "Crowdfunding. Exactly."

He turned toward her and nodded.

She nodded back.

"Okay. What's crowdfunding?" he said.

Sam smiled. "There are websites where you can upload pictures, a sad story. A need of some kind. People donate."

"Is that right? What kind of people?"

"All kinds. A girl I went to elementary school with got honored by the governor of Massachusetts at the State of the Commonwealth address because she crowdfunded so much. She had cancer, and she raised enough to pay her own medical bills and then crowdfunded for two or three other cancer patients she met while getting treatment."

George hit the steering wheel with the palm of his hand. "That right there is the Hollow Tree," he said. "Government officials taking credit for someone who is a victim of their policies. That poor girl shouldn't have had to raise that money in the first place."

Sam had never thought of it that way. She supposed he was right.

"Sorry for the strong reaction," George said.

"That's okay."

"I do like the idea. Crowdfunding. That's a new one. Thank you for keeping me in the loop."

"Thank you for never asking what I'm going to do after graduation," she said.

George's cheeks went red. He thought she was being sarcastic.

"I'm serious," Sam added.

"Are you worried?" George asked.

"I feel like I'm behind everyone else."

"Andrew had the same fears, and he landed on his feet. You should talk to him."

"He did? I mean, have these fears?"

"Sure. You two have a lot in common."

"How so?"

"Middle-class overachievers in a sea of rich kids."

He said it like it was obvious. Like two plus two equals four.

"On Elisabeth and Andrew's third date, know where she took him?" George said. "The ceremony for the Pulitzers. Her godfather won that year for his reporting in the *New York Times*. Andrew swears to this day that the guy had absolutely nothing to do with Elisabeth getting hired there, but come on."

"Elisabeth is really talented," Sam said.

"I don't disagree," he said. "But it never hurts to be born on third base."

"Her godfather, is he related to her?" Sam said.

"No. He was her father's roommate at prep school. Or maybe Harvard," George said. "You've probably heard Elisabeth's father is a big financial muckety-muck. He made his millions the old-fashioned way: inheriting wealth and screwing the little guy."

His millions.

Sam thought of Elisabeth's stories about being young and broke in the city. Four roommates in a two-bedroom apartment, waiting tables to get by. She never gave the impression that she came from money.

When Sam told her about her student loan debt, Elisabeth said, "Don't worry about that. Everyone I know has student loan debt. We all manage, one way or the other."

That *we*. She had included herself.

"I'm confused," Sam said, before she could think better of it. "I thought Elisabeth was a waitress after college."

George shrugged. "Was she? If so, I would assume it was just to piss off her parents. Or maybe she did *think* she needed to waitress. Elisabeth prides herself on not taking money from her father, but that's not the same as having a father who doesn't have money. She has a safety net most people don't. I love her, but that's her blind spot. Always has been."

Sam felt like some missing piece of the story had just been revealed to her, making everything else look different. Elisabeth wasn't the person she claimed to be. And here was Sam, taking her lies as proof that anyone could manage and pursue their art and somehow still end up with the beautiful house and the perfect baby.

George cleared his throat. "I love Lizzy, you know that. I hit the jackpot when I got her as a daughter-in-law. Maybe I'm just being bitter. Her parents rubbed me the wrong way at Christmas. They're clueless snobs, the both of them."

"I heard about the big fight," Sam said.

He looked surprised. "You did? Well, then. I don't have to tell you that, on some level, Lizzy knows she has a backup plan. Otherwise she never would have been so careless and gotten into that situation with her sister."

"What situation?" Sam said.

"Oh." He looked flustered, alarmed, like he'd said too much. "All I'm saying is that's how people like that operate. It's about who you know. If you don't know anyone, it might take longer."

Sam thought this over. George was right.

Isabella had only gotten her internship because a friend of her father's arranged it. When Lexi told them about her job offers and they congratulated her, she said, "My aunt is a big-deal literary agent. She called in a favor, that's all." So many of Sam's classmates had done unpaid internships during the summer months, when Sam was working to afford her tuition.

Still, somehow Sam hadn't made the connection until now that wealth wasn't only about money, but opportunity. She had thought her friends were being humble. There was no one she could call to find her a job, unless she wanted to be a nurse or a cop or a teacher. Except for Elisabeth. Elisabeth had offered, but Sam hadn't even considered taking her up on it. The offer hadn't seemed real. It seemed like too much to ask. Maybe that was how these things were done and Sam was the only one who didn't know it.

"The other day, Faye and I heard this story on the radio," George said. "The children of baby boomers will inherit more wealth than any previous generation. Faye said to me, 'So they're sitting around, waiting for their parents to die. Isn't that nice?' And I said, 'We're lucky we have nothing—Andrew has no incentive to wish us dead.'"

He grinned, but it wasn't convincing.

"I had mixed feelings after he went off to the city and got a big important job. Proud. But for a while, I swear, he was pissed at us. He started hanging around with all these rich kids, he met Elisabeth, and it was like he resented us for not being rich, as if it was our choice and we had decided against it on principle. We were only ever able to have one kid. That killed Faye. We put everything into him. Then, there he was, looking down on us. He used to go by Andy. Then all of a sudden, he's Andrew. Faye said to give him time, and she was right. Now he's back. Away from that city, away from that job, I see the old him coming through. Little things. Like he helped me switch out the screens for the storm windows. We had a few laughs, and a few beers, while we did it. I thought he'd tell me to just hire someone, but no. We went fishing together sometimes, when the weather was nice. I can even talk him into bowling on a really good day."

"I think I kind of know how Andrew felt," she said. "When I was in high school, everyone I knew was the same as me. Just, normal. But now, you wouldn't believe it. There's a Saudi princess in one of my art classes. My first year, this girl in my dorm invited a bunch of us home with her to Boston to celebrate her birthday. I grew up like ten minutes from her, but in the suburbs. Her family lives in a penthouse apartment in the city, overlooking the Charles River. An elevator opens right into their living room. Even Isabella. Her parents own three houses! I've had to learn how to be comfortable around rich people. The main thing is you're supposed to act like they're no different than you are. Even though they don't act normal. They always want to give you a tour of their house, like it's a museum."

George laughed.

"You can pretend you're the same when you all have rooms in the same dorm and eat the same food and go to the same classes," she said. "But then you see the way other people live, and—"

"Diego gave a very interesting presentation about first jobs after college at discussion group once," George said. "His oldest graduated in 1990. There were just no jobs to be had. Same thing happened six years ago, when the economy tanked. The economic climate you graduate into defines so much about your prospects, and yet if you happen to graduate at the wrong time, you end up feeling like a failure because you did everything right, you went to this elite school, and you couldn't get a job after. The fact is we're not as in control of our personal destinies as we imagine ourselves to be."

Sam nodded.

A lot of the people she knew from high school and college were planning on the Peace Corps or Teach For America or law school next year. She wondered now how many of them had a passion for it, and how many just needed a plan.

They were silent through the end of Tom Petty singing "Refugee," and "Gimme Shelter" by the Rolling Stones.

A song she particularly liked came on next.

"Who sings this again?" she said.

"Chuck Berry."

"I think Andrew was playing this song when I was over there for dinner recently."

"Probably. Kid left for college and made off with half my CDs. This here is a playlist of my favorite songs. I've decided life's too short for music that's just okay."

"I like that," she said.

A sign for the airport came into view. George hit the blinker.

Suddenly Sam felt embarrassed, remembering where they were headed.

"Did Andrew and Elisabeth tell you that Clive is—very old?" she said.

She sometimes found it helped to make a situation sound worse than it was so that the truth, which might otherwise be troubling, would instead come as a relief. Like in high school, when she wept to her parents that she had bad news and was ashamed of herself, allowing them to conjure up an unwanted pregnancy or a drug addiction, before telling them she had gotten a B in chemistry.

"Nobody tells me anything," George said. "How old is very old? My age?"

"Eww, no!" she said.

"Gee, thanks."

Sam grinned. "That's not what I meant."

George expertly navigated his way through the twists and turns of the airport. He didn't need to slow down or consult the signs to check which airlines landed at which terminal. The cars going in every direction felt to Sam like a video game. But George was unruffled.

He pulled out of a lane of cars stuck at a standstill, crossed to the far right, and sailed into the arrivals area.

"You're good at this," Sam said.

"I've done it a few thousand times," he said.

Sam saw Clive before he saw them.

He stood on the curb, a suitcase by his side. He was taller than everyone else around, and his hair was spiked up in that way he wore it when he was going out for the night. He wore jeans and leather sneakers and a red zip-up top that she knew had the Nottingham Forest team logo printed on one sleeve.

"There," she said, pointing. "That's him, that's Clive."

George pulled up right in front of him.

When Sam got out of the car, a smile spread across Clive's face.

"Babe!" he said. "You're a sight for sore eyes."

He picked Sam up off the ground, then placed her back on her feet and kissed her.

"Come on," she said. "I want to introduce you to George."

Sam walked around the car and got in back, leaving the front seat for Clive.

Before she could say anything, he opened the other door to the back and slid in beside her.

"Oh," she said.

"Hello, George," Clive said, reaching over the seat to shake his hand. "Pleased to meet you."

"Same here," George said.

He started driving.

She wished she could apologize to George without making Clive feel bad. Or somehow explain to Clive that George wasn't their Uber driver, that he was doing this as a friend. She had assumed that was understood.

Sam tried to ignore her irritation.

"It's so nice of you to do this, George," she said. "Taking the time out of your day for us."

"It's no problem," he said.

Before they even left the winding roads of the airport and got back on the highway, Clive was running a hand up her thigh. Sam pushed it away, meeting his eye, nodding toward George.

Clive looked injured.

She reached for his hand and held it, a small concession.

Every other time they had seen each other after being apart, they leaped right to the physical. When she arrived in London for the summer, he went down on her in a cab, something she thought of now with a mix of excitement and shame. On her most recent trip, they made out so brazenly on the Tube ride home from Heathrow that an old woman splashed water on them to make them stop. Without that element of the forbidden, Sam felt unsure how to begin.

"How was the flight?" she said.

"Dreadful. A small child kicked the back of my seat the whole way."

"That's the worst," George said.

"I've got a massive headache. Do either of you have any ibu-profen, by chance?"

The way he said the word bugged her. *I-boop-rofen.*

"Sorry, I don't," she said.

"Not on me," said George.

They were silent for a minute. "Pretty Woman" played in the background. If it were still just the two of them in the car, Sam would tell George how much she'd loved this song as a kid, how they blasted it at their neighborhood block party every summer, and all the dads danced around like fools, beckoning to their wives, who sat at picnic tables in the middle of the street, pre-tending not to see them.

Clive leaned forward. "George, mate," he said. "Would you mind changing the station? This song is so treacly, it makes my teeth hurt."

Sam's body froze. There was no way he could have known George had chosen the music, but still she felt horrible.

"I like this song," she said.

George switched to talk radio. A segment about an ICE raid in Texas, the mass deportation of a hundred people, some of whose children were left home alone, awaiting their parents' return from work.

"Obama won't let them get away with that," Sam said.

"Your Obama has deported more people than any other presi-dent in history," Clive said to her.

"Where did you hear that?" Sam said.

"I read it in this top-secret document called the newspaper."

She hated when he got like this. Perhaps he felt insecure, and so he had to overcompensate. When Clive was in this sort of mood, Sam avoided making any arguments about anything, because she didn't want to hear him say that her point was obvious, or simplistic, or that she was thinking all wrong.

"Clive, my man," George said. "Are you a fan of the English Premier League?"

They started talking about Newcastle United. Sam stared out the window.

She was almost certain George had no interest in soccer. He had probably looked it up online, done his research, so he'd have something to talk about with Clive. George was that kind of person.

Once they were at the dorm, Sam led Clive straight to her room.

She needed that reliable connection, her skin against his, to remind her of what Clive meant, to help them get back to normal.

He kissed her at the top of the platform stairs and dropped his bag just inside her room. Clive closed the door behind them.

15

Elisabeth

THE WEEKEND IN THE CITY was Andrew's idea.

Elisabeth saw it as an attempt to smooth over the fact that things between them had been terrible since Christmas. Her betrayal, which would otherwise have done them in, she was certain, had to be endured because they were married, they had a child. The god-awful tension might linger on for weeks or months or years, during which they still had to talk about what to eat for dinner and whether they needed paper towels. They both understood this without discussing it.

Elisabeth found it reassuring in a way. Things were rocky, but neither of them was going anywhere. At least not yet. She missed Andrew, though. He was there, in her presence, but not the same.

Since the baby, since the move, they'd had spats about money, and their parents, and whether to have another child, and who was doing more. The things they had heard married people argued about, and yet she remained surprised when it happened to them. But they always made up quickly.

This was something else.

Every time she allowed herself to think of how she had jeopardized *them* for her ungrateful sister, Elisabeth wanted to scream or cry or beg him to forgive her. Andrew kept asking why she'd done it. She didn't tell him that the decision had been a selfish one, that she couldn't bear to give her father the satisfaction of

Charlotte coming to him for help. When she thought of this now, Elisabeth could see how deranged her own thinking had been. Had the timing lined up, she might have tried to blame it on pregnancy hormones or postpartum psychosis or something. As it was, she'd given her sister the money long before all that, and so she could only sit with the fact that she had done a stupid thing for a stupid reason.

She hadn't spoken to any of her family members since Christmas, which wouldn't have been unusual under normal circumstances, but seemed noteworthy given how they'd left things.

In mid-January, Charlotte sent a text: *I'm doing a spiritual cleanse for the New Year. To that end, I want to say I'm sorry for the misunderstanding and I hope you know I still intend to pay you back someday.*

Elisabeth read it over and over again. She sent a screenshot to Nomi. They decided her sister needed an editor. If Charlotte had simply said she was sorry, without calling her own devious behavior a misunderstanding. If she hadn't mentioned the cleanse or added that amorphous *someday.*

Elisabeth didn't reply. By then, she knew for certain what she had probably known for a long time but been unable to admit to herself. The money was never coming back. Their savings were gone.

A week after Charlotte's text, a letter from their father's accountant arrived. It contained a check for three hundred thousand dollars, made out to Gil. The letter specified that the money was to be used for his education and living expenses.

Elisabeth was enraged. Even more so because her father had involved Gil.

"It just happens to be the exact amount Charlotte owes me," Elisabeth said.

"He's trying to find a way around that," Andrew said. "To respect your wishes, sort of."

The check now sat on her dresser, a question mark. Andrew thought she should accept it. Elisabeth couldn't believe he would ask her to. But she told him she would consider, if it would help fix things between them.

The situation at home was bad enough already when, the first week of February, Andrew received an email telling him he had not been selected to attend the conference in Denver he had been planning on for months. For a day or two, he seemed adrift, but then he doubled down, as if he would prove them wrong by sheer force of will. He was working harder than ever now, staying even later at work. Sometimes Elisabeth wondered if he was just trying to escape her.

She was pleased he had taken Monday off so they could stay an extra day in the city.

"I made an appointment for a couple's massage on Monday morning," she told him as they finished packing on Saturday.

Gil sat on the floor, pulling each item from the suitcase as soon as she placed it inside.

Andrew scrunched up his nose.

"A couple's massage? You really want to?"

"It's not for me and you, it's for me and Nomi."

"What time? I made us an appointment for noon that day."

"With who?"

"Dr. Chen?"

He said it that way, like he wasn't sure.

"You're kidding."

In all the months they had spent doing IVF, Andrew had never once been the one to contact the clinic. So this was why he wanted to go to the city, she thought. Not to smooth things over with her, but to accelerate the new-baby conversation. Or maybe it was both.

In one of their many arguments since Christmas, Andrew reminded her yet again that he had only agreed to IVF in the first place because she promised they wouldn't leave any embryos behind.

"We have two," she said when he brought it up. "If the first one works, then what? Will you be able to leave the other? Because *three* kids? I just can't."

"I don't know," Andrew had replied. "I guess we would cross that bridge when we got to it. We should be so lucky, right?"

Now she said, "You made an appointment without telling me?"

"We said we'd sit down with Dr. Chen the next time we were in the city. I figured I'd save you the call."

Elisabeth was trying to decide how mad she should be when the doorbell rang.

She went downstairs, thinking of how, under normal circumstances, she would have called Andrew on this odd decision. But after what she had done, he had all the power. She couldn't say anything.

She opened the front door. Sam was there, beside a guy Elisabeth could have identified as British without hearing him speak a word.

He was tall, so tall. Too tall.

"You must be Clive," she said.

"Pleasure to meet you, madam."

He extended a hand and a crooked, mischievous smile.

Elisabeth had an immediate, visceral dislike of him. His silly outfit. The way he addressed her, as if he were Sam's peer instead of hers. He looked all wrong standing next to sweet Sam, her baby face covered in makeup for the first time Elisabeth had ever seen.

Still, she said, "Come in. I'm so glad we're doing this."

Andrew came down with Gil and said hello.

What happened upstairs was forgotten, for now. Elisabeth was happy to focus on her husband, on getting out of the house. She couldn't look at Clive.

"Gil checklist," she said to Andrew. "Jacket? Stroller? Diapers? Wipes? Cream? Pack 'n Play? Toys? Puffs?"

"Check check check check check check check and check," Andrew replied.

The baby whined.

"He's tired," Elisabeth said.

She took him from Andrew's arms and began singing softly, the song she sang each night at bedtime: *Go to sleep, go to sleep, go to sleep, baby Gilly.*

Andrew came close. He joined in on the second verse: *Eyes are closed, eyes are closed, eyes are closed, my little sugar. One eye closed, two eyes closed, go to sleep, baby Gilly.*

Gil grinned up at the two of them. Elisabeth knew he would be asleep as soon as the car started rolling.

"Aren't they adorable?" Sam said.

"I'm taking notes," Clive replied. "That'll be us before long."

He stood behind Sam and wrapped his arms around her. Elisabeth wanted to snatch Sam away, to carry her to safety. For the first time ever, she wondered if she ought to call Sam's mother.

Elisabeth insisted that Clive ride shotgun, but he said he would rather sit in back with Sam.

Gil's car seat was on the passenger side. Sam sat behind Andrew. Clive was in the middle, knees protruding into the front seat.

For the first hour of the journey, Elisabeth kept glancing at them in the rearview mirror. They were holding hands. At one point, he whispered, "Give us a kiss."

Elisabeth looked away.

His accent was not the buttery Hugh Grant variety she'd been imagining, but something unrefined, coarse.

When the baby woke up, Clive was annoyingly good with him—he made Gil laugh. But he also kept sneezing. Elisabeth pictured the germs, collected on his transatlantic flight, now filling the air inside their car. Clive said it was only allergies, but no one had allergies at this time of year.

Even though Andrew was driving and should not be checking his phone, she knew he would, and so she sent him a text: *If this guy gets the baby sick, I will murder him.*

Andrew read it a few minutes later, but didn't look at her.

He was annoyed when she told him she had invited them.

"They won't be *with* us," she said. "We're only giving them a ride. This way, we get to go out on our own without Gil one night."

"Because there are no babysitters in Manhattan," Andrew said.

"None that he knows and loves."

The traffic was brutal. Brake lights as far as she could see.

By hour three, for no reason whatsoever, Clive began to whistle.

Elisabeth thought she might hyperventilate. They were trapped in a car, with this too-tall man, this creep, and it was her fault. She took out her phone for distraction. The BK Mamas were embroiled in a debate about whether to change the group's name to BK Caregivers, since the current name was sexist (ignoring dads) and elitist (ignoring childcare workers). They were taking a poll. There were already three hundred responses in the comments section from every angle of the argument. She began to read them, each so incredibly heated you might mistake this for an actual problem.

She had read through thirty or so and texted Nomi screenshots of the most hilarious ones, when Andrew asked, "Have you ever been to New York before, Clive?"

"No. Never even came to the States until I met Sam."

"You'll love it," Elisabeth said. "It's the greatest city in the world."

She put her phone in her purse, admonished herself to try harder.

"I've lived in London for years, and Barcelona before that. But I'm a country boy at heart," Clive said. "I want to convince Sam to move to a cottage after we're married, get some sheep and a few dogs."

Sam giggled, her meaning hard to decipher.

"Don't forget the honeybees," she said. An inside joke, perhaps.

Elisabeth ignored this, and said to Clive, "Did Sam tell you I met one of her professors and he thinks she's seriously gifted? One of the best he's ever seen?"

She could feel Andrew's eyes on her, wordlessly pointing out that she was stretching things. But Christopher had said that, or something like it.

"Of course he thinks so," Clive replied. "She's brilliant. I have one of her paintings framed in every room of our flat."

Our flat, Elisabeth thought. His and hers.

"It's true," Sam said. "The place is like a shrine to me."

Elisabeth faced front. It was worse than she thought. Sam wasn't some plaything for this guy. He actually wanted to marry her.

In an attempt to talk about something not related to their relationship, Elisabeth asked about the royals.

"Did you ever see Will and Kate out at a bar or anything, back when they were in college?" she said. "I've heard stories like that from people, and they make me so jealous."

Sam squealed. "She's so beautiful. I love her clothes. I would die if I saw her out at a bar."

"Why?" Clive scoffed. "The royals are a bunch of inbred parasites, mooching off the people and doing nothing for anyone but themselves."

"Oh, Clive," Sam said, like the statement was somehow adorable.

Andrew asked if anyone was hungry. They pulled over at the next rest stop. Elisabeth requested a turkey wrap and took Gil for a diaper change.

In the crowded ladies' room, hand dryers blasting, she put Gil down on the plastic changing table and smiled at him. He was a source of comfort she could plug in to at any time, a piece of herself outside of her.

"What do you think?" she whispered. "Not good enough for our Sam, is he?"

Gil looked up at her, revealing a new front tooth poking through.

When he was changed, Elisabeth went to find Andrew and tell him about the tooth. She spotted him in line at the sandwich place. Sam and Clive stood behind him, whispering, as if they were his teenage children.

Andrew had just gotten to the cash register when Elisabeth reached his side.

"So that's two large turkeys, a roast beef, a meatball, and four Cokes?" said the girl behind the counter.

"Umm, yes," Andrew said. He handed her his Visa.

Elisabeth looked to Clive and then to Andrew and back again. She met her husband's eye and he knew what she was asking—why was he paying for all of them?

Andrew shrugged, and Elisabeth understood. Clive hadn't offered to pay for his and Sam's.

It bothered her to a degree that was out of proportion with the offense. Were they to take Sam along on a road trip alone, they would buy her lunch, no question. But Clive was a grown man.

Sam deserved someone solid, someone her own age. A younger version of Andrew. Elisabeth remembered thinking early on in their relationship that he was dad smart. He knew about art and world history and the nuances of every country's political, economic, and social climate. If a child were to ask him anything, he could answer. While she had been known, when trying to make a point but fuzzy on the particulars, to say that something had happened "in the olden days." She looked at Andrew and thought: Husband. She looked at Clive and thought: Fling.

Sam had stayed too long at the fair, but she didn't realize. She seemed to think they could go on forever. Elisabeth recalled an email Sam sent over Christmas break, a sliver of doubt poking through. But she retreated quickly from it, and never raised the issue again.

Sam and Clive were staying with a friend way uptown for the weekend, but first, they accompanied Andrew and Elisabeth to the Algonquin.

They were going to see a Broadway matinee and have an early dinner. Sam and Clive would babysit at the hotel, in the room, if they wanted, or in the spacious lobby full of plush velvet sofas.

The kid at the front desk handed Andrew two room keys. The four of them, plus Gil in the stroller, and all their bags, crammed into the elevator and rode in silence to the top floor.

Elisabeth had paid extra for a small suite.

When Andrew unlocked the door and pushed it open, Sam and Clive gasped.

"Absolutely gorgeous," Clive said. "Look at that bed, babe. We should get one like that."

It was a four-poster, lifted high off the ground. Elisabeth was overcome by a sudden fear that they'd have sex in this room.

"This is the nicest hotel room I've ever seen," Sam said.

"I booked online," Elisabeth said. "I got a great deal."

It wasn't true. The room had been a splurge. She supposed she felt bad that Sam would likely be spending the weekend on a pullout couch or a futon.

She didn't think Andrew was paying attention to the conversation. But just in case, she didn't want him thinking about money right now. For the past two months, he'd been keeping close tabs on what they spent, worried in a way she'd never seen before.

He would periodically swing in the other direction and make a grand gesture that Elisabeth didn't really need him to make. He bought her gold earrings for Valentine's Day, and suggested the weekend away. At those times, it was almost like he was trying to convince himself that she hadn't ruined them after all. That they could still have the things they desired.

But more often, Andrew was panicked.

"We have nothing saved," he pointed out, again and again.

She thought it was passive-aggressive, how he made it sound like this was a circumstance that had occurred on its own. Like they had gone broke from natural causes. His refusal to come out and blame her when they both knew she was to blame only highlighted what Elisabeth had done wrong.

Clive picked Gil up and started dancing with him.

"*You put your right arm in, you put your right arm out,*" he sang. "*You put your right arm in and you shake it all about. You do the hokey-cokey and you turn yourself around. That's what it's all about!*"

Gil shouted his approval.

Sam said, "In England, they say hokey-cokey."

"What do you say here?" Clive said, still dancing.

"Hokey-pokey."

He paused, then continued, theatrically, "*You do the hoooo-key-cokey. You do the hooo-key-cokey.*"

Elisabeth wished he would shut up. Why was *cokey* so much more annoying than *pokey*? But it was. The English and Americans were so often like this. Such tiny differences and yet they amounted to something. Brits had that tendency to slip into baby talk. *Choccy bickies* and all that.

"We should change," Andrew said. "We don't want to be late."

Elisabeth unzipped her suitcase. Her dress was slightly wrinkled, but she couldn't be bothered to take out the ironing board. She hung the dress on the back of the bathroom door and ran the shower. In an attempt to make a bit of an effort while she waited to see if this would work, she pulled out her makeup bag and applied eyeliner, eye shadow, and mascara on top of her antiaging serum. She covered her dark undereye circles with concealer. She was adding lipstick when Andrew ducked his head in.

"Let's get going," he said. "The show starts in half an hour."

Elisabeth slipped the dress on. She couldn't tell whether the steam had helped.

Stepping back into the room, she told Sam, "Anything you need, text me. We'll be back early."

"Don't worry about us," Sam said. "Have fun!"

She held Gilbert on her hip, so natural with him. He had recently entered a stage where being in the care of anyone other than his mother brought on tears. The only exception was Sam.

Elisabeth waited until they were outside to say, "Well, he's terrible."

Andrew looked around. "Who?"

"Clive!" she said. "He's an old man!"

"I think he's younger than us."

"Compared to Sam, I mean."

Andrew reached for her hand. They walked that way up Eighth Avenue. She'd hated hand-holders when she lived here, two people taking up an entire sidewalk in the name of love. But this was the first time he'd taken her hand in the last six weeks. Elisabeth didn't want to break the spell, even if Andrew was forcing himself to do it, to try.

They passed the *Times* building and she looked up at the newsroom, staring for a minute as if her former self might come to the window and wave.

Elisabeth quickened her pace. She didn't want to run into anyone she knew.

"Doesn't it feel weird to be here as just another tourist?" she said.

"Yes," Andrew said. "I love it."

All through the show, she wondered what Sam and Clive were up to. She hoped it went without saying that she didn't want them to leave the hotel and go traipsing around Times Square with her baby.

Afterward, they took a cab downtown for dinner at the Little Owl, their old favorite. It was early. They had the place to themselves. They talked about the play, and what to order.

The waitress brought them a bottle of wine.

They clinked their glasses together.

Elisabeth took a sip. "That's good," she said.

Andrew tried his, and nodded in agreement.

"Do you know, I think Clive believes Sam is going to marry him," Elisabeth said.

She thought she saw a twinge of exasperation on her husband's face, but she kept going.

"If he gets his way, he'll whisk her off to England and she'll never get a job in the galleries."

"If they get married and she's a UK citizen, then who knows?" he said. "She could get a gallery job in London."

"You heard him! If they get married she'll be barefoot and pregnant, making jam in the Cotswolds in a year."

"You don't even know what the Cotswolds are," Andrew said.

"He talked her out of graduating Phi Beta Kappa," she said. "So that he could hang out with her more this semester. That's not what someone does when they have your best interest at heart."

She had tried to change Sam's mind, and Sam had said, *What's the point? So I can get bragging rights for one day when they call out my name at graduation?*

Elisabeth knew that was Clive talking. She should have said as much. She should have been more forceful.

"Sam doesn't know enough to know what a loser he is," she said now. "She's impressed by him because she's a child, basically. Anyone old enough to rent a car seems mature to her. He's taking advantage of her youth."

"Seems like he's crazy about her to me," Andrew said.

"Seriously? That's your takeaway?"

"Okay, fine, it's a slightly creepy dynamic. But I don't have to date the guy. What do I care? There must be something she sees in him."

"Yeah, he's hot."

"He is?"

"He's not my cup of tea. But objectively speaking, yes. He has that sleazy-hot thing going."

"Sleazy hot."

"And they have tons of hot sex."

"She told you that?"

"Not in so many words, but can't you tell from looking at them? But what does he want with her? If he wants to be married so bad, there are thousands of attractive, lonely thirty-five-year-olds in London he could call."

"Is that so?"

"I'm assuming. But anyone age appropriate would be too smart to get involved with a guy like him, you see?"

"You really hate his guts," Andrew said.

"I love Sam. I want the best for her."

"Do you think she's smart?"

"Yes. Why would you even ask that?"

"If she's smart, she'll figure out what's right on her own."

Elisabeth considered this.

"Once Sam described to me this big wedding she wants to have," she said. "It was all very childish, the kind of thing a little girl would come up with. I should have seen it then. She's caught up in a fantasy."

Andrew shrugged.

"But that's not like her, is it?" she said.

When he didn't answer, she said, "Your father thinks he's a weirdo, too. He said as much over the phone after he picked Clive up at the airport. He also said he thinks the whole going to London after graduation thing is a way of avoiding reality. Getting a job, facing rejection, all that."

"If George thinks it, then it must be true," he said.

"Yes. We have to find a way to get her away from him."

"I was kidding," Andrew said. "Can we talk about something else please? I sense you going over to the dark side."

He was right. Here she was, out with her husband, in the place she'd been longing to be for months, and she couldn't let herself enjoy it. She was fixated on her babysitter's love life instead.

Living in the city, you could easily blame it for your unhappiness—there was always a train delay or an angry stranger to accuse of ruining your day. One of the riskiest parts of leaving was that you might find out that, all along, the city wasn't the problem. You were.

"Sorry, yes, let's talk about something else," she said. "The grill? What's the latest?"

He'd been working on a prototype. She hadn't asked him about it lately. In part because he was still upset about Denver. In part because she knew it required more money than the college had agreed to give him, which led them back to that check from her father.

"I've been meaning to tell you," Andrew said. "The provost paid me a nice compliment. He said the students on my project are getting a lot out of it. He said I have a way with them that he doesn't see all that often."

"That's so nice," she said.

"Yeah. I know we joke about them, but I kind of love working with these kids. I'd been telling the provost how Cory came up with a really interesting idea. You know Cory? The tall kid with the mustache who you met at the Christmas party."

She nodded. "Ophelia."

"Right."

As Andrew talked details, Elisabeth drank more wine and tried to pay attention. But she felt her frustration rising when he mentioned needing a grant, searching for investors sooner than was customary.

She wondered if in every married person there was a pit of fear about whether a spouse had chosen him or her for the wrong reason. Andrew moved to the city and socialized with guys from Greenwich and Darien. Some part of him felt less than. Had he seen her as a way to become the man he wished he was, even as he pretended to understand why she rejected her father's money?

"Andrew," she interrupted without meaning to. "I'm not going to deposit the check."

He looked crushed. At least, she thought he did.

"We keep tiptoeing around it, but I can't do it. I won't take my father's money. Period. He's an evil bastard."

"Agreed," Andrew said. "But he will be one whether we keep his money or not."

"So that is what you want."

"Instead of losing all the money we've saved? Yes. If I get this grill off the ground, we could fix my parents' problems right away. It's killing me that they have to sell that house."

"And you're putting that on me?"

"Putting what on you? I was talking about what could happen if the grill is a success."

"Right. But we'll only know if it can succeed if I agree to take the money."

"He'd be paying you back what you loaned your sister. That's all."

"When the whole point of loaning it to her was that neither of us would have to be dependent on him."

"But she didn't abide by that."

"Yes, and your dad spends all his time in his man cave ranting on about the goddamn Hollow Tree, instead of dealing with what happened, trying to find more work, admitting that no one is ever going to buy that house and they can't afford to keep it. But I'm supposed to forget my principles and swoop in to save him?"

"I never said that," Andrew said softly. "Go ahead, rip up the check. Do what you want. That's what you always do in the end anyway, isn't it?"

Improbably, they had sex that night for the first time since the baby came. Not because either of them wanted to, particularly, but because it had been so long and they'd gotten a hotel room and it felt like it was now or never. The sex didn't hurt like she expected it to. It felt pretty much like it always had. She remembered now how nice it was to feel close to him in this way, especially when they were so far apart on everything else.

Elisabeth fell asleep beside Andrew, but woke up after a bit, restless. She didn't feel like stewing over their problems. She took her laptop into the bathroom and shut the door. She logged on to BK Mamas, where the fight about a name change was still raging, fourteen hours after it started. Around 6:00 p.m., Mimi Winchester threw in one of her grenades: *While we're on the topic of appropriate naming, can I just say—this is meant to be a board for BK Mamas. That is, moms who live in Brooklyn. I know for a fact LOTS of people here don't live in Brooklyn anymore.*

Twenty-nine women responded, accusing Mimi of elitism.

Sorry people like you came along and priced me out of a neighborhood I lived in for seventeen years, one of them wrote. *I may live in Queens, but I still think of myself as a BK Mama, and always will.*

Amen! wrote someone.

Preach, said someone else.

And then the woman in Queens announced the creation of a new group, the clunkily named Once and Always BK Caregivers.

Elisabeth clicked to see how many people had joined. One hundred and forty so far, though she doubted many of them had left the original group. She joined this one too. What the hell?

The clock on her laptop read 10:32.

Sam and Clive were probably out somewhere, beginning their night. Elisabeth wondered what Sam's friends thought of him. They couldn't possibly think he was good for her. There was something off about Clive, beyond the age difference, something she sensed but could not put into words.

She still had access to all her research tools from her days at the paper. There, sitting on the edge of the bathtub, she casually conducted a records search: *Clive Richardson, age 33, London.*

Nothing of a criminal nature came up. No bankruptcies or DUIs. But there was a marriage license, issued not even two years ago at the London City Hall. And divorce papers, signed six months later.

Elisabeth was almost positive Sam didn't know about this.

She searched online for the ex-wife—Laura Garcia. But it was too common a name, and it was getting late. Elisabeth closed her computer and tucked the information away, to be deployed at the appropriate time, whenever that was.

Before getting back in bed, she went and stood over her sleeping baby. He didn't yet know anything bad about the world, didn't know that people were so often something other than what they claimed to be. Gil woke up each morning with a smile on his face, expecting the best from everyone. When did that change? She hoped she could make it last as long as possible.

She was excited to show him her city in the morning. To take him to Central Park if it wasn't too cold.

How can you not want another when you're so great with him? Andrew had said.

She was stubborn; she knew that. Maybe she ought to consider what he wanted.

Elisabeth had always been ambitious, self-interested; you had to be to make it in the city. The first few months of Gil's life were easier than she'd imagined. Friends said the shock of having to be everything for someone else had depressed them. But in her case, it was simple when she gave her whole self over to him. Things got trickier when part of the old Elisabeth returned.

A month ago, she spoke to a class at the college. She arrived for Narrative Nonfiction 201 feeling far more nervous than she had expected to. The professor, Gwen's neighbor, read Elisabeth's bio aloud as an introduction. Elisabeth could tell the students were impressed.

They had a million questions. Afterward, they all wanted her email address.

Walking home that day, she thought about her nineteen-year-old self. If she heard all this, she would be amazed.

"They made me feel like I've made it," she said to Andrew later. "I never feel that way."

Ever since, Elisabeth had felt fiercely ambitious again. She wanted to work on her new book. She had ideas for articles, op-eds she might write, if she ever found the time. Whereas once having a sitter three days a week had seemed like a lot, she already knew that, after Sam graduated, she would hire someone full-time. She needed more hours to spend immersed in her work.

A second child would make that impossible, put her right back where she was nine months ago.

For an instant, looking at Gil, Elisabeth imagined two—riding down the driveway in their double stroller, babbling away to each other. But the image didn't stick.

She saw herself instead in her office, working again. It was a small space on the first floor of a building downtown. It had only one window. Her kitchen table might have been a preferable place to write, but at the office, she could be truly alone. She only rented the space from noon to four. Other people worked there at different hours of the day. They weren't supposed to leave stuff, but she sometimes caught traces of them. A CVS receipt. A Chinese takeout container in the trash.

There were days when she went into that room and fell asleep with her head on the desk. Days when she went to the BK Mamas page and typed something into the search box—*best infant booties* or *nine month sleep regression*—and found herself leaping from one post to another, to someone's personal page, to a link to *People* magazine, emerging hours later, disgusted, as if she'd gorged on the complete contents of her refrigerator.

But on the days when it went well, when she left with something to show for the time spent, Elisabeth felt proud, powerful. She was happy to be back in front of her laptop, wrestling with the best way to tell a story, listening to interviews she had recorded with female athletes and policy makers a year ago. Nothing else had ever consumed her the way writing did. When she was in the zone, she might look up thinking an hour had passed, when really she had been at it half the day.

Time now could be measured by the fullness of her breasts. She was still nursing, and often pumped at her desk while she worked. Once, a man burst right in, staring down at his phone and then up at her—Elisabeth had just finished pumping, and was about to transfer her milk into a baby bottle to bring home. She stood in the middle of the room, bra unhooked, breasts out. She held a rubber nipple in her mouth.

After the longest pause of all time, the guy said, "This is not the men's room," and fled.

Alone, Elisabeth laughed like she hadn't in ages.

In the morning, Andrew kissed her.

The sex, it seemed, had eclipsed the unpleasant dinner.

She was relieved that there would be no need for apologies, rehashing.

They spent a glorious Sunday that made her wonder why they ever left this place—an early haircut, brunch and the park and drinks with old friends, followed by dinner, just the three of them, at a French restaurant by the hotel. The waiter gave Gil three crayons, and before they could protest that he was too young, Gil was drawing a red line on the white paper that covered the table.

"He's brilliant, isn't he?" Andrew said, as if confessing something.

"I think so," she said, nodding.

She never could have predicted how moved they both would be by moments like this one. They had watched Gil grow from a blurry bean on a black-and-white screen into a human with arms and legs and ears; and then from someone who could not hold up his own head into the child who sat before them now, gnawing on a dinner roll.

"Oh!" she said. "I forgot to tell you. He got a new tooth."

"Where? Where?" Andrew said, and she was struck by the sensation that all she needed in the world were these two. That she would do anything to keep them.

On Monday morning, Elisabeth headed out to meet Nomi, feeling excited to an extent that bordered on ridiculous.

The air was cold, but she decided to walk downtown.

Passing certain street corners, she saw former versions of herself. The spot where, at twenty-five, she kissed a handsome bartender on the doorstep of an abandoned building, which had since become a ramen shop and then a bank. A sign advertised luxury apartments coming soon.

In Herald Square, she breathed in the familiar sweet smell of warm chestnuts, a food she had never tasted.

She passed the jewelry store where, at twenty-one, she spent an entire afternoon in the waiting room while her boss's watch got fixed. Elisabeth sat there, drinking a complimentary espresso, watching rich women in furs file in, this errand their only plan for the day. When the jeweler gave her the watch back, she tucked it into her coat pocket and wandered around SoHo for an hour before returning to work. A delicious feeling, like she was getting away with something.

Outside what used to be Mexican Radio, Elisabeth had a memory of a night in May, or early June, one of the first perfect summer evenings, warm, a sparkle in the air. She and her friend Rachel sat at an outdoor table, drinking margaritas at five in the afternoon. At the next table were two guys, one much cuter than the other. They flirted across the aisle, and then at some point, tables got pulled together. They went to a bar and another bar and another bar, until it was 3:00 a.m. at Pianos, and the cute one said, "Let's go back to my place. It's right around the corner."

He meant all four of them. He and Rachel disappeared into the bedroom for an hour while Elisabeth talked to the funny one out on the couch. They were both coming off heartbreaks. They commiserated, exchanged numbers, though neither of them ever called.

That previous spring, she had lost twelve pounds from grief. Nomi tried to force her to eat, but Elisabeth kept saying she couldn't taste anything since Jacob left.

Jacob. Memories of him were hidden around this city like Easter eggs. The night they met, at someone's birthday party, out in the backyard at Sweet and Vicious; their first kiss, standing in line for a movie at the Angelika. All the basement clubs and bars where she went to see his band play; the Strand bookstore, where he worked by day. He told her he loved her for the first time in his apartment on Saint Mark's. Not long after, he moved into her place. Two years later, he told her his father was leaving his mother, that Elisabeth's father was to blame, that he never wanted to see her again. There was nothing she could do to persuade him otherwise.

The memory of this brought on thoughts of Charlotte. Elisabeth couldn't say she missed her, exactly. She missed what she thought they had. That solidarity, that shared sense of purpose that began when her relationship with Jacob ended. Though now she wondered if Charlotte had ever stopped taking their father's money. Had he held the cards all along?

Her father's way of getting Jacob out of her life had sickened Elisabeth for so long. The way it happened sickened her still. But what would have become of the two of them otherwise?

Jacob, she realized, had been her Clive.

Over the years, Elisabeth had looked him up on Facebook from time to time. He still looked good. The band never took off. He worked in a bookstore in Seattle now. He had a rocker-chick girlfriend who seemed to own nothing but black bandage dresses. He held a beer in every photograph. As far as she could tell, Jacob had never grown up.

Nomi was waiting for her outside the spa.

They ran to each other, squealing, hugging tight.

In the lounge, they sat on a velvet sofa in fluffy white robes, gossiping and sipping cucumber water. They had arrived forty-five minutes early to do this. Nomi had instructed her assistant to tell anyone who asked that she was in her office, behind closed doors, on an important call that should not be interrupted for any reason.

Elisabeth's masseuse was a woman in her sixties with tight gray curls. She felt a bit jealous at first that Nomi had gotten the one in her twenties, with a pixie cut and yoga-toned arms. But the older woman proved to be stronger than she looked. Elisabeth felt herself relax under her touch.

When she was pregnant, and for a long time after, she felt like her body was no longer hers. She was in service to another life, a tiny stranger. Women complained that no one ever told you the specifics of birth. But by the time Elisabeth had Gil, she had heard it all. Friends told her how you bled for weeks after. How Pitocin might make you shake uncontrollably on the table, and that if they gave it to you, chances were you were headed for a C-section. One friend had the epidural needle stuck straight into a nerve and could never feel the urge to pee again. Another had a piece of her placenta left inside her and, months later, was forced to deliver it.

When it came time for Elisabeth's turn, the whole thing had been demystified to the point where she envied some young thing coming in with no idea of what was about to happen to her.

Gil's birth was easy, unremarkable, as births went.

Two days after getting home from the hospital, Elisabeth held a hand mirror between her legs, even though the nurses had warned her not to. She looked, and the words that came to mind were *Portal to Hell*. She didn't look again for six months.

Back then, the thought of another human being's hands on her body could not have appealed less. But here she was, whole again already.

The massage room was lit by tea candles. Soft music played.

Elisabeth lay facedown on the table, her forehead resting on a U-shaped pillow that smelled of eucalyptus.

She was just beginning to relax when Nomi said, "How's Andrew doing with the Denver news? What's going to happen with his invention?"

Elisabeth groaned. It was the last thing she wanted to think about.

"Who knows. I don't see it catching fire, if I'm honest."

"Was that a grill pun?" Nomi said.

"Ha. We've been arguing about it. Without actually arguing, for the most part."

"As you do."

Nomi was up to date on everything. Via text, she had distilled her opinion on the situation down to two sentences. *You shouldn't have lied to him, but shit happens. You can't have a second kid to make up for what you did.*

"Anyway," Elisabeth said now. "Let me tell you something far more interesting than that. I was up late on Saturday googling Sam's boyfriend and it turns out he was married before. I don't think she has any idea."

"Yikes," Nomi said.

"And the marriage only lasted six months. I'm dying to know what happened. Did she leave him because he cheated? Is he looking for a do-over with a younger, more naïve woman? I can't stop thinking about it. Do you think I should warn her?"

Nomi was silent for so long that Elisabeth thought she must have fallen asleep.

Then Nomi said, "Are you okay?" in such a concerned way that Elisabeth felt embarrassed that two other people were listening.

"Is it Andrew? Or your dad? Or all of it?"

"What do you mean?"

"You focus on someone else's problems when you want to avoid whatever's upsetting you in your own life. That's your thing."

The comment stung, but Elisabeth thought it over.

"Do not," she said, when she couldn't think of a more convincing response.

"Remember you had the cleaning lady who thought her husband was cheating, and you went full Nancy Drew on the guy? It was right after the *Washington Post* gave your book that bad review."

"Well, he was cheating."

"And when you were trying to get pregnant, that old man in your office died and you got kind of obsessed with taking care of his wife."

"Not obsessed," Elisabeth said. "I visited her a few times, and we talked on the phone a lot. She was lonely."

"You made her all those cakes and roast chickens."

"Andrew made them!"

"Because you forced him to," Nomi said. "You're an empath, you worry about people. It's good."

"Thank you."

"But sometimes, it's not that good."

"I see what you're saying, but honestly—I care about Sam because I like her so much. She's the closest thing I have to a real friend there. Maybe that's my problem. I have no friends."

"I don't have any either," Nomi said. "It's our age."

"Yes, you do, you have tons. What about that blonde in your building? And that funny one who's married to Brian's coworker?"

"But I never see them. Anyway. Most Brooklyn moms would drive you insane, believe me."

"We used to have so much free time," Elisabeth said. "Don't you miss having absolutely nothing to do on a Sunday? Or the excitement of going on a first date?"

"It wasn't exciting, it was sickening," Nomi said. "You're forgetting all the things a woman worries about on a first date—*Is my outfit cute? Will we have anything to talk about? Is this guy gonna murder me?*"

Elisabeth laughed.

"If I lived here, I would see you all the time," she said.

"You probably wouldn't," Nomi said. "We'd both be too busy."

"We'd find a way. We always did before."

"Maybe. But the same limited resources that make the city annoying for adults apply even more so to kids," Nomi said. "The competition trying to get your toddler into school. Christ, trying to get a swing at the playground is a struggle. Sometimes it feels like sixth grade, when everyone bought the same sweater because the most popular girl wore it to school the day before. They all have identical strollers. What's up with that? They truly think if you did not pay a grand for it, the wheels are going to fall off or something."

"But you love it here."

"I do. It's all worth it to me. It never seemed like it was worth it to you."

"I didn't think it was," Elisabeth said.

She wondered if it was in her blood, her cells, her DNA, this inability to be satisfied with what she had.

In sync, the masseuses whispered that they could slowly flip over for the second half.

The faceup part always made Elisabeth feel so much more vulnerable. Even more so since Nomi had decided to broadcast her troubles.

They lay in silence for a while.

Then Elisabeth said, "Andrew made us an appointment with Dr. Chen for later today. Without telling me."

"Ahh," Nomi said.

Elisabeth could hear her lifting her head.

"Now we're getting somewhere."

Everyone in the waiting room had funeral face. Closed-lipped expressions, resigned, gloomy.

In the past, when she had to be here every day, it made Elisabeth want to shout something inappropriate, or shower the crowd in armloads of confetti. Anything to change the mood. When, one morning, a man's phone erupted with "You down with O.P.P." and he could not seem to turn it off, it was the greatest thing that had ever happened, or would ever happen.

She sat now, looking around at the others with an air of superiority. This was a place for the desperate. But she wasn't desperate anymore. She didn't even want the thing they coveted. Andrew walked in a few minutes after she did, pushing Gil in the stroller. She used to think it was insensitive to bring a child here, like walking into a diabetes clinic eating chocolate cake.

A few women looked up from their phones or magazines to examine her, and Gil. If she was feeling more charitable, Elisabeth might have said, *He came from here! Don't give up!* But they didn't smile, and so she said nothing.

Nomi was right. The city had displeased her in a hundred different ways. It was good to remember that.

Andrew kissed her on the cheek and sat down.

"How was the massage?" he said.

"Good."

"And Nomi?"

"She's good. What have you guys been up to?"

"Went to that diner on Seventy-second for breakfast. Gil had pancakes."

"You did?" she said, looking at him, her voice full of cheer.

Elisabeth felt the eyes of the joyless upon her, but she didn't care.

"You didn't tell your parents about this, did you?" she asked.

"No," Andrew said. "Why?"

"Just curious."

The first time around, Faye and George let it be known that they thought IVF was a rich person thing, an urban affectation. Faye mentioned the names of celebrities she'd heard had done it. When Andrew calmly explained that the clinic would remove a single cell from each embryo for testing, Faye said, "What if the cell they take is the baby's arm?"

She was disgusted by the cost.

"It's highway robbery," Faye said to Elisabeth. "I wouldn't stand for it."

As if they had a choice. As if fertility treatments were a used car they could haggle over.

They were made to wait fifteen more minutes before being ushered into the doctor's office, where they waited another twenty. Gil was restless. They let him crawl around on the floor, poking his fingers in between the heating vents, trying to open a low drawer.

When Dr. Chen came in, he looked proud, taking in the sight of the baby. Elisabeth didn't like his expression, as if Gil were his creation, which she supposed he was in a way, but still.

"Hello there," he said. "What's your name?"

"Gilbert," she said. "Gil."

She knew from experience that this meeting would be as brief as he could make it, and she was happy about that.

"As soon as you're finished nursing, you can get started," he said. "A brother or sister for this guy in time for next Christmas, if you wish."

She wanted to make a crack about how much fun Christmas with her own sister had been this year, but this, like so many things, was a loaded topic.

The doctor looked at his computer screen, reading their file. "You have two grade-B embryos left," he said. "Given your age and the challenges we faced before, I'd say the chance of success with one embryo would be around seventeen percent. It will be much higher if you transfer both at once. But that will increase the likelihood of twins. So you need to do some soul-searching to determine if that fits with your plans."

"Absolutely not," she said. "I could never handle twins."

"I can think of worse things," Andrew said.

Elisabeth stared at him. "Like what?"

Dr. Chen cleared his throat. "You two have a lot to talk about. I'll leave you to it. Just—don't delay. The sooner you do this, the better. Wonderful to see you both. And to meet the famous Gil."

He looked down.

It was then that Elisabeth realized the famous Gil was chewing on the tassel of the doctor's patent leather wing tip.

"We'll be in touch," Andrew said.

He scooped the baby up off the floor with more dignity than she could have mustered.

Out in the hall, Andrew looked at her with such expectant eyes.

"What are your thoughts?" he said.

Elisabeth knew this might be the only way to win him back, to make things right between them. And yet, no part of her wanted to do it.

"I need to think about it some more," she said.

For the first time in a long time, Andrew looked satisfied by the words coming out of her mouth.

16

Sam

SAM AND CLIVE STAYED WITH Maddie for the weekend, in the Washington Heights apartment she shared with two other medical students. On Saturday, after watching Gil, they took the A train from Forty-second Street, pausing first to look at the neon behemoth that was Times Square. Sam knew from both Maddie and Elisabeth that real New Yorkers hated the place, but she thought it was sort of magnificent, those bright lights and gaudy flashing signs and people everywhere you looked.

On the subway, Clive read the ads for personal injury attorneys out loud to her.

"Is there any American who hasn't sued someone?" he said.

And Sam said, "Yes. Me."

She planted a kiss on his cheek. She was excited to see Maddie, and relieved in a way to be free of Elisabeth for the rest of the weekend.

Once they reached Maddie's, the three of them went to a bar in her neighborhood. Then, back at the apartment, Clive fell asleep, and Sam and Maddie stayed up talking.

Sam told her about the hotel room where they had spent the afternoon and evening with Gil.

"I've never seen anything like it," she said.

"Did you take pictures?" Maddie said.

"No, but I stole a bunch of shampoos from the maid's cart. Half for me and half for you."

Maddie nodded. "Sweet."

She was a year older than Sam. They met on the one day when eighth graders got to visit the town high school. Maddie was assigned to be Sam's tour guide. They had been best friends ever since, even though it was hard to find a place for their shared history in the midst of new friends, new lives.

Sam was more comfortable with Maddie than anyone. Their families were alike. Even their houses were nearly identical—modest white Colonials, distinct from each other only because the shutters on Sam's were black, and the shutters on Maddie's were red.

"Elisabeth thinks I should move here after graduation," Sam said now.

"Personally, I want to leave as soon as possible," Maddie said. "Go to a smaller city, where normal people can afford to live."

"That's pretty much what I told her, that I could never afford to live here," Sam said. "Elisabeth made it seem like she struggled when she was young, but it was worth it. Which is odd, considering the real story. Apparently she comes from a lot of money. Andrew's father told me the other day."

Sam pulled the shampoo bottles from her tote bag and lined them up on Maddie's coffee table.

"I thought she just had good taste. I didn't realize her father was a billionaire."

"An actual billionaire?" Maddie said.

"Probably not. But still."

"Still," Maddie said. "Sketchy."

"They lived in Brooklyn when they were here," Sam said. "I didn't know rich people lived in Brooklyn."

"That's where the undercover rich people live," Maddie said. "Like actual movie stars, but the kind who take their clothes to the laundromat because they think that's keeping it real. That's the thing about this city. So few people's lifestyles correspond to what they do for a living. You'll meet a poet, and she'll invite you over, and it turns out she has an entire brownstone. But it will never be mentioned *how*. You're supposed to pretend all poets live like that."

Sam hadn't said anything to Isabella about what George had told her. Isabella wouldn't get it.

She told Clive, who said, *Rich people are the worst. So predictable. I could sense that in Elisabeth, based on how you described her. You're too trusting, babe.*

She wished then that she hadn't told him.

But Maddie's reaction confirmed what Sam had already been thinking.

"This place isn't for me," Sam said. "It's so—big. And dirty. And crowded. No offense."

"None taken," Maddie said. "I didn't design it. It's not for me either, long term. But if you move here after graduation, we could live together for two years, until I finish school. Remember we used to talk about doing that? You working in a gallery, me in med school. Making dinner together every night. Watching TV in our pajamas. Dating identical twins named Chad and Brad."

Sam laughed.

"How fun would that be?" Maddie said.

"So much fun. Too bad you already have roommates."

"Calvin and Marisa graduate this spring. I'll need new roommates soon."

"Ooh."

"We should totally do it," Maddie said. "We'll live like an old married couple, at last."

Sam looked toward Maddie's room, where Clive was asleep on the air mattress.

When she crawled in beside him a few hours later, he woke up, groggy.

"I like New York City," he said.

"You've hardly seen it."

"What I've seen, I like."

"Elisabeth keeps saying I should move here," she said, testing his reaction.

"We should do, for a year or two. It'd be brilliant."

He kissed her and fell back to sleep.

Sam felt guilty. There was no space for him in the stories they had plotted tonight. She told herself that she and Maddie were only talking, having fun imagining what might have been had Clive not come along.

On Sunday, the Orthodox family in the apartment next door sat Shiva. A stream of mourners arrived. Their children spilled out into the hall, chasing one another, shouting like it was any other family party. Every so often, the children accidentally ran into Maddie's apartment. One little boy went straight to the bathroom, peed with the door open, and left without taking note of his surroundings. They could have turned the lock, but they found the situation too amusing.

Sam had made a list of places to take Clive, but they ended up spending most of their time at home, talking with Maddie and her roommates. Maddie made a frittata for breakfast and a big salad with walnuts and dried cranberries and goat cheese for lunch. Clive made salmon with fingerling potatoes for dinner. It felt so adult, a world away from dorm life.

After dinner, Sam and Clive sat on the sofa in the sunken living room. She pretended they were married, that the apartment was theirs. She could almost picture it.

Maddie and Clive developed an easy rapport that he had never managed with any of Sam's other friends. There was some special quality to the three of them together—Sam liked Clive better, liked their relationship more, when Maddie was around.

At some point on Sunday evening, the topic of Maddie's roommates leaving in a few months came up, and Clive said, "As luck would have it, Sam and I are thinking of moving here."

She was surprised he even remembered. He'd been half asleep when they discussed it.

Maddie looked confused, and Sam bumbled, "We were just talking, that's all."

Clive spent the whole weekend sniffling and coughing.

Allergies, he said.

"Sorry, it's probably the cat," Maddie said.

"It's okay," Clive said.

"It's not the cat! He was like this in the car on the way here!" Sam said.

She felt tense, like Clive had laid the blame on her friend, even though he hadn't been the one to bring up the cat.

"It's probably because you spend all day and night walking around London and it's freezing outside and now you're getting sick," she said, and then immediately felt bad.

"I never get sick," Clive said. "It's a fact."

On Monday, Maddie had a full day of classes. Sam and Clive went out for breakfast.

Their conversation was stilted. She felt like they were grasping for things to talk about. He didn't want to leave the waitress a tip, and Sam explained that such things were not optional in this country, at least not for decent people. Clive was cheap.

The other night, she had said as much to Maddie, who replied, "I think he's just poor."

Sam recoiled from that remark, but then said, "I think he's both."

After the awkward breakfast, they found a park by Maddie's place, where they made out on a rock on the far side of a little pond. They were surrounded by turtles, unbothered, unmoving, soaking up what they could of the weak winter sun.

Nobody talked much on the drive home.

"Please don't make me go back," Elisabeth said.

She sounded like they were taking her to prison.

Sam still sensed that things between Elisabeth and Andrew were fraught, even as Elisabeth described all the exciting activities they had done in the last forty-eight hours. How could they possibly have had a bad time staying in that hotel room, ordering as much room service as they wanted, going to Broadway shows and spa dates and dinners in fancy restaurants.

Sam wished she could unknow what George had told her.

At some point, Elisabeth said, "These friends we met up with on Saturday were telling us they just bought an eight-hundred-square-foot apartment for over a million dollars. They're using it as an office, not to live in. People in the city have too much money, I swear."

Clive nudged Sam and rolled his eyes.

So many people pretended at wealth they didn't have. Sam wondered why Elisabeth went to such lengths to seem average. She felt like she didn't really know her at all.

But an hour into the drive, Gil let out a squeal, and Elisabeth turned toward the back seat to look at him. Sam's eyes met hers and they exchanged a smile that felt so familiar, so comfortable, that Sam wished they could be alone, up in the den after a Sunday dinner, Elisabeth explaining whatever was going on with Andrew, Sam telling her about Clive.

Smooshed into Andrew and Elisabeth's back seat, subject to

their timing and on their terms, Clive seemed diminished. He could not keep still. He kept making a noise with his tongue. He tapped his fingers on his knees. He was used to being the one in charge on a road trip. In England, Sam never knew what route they were taking or how far it was. She was his passenger. They both liked it that way.

Now Clive kept asking questions about the car that Andrew didn't know the answers to, and then positing his own ideas.

"What kind of horsepower does this thing have?" Clive said.

"Two hundred, maybe?" Andrew said. "Three hundred?"

"One eighty-five, I reckon," Clive said.

Fifty miles from home, they pulled over at a rest stop so Sam and Elisabeth could pee.

Gil was asleep.

"I'll stay in the car with him," Andrew whispered.

"Me too," Clive said.

Sam wondered if Andrew found this annoying; if he was hoping for a few minutes alone.

She and Elisabeth went inside. They walked past the crowds lining up for Chipotle and Sbarro and Subway, all of which sounded delicious right now. Sam wanted dinner, but no one else was hungry, and she didn't want to be the only one eating.

Elisabeth started talking about the Central Park Zoo. She said she could never decide whether it was delightful or depressing.

"On the one hand, how incredible is it that you can see a polar bear in the middle of Manhattan?" she said. "On the other, that poor polar bear. He doesn't belong there."

They went into two stalls, right next to each other.

Sam paused and waited to see if Elisabeth was a stall-to-stall talker. She herself always let the other woman decide. She assumed Elisabeth would stop talking and resume their conversation at the sink, which proved accurate.

"Is everything going well with you and Clive?" Elisabeth said as they washed their hands.

Something about the way she said it made Sam uneasy. As if Elisabeth expected the answer to be no.

"Yeah," Sam said.

"You had a good time?"

"We did."

She considered mentioning how the conversation had been harder than she might have liked, or that Maddie had invited her to move in. But either thing felt like an admission she wasn't ready to make.

Instead Sam said, "I wish we'd gone to the Guggenheim."

She took in their reflection in the mirror.

Elisabeth always looked put together, even now, traveling in jeans and sneakers.

Sam looked rumpled. The arms of her plain striped shirt were wrinkled. Her hair was everywhere.

She noticed, with annoyance, her chubby cheeks. *Baby fat*, her mother would say. Elisabeth's were almost concave, a wonderful hollowness about them that Sam coveted. Clive had said he didn't think Elisabeth was that good looking, but Sam found her appearance endlessly appealing. Her big smile. Her elegant, protruding collarbones. Even the lines at the corners of her eyes that resembled the darting rays in a child's drawing of the sun.

Back at the dorm, they came upon Isabella and Shannon sitting on Isabella's bed with their laptops.

"How was the weekend?" Isabella said.

"Fun!" Sam said.

"Glorious," Clive said.

"We're gonna go to a late-night showing of the new Ben Affleck movie," Shannon said. "Buying tickets now. You two should come."

"I'm not overly interested in scripted films anymore," Clive said, before Sam could respond. "They're mostly rubbish, aren't they? You reach an age where that sort of thing stops being interesting."

He turned to Sam. "I'll only pay to go to the cinema if it's a really good documentary at the Barbican or something."

Isabella and Shannon both looked at him, and then down at their computers, without answering.

"We'd better leave you guys alone," Isabella said a few moments later.

"You don't have to," Sam said.

But they fled across the hall to Shannon's room anyway, and shut the door.

When she and Clive planned this trip, Ramona and her girl-friend hadn't broken up yet. Now that they had, Ramona was back to sleeping in her own bed, which meant Isabella would be on the floor. Everyone was sacrificing for Sam's benefit, and for Clive's. She wished he wouldn't default to snobby and arrogant whenever he felt uncomfortable.

Sam heard her friends laughing across the hall. So often while in their company, she had wished she was in London, with Clive. But now Clive was here and she wanted to be with them.

"I'm starving," he said. "Let's order something in."

"Any place that delivers around here closes by nine," Sam said.

Then she remembered her key to the kitchen, the one Maria gave her her first year, when she worked the early shift. Sam had never given it back.

"Come with me," she said, leading him by the hand down the back stairwell.

The dining hall felt foreboding with no one in it, and all the lights turned off.

"Where are you taking me?" Clive said.

"You'll see."

They crossed the room in the pitch black, his hand creeping down her back, squeezing her butt. Sam let out a squeal, and Clive said "What? What happened?" as if it hadn't been him.

When they reached the heavy metal kitchen door, she inserted the key, pushed it open.

"Dinner is served," she said as she switched on the light.

She went to one of the refrigerators and pulled out half a tray of leftover enchiladas from Mexican night on Saturday and three-quarters of an apple pie. Clive took a small bowl of mashed potatoes, looking guilty and gleeful, like the two of them were a pair of criminals.

Sam glanced over her shoulder before carrying the food to the microwave. It felt illicit, opening the door, closing it, pressing the buttons, each of which let out a loud beep.

Clive's lips were on the back of her neck before she had a chance to turn around. He wrapped his arms around her from behind, his hands on her breasts.

"Pull your pants down," he said.

Sam did so, watching the enchiladas spin. Her grandmother had once told her you could get cancer from standing in front of a microwave.

Clive slid one hand down between her legs.

"Spread them wider," he whispered.

She could hear him unzipping his jeans.

By Wednesday morning, Clive's alleged allergies had turned into the flu. He had a temperature of a hundred and two, the chills, a hacking cough. Sam went to class for three hours, and when she returned home for lunch, he had filled her trash can with dirty Kleenex.

She kept thinking she felt achy, waiting for it to hit her.

"Snuggle with me?" Clive said pathetically, and Sam curled her body against his like they were two Pringles in a can, all the while trying not to breathe.

When she returned from her afternoon classes, he was propped up on pillows in her bed, watching TV. A chair had been pulled up beside him. On it sat a bowl of chicken soup, a dish filled with crackers, lemon wedges, and honey packets, a mug, and a large silver thermos.

"What's all that?" she said.

"Tea," he said. "Soup."

"Where'd you get it?"

"I went down to the dining hall for a glass of water, and one of your friends took pity on me."

Sam felt some small sense of alarm. "Which friend?"

"Delmi. The cafeteria worker. She told me to get right back in bed and she'd bring this all up. She's a saint. We spoke a little Spanish. She tolerated my bad accent."

"Oh. Delmi," Sam said. Then, thinking it over, "That's not really her job."

Clive just smiled back.

At dinnertime, when Sam walked into the kitchen to thank her, Delmi was talking close with Maria. They were speaking Spanish, but Sam recognized one phrase, a favorite of Maria's.

"*Hay pericos en la milpa.*"

There are parakeets in the cornfield.

Two student workers were washing dishes, their backs to the room.

Were they the parakeets, Sam wondered, or was she?

"Hi, Sam," Delmi said, with no trace of her usual smile.

"You didn't have to do that for Clive," Sam said. "That was so nice of you."

"It was nothing," Delmi said.

She stared down at a cell phone in her hand, then showed Maria what was on the screen.

"Clive said he talked to you in Spanish. He lived in Spain for a while."

Delmi seemed agitated. "Hmm? Yes, he speaks very good Spanish."

"I hope he wasn't annoying."

"It's fine, Sam," Delmi snapped.

Sam thought of what she and Clive had done in this room the other night. It felt fun and harmless at the time, but now she wondered if somehow they knew. She regretted her behavior. It was thoughtless. Gross.

"Are you mad at me?" she said, sounding childish, feeling her face grow hot.

Delmi looked up from the phone. "What? No! Of course not."

Sam brought food upstairs for Clive and herself. She told him what had happened.

"Like she said, it's nothing to do with you," he said. "She's probably just having a bad day."

Clive looked pale. When he closed his eyes, she could tell it hurt.

Sam put a palm to his forehead, even though she could never determine anything that way.

"I'll get the thermometer," she said.

A few hours later, when Clive's fever still hadn't gone down, she took him to Health Services. The campus doctor kept looking from him to her and back again, as if trying to solve a riddle.

Sam went to work on Thursday, as usual. Elisabeth had told her to take the day off, spend it with Clive, but Sam insisted.

Privately, she felt eager for a break, but she didn't say so out loud.

She had never seen Clive sick before. He made a particularly pitiful patient. Sam tried to be nurturing, but as he coughed up phlegm and moaned throughout the night, she mostly wished he would go downstairs and sleep on one of the sofas in the living room. She felt an odd sense of surprise each time she opened the door to her room and found him lying there.

She had once viewed him as if from a distance, even when they lived together. Now it was like she had a magnifying glass suspended over his every flaw. Without his brightly colored zip-up tops, his designer sneakers, the product in his hair, he suddenly looked like a middle-aged man; a dad in a white undershirt.

Sam hoped the feeling would pass.

Walking into Elisabeth's house was a relief.

Still, when Elisabeth asked how the rest of their week had been, Sam said, "Great, mostly."

Elisabeth was effusive in her likes and dislikes. She had spoken several times about how fabulous Isabella was. But she hadn't said anything about Clive. It was an itch Sam wanted to scratch—to ask, *What do you think of him?* But she was afraid to know the answer. Weeks ago, Elisabeth had said Sam should bring Clive over for dinner while he was here, but now he was here and no invitation had been extended.

She passed an easy day with Gil, watching him toddle around the living room, doing a load of his laundry while he napped. Sam held each item up before tossing it into the machine. His sweet little shirts and pants and socks. Sometimes, in Gil's presence, she felt like she would explode if she had to wait much longer for a baby of her own. Other times, Sam felt like she was still a baby, so far from all this.

Her cell phone rang, her mother calling. Sam answered as she finished the laundry.

Her mother sounded tired, and a bit sad.

"I'm working as much overtime as I can," she said. "Six nights last week."

Sam thought of what her brother, Brendan, had told her about their father's job.

"How's Dad?" she said.

"He's okay. It's not the best time for him right now. The economy is good, which usually means his business is good. But for some reason, no one is putting additions on their houses. It's just the season, probably. Things will pick up in the spring."

Sam wanted to believe her, but she felt uneasy.

They talked a few minutes longer and then said their goodbyes.

Hanging on a clothing rack in the laundry room was a dress of Elisabeth's with the tags still on.

It had been there all year. Sam had seen it plenty of times. But now she felt that prickle at the back of her neck. She wanted proof of something. She walked toward the dress, looked at the price. Five hundred and fifty dollars. Elisabeth had never even worn it.

Next, Sam went to the powder room on the first floor. She looked up the price of the peony-scented hand soap online.

Forty-six dollars.

Sam felt her mother's eyes rolling in her own head.

Elisabeth had said she got it at a drugstore. But the Internet revealed that the soap was exclusively available at Neiman Marcus. (*Needless Markup*, as Sam's mother called it.)

Gil was in his high chair (seven hundred dollars), eating a mashed avocado, when Elisabeth came home.

She was on the phone, her face screwed up in annoyance, a stack of mail in her hand.

She smiled at Gil, then said into the phone, "But I still have three vials left over from last time. Why do I have to order new ones? I told you—it doesn't expire until June. Okay. Good. Thank you. The syringes will be included, right? And the extra needles? Good. No, no, it's okay. Thanks for your help."

She looked sheepish as she hung up.

"I have something to tell you," she said. "I'm going to try to get pregnant again. You're the only person I'm telling besides Andrew. Not even Nomi knows. She'll ask me about it constantly, and I want to keep the process as mellow and low pressure as possible."

"That makes sense."

Sam felt flattered to be included in the inner circle, but then she supposed it was necessary, since she spent so much time in this house.

"I know I've told you that I don't want more kids," Elisabeth said.

"What changed your mind?"

"I haven't changed my mind. But we have the two embryos, and Andrew wants to put them both in at once. Twins! I want zero additional children. Since neither of us could persuade the other to come over to our side, we decided to meet in the middle. One more kid—potentially."

Was this how it happened? Could the decision to bring a life into the world be reduced to a calculation, a compromise?

"There's a very high chance that it won't work," Elisabeth said.

Sam thought she sounded hopeful.

"We're going to start the shots next week. I'll be monitored by a doctor here. If all goes well, I'll go to the city in a month for the embryo transfer."

Her kids would be so close in age. Gil wasn't yet a year old. If

Elisabeth had been purely a friend, Sam would have asked if she was sure.

Clive was asleep when she got back to the dorm. He looked so sweet. By Saturday, he would be gone. Tomorrow she would try to block that out and enjoy the small amount of time they had left. Sam was never more in love with him than on the last night.

On Friday, Clive's fever broke. He was well enough to shower, get dressed, feel hungry again. Sam found herself touching him constantly, clinging to his T-shirt.

"Don't go," she said. And, "I'm psychically willing your flight to get canceled."

They went into town for dinner. She thought he looked particularly handsome, even under the fluorescent lights of the cheap Thai restaurant. When he asked if they should go to Herrell's for ice cream after, Sam shook her head and said, "I want to get you home."

Clive nodded. "I think that could be arranged."

Back at the dorm, voices floated out from the living room.

"What's going on down there?" Clive said. He was constitutionally incapable of missing a good party once he knew it was under way.

"Nothing interesting, I'm sure," she said.

It felt natural to be with Clive in Maddie's apartment, or on the streets of New York City, or even downtown, eating Thai food. But on campus, Sam still felt self-conscious. She didn't want to lead him down the hall and squirm as he tried to make conversation with a bunch of college girls.

Next year they would live in the real world again. The age difference wouldn't matter as much.

They climbed the stairs to her platform.

Isabella came running. She had mostly ignored them all week. But now she shouted, "Sam! Oh my God! Sam!"

Sam's heart rate quickened.

"What's the matter?" she said. "What happened?"

"Listen to this voice mail I just got," Isabella said. "Oh my God, my hands are shaking."

She set her cell phone to speaker. Clive and Sam leaned their heads down to listen.

Hey, little ho. This is Inez, Joseph's baby mama. You stay away from him, or I will claw your motherfucking eyes out. I'm not kidding. Don't try me, bitch.

At first Sam thought it must be a wrong number.

"Who's Joseph?" she asked.

"The stripper's assistant!" Isabella said.

"He has a baby mama? Who refers to herself as his *baby mama?*"

"Apparently."

"And he never mentioned this."

"Nope!"

"But didn't he get your name tattooed on his arm?" Clive said.

Sam felt touched that he remembered a detail like that.

"It was my initial," Isabella said. "The letter *I*."

"Inez," Clive said, nodding. "What a bastard."

Isabella laughed. "For real," she said.

Sam wondered if Clive had won her over, at last.

She took his arm. She was lucky to have found her person so early in life. Most of her friends would be searching for years.

In the morning, they were frantic, trying to get ready in time for George's arrival.

"What time is your flight again?" she asked.

"Half ten," Clive said.

Sam could never remember if it meant half past the hour or until.

"We need coffee," she said as he struggled to close his suitcase. "I'll meet you out front, okay?"

Sam went to the kitchen.

She pushed through the swinging door and found Maria and Delmi, not working, as they usually were when she entered, but looking down at something on the counter. Their heads snapped to attention when Sam walked in.

Maria put whatever it was behind her back.

"Come," she said.

She led Sam into the pantry.

The smell of the coffee conjured up memories of breakfast in her childhood home, and Sundays in bed with Clive in London, and early mornings here in this kitchen, talking to Gaby as they cooked at the start of the day.

"Look at this," Maria whispered. "Delmi heard a rumor it was coming."

Sam took the thin newspaper from her hands, its pages folded back.

There it was. Her letter, taking up half the page, which was divided in two by a vertical line down the middle. On the other side was a response from President Washington.

Sam's heartbeat quickened. She tried to look surprised, confused even.

"What is this?" she said stupidly, a smile forcing the edges of her lips upward.

"It's trouble," Maria said.

A jarring response; the opposite of what Sam expected.

"What? Why?" she said.

"Read it," Maria said.

Sam did.

Dear Student,

Thank you for your concern. And to the *Collegian* for providing this forum.

While it is impossible for me to address your specific accusations without knowing to whom you are referring (or indeed, if the individuals you're referring to are actual people, or if your complaints are of a more general nature . . .) I want to assure you that service employees are a valued part of this community, truly the lifeblood of the college. We are grateful every day for their tireless efforts. If that has not been properly conveyed, we must remedy the situation. To that end, Barney Reardon, head of Residence and Dining Services, and I have invited the support staff to join us for a frank and candid conversation about working conditions today at 5:00. The meeting will be closed, but details will be shared in these pages at a later date.

Thank you for caring enough to speak your truth.

Sincerely,

Shirley Washington

Sam looked up at Maria. "But this is a good thing, right? She's going to listen. She's great, I'm telling you. She'll make things better."

Maria sighed. "Some girl comes to this realization every few years and raises the issue with the college, and then nothing happens. There was even a big campus protest about it once. Maybe twice? I hope they don't do that again. It's a waste of everyone's time. This meeting today, they say it's mandatory. I don't want to go. Barney Reardon has never been out to help us. I don't see that changing now."

They heard footsteps outside the pantry and walked back into the kitchen, toward the sound. A sophomore whose name Sam couldn't recall was tying on an apron.

Maria's expression conveyed that the conversation was over.

"Hi, Sarah," she said. "Could you put out the cereal first?"

Sam walked out of the kitchen and through the dining hall.

The room was filling up with students, some in pajama pants and hoodies, sitting down to plates of scrambled eggs and waffles; others with coats and backpacks on, filling travel mugs with coffee, toasting bagels to eat on the way to class. All of them thought it was a day like any other.

It bothered Sam, though what did she expect? She and her friends didn't tend to start their day with intense conversations about what was in the college paper either.

She made her way outside. It wasn't until the breeze blew the flimsy pages in her hand that she realized she was still clutching the newspaper.

George's car was in the driveway, Clive already sitting in back.

The two men were talking, smiling, as if this was normal.

Sam made a point of climbing in front.

Her head was a jumble. Her heart raced.

"Where's the coffee, love?" Clive said.

"What?"

George started talking, but she couldn't make sense of what he said.

When he stopped for gas, Sam followed him with her eyes as he walked to the pump.

She said to Clive, "My letter is in the paper today. President Washington wrote me back, and she is going to meet with all the support staff to discuss the situation. Look."

She handed him the page.

"Well done," Clive said.

He was silent for a minute as he read President Washington's response. Then he looked up and said, "How arrogant is this? *Or indeed, if the individuals you're referring to are actual people?* It's like she's suggesting you made them up. What a twat."

Somehow Sam realized only then that she was upset not just because Maria had seemed so skeptical, but because what Clive said was true. President Washington's reply to her letter was dismissive, calculated, almost accusatory. It was as if the woman who gave the speech Sam had watched again and again was someone else entirely.

George pulled the pump from the tank and twisted the gas cap.

"I don't want George to know I did it," Sam said. "I don't want anyone to know yet."

"Why not? It was a great thing to do," Clive said. "Most college girls have their heads so far up their own asses they'd never even stop to consider someone else's needs."

It sounded like something Gaby would say.

Gaby. What would she make of what Sam had done? Gaby had told her Maria wouldn't want this. Why hadn't she listened?

Since she was a child, she had had a recurring nightmare about driving down a winding mountain road when she didn't know how to drive. Sometimes, the brakes went out. The way Sam felt now reminded her of that sensation. She wished she could wake up, relieved to find that none of it had actually happened. She suddenly had a terrible feeling about what she'd done.

When they got to the airport, George stayed in the car so Sam and Clive could say their goodbyes.

They hugged on the curb outside international departures. Sam stood on her toes to reach him.

Clive cupped her chin in his hand. "You're the best girl in the world. I love you," he said. "I'm proud of you for writing that letter."

"Don't be," she said.

"I'm going to miss you like hell."

"You too," she said. "I hate saying goodbye."

"I'm so glad we won't have to do it much longer," he said. "Soon, for the rest of my life, when I get on an airplane, you'll be sitting beside me, not waving me off."

Clive held on tight until a policeman walked by and told them it was time to move along.

That night before dinner, Sam walked into the kitchen and found it empty. Not just of people, but things. Delmi's plants were gone, and the statue of the Virgin Mary. Even the photograph of Gaby's baby had been taken down from the salad bar, just a speck of Scotch tape where it once hung.

Sam heard a noise from the pantry. She found Gaby, stocking cans of green beans and tomato paste.

"How did the meeting go?" she asked.

"It sucked," Gaby said coolly.

"What happened?"

"Your friend the president was pissed. Said whoever wrote that letter made her look bad. She actually accused the staff of being behind the whole thing. She said no student could possibly have known all those details. You know what I heard Delmi say to my aunt after? She said, 'That letter sure does sound like Gaby on a bad day.'"

Sam's cheeks grew hot.

Gaby went to her purse and pulled out a piece of paper.

"What's that?" Sam said.

"The new code of conduct all service employees have to sign."

Gaby read aloud. *"Section four: Employee satisfaction and communication. A positive and constructive relationship between the*

College and Staff is essential to the mission of the College. Thus, if the behavior, communication, or interaction on or off campus and/or online, of Staff Members reflects a loss of confidence in or serious disagreement with the College, Staff Members understand and agree that the College has the right to dismiss/terminate employment as determined at the College's sole and exclusive discretion."

Gaby met Sam's eye: "In other words, keep your mouths shut about what goes on here, or get out."

Sam started to reply, but Gaby went on.

"Section nine: Personal Belongings. Effective immediately, no personal belongings are to be kept in campus kitchens. Handbags, coats, and other small personal items should remain in designated storage lockers. Refuse is campus property and shall not be removed from campus other than by designated sanitation professionals. Food and beverage are property of the College and should not be taken from campus at any time, for any reason. Failure to observe these rules will be considered theft and result in immediate suspension."

Sam stood there, mouth agape.

"You wrote it, didn't you," Gaby said.

It was not a question.

"What the hell, Sam? I told you those things in confidence, as a friend. Not because I was looking for you to save the day. If I wanted the goddamn college president to know, I would have told her myself. Have I ever struck you as someone who has a hard time speaking her mind?"

Sam laughed gently. But Gaby wasn't laughing. She looked angry. Sam had never been on the receiving end of that look.

Gaby took a long, deep breath, just as Maria told her to whenever some entitled student was irritating her.

"By that definition of *theft*, I've stolen tons of stuff," Sam said. "So have most people I know."

Gaby shrugged.

"This is so messed up. We can stage a protest," Sam said. "People on this campus love to protest. I'm serious."

"Just let these women take care of themselves," Gaby said. "It's what they've been doing all their life."

"But my friend George, he's in that group. They help people who've been treated unfairly by the system. I could—"

Gaby shook her head. "Drawing even more attention to this is the last thing they would ever want to do. We don't have the luxury of crying about what's fair and what isn't. We're not like you."

Sam felt foolish.

"I'm so sorry," she said. "I feel terrible. I thought it would all be different. I should have signed my name. If anyone was going to get in trouble, it should be me."

"That wouldn't have mattered," Gaby said. "The school expects you to protest. And they expect you to move on and forget. They know what they're doing. They just don't care."

Gaby curled her hands into fists.

"I've got to get out of here," she said. "I need a new job. A friend of mine makes good money as a nanny and she's leaving her job soon. She said she'd put in a good word. I can't exactly picture myself doing that. But maybe if I could bring Josie."

Sam thought maybe Elisabeth would hire Gaby after she graduated. She couldn't quite see them together, but she could see Elisabeth being the type who would take pride in letting her nanny bring her own child to work.

"You know the baby I nanny for. Gil," she began.

Gaby's expression turned to revulsion, like she'd eaten something rotten.

"Stop saying you're a nanny," she snapped. "You were never a nanny, Sam."

Sam was confused. "Yes, I was. I am."

"You have no idea what this feels like."

Sam wondered if somehow Gaby had the wrong impression of who she was, where she came from. She thought of something George had said about Elisabeth.

"I don't have some safety net either, you know," Sam said. "I do get it. I'm worried about money all the time. My father's job has been—"

"Sam. Last year, your friend flew you to London because you were sad and it was her birthday. Who do you think you are?" Gaby said, voice rising. "You don't have a safety net? You don't have a family you can go home to, parents who would feed you and care for you if you needed?"

She stretched out her arms. "This place isn't a safety net for you? Maria has no safety net. Maria *is* the safety net, for so many people."

"I know that. I love Maria."

Gaby scoffed. "Don't say *love*. You just made her life ten times harder than it was to begin with. My aunt gets paid to be nice to girls like you."

The words stung. Sam felt tears prick at the corners of her eyes.

"You're gonna cry now?" Gaby said. "Am I supposed to make you feel better? After how you've treated me on top of everything else? Look. I get it. I was the temporary friend. Then your real friends came back and you didn't need me anymore."

"No," Sam said, "it was never like that. I've just been so busy."

"I have two jobs and a kid. Don't tell me how busy you are," Gaby said. "You'd better go. See? It says so right here. *Section twelve: No fraternizing with students.* Why don't you go find your princess? I'm sure she has all the time in the world."

17

WITHIN A FEW DAYS of her letter being published in the paper, things went back to the way they'd always been, as if the whole situation had never occurred. The student body did not rise up as Sam had imagined. The workers didn't do so either. Instead, they signed the college's contract and got on with it.

Everyone but Gaby. Maria said the contract had been the last straw for her. She'd gotten a new job as a hostess at a chain restaurant in Weaverville.

In the month that followed, Sam texted her several times, but Gaby never responded. When Sam checked Facebook, Gaby had unfriended her.

But it seemed Gaby hadn't outed her to the others. When Sam considered why, she figured Gaby felt responsible for telling her their troubles in the first place.

Sam missed her. She still went into the kitchen most mornings for her coffee. To not do so felt like an admission of something. Muscle memory made it so that pushing the door into the kitchen, she expected to see Gaby there, to smile at her, to laugh. Each time, it was a shock to find her gone.

Several times each day, sitting in a lecture hall or feeding Gil his bottle, Sam cringed, thinking back to the letter she'd written, how George had told her to consult Maria and Delmi and Gaby, but instead she had just gone ahead and done it, so sure that she knew what the outcome would be. She had only succeeded in making things worse for them. And she had been a terrible friend to Gaby. Her regret was a heavy object pushing down on her chest, making it hard to breathe.

She went out of her way to avoid walking by President Washington's house now. On the rare occasion when she had no choice but to do so, Sam had to look in the other direction. She kept thinking of the alumnae dinner she had agreed to work in a few weeks' time. She couldn't tell Maria that she no longer wanted to do it. Sam hoped that things would be different by then, though she couldn't imagine how.

The second Sunday in March, at six o'clock in the evening, Sam knocked at the open door of Andrew and Elisabeth's house.

In unison, they called, "Come in!"

She found them in the kitchen.

Elisabeth sat at one of the high-backed stools, a glass of red wine in her hand.

Andrew stood over a gleaming silver contraption on the counter. To the side of it was an open egg carton, a glass measuring cup, a bright yellow bag of semolina flour. The machine whirred. Long strands of dough flowed out through holes in the front. It reminded Sam of the Play-Doh Fun Factory she and her siblings used to fight over when they were kids.

"Sam!" Andrew said. "I got the old pasta maker out! Haven't used it since the move, but tonight's the night. We're having fresh fettuccine. Hope you're hungry!"

His tone was extra upbeat. He sounded like a mom in a television commercial.

"He's acting weird because you caught us in the middle of an argument," Elisabeth explained.

Andrew shook his head, rolled his eyes.

"What?" Elisabeth said. "It's Sam. She knows everything about us. She could probably hear us arguing from outside."

"I couldn't," Sam said.

She picked up the baby monitor and stuck out her lower lip at the sight of Gil in striped footie pajamas, sprawled on his back in the crib.

"I know," Elisabeth said. "Don't you want to eat him?"

"Wine, Sam?" Andrew asked.

"Sure, thanks. I can get it."

"Sit," he said. "I've got you."

Elisabeth said, "It's actually good news that brought on this disagreement we're having. We should toast. Andrew got invited to a conference for inventors in Denver. Lots of investors go. It's prestigious. Big deals are made there every year."

"That's great," Sam said. "Congrats."

They raised their glasses, clinked them together.

"I'm an alternate," Andrew said. "They didn't pick me first round, but I got the call today. Some guy who makes drum pants got meningitis, so there's an opening."

"What are drum pants?" Sam said.

Neither of them seemed to hear her. They were looking at each other, locked into a silent exchange she couldn't read.

"Only trouble is, he has to leave tomorrow at the crack of dawn," Elisabeth said. "He's abandoning me for my last week of shots. No big deal, I'm only doing the shots *for him*."

"Jesus," Andrew said with an exasperated smile.

"Kidding," Elisabeth said. "Sort of."

Lately, they seemed to be getting along again, though since Elisabeth started the injections, she had been off-kilter, not quite herself. She felt tired and bloated and irritable. Andrew was acting extra attentive. He was often still home when Sam arrived to work in the morning, giving Gil breakfast, getting him dressed, so Elisabeth could sleep in. He read up on the best foods for her fertility and slipped them into whatever he was making for dinner. Elisabeth said he never mentioned he was doing this, but she could tell.

"Last night, as a starter, he served me a bowl of bone broth," she had reported on Friday. "It tasted like shoes."

Now Andrew said, "I don't have to go."

"Stop saying that. You're going."

"Okay, so it's four more days of the regular shots and then the big one on the fifth day," he said.

"The trigger," Elisabeth said.

She looked at Sam. "They call it that because it feels like getting shot in the ass. I might be able to give myself the other ones, but not that. It's a three-inch needle. I'm afraid I'll pass out if I see it."

"Maybe we could ask my mother to come over and do the injections," Andrew said.

"Absolutely not," Elisabeth said. "I think we should just hit pause on this and try again another month."

"After everything you've gone through?" he said. "You're three-quarters of the way there."

"I could do the shots," Sam said. "I know how. I did them for Isabella."

"I wouldn't ask you to do that," Elisabeth said. "It has to happen every night at nine on the dot, after Gil is in bed, so you'd have to come over then. It would be such a pain."

"No, it wouldn't. I'm happy to help."

"We'd pay you for the hour each night," Andrew said.

"Andrew!" Elisabeth said. "Honey, she's doing this as a friend. Sorry, Sam, he's clueless sometimes."

Sam wondered what she would have said had Elisabeth not intervened. She might have taken the money.

"And what about the early morning appointments?" he said.

"I can make them work," Elisabeth said.

"You'll take Gil?"

"I guess so."

Elisabeth reached over and squeezed her hand. "Thank you. I feel so much better about this now."

"I'll come back on Friday night and we'll drive straight to the city the next day for the transfer," Andrew said.

Elisabeth nodded. "Good."

"I can't believe you might have two kids by this time next year," Sam said.

"Two under two," Andrew said, with wonder.

"That reminds me, Sam," Elisabeth said. "Gil turns one on May twenty-fourth. It's a Sunday."

"The day after my graduation," Sam said. "I've been meaning to tell you—each student only gets a handful of tickets to commencement. I'd love it if you could come, but I understand if you can't. Those things are always long and boring."

Elisabeth looked like she might cry. "Of course I'm coming!" she said. "What if we have a party here that Sunday? A combined first birthday and graduation party. Your family can come. We'd love to host them. And Andrew's parents. And—the neighbors? Your friends would be welcome, of course. My best friend, Nomi, will be here. I can't wait for you two to meet."

"I don't want Gil to have to share his birthday party with me," Sam said.

"You're his favorite person. He'll love it."

It was a generous offer, but somehow Sam couldn't picture the party Elisabeth had in mind. Her mother would want to host something when she got home. Whatever Elisabeth did would be so much nicer. Her mom would be intimidated, or embarrassed, or—something.

Sam couldn't imagine Elisabeth observing her in the context

of her family. Her parents still treated her like a child. Her mother would lick her thumb and run it back and forth across Sam's lips instead of saying, "There's something on your mouth."

"Think about it," Elisabeth said. "It would be my pleasure. We're going to miss you so much. There's only, what, eight more weeks of classes left?"

"I can't believe that," Sam said.

"Neither can I."

"I'll tell you who's gonna miss you," Andrew said. "My dad. We saw them yesterday and he couldn't stop talking about you."

Sam smiled, but the mention of George made her chest feel heavy. She had skipped the most recent discussion group meeting, telling him she had too much schoolwork. The guys in the group were excited about a Benjamin Ross article in the *Gazette*, all about them. Sam didn't think she could be alone with George in the car without telling him what she had done to Gaby and Maria and the others.

"Sam," Elisabeth said, drawing her attention from her thoughts. "Remember I wanted you to do that Madonna and Child painting of me and Gil? But with aspects of you in there as well. Something like that?"

"Oh God, you're serious about that?" Andrew said.

"Yes!" Elisabeth said. "It will be amazing."

"That is such a weird thing to ask," Andrew said. "You should just have her paint you and Gil."

"I could do that too," Sam said.

"No," Elisabeth said.

Isabella agreed with Andrew that it was an odd request, the idea that Sam might blend herself and Elisabeth into the image of one woman.

"You two couldn't look more different," Isabella said when Sam told her.

But Sam knew what Elisabeth meant. Not that she ought to

combine her own eyes and Elisabeth's chin, her hair and Elisabeth's nose. But rather that the woman in the painting should contain the essence of them both. Sam liked that only she and Elisabeth understood.

"We should take pictures this week, so you can get started," Elisabeth said. "We'll do it tomorrow when you're here. Sound good? I know you're busy, but don't say no. I have my heart set on it."

"You're bossy tonight," Andrew said.

Elisabeth stuck out her tongue.

"We can use my good camera, the Canon," she said. "Andrew, do you know where it is?"

Sam needed new paints, which she couldn't exactly afford. She wished she could say as much, but didn't know how to do it without embarrassing Elisabeth and herself in the process. Elisabeth had twice referred to the painting as something she planned to commission, though she had never specified a dollar amount. Sam had a sensation similar to the one she'd get as a child upon ripping open a birthday card from her grandparents to find a folded blue check inside. Experience promised that that check was in the amount of fifteen dollars. Hope suggested that perhaps they'd gone big, outlandishly so, just this once.

Her father's work situation weighed on her more and more as the end of the school year approached. She'd never imagined her parents would give her much money after she graduated, but she knew now that they'd have nothing to give her. She was trying to save as much as humanly possible for herself and, if need be, for them.

Later, after they'd eaten, they saw Gil fussing on the monitor. Elisabeth went upstairs to quiet him.

Andrew whispered across the table, "Does she seem off to you?"

Sam was used to being Elisabeth's confidante in this marriage, not his. Any response she could give felt like a betrayal.

"She's all over the place," he went on. "Almost—manic. I guess it's the drugs. Was your friend that way when she took them?"

"Isabella is always manic and all over the place, so it's hard to say," Sam replied.

She stood and cleared the dishes.

When Sam got to work the next morning, Elisabeth and Gil were in the living room. The shades were rolled up. Light streamed in. Elisabeth had pushed one of the armchairs to the center of the floor.

"I'm so excited for this," she said. "Come! Sit!"

Sam put her purse down and waved at Gil, who beamed in response. He was in his bouncer, wearing only a diaper.

She said, "Let me just hang up my jacket."

Elisabeth shook her head. "Sorry, I'll start over. Good morning, Sam! Can I get you some coffee?"

Sam smiled. "No, it's okay, we can get right to it. I can see you're eager."

"Thanks. Sorry. Andrew left at four for the airport and I couldn't get back to sleep, and now I'm wired and exhausted and I've had way too much caffeine."

She looked Sam up and down.

"Do you have anything on under that?" Elisabeth said.

Sam wore a green Celtics hoodie of her brother's. Underneath was the flimsiest tank top, something she'd had since high school, with spaghetti straps and two small holes in the front. It wasn't a shirt she would ever wear in public.

"An old tank top," she said. "You definitely don't want a picture of it."

"It's not so I can get your shirt in the photo, it's more so we can see the shape of your body. Your shoulders and clavicle and such. Does that make sense? You're the artist. You know best."

"I see what you mean," Sam said, though in every picture of the Madonna and Child she had ever seen, the Virgin Mary was covered in flowing robes, and usually a veil.

Sam pulled off the sweatshirt, feeling exposed, wondering why she could never say what she was thinking, whether that would ever change.

She noticed Elisabeth noticing the size of her breasts and had the urge to cross her arms up high and cover them with her hands, like she had done at the town pool the summer they first appeared.

"Are you sure you don't want me to just paint you and Gil, like Andrew suggested?" Sam said.

"My body is all wrong for a mother and child portrait," Elisabeth said.

Something in this made Sam feel sad for her. Elisabeth had spoken of her mother's obsession with being thin. She swore it hadn't had an effect on her. But wasn't this the effect? Feeling that her body wasn't what a mother's ought to be, even though she was a mother?

Elisabeth's second book was a critique of the diet industry. Sam tore through it. Though there were hardly any personal details in it, there was so much rage and resignation to the way she told the story; a sign of the toll it had taken. Reading it, Sam felt grateful for her own mother, who had never mentioned weight when she and her siblings were kids, who gave them ice cream every night after dinner and taught them how to drink the soupy remains straight from the bowl.

Elisabeth lifted Gil out of the bouncer.

For the next half hour, she photographed them in different

poses: Standing by the window, Gil's head on Sam's shoulder. In the chair, with him sitting on her left knee, her right knee, in the middle. With him lying across her lap.

Elisabeth stepped in from time to time, to tip Sam's chin up slightly, or to wrap Gil's golden curls around her finger, one by one, so that they fell in perfect formation.

When Gil started to rub his eyes, Sam was grateful.

"It's his naptime," she said.

"I guess we probably got enough," Elisabeth said.

Sam put her sweatshirt back on and went to heat a bottle.

Elisabeth puttered around the house for an hour, before leaving to try to get some work done in her office.

She came home right at five.

"Thanks again for indulging me with the picture thing," she said. "I'm so excited to have one of your paintings in our house."

Sam smiled. "Thanks."

"Have a great night," Elisabeth said.

"I'm coming back over at nine, right? For the shot?"

"You don't have to. I can do it myself. I was overreacting last night."

"Are you sure?"

Elisabeth nodded. "Totally."

Sam texted her at 8:45, asking if she was sure she was sure.

She was sitting in the dorm living room with a bunch of girls, watching a bad reality show about a family with six daughters who live at sea, on a yacht. Onscreen, teenage sisters in matching red bikinis and heels were bickering on the poop deck.

Elisabeth replied immediately. *You're so sweet to reach out. Honestly? Sam, I can't do it.*

Coming over, Sam wrote back.

On the floor sat a large tin of cookies someone's mother had baked. Sam grabbed four of them.

"My friend needs me," she said to no one in particular. "I've got to go."

On Elisabeth's kitchen table, there were two glass vials of liquid, a needle, a syringe, and a bottle of Cabernet, half drained.

She had been crying. Mascara pooled under her eyes. She wore glasses, which Sam had never seen before. She wondered if Elisabeth used contacts most of the time. It seemed like the sort of thing she should know by now.

"What are you thinking?" Elisabeth said.

Sam weighed whether to say: *I'm thinking that you usually look as put together as Grace Kelly, but tonight you more closely resemble Courtney Love.*

"I brought cookies," she said, adding them to the strange array of items.

"I shouldn't have bothered you," Elisabeth said.

"Why? I could never give myself a shot. I totally get why you can't do it."

"No, Sam. I meant I can't do this. Any of it."

Elisabeth sat down at the table and put her head in her hands.

"I feel like I'm losing my mind."

Sam sat beside her. She wasn't sure what to say. She pushed the stack of cookies toward Elisabeth.

"These are really good," she said.

Elisabeth picked one up, took a bite.

"That is good," she said.

She rolled her head back, stared at the ceiling.

"Fuck," she said. "What am I doing? I'll just do the shot. Let's do it."

"Okay," Sam said. She filled the syringe. "Butt, thigh, or stomach?"

With Isabella, they had rotated the injection site each night.

Elisabeth seemed to be considering the question. Then she shook her head. "No. No. I was right the first time. I can't."

Sam wanted to suggest that she call Andrew, or her best friend. She felt out of her depth.

"I don't want to be like my parents, with all that hostility," Elisabeth said. "I want peace in my marriage. I need Andrew and me on the same page. So I said I'd try for another baby. I guess if I'm honest, I was trying to make up for something I did wrong."

Sam wondered what it was. She held her breath, waiting to see if Elisabeth would say more. She thought of something George had said about a situation with Elisabeth's sister.

"But that's psychotic," Elisabeth said. "Nomi's right. I can't have a baby so he won't be mad at me. Andrew thinks I'm just scared. But every night I pray that this won't work."

"Oh, Elisabeth, that's a lot."

Sam's mom always said *That's a lot* when a friend confided in her over the telephone and she wasn't sure what to say.

"I can't do this, hoping against it. I have to make it clear to him that a second kid isn't in the cards. Right? And if he still can't get over the other thing, then, well, I don't know."

Sam swallowed. "Can I have some wine?" she said.

"Of course. Pour me another glass too?"

Sam did this, emptying the bottle.

She took a long sip. "So," she said. "I think you're right. Like you said, having a second child is a huge decision. If you already know you don't want it to work, like you said, then it seems like a bad position to put yourself in. Not to mention the baby."

Every word she said was deliberate, meant to emphasize that she wasn't making recommendations, only responding to what Elisabeth herself had said. Sam knew how these things could go. She didn't want to get blamed in the end.

Elisabeth nodded. "Thank you."

"I didn't do anything."

"Yes, you did."

They finished their wine. Sam was eager to get home. She had a strange urge to call her mother and tell her what happened, find out if she thought Sam had handled it well. But when Elisabeth suggested they open another bottle, Sam said that sounded great.

An hour later, Elisabeth was wasted. She'd been drinking before Sam got there, Sam remembered, too late. And she weighed practically nothing.

"What did you have for dinner?" Sam said.

"I don't remember," Elisabeth said. "Did I have dinner?"

Sam made a pot of spaghetti and forced her to eat a huge bowlful, covered with parmesan and melted butter.

Elisabeth was singing lightly under her breath by the time she was done.

"Let's get you to bed," Sam said.

She led Elisabeth upstairs, tucked her in. It was nothing she hadn't done a million times for Isabella, but it scared her to see Elisabeth like this.

"Sleep well," Sam said, trying to sound calm. "Good night."

Elisabeth looked up at her. "You're the best friend I have here, Sam. I don't know what I'll do without you when you're gone."

"I know," Sam said. "I'll miss you too."

Moments later, Elisabeth was asleep. She was still wearing her glasses. It seemed too intimate to remove them. But if she left them on Elisabeth's face, Sam thought, Elisabeth might roll over on them and break the frames.

Sam gently pulled them off, holding her breath.

She placed the glasses on top of Elisabeth's dresser, where she would easily find them in the morning.

It was possible Sam lingered there longer than was necessary, that she let her eyes scan the jewelry box, the photo of Andrew and Gil in a silver frame, the small pile of lacy things not yet put away. But she didn't dig. Didn't open a drawer or even an envelope. The check was sitting right there—made out to Gil, in the amount of three hundred thousand dollars. In the upper-left-hand corner was Elisabeth's father's name. Sam wasn't sure why it filled her with anger, why it made her think of her parents, of Maria and Gaby. Of Elisabeth never considering the cost of paint.

Once she was out of that room, Sam felt strangely free. She wanted to be in her dorm room, with the door open, telling Isabella the whole story.

She made her way down the hall, past Gil's nursery.

Gil.

He slept through the night now, most nights. But what if he woke up? Would Elisabeth even hear him crying, as drunk as she was?

Sam slipped into the room and lay down on the floor. She felt like crying herself. She rested her head on a giant stuffed rabbit with a satin bow around its neck and willed herself to sleep.

When she woke, the sun was rising. The baby was still asleep.

Sam crept downstairs, and out of the house.

Later, she texted Elisabeth to ask how she was feeling.

Fine! Elisabeth wrote back. *Thanks for checking. xx*

They saw each other again on Thursday. When Sam arrived for work, Elisabeth was her usual composed self. She said there was chicken and squash in the fridge for Gil's lunch, and a new music class at the public library at eleven, if they wanted to check it out. She gave the baby a squeeze and a kiss, and was gone.

The next morning was much the same.

By the end of the day, Sam's curiosity had taken over.

"I'm guessing you stuck with what you said on Monday? You didn't do any shots this week?"

Elisabeth shook her head. "No."

"How did Andrew take it?"

"I haven't told him yet," she said, looking down at the floor. "He's had kind of a hard week out there, so I decided to wait and tell him in person."

He would be home tonight. They were supposed to go to Manhattan tomorrow for the procedure. Sam wondered if Elisabeth had canceled; she wondered what Andrew would say.

"He'll understand," Elisabeth said. "Don't you think?"

"Sure," Sam said. "It's your body."

"That's right."

Elisabeth handed her a white envelope in addition to the usual stack of bills.

"What's this?" Sam said.

"You'll see."

Sam imagined a gift card to one of the restaurants downtown, or a letter thanking her for the other night. She waited until she was alone in her room to open it.

Inside the envelope were copies of the photographs Elisabeth had taken on Monday. Sam and Gil, skin to skin. Their posture far more intimate than any photo Sam had ever seen of her mother with her own children.

In most of them, Sam had a double chin, or flabby nun arms. But one shot was beautiful—sunlight beaming in through the window, Gil on her shoulder, Sam staring down at him, in love. She flipped the picture over. Elisabeth had written something on the back.

Inspiration for the painting! You look radiant here.

18

Elisabeth

EVERY MORNING THAT MONTH, Elisabeth had to be at the diagnostics center by six so they could draw her blood and perform an ultrasound and send the results to the clinic in the city.

She went in the yoga pants she'd worn to bed the night before, didn't bother to wash her face.

It was pitch black and bitter cold when she started the car each day. The roads were empty. Red lights seemed beside the point. The sleepy-eyed woman at the desk was always drinking a cup of tea, moving slow, when she arrived, as if Elisabeth had walked in on her in her own kitchen.

Afterward, she drove straight home and got back into bed like it had never happened, leaving Andrew to take care of things, which he was all too willing to do. He had forgiven her, it seemed. He never said as much, but she knew his feelings had changed because he had started making her coffee again, because he held her at night, instead of keeping to his side of the bed.

"I feel better than I have in ages," he told her.

Meanwhile, with each shot, each 5:00 a.m. alarm, Elisabeth felt increasingly unhinged.

She tried to distract herself with work. She was writing again, finally. It made her feel like there was at least one part of her life she wasn't messing up.

The day after she decided to stop taking her fertility drugs, she didn't wake until seven, when she heard Gil's cries. There were five missed calls from the clinic on her phone, and a text message from Andrew asking how the morning had gone. Her head felt like it had been slammed repeatedly between metal cymbals. She went to Gil's room, picked him up.

"Hello, my love," she said softly.

Elisabeth carried him downstairs and placed him in his high chair. She washed a handful of blueberries and cut each one in half before putting them on his tray. She had forgotten a bib, but she couldn't imagine going back upstairs, so she let him dirty his shirt. What was the difference? She'd have to soak one thing or the other.

Elisabeth swallowed three Advil and made coffee. She drank two cups, then fixed herself a piece of toast with peanut butter, and a scrambled egg for Gil. She could not remember the last time she'd been this hungover.

The previous night, before Sam came, Elisabeth had made the mistake of looking at Charlotte's Instagram for the first time since Christmas. It was like she was anxious over IVF and decided the best way to cope was to turn her attention to the only thing that made her even more anxious. She scrolled all the way back, through February and into January. The posts were the same as ever—sexy bathing-suit pics, asinine self-help sayings.

In one photo, Charlotte leaned backward off a moving train as it traversed the side of a lush, green mountain. She wore the shortest dress Elisabeth had ever seen. Charlotte's arms were outstretched, hands holding on to the sides of the open train door. A gorgeous man hovered over her. They were kissing. They looked like they were one sneeze away from falling off a cliff.

The caption read: *"Life is a daring adventure or nothing." I live by those words. Sri Lanka has reminded me that possessions don't matter, money doesn't matter. Only love matters. Only adventure. There are people who will never understand this. They believe money is everything. They hold on too tight to their small and boring lives. And for them, I sometimes weep. But not today, dear readers. Today, I SOAR.*

"Fuck you," Elisabeth said out loud.

She looked at the needle on the kitchen table and thought of how Charlotte was to blame for landing her here, in this position. Yet nothing had changed for Charlotte. There had been no consequences.

Almost two hundred commenters praised the train shot for its beauty, and Charlotte for being so brave. Elisabeth was fairly certain the quote was from Helen Keller, but Charlotte had probably seen it on a coaster and claimed it as her own.

Elisabeth pictured herself walking down the aisle of that train, feeling the warm air on her cheeks, and, *whoopsie*, shoving her sister right off.

After that, she started drinking.

The end of the night was a blank space. Elisabeth didn't recall saying goodbye to Sam. There was a pot of cloudy water on the stove, a colander in the sink, which suggested pasta, but she couldn't say what she'd eaten.

Sam texted to check in around nine. Elisabeth was tempted to ask her what happened. But she just responded that she was fine.

How much had she told her?

Eventually, she called the clinic back. Gil was speed-crawling up and down the front hall with a pen in his mouth, and she was letting him because she needed him happy and entertained above all else if she was going to survive this day.

"We got no results for you this morning," scolded the nurse on the line. "It's impossible to monitor the state of your uterus if you don't show up. Make sure you're there tomorrow."

"Will do," Elisabeth said.

That was all? She had never missed a single monitoring session when they were going through this the first time. They had once set out from Brooklyn in a blizzard at four-thirty in the morning, before the streets were plowed, to make it to the Upper East Side for seven o'clock.

She called Andrew during Gil's nap. She was on her fourth cup of coffee by then.

"How did it go this morning?" he said. "I feel awful that you had to get Gil up that early and schlep all the way to the blood-draw place."

"It was fine," she replied.

Elisabeth couldn't get into it yet. Maybe after she'd taken a shower, or a nap, or both.

"How's Denver?"

"Okay, I guess," Andrew said. "Hard to tell. There are definitely the cool kids in the room, who everyone's dying to meet. I'm not one of them."

"I think you're a cool kid," she said.

"Thanks."

Elisabeth tried to sound optimistic. "Keep it up," she said. "There are three days to go. It only takes one person."

"Did the clinic call with your levels?"

"Yup."

"And?"

"All good."

She willed him to stop asking questions so she could stop lying.

"You think we'll still be able to do the transfer on Saturday?"

"Sounds like it."

"I'm excited," he said.

She decided then that she would tell him in person what she had done, as soon as he got home.

On Wednesday, Thursday, and Friday mornings, Elisabeth went to the clinic and let them draw her blood. It made no sense, but she felt as though if she kept doing this, it meant she hadn't backed out entirely. Each day, the clinic called an hour later and said things weren't moving as fast as they should be. Her levels were too low. Each day, they told her to double her dose of everything that night, and she said she would, before proceeding to do nothing. The drugs had gone out with the garbage on Tuesday.

Andrew got home after eleven on Friday night.

She was reading in bed, waiting up for him.

When he came into the room, she said, "I'm so happy you're back."

He looked deflated.

"What?" she said.

"The grill. It's not going to work, is it?"

"What do you mean?"

"People were laughing during my presentation."

"No."

"I'm pretty sure one guy in the front row was playing Tetris on his phone. They were bored by the whole thing."

"That's because you didn't have enough time to perfect it," she said. "Maybe the prototype needs work. But that doesn't reflect on the idea."

"They hated the prototype *and* the idea," he said. "Most people there met with ten or twenty potential investors. Only two wanted to meet me. They both said the same things: people do barbecue on cloudy days, and people like the taste of meat seared in charcoal. Now more than ever, apparently."

They were the exact things she had worried about. But Elisabeth wasn't happy or smug. She felt sorry for him.

"There's another product like it that's selling gangbusters, already in stores," he said. "The inventor was on TV."

"If that one's selling gangbusters, maybe there's room for two in the market," she said.

"No. They said not."

"Adversity is part of it, right? You can't let two bozos in Denver decide your fate."

"Elisabeth. Seriously. What am I doing?" he said. "When do I ever even grill?"

She laughed. Something in her unclenched. Elisabeth realized only now that she'd been waiting months for him to come to this conclusion.

"I think I knew from early on that it wouldn't work," Andrew said. "But I had this opportunity. I got to do the thing everyone wants to do. I got to follow my dream. I didn't want to give up on that. Especially after what happened to my dad. It was like I was going to succeed for both of us, to make up for what he went through. No one ever says what you're supposed to do when you realize your dream was kind of stupid in the first place."

"You said yourself, you can come up with more ideas," she said.

Andrew shook his head. "As it turns out, I've got nothing."

Elisabeth stretched her arms out to him. "Come here."

Andrew got into bed, fully clothed, and spooned her, pressing his chest to her back, holding on tight.

"I don't know if it was even about the grill," he said. "I hated my job. I wish I could have just said that and saved us this wasted year."

"It wasn't wasted," she said.

She was thinking that maybe now they could return to Brooklyn, the grand experiment complete.

"You're right," he said. "It wasn't. I like living here. I like being near my parents, having a backyard for Gil."

Andrew got out of bed, went to the dresser, and picked up the check from her father.

Elisabeth's body grew stiff at the thought of him asking her to accept it one more time, but Andrew held it out to her and said, "Rip it up."

"What?"

"Go ahead. Rip it up. I wasn't listening. I was being selfish. I get it now."

Elisabeth felt like her husband had returned to her in some way she hadn't known he was gone.

She tore up the check and let the pieces fall to the bed like confetti.

"Now what?" she said.

Andrew shook his head. "I don't know."

We start over from scratch, she thought. *With nothing. Holy shit.* But she said, "Thank you."

They had sex then. The first really good sex since Gil.

Afterward, lying in the dark, he said, "All week at that conference, I kept thinking about me, you, and Gil in the car tomorrow, and of the amazing thing that's about to happen to our family. That kept me going."

Elisabeth needed to tell him. No more lies. But how?

"The odds are, it won't work," she said. "I don't want you getting your hopes up."

"I know," he said. "But at least we're trying. And, hon? I have a feeling it's going to work."

Elisabeth felt angry; it was his own fault. She had tried to warn him.

She cried on the way to have her blood drawn the next morning, and she cried all the way home, wondering what the hell she was doing. The window of time to tell him was nearly closed. She dreaded the moment.

He was in the living room when she got back, sitting on the floor with Gil.

The phone rang—the clinic calling already—and she rushed to answer.

It was the doctor himself on the line. As rare as a unicorn sighting.

"I know we have the transfer of one embryo scheduled for this afternoon," he said. "But I'm looking at your chart and I'm concerned about your body's response this week. It's almost like you weren't taking any hormones at all. I hate to tell you this, I know you're coming a long way, but the odds of a transfer working are basically zero. I'm afraid we should call it off and try a new regimen next month."

Elisabeth took the phone up to the bedroom and closed the door.

"I want to go ahead with it," she said.

"I can't advise that."

"It's my call, right? As long as I'm paying."

"Yes. But you pay me for my expertise."

"It will be fine," she said. "I know it."

"All right," he said. "As you said, it's your call."

Elisabeth was somehow separate from her body as she watched herself get in the car with her husband and child and head to the city. She was in awe of her own dishonesty.

Halfway there, Andrew said, "I'll only say this once, but I feel strongly that we should put in both embryos to improve our chances."

"Okay," she said, digging the hole ever deeper. "Let's do it."

She reached over, took his hand.

Elisabeth showed up at the hospital right on time, along with twelve other women. It felt like something from the fifties, how they were made to sit together in the waiting room wearing hairnets and paper gowns. When it was her turn, she followed a nurse down the familiar hallway, into a room that looked like the inside of a spaceship. The nurses strapped her to the table and tipped it back.

The doctor came in, the one who was scheduled to do procedures today. She didn't remember ever seeing him before. She was relieved that her doctor wasn't the one. He might try to talk her out of it again.

Elisabeth hung upside down while the doctor talked about the Mets and inserted a tube through the wall of her uterus, planting there her last two chances of becoming a mother again.

He said, "Good luck, I'll be rooting for you."

She thanked him, knowing that all the luck in the world could not possibly make it work.

Elisabeth was wheeled out on a stretcher, and made to lie still for an hour. The nurse gave her a black-and-white photo of two perfect circles. Their insides looked like the surface of the moon.

They spent the rest of the weekend at the Carlyle. Even the smallest room was absurdly expensive, but Andrew insisted.

"You've always wanted to stay there," he said. "You deserve it."

On Saturday night, after Andrew and Gil were asleep, Elisabeth went down to the lobby, to Bemelmans, and ordered a gin and tonic. She sat at the bar, watched as the dark room filled with people, impeccably dressed. In the town where she now lived, there was nowhere a person could go dressed like that. A jazz trio roared. The young man at the piano was gorgeous, not a line on his face. Nobody said a word to her. Elisabeth felt like a ghost.

At Andrew's insistence, he and Gil went out in the morning while she slept in. Then the three of them ate room service and walked through Central Park, and then they were heading home, to wait.

The following week was spring break. No Sam to talk to. She

was in London, with Clive. Andrew took the week off so Elisabeth could spend it on the couch, watching movies, free of any stress or responsibility. She had too much time to think. She wondered if the embryos had left her body yet, unprimed as it was to receive them. Or if they were still floating around inside her, searching in vain for a place to attach themselves.

She went to her Friday session with Violet, nervous that somehow Violet would intuit that she was holding back. But Elisabeth spent the hour talking nonsense—about her neighbors and her book deadline and a dream she'd had about an old boyfriend from high school—and Violet couldn't tell the difference.

She was supposed to take progesterone suppositories to increase her chances for success. Each morning, she removed one from the bottle and flushed it down the toilet.

Nomi texted her most days, as usual, about something trivial—an old classmate of theirs had lost eighty-five pounds; Nomi's kids were getting scooters and she and Brian were fighting over the necessity of helmets for toddlers. Elisabeth wanted to tell her, but she would have to start from the beginning. She wasn't sure she could say it out loud. Then one more person would know her secret. She wished she hadn't told Sam, that she could die without anyone finding out what she was capable of.

Elisabeth had always prided herself on knowing that she would never cheat on Andrew, as if that was the only way to deceive someone you loved.

She was disgusting. She was her father's daughter after all.

The following Monday was Sam's first day back.

She hadn't yet taken off her sneakers when Elisabeth confessed everything.

"I was going to tell him," she said. "But then he came home

from Denver and he was upset about what happened there, and I couldn't get the words out. The rest—I can't even explain. It turned into this runaway train."

"So Andrew still thinks there's a chance you're pregnant?" Sam said.

"Yes. I'll do one last blood test, the pregnancy test, on Friday, and that will be that. A few more days of this deception. Or the rest of my life, depending on how you look at it. I'm a liar, Sam. I'm terrible. I don't know what's wrong with me."

Sam didn't respond.

"I wish I'd never dragged you into it. You must think I'm the most awful person."

No reply. Elisabeth realized then that she wanted Sam to absolve her.

Elisabeth looked at her. Sam was crying.

"I think I know how you feel," she said, finally. "I did something recently that I really regret. I thought I was doing the right thing, but—I'll tell you, if you want. Then we'll be even."

"You don't have to do that," Elisabeth said.

"But I understand what you're going through. This thing I did. Now it's too late to fix it. I can't stop replaying it in my head. I think maybe I'm a bad person. I never thought I was, but I am."

Elisabeth reached over and touched her arm.

"Stop beating yourself up. There's no such thing as a good person. Or a bad one. There are just situations we get ourselves into that we never would have imagined, and we have to find our way out."

She wasn't sure if she was trying to convince Sam or herself of this.

They stared at each other.

Sam raised her left hand to wipe tears from her cheek.

That's when Elisabeth noticed the tiny diamond.

"Is that what I think it is? I thought you told Clive you didn't want a ring."

"I did! He said he couldn't resist." Sam shrugged. "He's a romantic."

That was one word for it.

The whole thing was controlling, a sign that he refused to take her as she was.

"And you're happy about this?" Elisabeth said.

"I don't think anything has changed, really."

"Sam, he proposed."

"Yes, but he already thought of us as engaged."

"But what do you think?"

"I love him. We're together. I guess I don't think defining it matters as much as all that."

Elisabeth wondered if she meant it. They were from different generations, maybe they viewed marriage differently. But no. She knew Sam. Sam was traditional; Sam painted her grandmother on a porch while her peers were pinning pubic hair to a corkboard and calling it art.

"So you'll definitely be going to London then," Elisabeth said.

"Yes. I've made my decision, and we'll see how it plays out."

"You'll see how getting married plays out."

"I've decided to take things less seriously," Sam said. "Clive pointed out to me this weekend that I tend to think one bad choice—one grade, one job interview, one decision—could derail my whole life. It's not true."

"Sometimes it is," Elisabeth said.

Burned in her brain forever: the year she was twenty-one, right out of college, and Nomi told her the story of a coworker at the foundation where she worked, a girl their age who got blackout drunk at a fundraiser and somehow ended up pooping on a white couch. That girl was never heard from again.

Sam probably wouldn't appreciate it if she compared marrying Clive to defecating in public, but Elisabeth had to say something.

"Has Clive ever been married before?" she asked.

She tried to sound neutral, detached, as if she had asked if Clive liked tomatoes.

"No," Sam said. "Why?"

"His age, I guess. And he's so good with Gil. He seems like the settling-down type."

"I don't think he's the type at all," Sam said. "It's just that he wants to settle down with me. He told me once that he didn't get married sooner because he hadn't found the right person."

"Isn't that sweet," Elisabeth said.

She knew now for certain that Creepy Clive had lied.

Later on, Elisabeth was at the drugstore, pushing Gil in the cart.

He greeted each person they passed with a wave and a shout, as if he was the mayor of the place.

She was debating which shampoo to buy when she heard someone call, "Hi, Gilbert!"

Elisabeth looked up. There was Isabella, wearing tiny shorts, though it was only sixty degrees out. Warmer than it had been in months, but even so.

"You're so tan. I'm jealous," Elisabeth said. "How was your spring break?"

"Great. I went to Tulum with my girlfriends from boarding school. One of my friends' dads has a villa there, right on the water."

"Sounds like heaven."

They talked for the next ten minutes about trips to Mexico each of them had taken, about the Mexican restaurant a few doors down from here that was pretty good, but had closed last month, only to be replaced by a Starbucks. The town had raised hell over that, but eventually Starbucks won, and now there was a line out the door at all times.

Elisabeth was ready to move on, but Isabella kept talking.

Gil's eyelids grew heavy, dipping closed, then snapping open like a paper window shade, until, at last, he fell asleep.

Finally, Isabella said, "You heard Clive put a ring on it?"

"I did."

Neither of them spoke for a long moment.

Then Elisabeth asked, "What do you think of that?"

"I'm worried," Isabella said. "I would have said something to her sooner, but—none of us thought it would last this long."

"I worry about her too," Elisabeth said. "I don't want her to do something she'll regret."

"He's clearly not good enough for her," Isabella said. "I mean, he gives walking tours for a living, and he makes up half the things he says on them. Just spouts fake dates and stories."

"Really?" Elisabeth said. "But he owns the company, right? He's making an app or something?"

"No. That's his friend who gave him the job. Clive lived in Spain until like two or three years ago, but he's never explained what he did there. It's shady."

"I didn't know all that," Elisabeth said.

"Yeah. Plus he's old, and kind of an annoying know-it-all."

"What do you think she sees in him?" Elisabeth said.

"Sam's never been good with change," Isabella said. "Or with endings. I think some part of her wants to let him go, but she can't." She took a bottle of shampoo from the shelf, popped the top open, sniffed.

"I never thanked you, by the way, for talking me out of it," Isabella said.

"Out of?" Elisabeth said. Then, "Oh. Of course. I'm glad you changed your mind."

"I can't wait until I'm your age," Isabella said. "It must be so nice to have your shit figured out."

On Friday morning, she went to the clinic one last time and stuck out her left arm, still bruised from all the pricks two weeks earlier. She took a deep breath as she watched the test tube fill with blood.

When the phone rang an hour later, Elisabeth let Andrew answer.

She heard him say "Mmm-hmm" and "I see" and "Okay, great, thank you."

He sounded happy. She was struck by the possibility that somehow it had worked, and he was about to walk into the living room and tell her they'd be parents again.

When he came to her with tears in his eyes, Elisabeth's stomach dropped with disappointment, a surprise to her.

"I'm so sorry," Andrew said. "I know how hard you tried."

The next day, Elisabeth went quiet.

Andrew assumed she was grieving. They were supposed to meet his parents at a new pizza place for an early dinner. He offered to take Gil, let her have some time alone.

She determined to use the time well, to ignore that she was horrid, that her husband was a better person than she would ever be.

She cleaned out the bedroom closet, and Gil's dresser drawers, and then set her focus on the bathroom. In the cupboard below the sink, Elisabeth found a brown paper bag, a gut punch.

She knew what it contained. All that remained of the items she brought home from the hospital after Gil was born. Why had she kept them, even through the move? What should she do with them now?

She went downstairs, poured a glass of wine, and sat in the living room with her unread stack of *New Yorkers*. She began with the oldest one, and skimmed through the table of contents, the event listings. She read a long article about prison reform, the film and book reviews, and all the cartoons, before moving on to the next issue.

This one featured a profile of Matilda Grey, champion of feminist art. Elisabeth began reading. A thought hung at the edges of her mind, where she couldn't quite grasp it.

Matilda Grey had a short silver bob and wore all black. Her London gallery was the epicenter of highly collectible art made by women.

Matilda Grey. Matilda Grey.

Elisabeth read on.

Matilda Grey had decided London was smothering. She was opening a new gallery in Brooklyn in the fall. She'd be moving there to run it.

It clicked for Elisabeth an hour later, when she'd switched to television, a show about a mother-daughter team renovating dilapidated houses in Baltimore.

The Matilda Grey gallery was the place Sam had applied to work in London. The place she wanted to work most in the world. They had rejected her because she wasn't British.

A possibly bad idea entered Elisabeth's head. Andrew often said her ideas should come with a mandatory waiting period, like buying a gun. She gave it half an hour, before sending emails to the handful of people she knew in the New York art world.

Andrew and Gil returned home not long after, Gil already asleep. Andrew put him down and joined her on the sofa.

"My dad had this whole speech prepared at dinner," he said. "About how the time I've spent on the grill is not a bad thing, because at least for all these months, I haven't been contributing to corporate greed like I did in my old job."

"Oh dear," she said. "The Hollow Tree."

Andrew nodded. "Indeed."

Elisabeth could not stop checking her phone. The lack of replies offended her, even though she realized it was a Saturday. She buzzed with anticipation, with an urge to see her plan come to something.

"You okay?" Andrew said.

"I am," she said, and it took her a minute to realize what he meant.

Elisabeth grew more and more antsy, until finally someone responded—the editor from the *Times* who covered Manhattan galleries.

Sorry, I don't know a soul there. Brooklyn is another world. I've heard Matilda is fantastic, though. Hope all's well!

She would have to cast a wider net.

Elisabeth logged on to BK Mamas for the first time in weeks. It was now called BK Families and Caregivers, in an effort to appease all sides.

She typed without stopping to think.

Hey mamas! My son's incredible babysitter is about to graduate college with honors. She's one of the brightest young women I've ever known, a super-talented painter, with amazing taste in art. It is her DREAM to work at the Matilda Grey gallery, which

I understand is opening this coming fall. Does anyone have an in? I can vouch for this girl—she is THE BEST. (Please help me stop her from making a colossal mistake and marrying her creepy British boyfriend and wasting all her talents!!)

She posted it, vowing not to check for responses for one hour.

Nomi texted after ten minutes: *Man, you are OBSESSED with your babysitter. You're not gonna leave me for her, are you?*

Elisabeth was pleased. If Nomi had seen it, that meant other people had. The post hadn't gotten lost in an avalanche of questions about bedtimes and diaper rash and horrible in-laws and Spanish immersion classes for kids under two.

When she checked, the post had one like—Nomi—and one comment, from a woman she didn't know: *Not a creepy Brit! Does he have bad teeth and everything? I dated one or two of those in my day.*

Not helpful, but still, Elisabeth wrote back: *Teeth right out of central casting. And a bad accent to match.*

It was mean, but the more activity a post got, the more people would see it. She added a second reply. This one just said *Ha ha!*

A moment later, another comment appeared, from Mimi Winchester.

Hi E! One of my dearest friends runs the place!! Email me!!

Anyone but Mimi, Elisabeth thought, knowing what it would cost her to ask this woman a favor. Mimi would hold it over her head for the rest of time, find a way to use it as proof of her own superiority.

But she thought of Sam. Sam had been there for her; Sam had listened. Sam had stopped her from making a huge mistake. When Elisabeth thanked her, Sam said she hadn't done anything, but that wasn't true. If not for Sam, she might be pregnant with twins right now.

Elisabeth composed an email to Mimi, telling her how Sam had applied to the gallery in London, how the gallerist there had loved her. She fudged a bit, saying, deep down, Sam had her heart set on New York, but this boyfriend was filling her head with other ideas.

Wouldn't it be perfect if they hired her? Elisabeth wrote. *She wants to be in New York, they're opening up in New York. Feels meant to be. But, and I realize this is a tall order, I feel like they would have to reach out to her . . .*

Mimi said she would see what she could do.

On Monday, Mimi followed up to say her friend had contacted the London gallery, and they remembered Sam and would add her to their interview list now that they knew she was headed for New York.

When Sam arrived to work the following Thursday, she did not stop to say hello or greet the baby. Instead, she said, "The craziest thing just happened. I got an email from Matilda Grey."

Elisabeth felt giddy.

"Who's that again?" she asked.

"It's not a person, it's a gallery. Well, it's a person too, of course. I applied to their London location. I think I told you? They couldn't hire me, but this email says the gallerist there remembered me and they're opening a space in Brooklyn."

"Brooklyn? Really?"

"Yeah."

"I wonder if it's near our old neighborhood."

"They want me to go down there and interview to be Matilda's assistant."

"What! That's fabulous," Elisabeth said. "You must have made an impression."

"I guess I did," Sam said, and she looked amazed.

"Don't be so surprised. They'd be lucky to have you."

"They want me to come for an interview tomorrow, in Brooklyn. I know I'm supposed to work."

"Of course you have to go. The only question is what are you going to wear?"

"I don't know," Sam said. "And I don't know what to say to Clive. Is it bad not to tell him yet? To wait and see what happens?"

"I might not be the best person to ask about withholding important information from your partner at the moment," Elisabeth said.

"I want this job," Sam said. "Have you ever been shocked by your own reaction to something? Like maybe you don't know yourself at all?"

Elisabeth thought of the moment Andrew came in and said she wasn't pregnant.

"Why don't you just see what happens?" she said.

Sam nodded. "I might not even get it."

She sounded both hopeful and fearful that this could be the case.

Sam

GIL WAS UPSTAIRS NAPPING when Sam got the call.
She and Elisabeth were sitting at the kitchen table,
drinking tea, making plans for the party. Outside, rain
pelted the windows.

Elisabeth had given a few chapters of her new book to her editor and agent and was awaiting feedback.

"This is my favorite part of the writing process," she said.
"The part where I get to do nothing for several days without feeling guilty about it."

She went for a run that morning, before the weather turned.
She ate a nice lunch out somewhere, alone.

"I can't wait to read the book once it's done," Sam said.

"Oh, Sam, you're the best," Elisabeth said.

"Really. I've read both your books now. They're so good. I think the second one is my favorite."

Elisabeth's face lit up. "Sam!" she said. "You always say the perfect thing."

The afternoon itself felt perfect, like so many things did now that the end was near. Lately, Sam attended classes with a sense of sappy gratitude, for getting to be part of a group of smart women, debating the meaning of literature and art. When in her life would she ever do that again? She inhaled deeply when she studied in the library stacks, wanting to memorize the smell of the books. She got into bed for her afternoon nap each day, knowing Isabella was in class, and that no one else would disturb her, because she had written *ZZZZZ* on the whiteboard that hung on the door, and her friends knew what that meant.

Things that had irritated her all year now made her smile. The sight of Isabella slicing oranges on her nightstand for sangria; the sound of Rosa next door playing the same Prince song on repeat for an hour; the fact that she could just appear in the dining hall at six and a warm meal would be waiting.

The campus was at its best in springtime. After a winter spent crossing the quad with their heads down, wrapped in heavy coats as they hurried past the frozen pond, the students took their time now. They stopped to chat, or to take pictures of the pink cherry blossoms that lined Paradise Road, or to have a picnic on the green, green grass behind College Hall.

The seniors were extra emotional. Somebody on their platform cried every night lately, about one thing or another.

Sam looked around Elisabeth's kitchen. This too would soon be over. She had loved their time together. Things had felt a bit strange after George told her about Elisabeth's family money, but that feeling had mostly faded now. After Elisabeth confessed what she'd done with the embryos, Sam spent a few days fixated on the deception. But she had to put that away. It didn't match the Elisabeth she knew. Maybe everyone had parts of themselves like that.

It was her new habit to get up at six each morning and go to the art building to work on the painting. Elisabeth had said not to worry if she needed to finish over the summer, but Sam intended to present it to her at the party. In part, so that she might get paid before moving to London. And in part because she wanted the painting on display at the party, both things representing their unique bond, the blurred lines between their lives. She wanted the portrait to be the best thing she'd ever created. She wanted to make Elisabeth proud. Sam sketched the figures out seven times before adding color.

This morning, she had entered the art building, which was usually empty at that hour, and bumped straight into one of her professors, Christopher Gillis. He looked like he'd just woken up, stumbling out of his office barefoot, in sweatpants, steel-gray hair pointing in every direction. She wondered if he had a girl in there.

He knew Elisabeth somehow. Sam didn't know their exact connection, but Elisabeth told her once how they had discussed her talent at a party.

Sam was weighing whether to mention the sighting when Elisabeth glanced up from her to-do list and said, "I can't believe Gil will be a year old in three weeks. And you'll be a college graduate."

She looked wistful, before turning back to the list and saying, "Does your family like shrimp?"

Elisabeth was going all out, even though Sam told her there was no need. Three cases of champagne had been purchased and now sat at the top of the basement stairs, ready to be ferried to the yard at the appointed hour. Elisabeth had ordered a balloon archway, twelve feet tall, the kind you saw at a prom or at the finish line of a 10K. A three-piece bluegrass band would play songs for both kids and adults. There would be cater-waiters serving endless hors d'oeuvres, and two cakes—one for Sam, and one for Gil.

Sam had yet to tell her mother.

"My family loves shrimp," she said.

Sam wondered about Elisabeth's family. She had said they were estranged, she had told Sam that terrible story about her father, but then they came and visited at Christmas. She hadn't mentioned them since.

There was no hint of them coming for Gil's birthday as far as Sam could tell.

Sam's cell phone rang. She looked down at the screen.

"It's a 718!" she said, immediately regretting her enthusiasm, in case the news was bad. How awful would it be for Elisabeth to have to console her, to feel compelled to say something reassuring, like the gallery didn't deserve her anyway.

"Answer it!" Elisabeth said.

Sam did.

"Sam?" said the voice at the other end of the line. "It's Natasha from Matilda Grey. Do you have a minute?"

Sam tried to steady her voice. "Sure," she said, thinking this could go either way. She thought the interview had gone well—the gallery was gorgeous. It looked just like the one in London. Mostly, Sam had talked to Natasha, but at the very end, Matilda herself came in to meet her and Sam gushed about her many visits to the Mayfair space, her favorite exhibitions. Matilda didn't say much, but after she shook Sam's hand and left the room, Natasha whispered, "She liked you."

Now Natasha said, "I'm calling to officially offer you the job as Matilda's assistant."

Sam rose from her chair and started jumping up and down. Elisabeth stood too, and danced in place. A hilarious, shocking sight.

Sam composed herself long enough to say thank you, and that she was thrilled to accept. They talked through logistics—when she might start, how much she'd get paid.

When she hung up, she said, "I got the job."

Elisabeth said, "I gathered that. Sam! Congratulations! Should we open a bottle of champagne to celebrate?"

It was one o'clock on a Monday, but before she could respond, Elisabeth had gone to fetch the champagne.

Left alone for a minute, she thought of Clive. The sweetness of this strange turn of events was cut through with the question of what would become of them now.

Sam twisted the ring on her finger. He had proposed in Leicester Square, in the exact spot where they met, down on one knee in front of hordes of onlookers. Half of them took out their phones and snapped photographs. Sam felt mortified, even as she tried to stay in the moment.

"It's only a cheap thing," Clive said as he showed her the ring. "I know you don't care, and that's one of a million reasons why I'm mad about you."

Elisabeth returned, clutching the champagne bottle by its neck.

"What's wrong?" she said. "You look sad."

"Thinking about Clive."

"People do long distance all the time."

"They *are* based in London," Sam said. "Maybe there would be a chance for me to transfer there eventually."

"Right," Elisabeth said. "Bottom line: Your dream job just fell into your lap. You've got to do it. Doesn't it feel meant to be?"

Sam tried not to express it for fear of seeming boastful, but she felt the fiercest sense of pride. Of all the applicants they must have seen in London, they remembered her. Elisabeth was right. It felt meant to be, like a gift from the universe she could not refuse.

She called her parents after dinner to tell them the news.

Her mother said, "Thank God. You're staying in America."

They hadn't talked much about her plans for next year. Whenever her parents brought this up, Sam said she was sending résumés out every week and left it at that. She hadn't yet told them about Clive's proposal.

Her mother's reaction annoyed her.

"They're based in London," Sam said. "So maybe I'll have

to go back and forth sometimes. But, yes, I'd be mostly in New York."

Her father's first question was about the money. When Sam told him the starting salary, he whistled and said, "I think that's about what our paperboy makes."

In the background, her mother yelled, "Don't listen to him!"

Sam knew he was kidding, but also not.

Her mother got back on the line. "Sweetheart, in all serious-ness, we are so proud of you."

"Thanks, Mom."

"While I have you, can I ask about tickets for graduation?"

"Sure."

"The five of us are coming, of course. I know you want Elisa-beth there. Nana and Pop-Pop would die if they couldn't come. So, that's eight. How many more tickets do we have? Enough to invite Aunt Mary-Ellen and Uncle Paul and Aunt Cathy and Lou?"

"Let me check," Sam said. "I get ten, and they're all spoken for, except one. But Isabella said she might have extras."

"Who's the ninth person in our group?" her mother said.

"Clive."

"Really? I thought he'd have to work."

"He's taking the Friday off."

"Is it worth doing that? You'll be so busy. You probably won't have time to see him."

"You guys are taking that day off," Sam said.

"We don't live in another country," her mother said. "And we're your family."

"So is he."

Her mother sighed.

"Please don't take this the wrong way, but maybe Clive could sit this one out. Your grandmother has no idea how old he is. Is that how you want her to find out? You've worked hard to get where you are, and it's been a stressful few months around here, as you know. Maybe it's selfish, but I just want this moment for us. Your dad and I are worried about it being less than perfect."

"Perfect for who?" Sam said.

She hated that she was engaged to someone her parents didn't approve of. She hated her need for their approval. Part of Sam wanted to beg her mother to try to like him, for her sake. She wanted to list all the sweet things Clive had done for her.

But none of this came through in what she said next. "Clive will be there. You'll have to deal. If you can't deal, don't come."

"Sam—"

"I need to go, because he'll be calling me any minute. We talk every night at this time. Not that you'd know that, since you never ask about him."

Sam hung up.

In truth, Clive wasn't calling her for another hour.

She grabbed hold of a pillow and screamed straight into it.

"You okay over there?" Lexi shouted from across the hall.

"I'm fine," Sam yelled back.

She needed to talk to Elisabeth.

Sam texted, asked if she was busy.

Just put Gil down for the night. Andrew's out with George. Come over! Elisabeth replied. *Let yourself in. I'm in the den upstairs. Hope everything's okay . . .*

When Sam found her, Elisabeth was sitting cross-legged on the couch, computer in her lap, some dumb real estate show on TV.

"What's up?" she said, patting the couch beside her. "Clive again?"

"Not exactly. I'm furious at my mother," Sam said.

"I didn't think you ever got mad at her," Elisabeth said.

Sam paused to think. "I don't very often."

When she was finished telling the story, Elisabeth said, "That sucks. But try to see it from her point of view. You're her little girl. I'm guessing you've never done anything wrong before in your life."

"You mean, before being with Clive? That's wrong?"

"Not wrong, just—cause for concern. From her point of view! I'm not saying it's rational. But I know your mother loves you and wants the best for you. Not all of us have that."

Sam nodded, not entirely convinced.

"It's been a hard time lately because my dad's business isn't doing well and my parents are stressed about money, but I feel like I'm being asked to fix everything. I'm not, really. But. It's annoying. They want their perfect day."

"Sam, I had no idea!" Elisabeth said. "I'm so sorry. Why didn't you tell me?"

Before she could respond, the baby started to cry.

Elisabeth groaned as she stood up. "Be right back. His new thing is throwing his pacifier out of the crib so I have to go in there and get it. Why couldn't I have a thumb-sucker? You can't lose your thumb."

Sam sat on the sofa and watched TV. When Elisabeth still hadn't returned several minutes later, Sam turned her laptop around to see what she'd been looking at.

The browser was open to Facebook. The page was one Elisabeth had made fun of in the past, full of overly analytical Brooklyn mothers, the type who started thinking about their kids' Harvard applications while they were in utero.

Elisabeth must have been in the middle of writing a comment on a post when Sam came in. The cursor hovered there, blinking, right after the words *So grateful to you, Mimi! You saved the*

Sam scrolled to the top to see who Mimi was and what exactly she had saved.

The original post was Elisabeth's. Sam's eyes rushed through the words: *My son's incredible babysitter . . . one of the brightest young women I've ever known . . . It is her DREAM . . . Matilda Grey . . . Please help me stop her from making a colossal mistake and marrying her creepy British boyfriend and wasting all her talents!!*

Someone had asked if Clive had bad teeth. Elisabeth answered in the affirmative.

Sam was shaking as she took it in. The job hadn't just come to her. Someone was taking pity, at Elisabeth's request.

Elisabeth had never let on for a second.

Sam got up, and stormed past Gil's room. Elisabeth, in shadow, stood over the crib.

Sam ran down the stairs.

Elisabeth called after her in a whisper, "Where are you going?"

She didn't reply. She reached the front hallway.

Elisabeth followed.

"Sam!" she said. "Wait! What's going on?"

Sam spun around and faced her.

"Thank you so much for trying to stop me from marrying my—how did you put it?—'creepy British boyfriend'?"

Elisabeth seemed to deflate right there in front of her. "Shit," she said.

"You must think I'm a complete idiot," Sam said. "Crying to you, getting so excited, and, all the time, you were the one pulling the strings."

"I believe in you, Sam," Elisabeth said. "I wanted to help."

"By forcing someone to hire me?"

"Come on. I don't have that kind of power. They hired you because you're great. I only made the meeting happen."

"I'm so sick of everyone thinking they know what's best for me. What did Clive ever do to you, or to anyone, to deserve those things you said? He's the kindest person I know."

"Maybe so."

Elisabeth's voice was soothing, as if she were trying to calm a child mid-tantrum. "But I know you, Sam. You have this great family, you love kids, you're super mature. You want to skip the big steps and be *there*. But everyone has to take those steps. It's all the mistakes you make in the middle that determine how strong you are at the end. You can't hide behind this thing with Clive forever."

"Who made you the authority on my life?" Sam demanded.

"I've lived longer than you, that's all. Clive is a sweet guy, but, Sam, do you really see a future with him?"

"What does that mean?"

"For one thing, he doesn't have two pennies to rub together. A man that age should be able to put you up in a hotel."

That she would take the details of Sam's life and turn them into an accusation. It was humiliating.

"Maybe money doesn't matter to me the way it does to you," Sam said.

"That's only because you don't know anything yet," Elisabeth said. "The people who know you best think he's wrong for you. Doesn't that tell you something?"

"Who?" Sam said.

"Your mother. Isabella. Me."

"You're not one of the people who know me best. You barely know me at all," Sam said. "And I'm not sure where you got that about Isabella."

"She told me."

"What did she say?"

"That she's worried. That nobody thought you and Clive would last this long. That she doesn't understand why you're marrying him. If I were you, I'd want to know why he's so hell-bent on marriage. Something tells me he hasn't told you everything about his past. I think Isabella feels the same way."

"Have there ever been two greater experts on marriage than you and Isabella?" Sam said. "Don't you have enough problems of your own to think about? Why are you so preoccupied with mine? You need me to go to Brooklyn because you regret leaving. I'm not you. I'm nothing like you. Do you know how oblivious you are? Your stories about struggling to make it in the big city. I know they're all bullshit. I don't even think you realize."

"Sam, you're angry. I get that. But I only want what's best for you. I wanted to be there for you the way you were there for me. You did me the biggest favor when you helped me decide not to go through with—"

"I had to do that," Sam said. "It's what you wanted and you're the boss."

She thought of Gaby's words, which had hurt so much—*My aunt gets paid to be nice to girls like you.*

Elisabeth shook her head. "I never saw it that way. I hope you didn't either."

"I stood by and watched you tell a huge lie to Andrew. I could have told him. At the time, I never would have thought it was my place. But you went right ahead and meddled in my life. Maybe I should do the same to you. See how you like it."

"Sam—"

"You may be older than I am, but you have no clue about relationships. You'd rather lie to your husband until you die than tell him what you want. You've just done to me what you stopped speaking to your own father for doing to you. Do you not see that?"

"You're right," Elisabeth said. "I mean—it's not the same at all, but I'm sorry."

"You look down on the rest of us. Me, George, probably even poor Andrew."

"George?" Elisabeth said. "I do not."

"You won't give his book idea the time of day, even though it's a good one."

"Really? This? Seriously?"

"You never once expressed any interest in what George and I were doing at that discussion group. You acted like you didn't want me to go."

Elisabeth sighed. "That's only because——" she began, but Sam didn't stay to hear the rest.

She went to the end of the hall, opened the front door, and walked out.

Clive called a few minutes after she got home.

Sam felt nauseated.

She said nothing about Elisabeth. She told him about the job offer, but not that she had accepted.

She wanted him to be the one to suggest it.

"I'm so confused about what to do," she said.

"The timing's rubbish," he said. "But soon we'll be married and you'll have a visa and then you can get a fabulous job just like it in London."

"I'm not sure it's that easy," she said.

"You didn't even have to apply to this one," he said. "That's unheard of. You're brilliant, babe. You'll get snapped up fast no matter where we are."

She envisioned herself at gallery openings, introducing him to her boss and coworkers. *My husband can't stay long, he's giving his Jack the Ripper tour tonight.* Then she felt bad. But when you were twenty-two and somebody's assistant, you were supposed to be dating some other twenty-two-year-old assistant, who lived with his college buddies and wasn't remotely interested in settling down yet.

"I thought we talked about maybe living in New York," she said.

"Someday. But not now. I couldn't just up and leave. We'll be married soon, that's all I care about."

"Why do you want to be married so badly?" she said.

Sam could tell from the silence that she had injured him.

"I'm sorry. I didn't mean for that to sound the way it did. It's just—I'm committed to you as it is."

"You're saying you don't want to marry me?" he said.

He sounded like a child. She thought back to the night they met, how assured he'd been, how drawn she was to him then.

"No," she said. "I guess—Clive. Have you ever been married before?"

Later, she would wonder why she asked the question then. Elisabeth had planted the seed much earlier, but somehow Sam's curiosity had not been piqued until tonight.

The pause was long enough that it served as an answer. Her heart sped up. Blood pumped in her ears.

"It was so brief, I honestly don't even think of it as a marriage," he said. "I thought things were fine. Then one day, I came home and Laura was gone."

Laura. The name on the empty folder in his email account. Sam was eager now to know what those deleted messages would have revealed.

"It was nothing like the kind of wedding we'll have," Clive said. "Laura had to be in control. I did whatever she said. She wasn't agreeable, like you."

"Agreeable?"

"We went to City Hall and then out for a curry with friends. That was it. That was our wedding."

Something he'd said on their first date came back to her now: *Here's City Hall, where the young brides get showered in rice each afternoon at two.*

At the time, she thought it sounded like poetry.

"Which friends?" Sam asked.

"Hers, mostly. And Ian and Chevy, Rowan and Dave B. A few others. I don't even remember who. My brother and Nicola."

"All of them knew. Your mom knew. The kids. Nobody ever let on in front of me."

"I don't think anyone thought it was relevant."

"An ex-wife? Irrelevant?"

"They were so happy for me when I found you," he said. "You're my soul mate. I'd been depressed over everything with her. It wasn't just the relationship ending. I was broke. I had to move out of our place and into this awful bedsit. Then into Ian's spare bedroom. It was humiliating."

"You two had your own place," she said, like a fool.

Of course they did. They were married. But she had never pictured him as someone else's.

"Laura made good money, but she's materialistic. She made me buy her this ridiculous diamond ring. I'm still paying it off. I felt worthless. Then I met you. You accepted me for who I am."

"When did she leave you?" Sam asked.

"It would have been the November before last."

"Five months before we met."

"I guess so."

"Why didn't you tell me?"

"At first, everyone thought it was a fling between us. I think even you and I thought so. I didn't think you needed to hear about that. I tried not to be with you, in the beginning. I purposely didn't ask for your number when we met. And then when I did call you that first time, I decided I shouldn't ask you out. I know you're too good for me, Sam. But I fell in love with you. I guess everything with her left my head. It didn't matter anymore."

"Were you divorced yet when we met? Are you even divorced now?"

Her teeth chattered as she said it.

"Yes, I'm divorced now," he said. "I wasn't then, technically. I was in every sense but the paperwork. I wasn't in touch with her. She'd already gone back to Spain."

"So all those years you lived there, you were with her."

"Yes. She wanted me to be some working stiff. I worked for her father's company in Barcelona. Then she wanted to be in London all of a sudden, so he sent us. We were happier in London, or I thought we were. We got married. Her idea. But we had only been married six months when she left. Sam, I swear to you, it's not a big deal. You're being childish."

"You lost your job because her father was your boss."

"Right."

"I need to go," she said. "My friends are waiting. Listen, my parents asked if you could maybe not come to graduation. They think it will be strange for my grandmother. Plus, there'll be too many people to wrangle, you know."

"You're joking," he said.

"It's not a big deal," she said. "Good night."

Sam woke to five text messages from him, asking her to call as soon as she was up. There was a text from her mother too, apologizing for how things had gone between them, but not going back on what she'd asked.

There was no word from Elisabeth.

It all felt like too much. When Sam saw her reflection in the bathroom mirror, her neck was covered in pink, splotchy hives. She lifted her T-shirt. They were all over her stomach too.

She heard footsteps, and then Isabella appeared in her fluffy blue bathrobe.

She was trailed by a sophomore wearing boxer shorts and an enormous T-shirt.

Sam ignored the presence of the sophomore.

"Please don't talk about me behind my back," she said.

Isabella blinked. "Sorry?"

"You know what I'm referring to."

"Sam. Is that you? Am I dreaming?"

"This isn't a joke, Isabella."

Isabella looked at the sophomore, who was pretending to be immersed in the application of toothpaste onto toothbrush.

"Elisabeth says you're worried about Clive and me. You think our relationship is a big mistake. How come you never felt the need to say anything to me about it?"

"Christ," Isabella said. "Why did she tell you that?"

"I wasn't aware that you two hang out," Sam said.

"I ran into her at CVS. It was a casual conversation."

"Do you know how often I hold my tongue when it comes to the shit you do?" Sam said.

"Yes!" Isabella said. "That's what friends do, isn't it?"

"Friends support each other," Sam said. "Real friends. Which, not surprisingly, you've never had, have you?"

Isabella looked for a second like she might cry, and then her face turned angry instead.

Sam pushed past her into the hall.

She called Maddie at lunchtime, not wanting to go back to the dorm to eat.

She sat in the grass outside the library, listening to the phone ring, terrified that it would go to voice mail.

Then Maddie picked up.

Sam heard an ambulance siren in the background. She heard Maddie walking down a windy city block, a sound like someone crushing a paper bag.

"Hey, what's up?" Maddie said.

"Not much. Just my whole life is falling apart."

Sam told her about the job offer, about her mother, about Elisabeth, and Clive and Isabella.

"In one day, I've gone from feeling like the luckiest person alive to like I can't trust anyone," Sam said.

"You can trust me," Maddie said. "Are you and Clive breaking up for real?"

"I don't know. What do you think I should do?"

"I can't decide that for you."

"Yes, you can. You know me better than anyone. Please."

Maddie sighed. "Come here. Take the job. Live with me. You don't have to stay forever."

"Now that Elisabeth and I fought like that, maybe she called them back and said not to hire me. Maybe I don't even have the job anymore."

"Sam. You do."

"I can't afford to live there on what they'll be paying me, and with my student loans."

She wanted Maddie to talk her into it.

"Can I?" she added with a smile.

Sam could hear Maddie smiling back. "We all feel that way when we get here, but we manage. You'll figure it out."

"No one ever thinks they have enough money," Sam said.

She plucked a gray, feathery dandelion from the ground.

"Good point," Maddie said.

Sam blew the soft petals into the air.

"Elisabeth told me that."

All day Tuesday and Wednesday, Sam wondered what would happen on Thursday, when she was next supposed to babysit. She waited for some sign from Elisabeth. She wasn't going to show up and pretend nothing had gone on between them. Then again, she couldn't imagine not showing up to work. She'd never done that in her life. And she needed the money. Not just her weekly pay, but whatever Elisabeth planned to pay her for the portrait.

By Wednesday night, she still hadn't heard anything.

In the morning, she thought she had a sore throat. Maybe she was too sick to work. Maybe fate had decided for her. But no. After a shower and a cup of coffee, to her great annoyance, Sam felt fine.

Her heart raced as she walked to Laurel Street. When she pushed open the back door, she swore she could feel Elisabeth's presence on the other side.

But she found Andrew in the kitchen instead, feeding Gil scrambled eggs.

"Elisabeth had an early call with her agent," he said. "She went down to her office a while ago. She seemed nervous."

Sam wondered how much he knew.

After a brief silence, she said, "I can take over from here."

"Okay," he said. "Great. Thanks."

Elisabeth didn't check in by phone or text like she usually did.

Sam was confused. She was the one who had been lied to, and yet she had shown up.

Andrew called the house while she was giving Gil his lunch.

"Can you stay late tonight?" he said. "Like six? Elisabeth has a friend coming into town for dinner, so I'll be getting home before her. Sorry, she only just told me."

"Sure thing," Sam said.

So Elisabeth was leaving him to deal with the mess she'd made.

Would they ever speak again? Sam was mad enough that she almost didn't care, but it made her sick to think of not seeing Gil after today. Was he old enough to wonder where she'd gone? All the times she had imagined the future, Sam thought they would send pictures and updates, maybe see each other once or twice a year, here or there, wherever *there* was.

She smiled through tears as she wiped his hands and face. She rocked him to sleep instead of letting him cry himself out, which was for some reason what you were supposed to do. Sam didn't lay Gil down in the crib for his afternoon nap. She held him to her in the rocking chair until he woke up. They played for the rest of the day. She didn't look at her phone once.

When Andrew got home, she said in a rush, "Would you mind paying me now for today and Monday?"

"Sure," he said. "Let me get my wallet."

While he went to find it, she whispered "I love you" to Gil, and kissed his soft, fat cheeks as many times as she could.

She got home a few minutes later and searched around for Andrew's cell number. She found it on the "In Case of Emergency" contact list Elisabeth had given her back in September, which sat crumpled at the bottom of her book bag.

She sent him a text.

Hi! It's Sam. I've just realized the rest of the semester is going to be super hectic. There's no way I can work tomorrow and next week. Sorry for the short notice.

Andrew replied, *Okay . . . hope everything is all right. Will we still see you Sunday for dinner?*

Sam didn't respond.

On Sunday, with two weeks to go until graduation, George arrived to take her to her final discussion group meeting. Sam thought of saying she couldn't make it, but when George called the night before and said he was going to pick her up, he sounded cheerful.

"We're having a bon voyage for you," he said.

He didn't mention Elisabeth. Maybe he didn't know, Sam thought. Or maybe the two things could remain separate.

But as soon as they were in the car, George said, "Andrew thinks something is up between you and Lizzy. Is that true?"

"I'd rather not talk about it," Sam said. "If that's okay."

"You two are such pals," George said. "Whatever it is, you'll work it out."

Neither of them said anything for a bit, and then George said, "You haven't mentioned your friend in the dining hall lately. How is she? Did she get her childcare issue worked out?"

Sam looked at him. "I need to tell you something. But it's really awful, so I'm going to look out the window when I tell you so I can't see the disappointed look on your face."

George chuckled. "All right. Out with it. You're making me nervous."

Sam still hadn't told anyone but Clive about the letter she'd written to President Washington. She hadn't been ready yet to own it. It was too shameful, too embarrassing.

But now she told George.

"Gaby didn't understand that I was just trying to help," Sam said. "Or maybe she understood, but she didn't care. I feel like she thinks I'm this privileged person. Like Isabella. Or Elisabeth. When really, I couldn't be further from it."

"There are a lot of different kinds of privilege," George said gently. "Education, for one."

"I'll be paying off my education until I die."

"Still," he said. "It makes all the difference. You should know that. Take it from someone who never dreamed of going to college. You've got your calling card now."

Sam felt chastened, even though she knew he wouldn't want her to.

"You meant well," George said. "I have no doubt. But you never should have sent that letter without asking them first."

"They wouldn't have let me send it," she said.

"Right," George said. "Exactly."

Sam had done to Gaby almost the same thing Elisabeth did to her, but with far worse results. Would George say that Elisabeth had meant well too? Sam wanted to be forgiven, but she didn't want to forgive.

They did not speak for the rest of the ride, until he pulled into the parking spot in front of Lindy's Bakery. Through the window she saw the old men seated around their usual table. Red balloons tied to an empty chair.

Later that night, Sam talked to Clive for the first time in a week. She'd been ignoring his calls.

"I'm sorry," he said as soon as she answered. "I should have told you sooner. Please don't let this come between us. I love you."

"I love you too," she said. "But I think I should take the job in Brooklyn. For now, at least. We can do long distance for a while. Okay?"

"Okay," he said. "If that's what you want."

They both cried. After they hung up, Sam kept crying. She told herself it wasn't over. They hadn't broken up. But she saw his niece and nephew, Freddy and Sophie, gone from her life. She saw the house in the country Clive had so often described, gone.

She thought of having to make an online dating profile and be out there, alone, like everybody else. Lexi had told Sam that every guy who liked her profile asked, "What are you?" or "Where are you from?" When Lexi said, "Chicago," they'd say, "But where are you *from*?" And then there was the guy who sent Isabella a picture of his penis with a ribbon tied around it on her birthday.

The idea of it made Sam cry even harder.

Isabella walked in then, and froze in the doorway.

"I'll kill him," she said. "What did he do to you?"

Things between them had been strained. But Sam laughed.

"Nothing," she said. "I did it to him."

Isabella came and sat beside her on the bed, hugged her tight. She didn't let go, and she didn't say a word, which was the perfect thing.

On the Thursday before commencement, Sam arrived at the president's mansion. Every light was on. The house glowed from within like a jack-o'-lantern. Out front, a banner reading CELE-BRATE WOMEN! obscured the second-story windows.

Sam went around to the back.

The dinner was meant to honor the college's top one hundred alumnae donors and their guests. Events like this were a show-case. The steak would be of the highest quality. The wine would cost fifty dollars a bottle. Five kinds of pie would be served. In a hundred and fifty years, it had never been otherwise.

Usually the best part of working an event like this was getting to eat the food. But tonight Sam wasn't hungry.

The kitchen was bustling when she entered. Women from din-ing halls all over campus were busy cooking, preparing, arrang-ing. They spoke to one another in Spanish, moving extra fast. One of them handed Sam a tray and pointed her down a long hallway, where other student waiters were coming and going.

"Smoked salmon and cucumber," the woman said.

Stepping into the packed living room full of women in neat suits and floral dresses, Sam felt unbalanced. Her hair was tied up in a bun. She wore a white button-down and black dress pants, per the instructions on the job sheet someone from RADS left in her mailbox. The shirt was old, and too tight. It strained open at her breasts. The pants needed ironing, but she didn't have an iron at school.

She lay in bed the night before, imagining herself confronting President Washington. She wouldn't, of course. The confidence she possessed when silently delivering a monologue to her pillow seemed to have left her now.

Months ago, she had been so excited to come here, to be in the woman's presence. Now Sam just wanted to get through it and get paid.

She approached a cluster of blondes in their sixties.

"Smoked salmon and cucumber?" she asked.

They waved her away.

Sam went toward a trio of youngish alums, each with a glass of white wine in hand.

"Smoked salmon and cucumber," she said.

One of them took a cocktail napkin from the tray and put a single canapé on top.

"Are you a student?" she asked, her voice full of excitement.

"I am."

"What year are you?"

"A senior."

"What house are you in?"

"Foss-Lanford."

"No way! One of my best friends lived there!"

Sam smiled wide, then turned toward the other side of the room. She knew from experience that she would have this exact conversation at least ten more times tonight.

She wished she had gotten the chicken skewers with peanut dipping sauce, or the mini-sliders. Then the women would have approached her, instead of the other way around, and she could have gotten away with making less conversation. She didn't feel like talking.

Fresh flowers sprayed forth from every surface: cherry blossom branches as tall as she was on the sideboards, white roses cut down to just a few inches stuffed into round white vases on the end tables, and long-stemmed roses, hundreds of them, in larger vases, filling the surface of a table in the center of the room. Sam wondered how much the flowers had cost. How much this whole evening had cost.

The crowd parted. There, by the fireplace, stood President Washington in a navy skirt-suit and pumps, a silk scarf tied around her neck. She seemed to be lost in conversation with two white-haired women beside her. Sam watched as President Washington kissed each of them on the cheek and then excused herself.

The president stood alone for just a second. She looked in Sam's direction, met her eye. Sam imagined some other, braver reality. She imagined running toward her, making demands that could not be ignored.

While it is impossible for me to address your specific accusations without knowing who you are—

She wished she could say: *Here I am. Now you know.*
The words she'd recited in bed came back to her.

President Washington, you claim to celebrate women, but there are women who have worked on this campus for decades and have nothing to show for it. Shouldn't we feel ashamed? Why won't you make it right? What's the point of shining a light on the truth, if the truth just sits there, unchanged. Tell me. Please. Tell me.

The president clinked a silver spoon against a glass.

The room fell to a hush.

"Good evening!" she shouted, her voice full of energy. "Welcome home!"

The alums hooted and cheered.

"We're here tonight to celebrate *you*," President Washington said. "Your generous donations helped us reach an all-time fundraising goal this year. We were able to break ground on the new engineering building; to begin talking about a state-of-the-art library. To welcome the largest class yet of our Lucretia Chesnutt fellows. Raise your hands, ladies. Don't be shy."

From their spots throughout the crowd, ten or twelve fellows put up their hands. They were the only black women in the room, other than the president herself. If there was something uncomfortable about that, President Washington didn't seem to notice.

Sam saw Shannon among them. Shannon noticed her at the same time. She rolled her eyes.

Something occurred to Sam then. The president's mansion was a place to go and draw hearts in chalk on the driveway, on her birthday, on Valentine's Day. They all loved her, and showed their love with abandon. It felt personal. But President Washington had never shown them anything like it in return. She was playing her part, doing her job.

She works for the company, not us.

Gaby was supposed to have been here tonight. But even if she hadn't quit, she wouldn't be in this room. All the workers passing canapés were students. The full-time staff was hidden away in the kitchen.

Saturday morning, they sat in folding chairs on the quad in their black caps and gowns, under a cloudless blue sky.

Out of a class of seven hundred, Sam was graduating with the tenth-highest GPA. Some kind of magical thinking made her wonder if she might still get called for Phi Beta Kappa, handed that golden key, which had once seemed so important, and then had seemed superfluous, and now seemed like something she had earned but for one mistake. Maybe just this once, they would make an exception. But when the Phi Beta Kappa names were called, hers was not among them.

When Sam crossed the stage to get her diploma, her family cheered, louder than anyone else's, and she was slightly horrified, but also kind of proud. She walked slowly back, searching the faces. She realized once she was in her chair that she'd been looking for Elisabeth.

That night after dinner, Sam walked to the corner of Laurel and Main, hoping she might be there. She stayed for a long time, watching cars zip past. She wondered if Elisabeth would still throw a party tomorrow, if there would be a balloon archway and champagne, all the things they'd talked about, just without her. Finally, Sam went home, the last night she and Isabella would ever spend in their room.

Music blared. She could hear Isabella and Lexi and Shannon singing from halfway down the hall.

When Sam reached the platform, Isabella nodded toward their room.

"Look what came for you."

The door was open, exposing a vase of long-stemmed roses on Sam's nightstand. The note read *So proud of you, babe. Can't wait to celebrate in person. Love, Clive*

Sam went out to the hallway, closed the door, and turned toward her friends.

Before they got in the car to leave the next morning, she went to the kitchen for her last cup of coffee. It was early. Only Maria had arrived so far.

Sam started to cry.

Maria hugged her.

"No tears!" she said. "This is a happy day. We're so proud of you."

"I'll miss you," Sam said.

"We're going to stay in touch," Maria said.

Sam wanted to tell her that she had only wanted to help, that she was sorry.

She said, "Will you please tell Gaby goodbye for me? And tell her to call me."

"Oh yes, she said to say congratulations," Maria said.

Sam could tell she was lying. Probably, Maria was trying to make up for what she had taken as Gaby being rude, or less than thoughtful. She didn't suspect Sam of having done wrong for a second. That was the worst part.

Later, smooshed into the back seat of her parents' minivan between her television set and her suitcase and her siblings, Sam remembered the painting and felt a stab of regret. She had worked hard on it for weeks, tried to make it perfect, only to leave it propped on an easel, half finished, undone.

Elisabeth

E LISABETH PUSHED GIL'S STROLLER across campus, listening to the birds.

There was no one else around, not a single person. Overnight, the place had emptied out. The folding chairs, the stage, and the tent had been cleared from the quad. The grass was an unblemished green, as if the ceremony had never happened, as if the girls in their black caps and gowns hadn't sat there in rows, fidgeting in nervous anticipation, high heels sinking into soft ground.

Elisabeth could only be certain they had because she had seen them, briefly.

Her invitation was postmarked the day of her terrible argument with Sam. It arrived two days later, a Wednesday.

The morning after that, Sam was supposed to watch Gil for the first time since they'd argued. At the last minute, Elisabeth escaped to her office, telling Andrew to tell Sam that she had an important phone call with her agent. It was true, and yet she knew that had they not fought, she would have taken the call from home. She was being a wimp; she could admit that. She wanted Andrew to take the temperature of things and report back before she saw Sam later that evening.

As soon as she reached her office, Elisabeth thought of the threat Sam had made and wondered if it had been wise to leave her alone with Andrew.

Maybe I should do the same to you. See how you like it, she had said. The words so hostile, so unlike Sam.

Elisabeth had told Andrew that Sam was mad at her because she had meddled in her relationship with Clive. She didn't tell him the rest. Now she let herself imagine the worst. She pictured Sam and Andrew in the kitchen, the baby on Sam's hip. Sam saying, *There's something you need to know about your wife.*

Andrew might actually leave her.

Elisabeth was so consumed with dread over this that she didn't pause to wonder what her agent would think of the chapters she'd sent. So when Amelia sighed and said, *"Look,"* just that one word surprised her. She knew what *Look* meant.

"The book is technically good," Amelia said. "It's great. Everything you write is great, you're a great writer."

"But?"

"But we can tell your heart's not in it."

"I wouldn't say that," Elisabeth said. She felt offended, even though it was true.

"Why is this the book you're writing now? What does it have to do with you, with your world, your obsessions?"

"Not every book needs to be autobiographical," she said. "My others aren't. I'm a journalist."

"Sure. Of course," Amelia said. "But let's be honest. Women in sports? You hate sports."

Elisabeth was supposed to write about her obsessions? A book about women who commit fertility fraud against their husbands. A book about a woman unable to be normal, as much as she wished she could be. A book about a woman who meddled in a girl's life when she should have been paying closer attention to her own.

"What scares you?" Amelia said. "What would you give anything to stop thinking about?"

It was all too much, the book and the situation with Sam. Elisabeth decided to hide out awhile longer in her office. She asked Andrew to get home early, make some excuse. She would face Sam tomorrow.

But after that day, Sam never came back. In the week that followed, Elisabeth must have picked up the phone a dozen times to call and apologize for overstepping. But when she remembered things they both had said, she wasn't sure how to talk about any of it. It was so raw, so awful.

She decided she would go to the graduation ceremony, give Sam her gift, and say she was sorry. Nothing drawn out, just a simple *I shouldn't have. Forgive me.* Maybe it would be bad—maybe Clive would confront her for interfering, or Sam's mother would tell her she was a terrible person. But maybe all would be well, and they'd celebrate at her house the next day, as planned.

Elisabeth wore a red shirtdress, flats, and sunglasses. She stood off to the side, away from the groups of family members, feeling out of place and a bit lonesome. It was a glorious sunny day. The blue sky set against the brick buildings gave the place a sharper focus and made everything look clean, perfect.

When the grads filed in, she caught sight of Sam from a distance. She looked serious, determined, until her face broke into a smile, and she started to laugh. Elisabeth had never seen her laugh like that. Sam pulled away from the procession just fast enough to hug and kiss her relatives. They held a homemade sign. Elisabeth couldn't make out what it said.

She had miscalculated. She wasn't wanted. She shouldn't have come. She turned and walked away. When Andrew asked why she was home so soon, Elisabeth told him she had a headache and needed to lie down.

Now, two days later, she was back. Headed for the white Unitarian church tucked behind the science building. Specifically, the College Children's Center day care, located in the church basement, and run by Maris Ames, a soft and cheery woman with thick, almost-purplish hair.

She met them at the door with a smile. Gil grinned back appreciatively.

As of three days ago, he could walk. A step or two at a time, and then he'd fall down or grab hold of a piece of furniture. It was a milestone every child reached somewhere around this age, and yet Elisabeth and Andrew were awestruck.

While Gil perused the classroom, pulling blocks and books and bins from where they belonged and dumping them on the floor, Maris explained that during the academic year, the school was staffed by students from the Early Childhood Education Department.

"Lovely girls. Each handpicked by yours truly, and not a dud among them," she said. "I can sense a hard worker when I see one. I've been at this for forty years. In summertime, we have excellent help as well. Older gals with experience. Grandmotherly types."

Elisabeth smiled. She liked this woman.

Her neighbors said the school was overpriced. But one of the good parts about living in the city for so long was that she had a skewed sense of what things ought to cost. To her, almost everything here seemed reasonable, if not downright cheap.

"And you'd have room for him soon?" she asked.

"As soon as you'd like."

Elisabeth had been thinking of having Gil start the following week, but now she said, "Maybe at the end of July?"

"Sure," Maris said.

It would give her that much more time with her baby, who felt less like a baby every day. Maybe Faye could sit with him some, since she'd be off for the summer. Elisabeth had vowed to herself to try and let her mother-in-law in more. They had no longer just moved here. They lived here. She ought to make a go of it.

Things would be different, having Gil away from home all day, not being able to look in on him whenever she wanted. She thought he would thrive in the presence of other kids his age. But she would miss what they'd had this first year, the cocoon of the two of them, plus Sam.

Sam had only been with them three days a week. Day care would be full-time. Elisabeth felt overcome with regret, knowing how much of his life would have nothing to do with her. It made her want to quit work and stay home doing arts-and-crafts projects with Gil for the next ten years, even as she knew that she'd lose her mind.

Andrew's fellowship was soon to end. He had no plan for what might come next. The provost at the hippie college had hinted at keeping him on in some kind of mentor capacity, but who knew where that would lead. She needed to write a book.

When Elisabeth thought of Sam, she felt like she had ruined something, even though their arrangement would have come to an end anyway. She would still be standing here, scanning the brightly colored room for choking hazards as she pretended to listen to Maris Ames's thoughts on the Montessori method.

Elisabeth assumed Sam, like the rest of them, had gone home by now. She couldn't believe there had been no goodbye.

All day yesterday, she'd half expected her to show up.

The party had not gone as planned. When they woke, the sky was dark and heavy with rain. Elisabeth tried not to care. There was nothing she could do about the weather.

Even as she told herself this, she said to Andrew, "Today is going to be a disaster, I can tell. Yesterday was perfect. Why didn't we do this yesterday?"

"Because it wasn't Gil's birthday yesterday," he said.

"We should have canceled," she said. "Done something just the three of us."

"It's going to be fine," he said.

Nomi's train was due to arrive at eleven. She was coming on her own and staying with them for two nights. Elisabeth had imagined her best friend looking on, admiringly, as she hosted a large, joyous affair. The kind of thing you could only do when you had a house and a big backyard.

Elisabeth had had until a few days ago to change the order with the caterers. She waited because she thought there was a chance she and Sam would reconcile. Before she knew it, a man with one hundred and twenty shrimp puffs was asking if she preferred silver or Lucite trays for passing.

There was enough food to feed Sam's giant family and all her friends, when the only people coming were Andrew's parents and a couple of his coworkers and whichever neighbors chose to attend.

As Andrew was leaving to get Nomi at the station, a UPS guy delivered a giant blue-wrapped gift box. Elisabeth opened it. A present from her mother. The box contained expensive baby clothes, the kind that were gorgeous and that no baby would ever have a reason to wear.

The card read *Love, Gigi.*

"When did we decide that would be her grandma name?" Andrew said.

"She decided, I guess."

Elisabeth smiled, in spite of herself.

Andrew kissed her goodbye.

Soon after he left, three guys with scraggly beards and straw hats arrived. One dragged an upright bass; another had a drum in his arms.

"It feels like rain, doesn't it?" Elisabeth said to them. "Should we be putting you inside, do you think, or would that be too loud?"

They shrugged, indifferent.

"Maybe start in the yard and we'll play it by ear," she said.

The men from the balloon company were setting up out front when Nomi got there forty minutes later.

She pushed past them, looking exasperated, and found Elisabeth in the hall.

"I'm so sorry," Nomi said. "I planned to bring wine. I thought we could stop somewhere on the way from the train. I had no idea there were still places where liquor stores are closed on Sunday. Are women allowed to vote in this town yet?"

"Ha ha," Elisabeth said. "Hi!"

When they embraced, she willed Nomi to look around, to say something nice about the house.

"Your living room is a re-creation of the one in Brooklyn," Nomi said. "That's hilarious."

The balloon men needed a signature and her credit card. Elisabeth went to find her purse.

Within five minutes of the men's departure, two separate couples walked in without knocking, assuming a balloon archway signified an open house.

"Where *are* we?" Nomi said. "Do you not have locks?"

Elisabeth offered the band members fifty bucks to drag the archway out back, where nobody would see it, other than people they'd invited.

By noon, everyone had arrived. There were twice as many cater-waiters as there were guests. They circled the yard, trying to look busy. The Laurels had all come and were downing flutes of champagne, standing in the corner, whispering.

"Terrible women," Nomi said, watching them from across the yard. "You can tell by looking. Who makes that dress the chunky blonde is wearing? Peg Bundy for Spandex?"

Elisabeth had dreamed of this—having her best friend by her side to make fun of the Laurels with her. So why did she wish Nomi could try to blend in, and keep some thoughts to herself?

In a way, she thought there was something to appreciate about how the Laurels always showed up for one another. And now, it seemed, for her as well. They could have easily skipped this party, but they were here, and making the best of it.

The goth couple they had seen get married in the fall sat at the picnic table, holding hands. Elisabeth could not remember their names. The day of their wedding, Andrew got mad at her for making fun of them, for suggesting that they'd be divorced soon. It was kind of awful of her, now that she thought of it. Elisabeth gave them a wave. Maybe they had as good a shot as anyone.

Still, she wondered if their weird energy was keeping people away from the food—right in front of them were platters heaped with charcuterie and crudités, sandwiches cut into triangles, bowls of fresh salad. In the middle of it all, a tower assembled from thirty blue-frosted cupcakes.

On her way to get more to drink, Debbie from across the street commended Elisabeth on the dessert choice and said it was all the rage at kids' parties this year. Elisabeth told her the truth—the cupcake tower had been the caterer's idea.

When Debbie walked away, Nomi said, "Brooklyn moved on from that particular trend five summers ago."

Elisabeth wondered if this was what she sounded like. It bothered her, even though she had been thinking the same thing. She wondered if this tendency toward snobbery would ever leave her, or if living in the city had ruined her for life.

She kept glancing at the sky.

"Looks like rain, doesn't it?" she whispered to Nomi.

Nomi shushed her. "Don't conjure it!"

"I don't think that's how rain works," Elisabeth said, feeling injured, wishing she hadn't said anything.

Wind whipped through the yard. The balloon arch swayed.

Elisabeth looked at Gil, happily crawling in the grass, chasing Debbie's two kids. She took in a deep breath. He was having fun. That was all that mattered. So the first party they threw in this house was an odd one. So what.

From her spot in the yard, she heard the home phone ring.

Her father-in-law must have answered it, because a moment later, he called out the open door, "Lizzy! It's for you."

Her first thought was that maybe it was Sam. Maybe George had talked to her, and she would be here with them soon.

Elisabeth dashed inside.

"Your dad," George whispered. He handed her the phone.

"Calling to wish my grandson a happy birthday," he said. "Put him on, will you. I want to talk to him."

Elisabeth was tempted to point out that Gil couldn't speak yet, but instead she said, "Why don't we call you back in a bit? We're having that party now. Remember? I invited you and Gloria to come."

"Yes, yes," he said. "You go enjoy."

He hadn't bothered to come up with a reason why they couldn't make it, nor had her mother. Neither of them RSVP'd one way or the other. Elisabeth supposed that for her parents, a one-year-old's backyard birthday celebration didn't rise to the level of things important enough to acknowledge, let alone consider attending.

She <u>hadn't</u> invited her sister. She was still too angry. She put Charlotte's email address on the list for the Evite, then erased it, then added it again, then erased it and left it at that.

Charlotte sent a toy fire truck via Amazon. After that disastrous Christmas, Elisabeth figured they would now go back to being this kind of family. The kind who sent gifts in lieu of ever spending time together. She was fine with that.

"My accountant sent the birthday boy a little something for college a few months ago," her father said.

"Yes, I know," she said.

"Will he be depositing it anytime soon?"

"No," she said.

Elisabeth didn't elaborate.

She knew he wouldn't get it, that the wound was deeper than he'd be willing to admit.

"You know, he doesn't need your permission," her father said, an absurd threat that she refused to get worked up about.

"Talk to you later," she said. "Hi to Gloria."

"Gloria's gone," he said.

"What happened?"

He paused, and then, in a voice that sounded amused by itself, said, "I'm afraid I strayed."

Why was he telling her this, today? Or any time, for that matter.

"I argued that technically it shouldn't count as a betrayal," he said.

Elisabeth wanted to say *That's nice, goodbye* and slam the phone down, but instead she said, "Why's that?"

There was an open bottle of champagne on the counter, half full. She took a swig, not bothering with a glass.

"Technically, I wasn't cheating," he said. She swore she could hear his grin. "Because. I ask you: Is it possible to cheat with your own wife?"

Elisabeth closed her eyes, took another drink. She didn't say anything.

"It was your mother," he said, in case she hadn't understood. "I had a fling with your mother."

"Good for you," she said. "I'd better go, there's someone at the door."

"I'm not saying we're going to get back together, Boo, so we're clear."

"Sure, fine. Whatever."

"Don't want to get your hopes up. But I'm not saying that we're *not* getting back together either. Love is mysterious."

Andrew walked in then, as she was draining the bottle.

She froze, having been discovered, then grinned.

"Bye, Dad," Elisabeth said.

She hung up.

"My father's having an affair with my mother," she said.

Andrew nodded. "Sounds about right."

"Does this party suck?" she said.

"It does," Andrew said. "Want to go hide upstairs?"

"Yes," she said. "But no. We'd better get out there."

They reached the back door in time to see the balloon arch pull away from its moorings, skim the cupcake tower, and float up into the sky.

When Elisabeth got home from the day-care visit, Nomi was at the kitchen table, reading the paper.

"Remind me to abandon my children more often," she said. "This is heaven. The light in this room is perfect. It's so quiet. I could sit here all day."

"Finally!" Elisabeth said. "Something you like about this place."

"What do you mean?"

"Yesterday it felt like you were judging everything about our life here and finding it lacking. Which, I get it, this isn't exactly a world capital. But still."

"Sorry," Nomi said. "I was only saying things you've said to me a million times. Maybe it's like how you can make fun of your own family all you want, but someone else does it and you are duty bound to defend your people. It's kind of sweet. You like it here."

Her tone was teasing, singsong, as if they were in the fourth grade and she was talking about a boy Elisabeth had a crush on.

"I do not. Well, I like some things." Elisabeth sighed. "I don't know how I feel. I think I maybe wanted to impress you."

"That's adorable," Nomi said. "And sad. You don't have to prove anything to me. Maybe I'm not totally over losing you to this place. But I'll get there."

"For the record, you can make fun of my family whenever you want," Elisabeth said. "I knew my parents wouldn't come this weekend. But then I went to Sam's graduation. I saw her parents, her grandparents, the whole gang. I think that might have been part of my thing with her. I wanted what she had, in that way. Sam's so normal. She comes from this perfect family."

"How many perfect families do you know?" Nomi said. "Maybe she just hasn't figured out yet what's fucked up about hers. Look at you. You do a very convincing impression of a normal person. If I just met you, I'd have no idea your parents are so twisted."

"Thank you," Elisabeth said, and she meant it.

The doorbell rang.

"Who's that?" Nomi said.

"I don't know."

"A neighbor coming to borrow a cup of sugar? You don't think Lassie's fallen down the well again, do you?"

"Shut up," Elisabeth called over her shoulder as she went toward the door.

When she opened it, a hugely pregnant Gwen stood there, smiling.

"Is this an okay time?" she said. "I wanted to drop off a gift for Gil. I'm sorry I couldn't make it yesterday."

"You didn't miss much," Elisabeth said. "Come in. It's great to see you."

Gwen followed her into the kitchen.

"Gwen, this is my best friend, Nomi," Elisabeth said. "She's visiting from the city."

"Sorry," Gwen said. "I should have called first."

"Sit," Nomi said. "How far along are you?"

"Six months."

Gwen sat down across the table from Nomi, her body pouring itself onto the chair.

"I had no idea you were expecting!" Elisabeth said.

"You hadn't heard? I was positive it must be the talk of the neighborhood."

"I'm sure it is. But nobody tells me anything."

Gwen laughed. "So I guess that means you haven't heard the other part either."

"What other part?"

"Christopher left me. I'm having this baby alone."

"What?"

"He's gone. He got a teaching job at some place you've never heard of in Arkansas. I'm pretty sure he took one of his favorite students along for company."

"No."

"I can't believe the Laurels haven't told everyone in town yet. Don't hate me, but honestly, I skipped the party yesterday to avoid seeing them." Gwen inhaled deeply, then released the breath. "One good thing about my marriage ending is I won't have to go to book club anymore. You probably noticed I didn't come to the last few. It felt great!"

"Oh no, please don't leave me," Elisabeth said. "Though truth be told, I always wondered why you wanted to be a part of that book club."

"Christopher pushed me to go," Gwen said. "He said since his coworker's wife had invited me, it would be rude not to. Turns out he had a standing date with one of his undergrads at our house whenever I was here on Laurel Street."

"What a bastard," Nomi said.

"Yeah," Gwen said.

"But why did you do what he said?" Elisabeth said. "You're such a badass."

Gwen laughed.

"I was always the more successful one. I had tenure, he didn't. So I had to act sometimes like he was the boss. How refreshing not to have to play that game anymore. We were trying to have a baby for so long that I forgot about the two of us. Everyone said that was normal. That fertility stuff is hard on a marriage. Then I got pregnant and realized a baby wasn't what was missing between us."

"I'm sorry."

"It's for the best. I can't imagine raising a child with him."

Elisabeth wasn't sure if she should push further, especially with Nomi here.

"I have so much to give you," she said. "A bassinet, a stroller. Tons of clothes—do you know what you're having?"

"No. Going to be surprised. Because I haven't been surprised enough lately. Do you have a pediatrician you like?"

"Dr. Gordon is the best. I'll give you her number."

"Thanks. What are your thoughts on swaddling? A friend of mine swears by it, but then I read a story about how it can be bad for the baby's hips. Sorry, I have way too many questions."

"I'm so happy to answer them and feel like I know something for once," Elisabeth said. "I was standing where you are a year ago. You'll be a pro in no time. You'll see."

"It's overwhelming if I think about it too much," Gwen said.

"Stephanie added me to that Facebook group for moms who live in town. She's sort of the queen of the whole thing. It's deeply annoying. I had to mute it."

Elisabeth looked at Nomi. "I didn't know there was a Facebook group for moms here," she said.

She had been so consumed with BK Mamas that she hadn't even thought to look.

Gwen turned to Nomi. "Sorry. My life isn't usually this much of a soap opera. I must sound crazy to you."

Nomi smiled. "No," she said. "You sound like one of us."

Two weeks later, Elisabeth and Andrew went to Faye and George's.

Faye made pot roast. The four of them sat at the table longer than usual, talking and eating.

It would be their last dinner together in this house. Faye and George were moving in a few days, to a two-bedroom condo in town. It was a small miracle that they found a buyer. They hadn't gotten much for the place, but they were out from under.

Faye said it was a relief, mostly. Though she would miss the garden she had planted out back; and the signs of a younger Andrew that she still saw everywhere—the old treehouse, the pencil notches on the basement doorframe, denoting his height over the years.

All around them were cardboard boxes, full or half full, labeled in black marker: KITCHEN GADGETS, G'S TOOLS, A'S YEAR-BOOKS. Gil wandered from one open box to another, removing items, before he settled on a metal potato masher, which he then banged against the linoleum floor for ten minutes.

When the plates had been cleared, George excused himself and slipped into his office to do some packing.

"He's not packing," Faye said. "He's working. He's still at it. He and the guys from his discussion group are planning yet another protest. Ever since that article in the *Gazette* about them, people are calling and asking for their help."

Faye shook her head. "I'm proud of him. But don't tell him I said so."

Elisabeth got up to use the bathroom in the hall. When she came out, instead of turning left to go back to the kitchen, she went right and knocked at George's office door.

"Come in!" he called.

He grinned when he saw her there. "Lizzy," he said, "to what do I owe the pleasure?"

"I want to apologize," she said.

"For what?"

"I made a huge mistake when I gave that money to my sister. If it hadn't been for that, we'd have it to offer you, to save this house. Now it's too late. I'm so sorry."

George shook his head. "We never would have taken it."

"Aren't you going to miss this place?"

"Yes," he said. "But everyone I've spent time with here, everyone I love, is still with me. So who cares about a house?"

It occurred to Elisabeth then that she had spent so much time worrying about the dark legacy of her own family that she hadn't considered that this too would be Gil's inheritance. Good men like George and Andrew. She hoped he would turn out like them.

"Have you heard from Sam at all since she left?" Elisabeth asked, trying to sound noncommittal; just making conversation.

George shook his head.

She felt relieved.

"Did you two make up?" George said.

"Not yet."

"You should. She's a great girl."

"She is."

"And so are you," he said. "That goes without saying."

Elisabeth smiled. "Thanks. Faye mentioned that all these people are coming to you for guidance after that article in the *Gazette*," she said. "I'm proud of you, George."

The part of her fight with Sam that played over and over in her mind was what she'd said about Clive having no money.

He doesn't have two pennies to rub together.

You don't know anything yet.

It shocked Elisabeth, how much she sounded like her parents then. The meddling was like them too. So certain that she knew best. Sam had recognized this. How could it be that Elisabeth had made it her mission in life not to become them, and yet somehow, still, she'd done just that.

The hardest lessons were the ones you had to learn over and over again. So again, she was going to try. She'd deactivated her membership to BK Mamas, then deleted her Facebook account altogether. She had no idea whether Sam had taken the job in Brooklyn, or gone to London to be with Clive, and no intention of finding out. Best to seal off this past year in her mind and move forward.

Sam had often spoken of her summer abroad. A time out of time, in between, when she became some other version of herself. Elisabeth had started to think of the months they spent together in this same way. There was no other year of life when the two of them could have grown so close, or fallen out so spectacularly. Secrets that ought to remain hers alone would move about the world inside of Sam now too. Sam had the power to tell them, or not.

Elisabeth glanced at a stack of library books on George's desk: *Workers' Rights as Human Rights; Labor's Untold Story; Nickel and Dimed: On (Not) Getting By in America.*

Another thing Sam had been right about. Elisabeth and Andrew didn't dismiss the Hollow Tree because it was silly and obvious, as they always said, but because it implicated them. They had been blind to something. They'd chosen to be blind.

What would you give anything to stop thinking about? her agent had said.

Her shame and anxiety about her family's wealth made her never want to discuss it, as if by not mentioning money, she could make all the complexity go away. The same could be said of the conveniences they relied upon to get through a day, a week, a year.

That was why she'd never asked him to elaborate. Because it might be too painful.

Elisabeth put her hand on top of the books.

"George," she said. "Tell me."

They stayed late that night.

They took photos in Andrew's childhood bedroom. He showed Gil where he'd carved a shamrock into the floor of his closet, and where he used to stand and sink baskets on the hoop attached to the back of the door.

His parents' voices drifted up from downstairs. Elisabeth thought of what it must have been like to be a little boy alone here, listening.

A pang of remorse shot through her.

Eventually, Gil rubbed his eyes, and Andrew picked him up, carried him over to the window. They rocked back and forth, the baby's head on his shoulder.

"That's the Big Dipper," Andrew whispered. "The really bright one is Venus. And I think that one over there is the one I paid to have named after my girlfriend freshman year of high school. Got a certificate and everything."

Elisabeth sometimes wondered if she belonged in her own life, a strange sensation. She still didn't think she was very good at it. But she cherished the little family she had made beyond reason. For years to come, she would remember this sight: her Gil and her Andrew, staring out at a sky full of stars.

EPILOGUE

2025

I T WAS ISABELLA WHO INSISTED they go to their tenth reunion. Neither of them had attended the fifth, feeling that five years were too few for anything significant to have happened to anyone.

But ten years felt impossible. How could so much time have passed so quickly?

"Do you think everyone will be married with children?" Sam said on the phone.

"Only the tragically boring people," said Isabella, who was herself married with two boys under three.

"Will you bring Steve and the kids?"

"No way. This is for us."

"We could go somewhere on our own," Sam said.

They did this once a year, met up in Jamaica or San Francisco or Maine for three or four nights. Years had passed since they spoke often. In their first jobs, they exchanged several emails a day, paragraphs long, about how busy they were. Now they were too busy to do anything like that. But when they saw each other in person, they clicked right back into place and talked nonstop until it was time to part ways, making up for all the lost conversations they should have had.

"Sam, you look incredible, and you're probably in the top three percent of successful members of our class," Isabella said. "You're going to the reunion."

So Sam sent in her check and her forms, and even got a little bit excited about staying in the dorm for old times' sake. But then Isabella finagled the use of her father's friend's condo at a nearby ski resort. It was an hour from campus, but it had a hot tub and a deck and a fireplace in every bedroom.

The reunion began on Friday afternoon. They met up on Wednesday evening to have some time alone beforehand. They drank wine and watched the sun set and agreed that life would be so much better if they lived closer. They talked until three in the morning.

On Thursday, they hiked and went to lunch, talking all the while. It seemed impossible that they could ever run out of things to say. At some point, Sam wondered why her jaw hurt, and then realized it was from laughing. She wished she had understood during their school days that she would never experience friendship in such a concentrated form again, except in small doses, like this.

When Isabella got depressed after the birth of her first son, they instituted the Bat Signal—a way of letting each other know that an urgent response was required. If one of them truly needed the other, she'd be there. But for the most part, their friendship was guilt-free. Voice mails sometimes went unanswered. A birthday present might arrive two months late, or not at all. There were no hurt feelings on either side.

The plan for Friday was to get to the college early, hours before the festivities began. To remember the place on their own terms. But that morning, when Sam walked into the kitchen, Isabella didn't even look up from her phone. She was typing furiously.

"Fucking fuckheads," she murmured.

"Work drama?" Sam said.

"Yes. Ugh. I'm sorry."

"Don't be."

Sam said she'd take her own car to campus. They could meet up later.

On the drive, she listened to the radio, left the window down, and breathed in the air. Ten miles outside town, she started to feel nervous. She wished she had waited for Isabella after all.

Sam made a mental list of her achievements, as if she could build a wall out of them and hide behind it—she weighed fifteen pounds less than the day she graduated. She knew how to dress now, in clothes that flattered her figure, rather than shapeless things meant to hide it. She had a two-hundred-dollar haircut and had recently been profiled in the *Alumnae Quarterly* for her work in the art world. So why did she feel so insecure?

She parked in front of Foss-Lanford Hall. The dorm looked exactly as it always had, the name embossed in stone above the entrance.

Once, lying poolside on one of their trips, Isabella asked, "Who was Foss Lanford?"

"Was it a person?" Sam said. "I thought it was two people."

Isabella shrugged, and moved on to another topic.

Back at work a few days later, Sam went online for answers.

Eleanor Foss, class of '47, had married George Lanford in 1950. Together, they made a fortune designing popular board games, none of which existed anymore. When Eleanor died, George gave enough money to the college that they named a building in her honor, albeit a dorm at the far end of campus. Sam felt bad for not knowing sooner, for passing under her name every day for years without so much as wondering. The appeal of having your name carved in stone, she would imagine, was that you would never be forgotten. But that assumed curiosity, care, on the part of those who came after.

She got out of the car now and noted the second-to-last window on the third floor, which had once been hers and Isabella's. From out here, it looked like all the others.

In the dining hall on the first floor, bodies moved around.

Sam couldn't make out the faces.

Maybe this was why she'd been reluctant to return, the sensation that still showed up every once in a while when she thought of what had happened. Not only what she'd done, but how she'd been. All the things she didn't understand until later, made worse by the fact that she believed, at the time, that she understood perfectly.

There was shame in knowing how easy it had been to walk away from the mess she made. A childish mistake on her part that would make every day that much harder for the women in the dining hall, women she claimed to love.

Sam never spoke to them again after graduation. She left this place with promises to keep in touch with so many people, never imagining that she'd stop knowing them that day, or soon after. Her life would fill up with new names and faces, until the ones she knew here were only memories, and in some cases not even that.

She gave Maria her parents' address, but never heard from her, which made Sam wonder if Gaby had told Maria the truth once she was gone.

She did try to track Gaby down a few years back. Sam found her photograph on the website of an upscale Salvadoran restaurant where, at the time, Gaby was working as the general manager. Sam thought she looked happy. She sent an email, but got no reply. She had wanted to make it right, whatever that meant after so much time.

Thinking on it now, she vowed to try again.

She began walking across campus. When she passed the president's house, an old resentment rose up in her, even though the school had a new president now. Four years after Sam graduated, there had been an uproar among students and alumnae when the full story of Shirley Washington's business dealings emerged in a documentary commemorating the tenth anniversary of the financial crisis.

Sam didn't know how it was possible that the issue hadn't been raised until then. The stories were there, for anyone to see, but they had required pointing out, highlighting, by a third party who had no particular interest in seeing Shirley Washington as a hero.

It's so disappointing, Isabella had written in an email. *To come from nothing like she did and get so far, only to become so corrupted.*

Sam chose not to reply. It seemed useless to point out that someone who came from nothing had just as much incentive as anyone else—probably more—to let herself be seduced by the system. But it was disappointing. Heartbreaking, really.

The bill Sam received in the mail each month was a reminder of the price she had paid for her education, and was paying still. As were the semiannual solicitations from the development office, which annoyed her, seeing as the money she owed this place was a large part of the reason why she'd probably never own a home or know what it was like to live debt-free. And yet, Sam was grateful for her time here. She thought of those as some of the best years of her life.

She reached the pond now. A student center had been built on its banks, a modern white building that looked all wrong.

Sam kept going. She was headed for the library.

Once inside, she retraced her old path to the carrels downstairs. Sam was stunned to find them gone, replaced by two long, sleek wooden tables and several chairs. She would have hated to work like that, so exposed to everyone else.

Wherever she went, students looked at her, suspicious.

They saw this place as theirs, just as she once had. They didn't realize they were only borrowing the stately brick buildings and the two-hundred-year-old oak trees, which were older than the college itself.

There were far more black and brown faces among them than there were when she was here. Ten years on, the campus looked more like the world. The college was proud of this; touted it in every fundraising letter. Still, when Sam passed the white tent being set up outside College Hall, the staff looked the same as ever. She searched for Maria and Delmi, unsure whether she hoped to see them or not.

She supposed it was childish, simplistic, but Sam still could not square the discrepancies of lives that overlapped with one another every day. She looked at the people digging up roads and busing dishes and caring for other people's children—holding up the world—and wondered what they'd rather be doing. She was thirty-one years old, and she couldn't quite accept that some people would be allowed and encouraged to pursue their passions, while others never would.

But she knew that whether she accepted it or not did nothing to erase the fact of it. Every year it seemed the country moved closer and closer to a place where there would soon be very rich people and very poor people, and very few in between.

Sam walked on. She went through the campus gates. There had long been a legend that any girl who did this before graduation would never marry. Ridiculous, but back then Sam hadn't taken the chance. She always went around, in case.

She had recently started telling people she wasn't sure she ever wanted to get married. Each time she said it, she wondered if it was true. In the last two years, she'd been a bridesmaid five times. She had gone to three dinner parties where she was the only uncoupled attendee. When Isabella got married, Sam didn't feel any twinge of jealousy. But when Isabella had a baby, bought a house, she suddenly grew aware of how behind she had fallen.

Sam lived alone now, in an apartment on the top floor of a house built in 1790. She sensed the ghosts of its past hanging around when the hardwood creaked beneath her bare feet each morning, when the light in the kitchen flickered for no reason.

Sam continued on until the downtown came into view.

When she lived here, there wasn't a single chain store besides CVS and, at the end of senior year, a Starbucks. Now almost every storefront advertised a familiar restaurant franchise or clothing brand. The historic old movie theater had been converted into a Citibank.

She stood at the crosswalk at Plum and Main, waiting for the light to change. As it did, and the WALK sign lit up, a black SUV slowed to a stop in front of her. The woman behind the wheel was slight, eclipsed by her automobile. She swiveled her head and said something to the children in the back seat.

Sam started to cross as the driver faced forward.

Elisabeth.

It was her, there was no doubt. She looked exactly the same.

After college, for a while, Sam kept track of her.

She had the urge to tell Elisabeth when she learned that Clive had gotten married, a year after they broke up. It stung at the time, even though Sam had been the one to end things. Those first few months in the city, she relied on their unclean break, on the fact that she could always call him or run off to be with him if she wanted. When the option was no longer hers, she grieved over it, if not over the loss of Clive himself.

Sam was now almost the age he had been when they met. She had college interns at work. She marveled at how young they were. Just babies. She had never felt exploited by Clive, or taken advantage of. He was kind and encouraging and loyal. He had loved her. But it did occur to her that at the time it had seemed like no one else understood, when maybe she was the one who didn't.

Once, when she was twenty-six, eating dinner with friends at a café in the West Village, she saw a poster advertising a reading by the poet Julian Wells.

There he was, smiling in his photograph. Julian, the Mollusk, from the campus library. He looked good. He'd figured out what to do with that tight, curly hair, letting it grow out a bit. He wore glasses and had a beard. Nerds were having a moment in the city, and Julian looked as if he was making the most of it.

The bio on the poster said he had published a poem in the *Atlantic* and had a forthcoming book. He was teaching at Columbia that semester. Sam was at a particularly lonesome point. Staring at the poster, she wondered if she had taken a wrong turn all those years ago, one that she would never be able to correct. She went so far as to email Julian at his Columbia address after a few glasses of wine. She tried to sound breezy—how funny they had both landed in New York at the same time, maybe they should meet for coffee. He never wrote back.

That same year, Elisabeth published her book *The Hollow Tree* to much acclaim.

Sam found it on the new nonfiction shelf at Shakespeare & Co. one snowy afternoon. She flipped through, searching for some mention of herself, but there wasn't one. There was a chapter about a discussion group, made up of old men who met at a small-town coffee shop to talk through the ills of the world. Elisabeth quoted them, but used fake names. Sam tried to guess who had said what.

The last five pages of the chapter focused on a man she called

Larry, who ran a lucrative car service, until Uber put him out of business. After building a name for himself as a volunteer advocate for workers' rights, Larry got a job as a union organizer.

That had made Sam smile.

She still saw examples of the Hollow Tree everywhere, even more so after they lost touch. George used to shake his head and say, *Where can this possibly be headed?* Sam thought of that when she read about the ever-worsening state of the country, when the members of her family who had always loved debating politics had to stop talking about the subject, or else stop talking, period. When so many of the things George had predicted came true.

Even though she did not name him in the story, Elisabeth acknowledged that her book wouldn't exist without George. *The Hollow Tree* was dedicated to him.

Elisabeth crossed Sam's mind again months later, when Sam was moving out of the apartment she and Maddie shared in New York. As Sam filled a box with books, a photograph slipped out of one—in it, Sam was holding Gilbert, the strap of her top obscured, the baby visible only from the waist up, so that it appeared both of them were naked. Inspiration for a painting she had never finished, never delivered. She wondered what happened to it and, in turn, to Elisabeth. Had she ever told Andrew the truth? Were they still together?

Sam was almost certain that was the last time she thought of her. The years passed faster, the older she got. There was less time to ruminate, less time for everything. Less time.

But now Elisabeth was in front of her, looking confused as to why some random woman was waving.

Until she seemed to realize. She rolled down her window.

"Sam?" she said. "I didn't recognize you. You look fantastic. You're all grown up."

For a moment, it was just the two of them, as it had been years before.

Elisabeth turned and said, "Gil! This is Sam. She was your first babysitter."

The boy in the back seat was tall and lanky. He wore a shiny green basketball uniform. His blond curls were gone. He had shaggy brown hair now.

"Say hello," Elisabeth said.

"Hi," he said, bashful.

Sam was a stranger to him.

She could remember what it felt like to cross a room with the weight of his body pressed against her shoulder; the sensation of popping Cheerios into his mouth, one by one.

"And this is Willa," Elisabeth said. "Willa, you weren't even born yet when we knew Sam."

The girl looked like Elisabeth. The same slender build, the same eyes.

Sam almost expected her to explain. The Elisabeth she remembered would have blurted out, *Willa was adopted,* or *I ended up getting pregnant by accident after all that. Can you believe it?*

Instead, in a voice that was warm, but somewhat formal, Elisabeth said, "What are you up to these days?"

Sam felt flustered, as if she were not an authority on her own life.

"I'm here for my tenth reunion," she said finally. "I opened my own gallery last year."

"That's amazing. In Brooklyn?"

"No. Providence."

Sam had first gone there to visit her sister Caitlin when she was a student at the Rhode Island School of Design. She fell in love with the city—with its gorgeous old mansions and tacky Italian restaurants and proximity to the beach. She decided to stay.

Caitlin stayed on too, after she graduated. They lived only a few blocks apart. She was making it as a painter now, almost. Supplementing her income by bartending a few nights a week. She looked like Sam had at that age, but for the sleeve tattoos of birds and butterflies. Caitlin was the artist Sam had almost wanted to be, but not badly enough. A more independent, self-assured version of the original. They met most mornings for a walk along the river.

Sam had lasted six years in New York, doing everything for Matilda—from helping her choose the art, to giving her Chihuahua his host of daily medications. That had set her on her path. Matilda promoted her twice, and would have done so again if Sam had wanted to stay. But Sam never felt she belonged in the city the way some people did.

Once, when her mother was visiting, they went to dinner at a bustling place in Tribeca. The tables were close together. A Midwestern businessman sat alone beside them. Sam's mother made small talk with the guy when Sam excused herself to go wash her hands. From then on, he kept interrupting their conversation.

Sam responded to his questions in short, clipped sentences, wanting her mother to herself. In her entire life, she had almost never had that. When their brussels sprouts arrived, the man said he had wanted to order them, but the portion was too large for one person.

"Have some of ours!" her mother offered.

Sam shot her a look.

After dinner, walking up West Broadway, her mother said, "New York has hardened you."

Sam knew people who might wear this hardness as a badge of honor, but she didn't want to be one of them.

The things she could tell her mother, the things she had seen. The Saturday night when she sold her first painting and walked down into the subway full of pride, content, only to see a drunk kid punch an old homeless man in the face, knocking him out cold.

One's mood in New York was dependent on everybody else's—a hard look in response to a smile was enough to make her want to cry at first. At some point, she stopped making eye contact with people in the street and was genuinely surprised when anyone said *Hello* or *Good morning* or *Have a nice day*. When she finally left, she didn't know what had taken so long. But because she had put in the time, she could now go anywhere.

"I wondered if you might have moved back to Brooklyn," Sam now said to Elisabeth. "I remember how much you missed it back then."

"Counting down the days until these two move out, and then we'll see," Elisabeth said. "This is a good place to raise kids, though. It's easy here. Andrew's working at the college now."

"Please say hi to him for me. And George. How is he doing?"

"He's good," Elisabeth said.

Sam wished she would say more. Elisabeth's smile didn't seem real.

"I loved *The Hollow Tree*," Sam said.

"Thanks. That means a lot."

She wondered if Elisabeth remembered that she had been there when the idea first came up, that Sam had encouraged her to do it.

There was something Sam had imagined telling her, but now that they were face-to-face, it felt like too much. She wanted to say that Elisabeth's pushiness, her flawed advice, her meddling, had been wrong and problematic, and yet all of it had propelled Sam into her future. For that, she was grateful.

The car behind gave a short honk. The light was green again.

Sam thought Elisabeth might pull over, talk awhile.

But she said, "We're holding up traffic. We should go. If you're ever in the area again, look us up, come for dinner."

"I'd like that," Sam said, though she knew it would never happen.

Elisabeth looked like she wanted to say more. But she only said, "See you, Sam," and then was gone.

Acknowledgments

TWO YEARS BACK, I published an essay in *Real Simple* magazine that ended with the line: *Every child began as a story one woman told to herself.*

Perhaps the same can be said of every novel. This one began as a story I told my friend Jami Attenberg over drinks one night, seven years ago. She said, "That should be your next book." I wrote another book instead, but her words kept rattling around in my head. And when I finished that other book, I was ready.

I started off writing from Sam's point of view. I was pregnant with my first child at the time, and had no idea what Elisabeth's thoughts on new motherhood would be. I left those sections blank, aware that soon enough, I'd know how to fill them in.

In June 2017, my son, Leo, was born. I took notes here and there for six months, and wondered if I'd ever write actual chapters again. Then I met Radha Khan, without whom there would be no book in your hands.

That winter, my friends Bryan Walsh and Siobhan O'Connor offered the use of their apartment, two blocks from ours, while they were away on an extended trip. I only had to water the plants, and Siobhan said she didn't mind if I killed them all, which set the bar appropriately low for my plant-care abilities. In that lovely, sun-filled space, I wrote again. It was glorious. I cranked out page after page. I wrote faster than I ever had before.

Toward the end, I began taking long daily naps on the sofa. I was exhausted, it turned out, not only because I had a seven-month-old at home, but because I was pregnant again.

I gave the first hundred pages to my agent, Brettne Bloom, and my editor, Jenny Jackson. They provided their usual brilliant feedback, and the three of us had a brainstorming session. Two days later, Jenny's second child was born. She went on maternity leave. I joined the Brooklyn Writers Space, where many nights I stayed late, working until midnight while my wonderful husband, Kevin Johannesen, handled the home front, so that I could get a draft done before the baby came.

I sent Jenny and Brettne the first full draft when I was nine months pregnant and Jenny was just back from leave, a sort of baby-and-book relay race. In November of 2018, my daughter, Stella, was born.

When Stella was three months old, I started working on the second draft.

Ann Napolitano, Liz Egan, Rachel Fershleiser, Jami Attenberg, Courtney Sheinmel, Meg Wolitzer, Hilma Wolitzer, Hallie Schaeffer, and Maris Dyer read subsequent drafts, each making the book stronger and smarter than it was before. Alexandra Torrealba came in at the eleventh hour with valuable wisdom. Karin Kringen read with generosity and the keen eye of a woman who can guess the ending of any Lifetime movie within the first five minutes. Her friendship also provided inspiration.

I'm grateful to my cousin, Pauline Hickey, and her friends, for answering my questions about their age group. To Jess Bacal, Shayla Bezjak, Riana Olson, Margaret Barthel, and all the Smithies who took the time to discuss post-graduation job prospects with me. To Brooke Hauser and Dusty Christensen at the *Daily Hampshire Gazette*. To my sister, Caroline Sullivan, for Trinket; to Kirsty Calvert Ansari for British assistance; to Julie Schwietert Collazo and Micaela Coellar-Coiro; to Melissa Johnson for letting me describe the whole plot after dinner one night, and making it clear where the holes were, without saying a word; to my father, Eugene Sullivan; to Laura Smith; Aliya Pitts; Lauren Semino; Olessa Pindak; Hilary Howard; Rebecca Ruiz; Lucie Prinz; the Garden Street Girls; and the fierce women of Immigrant Families Together.

I'm extremely lucky to be publishing my fifth novel in a row with Knopf and Vintage. Thanks to everyone there for everything these past ten years, especially Sara Eagle, Paul Bogaards, Christine Gillespie, Emily Reardon, Jason Gobble, Maria Massey, Kristen Bearse, Nicholas Latimer, Kate Runde Sullivan, and the late Russell Perrault and Sonny Mehta.

Thank you, Grace Han, for the gorgeous cover art. Thank you to the Book Group. To Jenny Meyer and Heidi Gall at the Jenny Meyer Literary Agency. To Jason Richman at UTA. And to Christie Hinrichs at Authors Unbound.

The members of Bococa Moms and Smithie Parents have been a source of comfort and wisdom. What happens in a closed Facebook group stays in a closed Facebook group, and all posts and replies herein are entirely fictional. Except for Jamey Borell's comment about the dangers of doing multivariate regression analysis on the impact of eating an Oreo, because there is nothing I could come up with that would improve upon that.

Finally, thank you to my mother, M. Joyce Gallagher. She told me about the Hollow Tree, and just like George, I've seen it everywhere ever since.

SAINTS FOR ALL OCCASIONS

Nora and Theresa Flynn are twenty-one and seventeen when they leave their small village in Ireland and journey to America. When Theresa ends up pregnant, Nora is forced to come up with a plan—a decision with repercussions they are both far too young to understand. Fifty years later, Nora is the matriarch of a big Catholic family with four grown children. Estranged from her sister, Theresa is a cloistered nun, living in an abbey in rural Vermont. Until, after decades of silence, a sudden death forces Nora and Theresa to confront the choices they made so long ago. A graceful, supremely moving novel from one of our most beloved writers, *Saints for All Occasions* explores the fascinating, funny, and sometimes achingly sad ways a secret at the heart of one family both breaks them and binds them together.

Fiction

THE ENGAGEMENTS

Evelyn has been married to her husband for forty years, but their son's messy divorce has put them at rare odds; James, a beleaguered paramedic, has spent most of his marriage haunted by his wife's family's expectations; Delphine has thrown caution to the wind and left a peaceful French life for an exciting but rocky romance in America; and Kate, partnered with Dan for a decade, has seen every kind of wedding and has vowed never, ever, to have one of her own. As the stories connect to each other in surprising ways, *The Engagements* explores the complicated ins and outs of relationships, then, now, and forever.

Fiction

MAINE

For the Kellehers, Maine is a place where children run in packs, showers are taken outdoors, and old Irish songs are sung around a piano. As three generations of Kelleher women arrive at the family's beach house, each brings her own hopes and fears. Maggie is thirty-two and pregnant, waiting for the perfect moment to tell her imperfect boyfriend the news; Ann Marie, a Kelleher by marriage, is channeling her domestic frustration into a dollhouse obsession and an ill-advised crush; Kathleen, the black sheep, never wanted to set foot in the cottage again; and Alice, the matriarch at the center of it all, would trade every floorboard for a chance to undo the events of one night, long ago.

Fiction

COMMENCEMENT

Assigned to the same dorm their first year at Smith College, Celia, Bree, Sally, and April couldn't have less in common. Celia, a lapsed Catholic, arrives with a bottle of vodka in her suitcase; beautiful Bree pines for the fiancé she left behind in Savannah; Sally, preppy and obsessively neat, is reeling from the loss of her mother; and April, a radical, redheaded feminist wearing a "Riot: Don't Diet" T-shirt, wants a room transfer immediately. Written with radiant style and a wicked sense of humor, *Commencement* follows these unlikely friends through college and the years beyond, brilliantly capturing the complicated landscape facing young women today.

Fiction

VINTAGE CONTEMPORARIES
Available wherever books are sold.
www.vintagebooks.com